THE PHARAOH OF VENICE

2

Also by Owen Trevor Smith

Seven Roads To Travel
The Day Bonny Blue Raced For The Cup
Lindisfarne: Fury of the Northmen
(Feran Chronicles: Book 1)
Westerling: Prince of Wessex
(Feran Chronicles: Book 2)

THE PHARAOH OF VENICE

TALES OF A MINOR GOD: Book One

OWEN TREVOR SMITH

Owen Trevor Smith

Cover Image: Steven Novak
Novakillustration.com

CHAPTER ONE

A strange encounter in a café in Venice…

Friday 10:15 am

'You wouldn't believe me if I told you.'

Her eyebrows raised. She said: 'Try me.'

The man regarded her thoughtfully.

'It's not a normal occupation.'

His tone was pleasant, but he seemed to consider the topic closed and busied himself sorting the papers he had gathered from the table. He studied one of the sheets, his face hidden behind it. She could hear him muttering to himself but the words were meaningless. Was he annoyed at her intrusion?

She lifted the glass of lemonade for which the café was justly renowned, leaning back in her chair to survey her table companion, automatically assessing him. Despite his reluctance to provide information about his profession, his face was open and honest, with no trace of an attempt to be secretive. She would have detected that in an instant. He had the air of a businessman but his thick black wavy hair was too long for the corporate world. His clothing gave little away, casual and neat, an open-necked white cotton shirt, short-sleeved, and light brown trousers – his exposed skin was tanned and muscular. What he wore was good quality, which probably marked him as successful. He was young, around thirty perhaps, but he had a calmness about him, and his eyes told her he was experienced. He was handsome – in a European way.

He wore an expensive gold watch and on his right wrist were several bracelets made from leather and metal bands featuring mineral stones and carved figures. A man wearing charm bracelets? On his right middle finger was a gold ring, the type that usually displayed initials, but on this one she glimpsed tiny engraved writing. An inspirational phrase, perhaps? A dedication?

The outside of her glass was frosted and felt pleasingly cold to her fingertips as she brought it to her lips.

In the narrow street off St Mark's Square, with no wind to move it along, the late afternoon air sat motionless and heavy between the buildings, muffling the conversational murmurs from the nearby tables. She breathed deeply and felt relaxed for the first time since stepping off the plane.

It was an unsatisfactory reply to her question. Asking someone's occupation usually prompted a predictable exchange, at a sufficiently superficial level, that met the courtesy expectations of both parties. Madeleine categorised their current situation as being at the third level of communication between strangers. The first level was an acknowledgement of presence – eye contact and maybe a nod or a smile. The second level was usually an observation about the weather. The next level, the third, was only entered if a reasonable degree of interest still remained.

He had agreed that it *was* unusually hot, even for the season, so she had asked her third-level question. She was not really interested in whether the man was a locksmith or a lawyer. She was continuing a polite conversation as a way of thanking him for allowing her to share his table.

The small café was a favourite whenever she was in Venice. It was some distance from her usual hotel, but she enjoyed the walk and it gave a purpose to an afternoon stroll. The setting was picture-book perfect; a small cobbled triangular courtyard surrounded by the yellowed terracotta walls of the café on two sides and a waist-height brick wall on the third, separating the courtyard from the street. The waiter was a delight; there was a view of a small part of *la Piazza*, and the narrow street provided enough passers-by to satisfy her pastime of observing without being noticed.

She was happy to be in familiar surroundings again.

The other four outdoor tables of the café were occupied and she had been pleased and relieved when her request to share his table was accepted, albeit after a hesitation. He had been deep in concentration and her interruption was unexpected, but he quickly recovered and moved to collect several scattered sheets of paper to make room on the table for her lemonade glass. She glanced at one of the papers as he picked it up. It was folded in half and she could just see the names of several countries – with lines drawn down to the fold, connecting the countries to something on the hidden part of the paper.

If he had refused her request, she would have been left awkwardly standing in the tiny courtyard with her glass of lemonade in one hand and her phone in the other with nowhere to sit, like the odd one out in a game of musical chairs.

Madeleine thanked him and sat down. As soon as she'd freed a hand by placing her glass on the table, she quickly completed the reply to a text message that had been received just as her order of lemonade arrived while she stood at the counter, transmitting her confirmation of attendance at the symposium on Tuesday. She placed the phone on the table beside her glass and remarked about the heat of the day – her 'weather' observation; followed by the question about his occupation which had elicited the enigmatic response.

'I DIDN'T MEAN TO PRY,' she said after sipping her drink. 'I noticed your papers and thought you might be a researcher of some sort, an academic, but it's none of my business.'

'You read my papers? What did you see?'

'Oh, nothing really.'

His voice had an edge to it. It wasn't anger, just concern, but coupled with – it took her a moment to recognise it – with *interest*.

'I'm sorry…' she began to apologise but stopped when he lifted his eyes to look directly at her. His smile confirmed it was just a polite enquiry.

She shrugged. 'I saw the names of four countries ending with '*Italy*,' and there were lines extending from each name, but the rest of the paper was folded underneath.'

She saw the man register surprise but further conversation was interrupted by the arrival of a black cat from under the table. The creature jumped onto her lap, rubbing its head insistently against the inside of her arm. Madeleine hastily returned her glass to the safety of the table before the enthusiastic greeting caused an accident.

'*Ciao* Bastia…' she said happily, fondling the cat vigorously. 'You remember me!' The cat looked up at her and purred loudly.

'Do cats like you?'

'They seem to. This one does, anyway. We're old friends.'

'A window to the soul…' the man said.

Madeleine looked up. He was watching the cat.

He waved his hand. 'The opinion of a very wise Japanese gentleman I've had the pleasure of knowing for many years.' He saw her expression was still puzzled and explained: 'Akihiro says – the behaviour of a cat, especially a black one, towards someone, is a window into that person's soul.'

She thought about it. 'An appealing idea,' she said.

The cat turned in a circle, preparing to settle. It paused to stare across the table at the man, holding that pose in a half-turn for a moment until, its assessment complete, it flopped down in her lap and lifted a paw for a pre-wash inspection.

'Your cat has an interesting name. Did you say Bastia?'

'Yes. Why is that interesting?'

The young man paused. He picked up the pile of papers from the table and bent to place them in a briefcase at his feet. When he straightened, he half rose from his seat and reached across the table.

'Allow me to introduce myself first. My name is Logan Milan.'

'Madeleine Galli.' She briefly clasped his hand.

Logan's response was not what she expected. His eyes widened. He was surprised for some reason by her name. He repeated her name as he sat down, then slowly nodded and laughed softly as if he were enjoying a private joke.

'I'm not intending to be personal, but how do you spell your name, Madeleine?' he asked.

She spelt it for him.

'I see,' he said. 'That's the French spelling, but you are not French.'

'No, American. My mother preferred that spelling.'

'I see,' he said again. He leaned back in his chair.

'Your surname – how do you spell that? With an 'EY', like the ship?'

'With an 'I'. G-A-L-L-I.'

'Does your family have a connection to this country?'

'Yes, my grandfather was from here, from this city in fact. Tolentino Galli.'

He nodded but said nothing.

'First, the cat's name interested you, now *my* name,' she said. 'Are you a student of names?'

He didn't answer the question directly. 'Names are important.'

'In what way?'

He didn't reply. Instead, he regarded her as if trying to decide something. She held his gaze and, without looking, reached for her glass. She located it and lifted it, her eyes not leaving his. He made his decision.

'Did you know your name derives from Magdalene – from Mary Magdalene, the…' he hesitated, '…the *companion* of Jesus?' He placed a slight emphasis on the word 'companion'.

'I've heard that, yes.'

'And that the surname Magdalene indicates that Mary came from Magdala, a village on the Sea of Galilee, and here we have you – Madeleine Galli – almost 'Magdalene Galilee'. I think that's interesting. Don't you think so?'

Madeleine sipped from her drink and replaced it on the table. She noticed for the first time – now that the table was cleared of his papers – that he didn't have anything to eat or drink in front of him. That was unusual. Mario was very efficient and wouldn't tolerate his tables being occupied by customers who didn't order.

'I suppose it is,' she agreed. 'I hadn't thought of it like that before. And Bastia?'

'Ah yes, Bastia.'

She waited, and when he leaned back, looking thoughtful, she asked: 'What's interesting about Bastia?' She tilted her head, attempting nonchalance, but she had to admit she was intrigued. 'Does her name have a biblical origin, too?'

'Way beyond biblical,' he said. '*Bast* was an Egyptian goddess; at first a sun goddess of war when she was portrayed as a lion but she later became a moon goddess of fertility and was identified as…' he waved his hand at Bastia, '…a black cat.'

'A black cat,' Madeleine repeated. She looked down at Bastia. The cat was regarding Logan over the rim of the table, her ears pricked forward as if listening to his words.

He glanced at his watch then reached for his briefcase and stood up.

'Madeleine, I'm pleased to have met you, but I have an appointment that cannot wait.' He extended his hand again to her.

She accepted his handshake. 'I'm glad that chance brought us together at this table,' she said. 'It's been very…' she searched for the word, '…*informative* meeting you.'

He held her hand longer than was necessary. His skin was smooth and warm.

'In my experience,' he said, 'nothing much happens by chance.' He moved his hand until he was just holding her fingers, lifting them. 'In ways that you cannot know, Madeleine, you're a very interesting person to me. I'd like to continue this conversation. Can you dine with me tonight? I can pick you up at your hotel at nine.'

Later, she couldn't understand why she accepted without hesitation.

'On one condition,' she said.

'Which is…?'

'My condition is that you answer the question you evaded earlier and tell me what it is you do.'

He smiled. 'We can get to know each other better tonight. For now, let me just say I'm a collector.' He released her hand with a slight bow. 'Until nine.'

'*Bella* Madeleine!' A voice from behind made her turn her head. 'Why you not tell me you are here?'

Mario glided briskly up to clear the table behind his departing customer and was surprised when there was nothing to clear. He looked about in obvious bewilderment.

'*Ciao,* my dear Mario – I arrived this morning.'

A tune snippet from her phone announced the receipt of a text. That would be an acknowledgement of her symposium confirmation. She reached for the phone and tucked it into her bag, her eyes on Logan as he stepped into the street and headed towards the square.

He didn't look back.

She turned to Mario and returned his warm smile. 'I hope you've been well…' she said.

It took five minutes for her to realise she hadn't told Logan where she was staying.

CHAPTER TWO

A beautiful night, the Magari, and the power…

Friday 8:40 pm

The woman staring at her from the bathroom mirror was a little taller than she'd like to have been. Being tall tended to intimidate shorter men, which sometimes made for difficult relationships, both personal and professional. She was pleased, however, that the woman had a trim and, yes, attractive figure, not too thin – 'with meat on her bones' as her father liked to say. *Also*, she thought wryly, *neither top heavy nor bottom heavy.* She turned sideways and smoothed her dress around her hips. She'd chosen a simple black knee-length dress with a round neck accentuated by a single string of pearls. She noted appreciatively the straight back and full legs in the reflection. Both dance and college track had contributed to her firm shape, with her ballet teacher, Miss Emilie, responsible for drilling into her the 'proper posture' she now carried without thought.

'You're in charge, Miss Galli, don't let gravity take over. Control is the key, girl. Walk *boldly*, as if you own every step.'

Madeleine could easily recall Miss Emilie's surprisingly deep-voiced instructions issuing from her stick-like frame, even now, almost ten years later. The teacher had repeated those or similar words over the years until they resonated like a broken record, but they had done their job.

Madeleine leaned forward to check her eye-liner and pressed her lips together to smooth her lipstick. She tilted her head, pushing aside the ebony-black hair that fell as straight as a waterfall onto her shoulders, to inspect her matching pearl earrings, then, satisfied, she took a step back.

The woman's emerald green eyes returned her look with confidence. She glanced at her watch.

What did she know about Logan Milan?

As always, she trusted what she called her 'instincts', although she knew her talent – the combination of training and natural ability – was at a much higher level than instinct. She had detected nothing negative, which, of course – she rationalized with a smile – she could legitimately interpret as a favourable verdict. Also, she looked forward to meeting him again because there were some unanswered questions in the air. When she reviewed their encounter at the café, there were moments she didn't understand. Why had he not ordered anything? Strangers didn't get to sit more than a few seconds before Mario was 'on their case'. What was his actual occupation? She wanted to follow up on his vague answer of 'a collector' by asking at least the question – of what?

She stopped in the doorway between bathroom and bedroom. Why was she so obsessed with his occupation? She *wasn't* obsessed, she told herself, just curious. *Justifiably* curious.

'And…' she said aloud, wagging her finger for emphasis, '…you made some statements I would like clarified. 'Black cats – windows to the soul?' What was that about? What was the other one? 'Nothing much happens by chance'. Oh no, Logan Milan, you're not going to get away…'

She stopped in mid-sentence. Calm down. He may not even show. How could he? How could he know where she was staying? Why was she acting as if he would arrive at nine? More likely, he will now be annoyed, realising he hadn't asked her for the name of her hotel.

She shook her head. Are you in control, Miss Galli? Yes, Miss Emilie. Then behave like it, Miss Galli.

She bent to pick up a small black bag from the bed and slipped the thin silver chain over her shoulder.

AT PRECISELY NINE O'CLOCK, Logan Milan entered the lounge of the Hotel Moresco. He was dressed in a charcoal suit with a white shirt and dark blue tie. His hair, which she had thought long at the café, now perfectly suited the image he presented – what was the phrase? – 'a sophisticated man about town'; no – he was a man *of* the town.

Without hesitation, he crossed to where she was sitting and held out his hand to help her rise from her chair.

'Madeleine,' he said. 'You look very beautiful.'

'Thank you, *Signore.*' She took his offered hand.

'Please…' he inclined his other hand toward the entrance. 'I don't want to waste a moment. I have a gondola waiting on the *Rio Nuovo.*'

She was relieved to find that Logan was an inch or so taller than her.

'How on earth did you find me…?'

He held up a hand. 'Outside…' he said, with a theatrical tone, '…dusk has just turned to twilight. It's the perfect time for a journey along the canals – an experience only our wonderful *Venezia* can provide. A beautiful night and a beautiful city await us. Time enough for questions later.'

In less than a minute, he steadied the gondola as she stepped from the landing. Logan introduced the gondolier as 'Nico', a broad-shouldered young man with a mop of tousled blond hair who flashed a broad smile as a greeting, his perfect teeth shining in the dusky moonlight. Madeleine was helped into a double seat in the middle of the gondola.

Logan was about to join her when a loud voice said: 'Hey, buddy, is this boat for hire?'

She turned her head to see a large man standing on the landing. He was overweight, but his short-sleeved shirt revealed thick, powerful arms, and from his knee-length pants emerged two solidly muscular legs. He looked like a weightlifter or a wrestler. Two cameras on straps around his neck rested on a colourful Hawaiian-style shirt. Behind him, a small woman with dyed blonde hair looked embarrassed. She put her hand on his elbow and said: 'Robert, please…'

The man shrugged her hand off. 'I'm just *asking*. No harm in that. What about it, son. I'll pay double your fee. The lady can get the next one.'

Madeleine heard Nico say calmly: '*No, Signore.*'

The man noticed Logan and addressed him.

'Hey there! We've made a wrong turn somewhere, and I just wanna get back to the hotel. Let me have your boat and this young paddler, and I'll make it worth your while.'

Nico started again: '*Signore…*'

The man rounded on him, his voice tight. 'Look, sonny, just keep outa this, OK? I'm talkin' with the man now.'

Logan said softly in her ear: 'Excuse me.'

Nico wiped his hands on his trousers and took a step toward the man, but Logan quickly moved to his side and lightly touched his shoulder as he passed by. A look of disappointment appeared momentarily on Nico's face, but he moved back as Logan jumped nimbly onto the landing. He was fingering his bracelets as he stepped up to the man. Madeleine could see it wasn't nervousness; he had a confident air.

He stood close to the man, taking him by the elbow, just as the woman had, and talked to him in a low voice that Madeleine couldn't hear. The man's face had flushed at Logan's approach, but Logan's words somehow quickly soothed that anger.

After only a second or two, the man relaxed and became surprisingly calm. He nodded to Logan.

'Of course,' he said. 'I understand completely. Thank you.' He looked down at Madeleine. 'Ma'am, I'm sorry to have disturbed your evening. Please excuse me.'

Madeleine could see that the apology was genuine but so out of character that she could only nod dumbly at him. He took the woman by the shoulder, gently turned her around, and with a hand on her back, he guided her away from the landing, leaning down to talk to her. She threw a bewildered glance over her shoulder and then had to hurry to keep up with him.

Logan stepped from the landing and stayed for a moment talking with Nico, patting him on the shoulder, then returned to sit alongside her and at his signal, they were smoothly underway.

Madeleine leaned against the back of her seat, took a deep breath and closed her eyes.

The confrontation had made her heart race, and she wondered briefly what Logan had said to the man to make him change his mind. It was remarkable that the man's belligerence had been overcome so swiftly. *That man was used to getting his own way.* Logan's smooth handling of the situation was impressive, but there was still something odd about the outcome.

For the second time, she asked herself if she was being foolish – heading off to an unknown destination with a man she had only met for five minutes – a meeting which could hardly be considered normal and at which almost everything he said was strange. After a moment's reflection, she chose to trust her instincts. She didn't view the strangeness as alarming but rather as an intriguing set of responses that invited further exploration.

She opened her eyes to glance at Logan and received a warm smile in return and a wave of the hand encompassing the canal and the surrounding scene. His expression was open and genuine. He had plainly dismissed the incident and was again at ease, saying as clearly as if he had spoken: *I told you it would be beautiful. Just sit back and enjoy.*

It was not completely quiet – they were surrounded by sounds – but she felt isolated as if being on the water separated her from the other inhabitants of the city. She was part of an exclusive group – those who were at this moment travelling along the canals of Venice. Nico began to hum a familiar tune which Madeleine initially could not place, but after she had joined in for a few bars in her head, she recognised *Santa Lucia*.

'You found a musical Gondolier,' she whispered to Logan. 'How wonderful.'

'He is the Neapolitan boatman inviting you to enjoy the cool of the evening on his boat, an escape from the heat of the afternoon – that's what the Italian version of the song says, but you may have already known that.'

'No,' she said. 'I didn't know that.' She knew the tune well but, while her command of Italian was adequate and grew with every visit to the country, she had heard it sung almost exclusively in English and hadn't tried to translate the Italian words.

Nico started to softly sing, his voice a beautifully smooth and clear tenor. He sang easily, holding the tune comfortably and releasing it into the clear night air with perfect phrasing; a note held a fraction long, followed by a pause to build the anticipation, in true Italian style. After Logan's explanation, she listened to the words and lifted her hand to feel the night air when he sang *Con questo zeffiro, cosi soave* – 'with this breeze, so sweet'. *Santa Lucia* thought Madeleine – Saint Lucy. She hadn't heard of Saint Lucy, but she would have bet good money that Logan knew all about her.

She was soon lost as they glided past streets she had never visited, past doorways lit by pale yellow lights where men sat on steps, cigarettes held limply in their hands, trailing smoke towards the rooftops. The soft voice of a mother reading to an unseen child, her back catching the cool of the evening through an open window. Two cats sitting on the edge of a wooden pier as still as statues, moving only their eyes to watch the gondola slip by until distracted by the flop of a fish. A young couple, teenagers, embracing against an advertisement painted on a brick wall, their shadowed privacy exposed by the searchlight of an opening door. Each vignette appeared and disappeared as they passed by, lit by street lights and by the pale moon, like a stage show presenting a series of scenes each visible for only a few seconds.

Her reverie was interrupted when the gondola slowed. She had no idea how long it had been since she had stepped from the hotel landing; it could have been fifteen minutes or fifty. She waited for Nico to complete the mooring of the gondola before rising and thanking him earnestly.

'That was wonderful. Thank you. I'll never hear that song again without thinking of you,' she said, squeezing his hand between hers. Although his skin was smooth to her touch, beneath the skin his hand felt incredibly firm.

'It was my pleasure, ma'am,' Nico replied, surprising her with both his use of English and his American accent.

'Oh, but... I thought...'

Logan's hand took her elbow to help her onto the landing.

'I know,' he said conspiratorially, his face bent close to hers. 'When I first met Nico, he surprised me too, but in a different way.'

Madeleine stared at him as she stepped onto the wooden planks, pleasantly piqued at his introduction of yet another mystery. She kept her voice neutral: 'You must tell me about that sometime.'

He smiled at her and nodded. 'Perhaps I will.'

THE SETTING THAT GREETED her was similar to the one outside her hotel – a brightly lit frontage illuminating a narrow cobbled street that separated the building from the canal, with the stones worn smooth by the rubbing of countless feet. The entrance Logan now led her through was smaller but the closeness of the walls and especially the golden glow of the antique lantern above the door only served to make it seem more homely and inviting.

Above the door was painted a single word: *MAGARI*.

It was an unusual name for a hotel. Madeleine translated the word as 'Maybe' or 'If only' – a look into the future with a feeling of hope. *But*, she thought, *on this night, the unusual was becoming common.*

A small man with wizened features and a hawk-like nose stepped out from behind the reception desk. He wore black perfectly-creased trousers and a gold-trimmed black waistcoat covering a red and white striped shirt. Age had whitened his hair and bent his back but his pace was brisk and his eyes sparkled as he hurried to meet his guests, wringing his hands with pleasure.

'Exactly as you described her, *Signore* – a flawless diamond worthy of the Queen of the Nile herself.'

Logan smiled broadly. 'That wasn't meant to be repeated, Pietro…'

'Oh, I'm sure it was, *Signore*, I'm sure it was.' Pietro turned his attention from Madeleine to Logan. 'You'll find that everything is ready upstairs, but you don't *need* to take the stairs if you don't wish to; the elevator is at your disposal and is, as you know, very reliable. If it were my choice…'

'Allow me to introduce…' interrupted Logan, '…and also apologise for, the man without whom my humble hotel would crumble to dust, and…' he added good-naturedly, '…a man who talks far too much. This is Pietro, who has known this hotel for…'

'More years than you can count,' finished Pietro. He bowed deeply. '*Signora*, please allow me to escort you…'

'We can do our own escorting, thank you Pietro. You may be needed if other guests arrive.'

Madeleine was amused to note that the last comment had surprised Pietro, and consequently, since the time she had entered the foyer, this was the first sentence to have been completed without interruption.

'Other guests?' said Pietro, 'There are no…'

'A night like this – who's to say? Someone may come in at any time,' said Logan. He thought a moment, then asked: 'When are the Rosenbergs due?'

'Not until Tuesday evening.'

'Good. We'll let you know if we need anything.' He called over his shoulder: 'Nico, we'll take the elevator. We'll be in the Blue Room.'

Taking Madeleine's elbow once more, he said: 'You'll find the elevator quite cosy. It was definitely *not* designed for large parties.'

LOGAN DIRECTED HER TO a table positioned in a bay window with a view over the rooftops of the old city. If Madeleine's sense of direction was accurate, the canal would be below the window although it was out of sight. In any respectable Venetian restaurant, a table with a view like this would be difficult to obtain without special connections or a prior booking made months ahead. In this restaurant, there was no such problem. Although there were ten other tables decorated and set in the same manner as theirs; they were the only guests. One difference was that the other tables were set for four, but theirs for only two.

As suggested by the name Logan had used, the predominant colour in the room was blue. Lush thick velvet floor-to-ceiling curtains hung in the bay window to either side of their table, the deep hue matching both the table cloths and the carpet, with the table-top napkins a lighter colour for contrast. A lit candle in the centre of the table supported the shade of the napkins and released a delicate fragrance of jasmine into the air.

After seeing Madeleine to her seat, Logan seated himself and drew a bottle of white wine from the ice bucket on a stand beside his chair. He checked the label and then removed and examined the cork. He poured a tasting amount into her glass, then waited patiently while she swirled the wine and put her nose to the rim before tilting the glass to take a little on her lips.

'It has the colour of chardonnay but a taste more like sauvignon, and – something else – is it a blend?'

'Bravo,' he said. 'Yes, there are several other grape varieties added.' He poured the same amount into his own glass and repeated her actions, spending a long time assessing the bouquet before tasting.

He held the glass before his eyes, swirling the liquid and letting it catch the light of the candle. His eyes, Madeleine noted, were a pale blue, a contrast with his tanned face that she hadn't noticed in the sunlight at the café.

'After years where Italian white wines have languished a distant second behind the reds,' he mused, 'I think with this vintage, they have at last produced one that's worthy.'

She held out her glass to be filled, but he said: 'We'll order first – this wine should *accompany* the meal.'

As if waiting for those very words, Nico appeared at the table. Somehow, Madeleine was not surprised to see him.

'What would you like to order, ma'am?' he asked. Even when speaking, his full voice made her think of the rolling hills of… somewhere. Wales? She imagined a place where his beautiful singing could be heard for miles across the valleys.

She looked around. 'I don't have a menu.'

'Order whatever you like,' said Logan. 'If we don't have it we can quickly get it.'

Her smile was mischievous. 'Crocodile?'

Logan's face remained calm. 'Overrated,' he said. 'Anything else?'

Madeleine gave his request some thought. 'With this wine… I would like fresh salmon stuffed with melted parmesan.'

Logan nodded his approval. To Nico, he said: 'I'll have a rib eye with…' he paused, '…garlic and cream, I think. We'll start with langoustine bisque, not…'

Nico said: '…too spicy,' in perfect unison with Logan.

Logan smiled. 'Indeed,' he said, '…and some vegetables…' He looked at Madeleine. Did she want anything in particular? She shook her head.

'I'd like some snow peas, but have ShangWu choose the rest.'

As he finished the order, Logan glanced at the wine bottle. Nico acknowledged with a nod and left the table.

'Something about the wine doesn't meet with your approval?' asked Madeleine.

'Quite the contrary. I was just reminding him, although I'm sure he didn't need it, of the particular bottle we are starting with tonight. He'll have our food prepared accordingly.'

'Please don't tell me he's going to cook it too.'

'He's an excellent cook, in fact, and enjoys creating extravagant dishes, but no, tonight we have a chef for that task. Nico will, however, make sure the food meets our expectations.'

There was a pause and they both began to speak together, stopping and smiling at the same time. Logan indicated she should continue.

'Several times you've said 'we' or 'my' when referring to this hotel. Do you work here or stay here or have some sort of interest...?'

He sighed. 'I own this hotel. For better or worse, the *Magari* is mine.'

'Oh,' she said appreciatively. 'So, is your occupation 'Hotel Owner'? How many hotels do you own?' She said the last light-heartedly, but his reply was serious.

'Several. Throughout Europe, from Spain to Russia and in the Middle East and India. Two in Egypt. A few also in North America.'

She took some time to digest his statement. The unexpected answer had, as her father would have said, 'taken the wind out of her sails'. Was this what he collected? Hotels?

'You don't seem worried that there are no other guests. Is this hotel not doing well?'

His reaction was again not what she expected. He was amused.

'You won't find the *Magari* in any travel guide,' he said. 'We are registered and we pay the required taxes, and we do have guests occasionally, people from the street and some referrals, but my hotels are not for commercial profit. I use them for other things.'

'Like entertaining ladies for dinner?'

'Exactly.'

Her hand reached absentmindedly for her wine glass. To keep a hotel, even a relatively small one such as this, operational but not actively seeking custom must be very costly. And he said he has several. Another unresolved mystery to be tucked away.

She asked: 'What were you going to say, before, when we...?'

'I was going to say that you have impressed me tonight.'

In the face of his revelation about hotel ownership, her first thought was that he was trying to pamper her ego.

'How can I have impressed you?'

'In many ways that, for the moment, you will know nothing about, but I'll start with the obvious.' He ticked off the items on his fingers. 'First, you freely came with me tonight, a person you did not really know, to an unknown destination, and you came relaxed and with confidence and poise. Second, you understood the words to *Santa Lucia*...' As her eyebrows raised, he grinned, '... or at least some of them. Third, you were not worried when you saw we would be alone in the restaurant. Fourth, you can appreciate good wine, and, from the order you gave to Nico, I have no doubt – also good food, and, fifth...' he paused. 'I'm running out of fingers, so this will be the last.' He placed his hands on the table.

'Fifth, I know this day has been strange for you. I know you have questions and I've asked you to delay them several times. I'll answer your questions, all of them, tonight, but I'd like to do that when the time is right – *after* we've eaten. Through all this strangeness, I know you're enjoying yourself and have maintained your humour.'

He smiled at her. 'I only wish we'd been able to give you a fillet of crocodile tail.'

NICO PLACED A CUP of coffee in front of her and enquired: 'Was the meal satisfactory, ma'am?'

'Beautiful. Please call me Madeleine. The bisque was delicious as was the salmon – but there was something else with the parmesan...'

'A small addition of artichoke – the chef's suggestion.'

'It was perfect.'

'I'll let him know.'

He set Logan's cup on the table. Madeleine touched her hand to her cup to gauge how hot it was, expecting to need to leave it for a while until it cooled. It was hot but not too hot. She brought the cup almost to her lips, testing the heat by holding the steaming liquid close to her skin, enjoying the aroma. It was the perfect temperature, ready for drinking, and she took a mouthful. There was a chocolate taste mixed with the coffee. She made an appreciative face.

Nico was watching her, and he smiled when he saw she approved.

'It's unusual, isn't it?' He turned to Logan. 'To follow…?'

'Brandy, I think.'

'Of course.'

They waited while Nico efficiently and unhurriedly gathered the plates and the used cutlery.

Logan lifted his coffee cup and sat back in his chair. He regarded her over the rim.

'Where would you like to start?'

While Madeleine took a few seconds to organise her thoughts, Logan drank from his coffee.

'I'll start with your hotels,' she said. 'If you wanted a place to stay or entertain, or whatever, in different locations, surely a house or apartment would be better. For one thing, it would be a much cheaper option.'

'Apartments and houses, even remote ones, have neighbours. People arriving for short stays and then leaving are noticed. But people coming and going from a hotel is not unusual – it's expected. Hotels are in handy locations – near the city centre. Also,' he shrugged, 'I *like* hotels.'

'But you can have guests staying at your hotels. Don't they interfere with your private activities? Don't they notice anything strange?'

'Any guest who stays at any of my hotels has a very enjoyable and very normal experience.'

'But,' Madeleine persisted, 'in this hotel, for instance, wouldn't a couple wonder why they were the only people dining?'

'If necessary, Pietro would arrange other diners for such an occasion. We are well practised at this. I can show you dozens of letters giving this hotel, and all my hotels, glowing reviews. We do, in fact, have return guests like Eli Rosenberg and his wife Eleanor from Philadelphia who've stayed here four or five times now.'

Her mind whirled at the expense of maintaining such contingencies.

'OK,' she conceded. 'You said you use the hotels for entertainment, but there must be more to this arrangement than that?'

'It's a matter of convenience, and other requirements which the hotels satisfy very well.'

She couldn't help but feel she was playing a game. He was being both open and a little secretive. She thought of the questions she had wanted to ask when she was in her hotel room – the moments from their meeting in the café that had puzzled her. She leaned forward.

'Why did you invite me here tonight? Our meeting was by chance – wasn't it?'

'I invited you because I wanted to learn more about you. I didn't engineer our meeting, if that concerns you, but I don't attribute it to pure chance. Chance is an elusive concept. Philosophically, I would argue that nothing occurs completely by chance.'

She met his gaze across the table.

'Allow me to ask a question of my own,' he said. When she nodded, he continued: 'Madeleine, when you approached my table at the café, how did you feel?'

'What do you mean?'

'The table was covered with papers; did my table look inviting to you?'

'All of the other tables were occupied. It was the only free chair.'

'OK. When you sat down, you still felt nothing unusual?'

'Not that I can recall.' She thought for a moment. 'I was mildly surprised that you did allow me to share. Why did you? You were obviously in the middle of something.'

'Yes, something important. But the fact that you were able to *ask* to share my table made you literally stand out from the crowd. It made you very interesting to me. It's one of the reasons why I invited you here tonight.'

'That doesn't make sense.'

'Would it surprise you to know that, before you, several other people had approached my table in the same circumstances, but none had asked to share? In fact, all of them left the café.'

When she didn't reply, he said: 'When they got near my table, these people felt uneasy, and the closer they approached, the worse they felt. If they had attempted to sit down, they would have become quite nauseous. But you didn't feel like that, did you?'

She shook her head. 'No, I didn't.' When he didn't speak immediately, she added: 'I presume that also applied to Mario, the waiter.'

'Yes, it would have.'

'But how…? Why?'

Logan leaned forward, resting on his elbows, and linked his fingers together. He didn't speak for a few seconds, contemplating either what to say or how to say it.

'Let me start from the beginning. Before this moment, I wasn't sure how much I would tell you this evening, but I think you deserve an explanation because I believe our lives have intersected for a reason.'

'What I'm about to say, you're going to find hard to accept.' He paused to assess her reaction. 'Please… all I ask is that you suspend your disbelief until you've heard me out.'

She took the time to drink the last of her coffee and replace the cup. She studied him. His face and manner held no trace of deception or dishonesty. She nodded slowly.

'What do you know about hypnosis or the power of suggestion? Have you seen stage hypnotists?'

'Yes, I have. Amongst the silly stuff, I've seen some things that were quite incredible.'

'What incredible things have you seen?'

28

'Evidence of unusual strength, unnatural reactions such as stiffening of the body. Elimination of pain… enhancement of memory, and… control over the senses like taste and smell. That sort of thing.'

'Good. Anything else?'

'Oh yes – involuntary reactions to phrases. The hypnotist says a phrase – or he could play music, I think – anyway, something he has previously pre-programmed into the subject, and a person who has returned to his seat jumps up and crows like a rooster.'

He chuckled. 'That's right. So… words have been spoken – a 'suggestion' has been made – and, in the example you mentioned, the words have had a mysterious influence on someone with a distance and time separation.'

'That's putting it very formally, but yes – that's what happens.'

'Do you believe it's genuine, or is there some trickery involved?'

They both sat back as Nico arrived with two large brandy glasses, each containing a generous amount of liquid that was the colour of a beautiful deep amber. He carefully placed one in front of Madeleine and then Logan, collected their coffee cups and retired immediately. Madeleine was impressed with his professional manner. He seemed to have many talents.

She picked up her glass, cupped the bowl in her hands to warm it and swirled the brandy.

'What do we have here?' she asked. 'An XO Cognac?' The evidence of her eyes and nose indicated a superior quality.

'An *Hors d'âge* Armagnac, actually.'

'I can only presume that *Hors d'âge* is an excellent mark.'

'The best. It literally means 'ageless'.'

'Yes,' she said, 'or, *more* literally, 'without age'.' She smiled at him and he returned her smile with a nod to acknowledge her point. She lowered her eyes and regarded the fractured reflections of the candlelight moving on the surface of the liquid as if trying to pry out its secrets using her gaze alone.

'Both,' she said, giving a delayed answer to his question about hypnosis. She raised her eyes to meet his. 'I believe the effects of hypnosis are real but there may sometimes be trickery involved. I accept a stage show may have paid accomplices to provide the expected reaction, but I know that hypnotherapy is also used seriously both medically and psychologically.'

'That's true,' he said. 'Now, let's take a step in a different direction. You've heard stories, of course, of witches and the spells they use. What do you think of these stories?'

'They're just stories. A product of superstitious minds. Women have been persecuted as witches in the past through fear and ignorance but in this more enlightened time we know witches don't exist and their spells only appear in scary stories meant for children.'

'That's a fair assessment. But...' He paused. 'Let's assume for the moment that witches *did* exist – would you accept that their spells could work in a similar way to a hypnotic suggestion? After all, both involve an attempt to influence someone using words.'

'The witches also use eye of newt and toe of frog if I remember my Macbeth.'

'Yes, exactly. In the folklore, strange and unfamiliar objects can be used to enhance the spell and give more power to the words. An object that performs this function is called a talisman.'

'Well, OK, for the sake of argument, I can see a connection.'

Logan's face became serious. He leaned forward and again clasped his hands in front of him.

'What if I were to tell you that the use of hypnosis or suggestion – the power of words said in the right way at the right time, just like a spell in fact – is an ancient art and many of the old stories and myths that different cultures have about the abilities of witches or wizards are sourced from those ancient times. Even today, the stories we hear often contain gems of truth, although they're usually twisted almost beyond recognition.'

Logan picked up his brandy glass and stared into the liquid as if looking into a crystal ball.

'From my own investigation,' he continued, 'I know that the knowledge and use of this hypnotic power dates back to around three thousand years *before* the birth of Jesus – to Egypt, and to the time of the rise of a man named Menes; a very powerful man who united Upper and Lower Egypt and became the first Pharaoh. I could talk all night about Menes and also two sisters who were influential at the time and, as fascinating as I'm sure you would find the story, we'll leave it for now – in the past.'

He looked up at her and waited for her to process his words.

'I'm sure you know where this is leading. Throughout history, there have been people who have used this 'power', let's just call it that, with both good intentions and bad. And, yes, there are people today who have studied it and become skilled in its use.'

Madeleine studied Logan's face but didn't say anything. He didn't flinch under her gaze.

She lifted her glass and was just about to drink when she lowered it a fraction and said: 'Have you been using this… this *power* on me? Is that how I was persuaded to be here tonight? Am I under your spell?'

He shook his head. 'No, I have used no persuasion as such on you, and I never will, not without your permission. In your case, actually, I'm not sure I could.'

'So…' She took a sip of the Armagnac and held it in her mouth for a few seconds before allowing it to trickle down her throat, '…you admit to being one of these skilled practitioners you've just mentioned?'

He inclined his head but didn't reply.

'And what did you mean, just now, when you said: '…used no persuasion *as such*?'

'I have not used the power to persuade you, but I did tell you about the meaning of your name in the hope you would be interested to learn more and agree to meet again.' He gave a quiet laugh. 'I almost asked you if your middle name was 'Lee' because the name Madeleine Lee Galli would have been a nice twist on 'Galilee'.'

'No,' she said with a smile. 'My middle name is not 'Lee'.'

The Armagnac was heavenly, worthy of its 'ageless' name, and she took another sip, mulling his words and appraising him while she savoured the delicious flavour and enjoyed the tingle on her tongue. The evening was pleasant, very much so, but was there any hidden agenda here? She had made a profession of her ability to see past the exposed layers that people presented and recognise what lay behind; the deviousness, dishonesty and lies – or, alternatively, the genuineness and truth. She searched his face and posture for decisive clues. Once again, he met her eyes openly. She saw only sincerity. He believed the words he was saying.

He took her silence as an invitation to continue.

'When I asked if you had seen anything on one of my papers, you mentioned you had seen some country names – do you remember now what they were?'

'Yes. I saw 'Iceland', 'Japan', 'America', and 'Italy'.'

'How certain are you of those words?'

She took a moment to think. 'Very certain. What's this about?'

Logan raised his hand and Madeleine turned to see Nico approaching with a briefcase, right on cue, as if he had been waiting for the signal. She watched him and noticed that he moved with a remarkably smooth gait, seeming to glide across the floor with no effort, his upper body quite still. He caught her watching and gave a broad and honest smile which she could not help but return.

Logan opened the case, extracted some papers and selected the top one. Nico remained at the table.

'These are the papers I had on my table in the café this afternoon and this is the page you glanced at.' The paper was still folded as she had seen it but he unfolded it and passed it to her.

She looked at the page. Written across the top half of the page was: '*Iceland, Japan, America, Italy*'. Below the fold, aligned underneath the country names and connected by a line to each, were the words '*Kjarval, Akihiro, Kimi,* and *Sapphire?*'. Below the last word was written '*Venice?*'.

'As you can see,' Logan said, 'you saw and recalled the countries correctly, but – and this is the part I find intriguing – I would have sworn that I removed the paper before you had time to *consciously* see anything written there. Do you have an eidetic memory?'

She continued to stare at the page.

'Is this some sort of trick?' Her voice sounded a little harsher than she intended.

Had everything since the café meeting been orchestrated to get to this point? Just to present a cheap magician's trick? She was mildly annoyed but also intrigued. If it was a trick, it was a very elaborate one – and for what purpose?

She lowered her glass to the table. She looked at him closely, professionally. His expression was open and genuine.

'How could you possibly know that?' she asked.

The only reaction from Logan was to also place his glass on the table.

'Know what?' he said, his voice even.

So, for some reason he wanted her to spell it out.

'That my middle name is Kimi. It's a very unusual name and an unusual spelling. We've just talked about my middle name a few minutes ago but there's no way you could have known what it was.'

He stared at her and then a smile formed at the corner of his mouth. He gave that soft chuckle she had heard before.

She sighed and relaxed. Maybe it *was* just his little joke.

'You got me,' she said, 'I didn't see it coming. How did you do it?'

'Madeleine, please believe me when I tell you I'm not playing tricks on you. I didn't know about your middle name. But it's another piece to fit into the puzzle.'

'You see,' he continued before she could speak. 'I've asked myself a similar question to the one you asked earlier. Why did we meet? More light is being shone on that question with every passing minute. I'll explain what I mean, but indulge me a moment longer. You said your grandfather was Italian. I assume from your surname that would be your paternal grandfather and that on your mother's side you have an ancestry that is American to the core. *Native* American – is that true?'

'Well… yes, one-eighth or one-sixteenth or some such number.'

'Then I can further state with confidence that your family – your *mother's* family – is almost certainly from the eastern seaboard of North America and that your Native American ancestry is Algonquin.'

Her mouth opened in astonishment.

He held up a hand. 'It's not a trick. I'm just using information and deduction. *This* Kimi…' he pointed to the name on the page, '… is a wonderful woman in her eighties, and she was well and still possessed of her wicked sense of humour when I last visited her. She's also of Algonquin heritage, one-half I think.'

'You're telling me my name appearing on the paper isn't a trick?'

'Not at all. Kimi lives in Charlotte, North Carolina.'

'Really?' She felt a slight suspicion returning, but how could it be anything more than coincidence? 'Now I have a 'did you know',' she said. 'Did you know that I am from Charlottes*ville*, Virginia? I imagine you'll find that 'interesting' too. He nodded, and she said: 'So all this is just a set of amazing coincidences?'

'Oh, it's no coincidence – of that I'm certain. It's pieces fitting together. I was able to guess your heritage because Kimi told me her name is an Algonquin name. She said it actually means *secret* in the Algonquin language. Did you know that?'

He smiled, realising he was continuing the 'did you know' game. His smile relaxed her.

'No. It's an inherited name in our family; a tradition – the oldest girl in each generation is given Kimi as a middle name.'

She looked up at Nico, still standing beside the table, his manner both relaxed and attentive, and saw he was watching her with an expression of… it took her a moment to recognise it… of sympathy. He sympathised with her bewilderment. She intuitively knew that he believed Logan's incredible tale but he also understood her position.

'Ah. More light,' said Logan. 'I wonder if you're related to my Kimi?'

She shrugged, reached for her glass and sat back in her chair, holding the glass of Armagnac between her hands. He leaned over and picked up the paper from where she had placed it, moving it into the centre and smoothing it. He handed the other papers to Nico, who replaced them in the briefcase and left the table.

Logan lifted his eyes from the paper back to Madeleine.

'As you suspected,' he said, 'I've studied and practised what you call hypnosis or suggestion, which I call the 'power', and I've attained a level of proficiency in its use. Before I can explain further, however, there's some background you need to understand. I'll try to be brief.'

He waited for her nod before continuing.

'Several years ago, I finally acquired a manuscript I'd been seeking for some time, a manuscript purporting to be a copy of a papyrus originating in the old city of Bubastis in Lower Egypt, which detailed the requirements and expectations of a practitioner of the power and the rules governing its use, much like the Rule of Benedict did for medieval monks in the eighth century. The manuscript divides practitioners into four levels of proficiency: Initiate, Advocate, Sage and Master. I have only recently, after a twelve-year journey, attained the level of a Master.'

'The paper you saw lists the country of residence and the name of the three other people I know in the world who have achieved the highest level. Two of them I know well: Akihiro in Japan and Kimi in North Carolina. Kjarval, from Iceland, I've only met once, but we all correspond frequently. Importantly, we four share the same philosophy regarding the power and its use.'

He leaned forward. 'Recently, there's been a series of disturbing events in Asia and, more recently, also in Europe, which lead me to believe there is a fifth person using the power at the level of a Master. Based on information I've received from a friend, I've added Italy to the list. Despite a concentration of his activity initially in Asia, I have reason to suspect this Master is based in Italy.'

He rubbed his chin with his hand, momentarily distracted.

'The waves created by the Italian Master, in fact…' he said to himself, '…are increasing at a worrying rate.'

He looked up, and his focus returned.

'Now, let me mention three related things you would have heard of, I'm sure.'

He held up his hand as he had done before and ticked each item off on his fingers.

'*One*. I'm talking about hypnosis, and you will have heard that people can't be hypnotised against their will. The truth is that people have varying degrees of resistance, but, even then, to guard against being hypnotised, you must be aware of the attempt, and there are several ways to circumvent that.'

'For instance, number *two,* you will also have heard of unconscious learning, subliminal advertising and so on – influences that happen below the level of consciousness. Some of this works, but most doesn't, simply because the people don't know what they're doing.'

'And *three*; you're no doubt aware that the brain filters the information it receives, allowing our conscious mind to receive only a part of that information, and you've also probably heard it said that our brain only works at a fraction of its potential.' He smiled. 'I suppose that's really *four* things.'

Madeleine acknowledged each of his points and smiled at the last two. In her briefcase at the hotel was a recent research paper on the topic of brain stimulation and consciousness.

Logan lowered his hand and leaned back.

'You may ask – what's the connection? Well, regarding the filtering… All our senses – vision, hearing, smell, even touch and taste – provide the brain with a much wider range of input than our conscious mind recognises. We actually hear sounds for instance at much lower and higher frequencies than we realise and also much quieter sounds than you would think it is possible to hear. Your brain simply interprets this extra 'noise' as meaningless or unimportant and discards it. *But*, and this is the important part, the sounds *are* received, and certain sounds, or I should say, certain *sequences* of sounds, do still have an effect on the brain even though the person may be entirely unaware of it happening and therefore powerless to resist it. These sounds do not even need to have meaning, in the sense of a language, to be effective.'

She nodded to show she was following him.

'While I was working at the café, I didn't want to be disturbed, so when a person approached me, I uttered a few words – you could legitimately call it a 'spell' – and they would feel unsure or uneasy and lack the confidence to ask to share my table.'

'Then you arrived. You ignored my spell as if it wasn't there. At first, I was suspicious and thought there must have been some temporary aberration, that you somehow hadn't received my words. Maybe you were deaf. But when you asked to share my table, I could see that wasn't the case. I repeated the spell, adding a little more persuasion, expecting you to quickly leave. That didn't happen. Then you told me you had seen some words on one of my papers – words I knew were visible to you for such a short time you shouldn't have been able to register them.'

'Even so, I would still have dismissed that as just keen observation until you told me your name, which was quickly followed by an introduction to *Bast,* the black cat. These were two signs that I couldn't fail to notice.'

He paused, and Madeleine corrected him: 'The cat's name is *Bastia*. But I don't understand. What signs?'

'The names were the signs. Your name was a beacon illuminating the man the christians call Jesus, who was a great practitioner of the power, possibly the greatest; his followers called him Master for a reason.'

'I remember my name reminded you of Mary Magdalene, but that's hardly a *beacon* to Jesus. She was only his companion as you called her.'

'Mary was not his companion; she was his *wife*. Many ancient texts mention this – not the ones chosen by the early christians, though. It's probable she was as adept as he was in the power.'

'OK, so Bastia's name happens to be similar to *Bast*, a minor goddess of ancient Egypt. These are very tenuous signs it seems to me.'

'Not if you know that *Bast* was depicted as a black cat, and she was not always a minor goddess. She was the goddess of war at the time of the rise of the first Pharaoh Menes – I mentioned him earlier. Bast was at the top of the tree right at the time of the emergence of the power. She's an integral player at the point of origin, one of the two sisters I also mentioned. Her influence waned after a struggle for supremacy amongst the gods.'

'You're making it sound like you believe these ancient Egyptian gods were real.'

Logan thought before he answered.

'Let me put that a different way.' He leaned forward to emphasise his point. 'I believe a group of people became so powerful they were given godly status and treated as such. Since Menes' time, the Pharaoh was considered to be a living god, known as Horus in life and Osiris in death. Subsequent Pharaohs were reincarnations of Horus, who, like Bast, was related to the fertile earth of the Nile. The struggle I just mentioned is told in a persistent Egyptian myth which depicts a mighty battle with Horus and Bast allied against Sekhmet, who was associated with the desert. I mentioned two sisters earlier. In the myth, Sekhmet was Bast's sister. So, it's a conflict between the fertile black earth, the *good* earth, and the bad influence of the desert. I believe this battle is a depiction of the struggle for control of the power.'

He sat back and took a sip of his Armagnac, creating a deliberate pause to assess her reaction. When she didn't comment, he continued.

'To return to your question – your name and the cat's name got my attention. Add in your reaction to the power, or, rather, your amazing *lack* of reaction, and I told myself I should not ignore this woman. I wanted to find out more about you.'

Madeleine considered his words. 'So, now I know why you invited me here. Do you belong to a society or something similar?'

Logan nodded. 'In the course of my research, I've encountered some like-minded people and together we have formed a coalition, a society if you like, and set up some rules of behaviour. I've told you about the Masters, but there are several more, a dozen or so that I know of, at lower levels of proficiency. Those at the higher levels, the Masters and Sages, try to mentor these people and guide them. We know how the power could easily be misused, and we are determined to prevent its misuse.'

'You suspect this unknown Master is misusing the…' she hesitated, '…the *power* as you call it? I presume you mean using it to do someone harm?'

'Yes, exactly. Or for dishonest personal gain.'

He touched his finger to the word *Italy* on the paper.

'I suspect there's a Master in Italy, possibly even in Venice, whose influence has appeared fairly recently throughout Europe and Asia.' He tapped on the paper. 'In Europe, wealthy businessmen have suddenly lost all memory for extended periods – several days, usually. I have a friend looking into these incidents and trying to connect them. He was the one who traced their origin to Italy.'

'Even more disturbing…' Logan continued, '…are incidents occurring sporadically over the last year or so in Asia, particularly India and Sri Lanka.'

'What sort of incident?'

'The European episodes you may not have heard about because these businessmen withdrew large sums of money from their own or their firm's accounts and then had no idea what they did with the funds. I've talked with some of them and enhanced their memory. I traced their actions and discovered that in each case, they left the cash in a specific location, but that's all they know. Naturally, they're keen to keep these events quiet, not wanting their folly to be exposed.'

'The incidents in Asia are of two types. The first type differs from the European in that the events *are* public; you may have read about them in the newspapers. Over the last couple of years, there have been several reported thefts of large quantities of precious stones – rubies and emeralds from India and sapphires from Sri Lanka. The connection is that the thefts occurred with the *cooperation* of senior members of large jewellery houses who then remember nothing. My friend suspects similar incidents may, in fact, have been happening for many years, maybe as long as a decade. The most recent theft occurred in Vavuniya, Sri Lanka, a week ago. Just as with the European businessmen, the trail quickly comes to a dead end.'

He waited a moment, then said: 'The second type of incident in Asia is different in nature, involving bank officials also with unexplained lapses of memory, but strangely, considering their profession, these cases don't seem to involve money. It's only the memory lapses that connect them. Again, the most recent of these episodes was in Sri Lanka.'

His brow furrowed. 'Whoever is behind these affairs keeps himself carefully out of sight. I've given him a name. I call him Sapphire.'

'Sapphire…? Because of the connection to Sri Lanka?'

His smile contained a touch of embarrassment. 'Yes. My mother has an extensive collection of Ceylonese sapphires – when the recent events in Sri Lanka came into focus, it seemed appropriate.'

His tone lightened. 'The pearls you are wearing tonight also have a connection to the island of Sri Lanka – known, of course, as the 'Pearl of the Orient' – but…,' he said, holding up a hand in a gesture of acceptance as a slight frown appeared on her face and she lifted her hand to her necklace, '…that may indeed be seeking a link where none exists.'

She laughed at his concession and sat back, turning the idea of hypnosis being deliberately used as a power over in her head. If it *were* possible, it could be a very powerful tool. Or even a weapon? There certainly was potential for its misuse – to control someone against their will.

A thought occurred to her.

'The man on the landing who wanted to hire the gondola, what did you say to him? Did you use your power to make him change his mind?'

'In a mild fashion. I used some words that calmed him and told him where he could hire a water taxi. I also suggested he should apologise for disturbing the lady.'

'You touched his elbow, was that…?'

'Yes, touch helps significantly.'

'Was it significant that you touched him exactly where the woman had recently held his elbow?'

Logan drew in a breath and raised a finger in the air.

'Yes, it *was*. Now I'm really impressed. Is there nothing you don't notice?'

'I noticed you touched one of your bracelets as you stepped onto the landing. I suspect, now, that wasn't an absentminded gesture.'

Logan lifted his glass and sat back in his chair. He regarded her for a few seconds.

'What do you know about talismans?'

'They're helpful items used by witches, you said. Like an amulet or a charm – worn for luck.'

'No, those are different things. An amulet is supposed to *protect* the wearer, but amulets are, almost entirely, the product of superstitious folklore. A talisman, sometimes mistakenly called a charm, however, has nothing to do with luck. Instead, it *enhances*...' He paused.

'Enhances what?' She already knew what his answer would be.

'Enhances *spells*, Madeleine. These...' he held up his wrist, '...are a collection of some of the most effective talismans – you could call them a set of talismans for everyday use. There are more effective aids like aromas or certain potions to be ingested, but those items require considerable preparation, which takes time. For on-the-spot effectiveness...' he jiggled his hand '... *these* are the ones that work.'

He extended a finger from the hand holding his glass and touched a carved wooden figure shaped like a stick with a head and arms, attached to one of his bracelets.

'This talisman, for instance,' he said, 'in the shape of the hieroglyph *ankh*, the symbol for 'life', is called *Manipthset*. It was the one I touched before I confronted that man. It enhances persuasion spells.' He swirled the liquid in his glass. 'I don't know *how* exactly. I study and follow the writings and I do know, from experience, that the power is significantly more effective.'

A small chuckle. 'Actually, you were wrong when you said my gesture wasn't absentminded. I don't really *need* to touch the talisman with my fingers, so it *was* absentminded in a way. I just do it to remind myself that the talisman is there – like a habit. It's already close to me, which is enough.'

Of all of the ideas Logan had talked to her about tonight, this sounded the most far-fetched, but she could see he believed it. His ability to quiet the loud man had been impressive, but regarding the use of talismans, Madeleine decided she would need more convincing.

'Sounds very much like superstition,' she said. 'Do you also have a rabbit's foot hidden somewhere…?'

'Actually, rabbit's feet are…'

Madeleine held up both hands in protest, which Logan acknowledged.

'Sorry. I know my passion for the subject can be overwhelming.'

She picked up her own glass, and they both sat in silence, contemplating the dark liquid.

'Actually, I did notice something else.' She waited expectantly and was rewarded with a look of surprise.

'What?' he asked, intrigued.

She smiled. 'Nico was disappointed that you stepped in. He was about to confront the man who was very big and strong and outweighed him by some margin. Were you afraid Nico would get hurt?'

Logan laughed out loud. It was the first time Madeleine had heard more than a soft chuckle from him.

'Afraid for Nico? Let me tell you this. I would not be afraid for Nico against any man in the world. He is nothing short of extraordinary in that respect.'

Madeleine remembered Logan had mentioned earlier that he had met Nico in unusual circumstances. She knew intuitively that Nico's story would almost certainly match any of the other amazing things she had heard tonight, but she wasn't sure she could handle any more amazement. She shook her head and forced herself to change the subject, bringing the conversation back to something that was still unresolved.

'Logan, what is it *specifically* that you collect?'

Logan drew in a breath and slowly let it out again. 'I collect *knowledge*, Madeleine; knowledge from the far distant past, especially ancient spells and their associated talismans that have been deliberately lost — scattered and hidden, sometimes broken, to ensure their power could never again be used — or should I say — could never again be *misused*.'

She wanted to ask — *who* tried to conceal the spells? But that, she was sure, would be opening a door to another level which, tonight, would not be welcome in her already overloaded mind.

Instead, she said: 'And you think *I* somehow fit into this wild story?'

'I believe we met for a reason, and I think *you* are a very extraordinary person, Madeleine Galli.'

CHAPTER THREE

Vatican City…

'Where is he now?'

'Still in Venice, Your Eminence.'

'*Where* in Venice?'

'Inside his hotel. In the company of a young woman, apparently.'

'Who is she?'

'We are looking into that now. We have a photo and I will soon have a copy of her passport.'

The old man fingered his blood-red robe while he considered the information. It was new, and the stiffness of the cloth irritated him.

He sighed and placed a hand on the other man's shoulder. The man winced. The grip was surprisingly powerful.

'I'm tired. I'm going to retire to my chamber,' the old man said. His voice stiffened to match his grip. 'I have only recently acquired your services, so I'll allow that you may not be aware of this yet, but I'm *not* a patient man. In the morning, I will want to know all about her.'

'Of course, Your Eminence.'

CHAPTER FOUR

Sir Brian sets the scene…

Friday 11:20 pm

They had moved to another room on the same floor of the hotel, a lounge with soft lighting in subdued colours emanating from standing lamps and also from a small corner bar. Another bay window, this time open, allowed a refreshing draught of the cool night air to circulate. Madeleine had just reclined into a huge luxurious leather armchair, it's curved back towering two feet higher than her head, when Nico appeared with a replacement for her glass of Armagnac. She considered refusing but the previous glass *had* been delicious. Logan sat opposite in a matching armchair. He had just invited her to continue the conversation they had left at the dinner table by asking if there were any questions he hadn't yet answered. He also accepted a glass from Nico.

Madeleine sipped from her glass before speaking.

'You said we met for a reason,' she said. 'If it wasn't by your design, was I hypnotically programmed by someone else to meet you at the café this afternoon?'

'I don't think you *can* be affected by the power or 'programmed' as you put it. My attempt certainly had no effect, which is the first time that's happened. I've made a special study of resistance to the use of the power, and I've never met anyone with your level of natural resistance. As I said before, some people have different degrees of resistance, which, with the proper procedures, can be overcome, but I didn't think total resistance was possible. That's *one* of your strengths. I suspect you have others. Your powers of observation, for instance, are remarkable.'

He paused, then added: 'As for there being a reason behind our meeting, well, let me put it this way… Strange things have happened to me recently and I'm beginning to think they're all connected. Pieces seem to be fitting together, but I can't yet see what's being formed.' He turned his palms up. 'I know that sounds weird and an unsatisfactory explanation. It sounds weird to me, too. But, whatever it is, I believe you're part of it.'

His eyes met hers. 'If you don't mind telling me, what do *you* do, Madeleine, and why have you come to Venice?'

'I'm here for a symposium, and I've also come to visit my aunt. She's staying with a friend in Ravenna at the moment, but she'll be back in Venice on Monday. I've taken a month's leave, so after the symposium, I hope to see some of the marvellous Italian historical art, something I never seem to have had time for in the past.'

'Anything in particular?'

'The Sistine Chapel in the Vatican is at the top of my list – and the Uffizi Gallery in Florence.'

Logan nodded. 'A worthy ambition. But, I must point out, it's the height of the tourist season…'

She nodded in agreement. 'I know, but I've planned to visit the Sistine Chapel several times before and not made it for one reason or another. So this time, I'm determined.'

He leaned forward. 'You mentioned a symposium. I'm intrigued to know your profession.'

'I'm a forensic psychologist. My father and I have a small business, working with large companies and law enforcement agencies. We do key appointment profiling, criminal profiling, commercial negotiations – that sort of thing. I also do some lecturing at Virginia State.'

'Ah, so my lecture about the brain and consciousness was unnecessary.' Madeleine smiled and nodded. He leaned back, appraising her with renewed interest. 'I'm picking you're very good at your job.'

'We certainly have no lack of clients; yes…' she nodded, '…we're doing well.'

'No,' he said, 'I wasn't speaking of your firm. I meant that I'm certain *you* are good at what you do.'

She smiled at the compliment but made no reply.

'So… you're able to combine attendance at the symposium with a family visit?'

'Yes. There's a… a *matter* that my aunt wants me to help her with.'

He nodded, then said: 'What's the subject of the symposium?'

She laughed. 'Actually, it may interest you. This year, it's a combination of physics, medicine and behaviour.'

'How might it interest me?'

'Well, the key speaker will propose that the brain's processing of stimuli is *quantum* in nature, and I know you're interested in brain processes.'

'Are you speaking or just attending?'

'I'm speaking.'

He waited, then smiled at her reluctance to elaborate. 'On…?'

'My speech is titled 'The effect of electrical pre-activity and brain processing time delays in the interpretation of overt responses'.'

'Now I'm really interested. Can you summarise your speech into a couple of sentences?'

She raised her eyebrows. 'Are you sure? It's quite specialised.'

'Yes, please.'

'OK then. Let me think. I wrote a summary for the Speakers List.' She gathered her thoughts.

'It's generally agreed…' she began, speaking slowly, '…that there's a delay of a half-second or so between a stimulus and a conscious reaction. It's the time taken by the brain to process the information. Recently, researchers have found that this delay may be several *seconds* in certain situations, during which the brain registers significant electrical activity, so it's doing a lot of work. My paper discusses the processing that occurs during the delay and argues that such time delays need to be taken into account when interpreting a person's responses.'

'Interpreting a person's responses is something you do in your profession?'

'Yes. Conscious and unconscious responses.'

'And you're asking the question – is the response you are seeing a response to something that has just happened or something that happened several seconds ago?'

'Exactly.'

He nodded thoughtfully.

'Fascinating. It's an interesting question.'

She sipped her drink. 'Yes,' she agreed, 'it is, indeed, an interesting question.'

Logan sat back in his chair, regarding her.

Her own remark reminded her of another interesting question, one she had asked when he picked her up at the Moresco.

She leaned forward. 'Logan, how did you know where I was staying? How did you even know I was staying at a hotel? I could have been staying with my aunt.'

'Ah. I promised to answer that, didn't I? It wasn't magic. I noticed the Hotel Moresco app on your phone when you put it on the table, and you didn't correct me when I suggested I pick you up at your *hotel.*'

She smiled. 'Very good, Sherlock.' She waved a hand at him. 'Your turn.'

He momentarily looked puzzled, then said: 'Oh, you mean why am I in Venice?'

'Yes. Is Venice your home town?'

'In a way, I suppose it is. My mother is French and lives in Paris, but my father is English and I was raised in Southern England.'

'English? With a surname like Milan?'

He shrugged. 'The English have a varied ancestry.'

'So, in what way is Venice, you *suppose*, your home…?' She felt the question was close to prying, but he had asked the same of her.

'I'm not sure I *have* a home in the normal sense – I spend much of my time travelling. But Venice is the most beautiful city in the world, and it's special for me because the *Magari* was my first hotel, so in that respect it feels like home. I returned to Venice a few weeks ago because I needed permission from the City Council –my appointment this afternoon –to explore the foundations of a certain part of Venice. Getting that permission is proving complicated. I'm searching for some ancient artefacts.'

'Do you mind telling me what items you're looking for?' After his reluctance to divulge his profession, she was not hopeful of a straight answer, but he surprised her.

'A container with a manuscript inside, and perhaps another object, that I believe is buried in the mud beneath the city. The papers you saw were my research notes, and I was trying to complete a last-minute review and check my conclusions before you rudely interrupted me.'

He smiled at her and she tilted her head in acknowledgment.

'The foundations of Venice…' she repeated slowly.

'Yes. Most of the city is built on a network of wooden piles sunk into the mud of the hundred or so islands that make up…'

She interrupted him with a raised finger. 'Sorry, yes, I know that.' She shook her head. 'It's just that… my aunt has asked me to help her with a problem that also involves the foundations of Venice, or more specifically, of her building. She has had to move out of her apartment because the building is subsiding and, according to the Council, in danger of collapse. The Council are going to demolish the building. She wants me to accompany her when she meets with the Council on Monday. I'm trying to decide whether this is another coincidence or part of your puzzle.'

He spread his arms in a 'who knows' gesture.

'If getting permission is complicated, can't you just force the officials to do as you wish?' Madeleine said – and immediately regretted it as a concerned look appeared on his face. The suggestion did seem to border on being criminal.

'I'm sorry…' she began, but he waved her apology away.

'Yes, it's a fine line, but that's exactly the misuse of the power to manipulate others for personal gain that I'm keen to avoid and, indeed, prevent.'

She heard someone approaching and turned her head to see it was Pietro.

Pietro nodded to Madeleine to apologise for the intrusion. 'Excuse me, *Signora*,' he said, turning to Logan, ' *Signore*, Sir Brian is requesting a video link. Shall I tell him you're occupied…?'

'No, that's OK, it may be urgent. I'll take it. Is he calling from Brussels?'

'Yes,' said Pietro. 'From his office. Will you take it in your room?'

At Logan's nod, he glanced at the brandy glasses and asked: 'Can I bring you anything else?'

'No, thank you.' Logan looked at his watch. 'It's almost midnight on a Friday. Does the man never go home?'

Madeleine leaned back, nestling into her chair, expecting a short delay. Logan stood up and beckoned to her.

'Madeleine, I'd like you to come with me – I think you should meet Sir Brian. I'll be interested to see what you think of him. Leave your brandy; we shouldn't be long.'

He led her through the lounge doors and down a long hall with doors spaced at intervals – a typical hotel hallway. He slowed so that she was walking alongside him.

'What you've told me tonight is more than interesting,' he said. 'It's fascinating. I believe you and I may be very complementary people.'

'I don't really know what you mean,' she said, and couldn't resist adding: '…but I'll take it as a compliment.'

'Oh, it is,' he said, pleased with her play on the words. 'It certainly is.'

They turned a corner into a much shorter hall with only one door at the end. Logan drew a key from his pocket attached to a solid chain. She noticed his thumb fitted into a small depression on the key. He inserted the key, waited for a small click, and slowly turned it. When the door unlocked, there was the sound of bars moving behind the door as if they were entering a bank vault. As the door opened, the lights in the room came on.

'No electronic entrance card?'

'A matter of security,' said Logan.

The predominant feature inside the room was a large central desk, solidly constructed, with thick, beautifully carved legs. Five wide computer screens were arranged in a semicircle on the desktop facing away from the door. Beside the main desk stood a smaller one on which banks of modems and other equipment were arranged. Against one wall, she recognised two large side-by-side printers and a cupboard probably containing printing supplies. Next to the printers, a floor-to-ceiling bookshelf was packed with books except for the bottom shelf, which held stacked file boxes. On the opposite wall, a tall metal rack contained equipment that looked like CD music players. Three towers resembling tall audio speakers stood within easy reach of the large high-backed chair behind the desk. Solid dark-wood shelves curved in a semi-circle behind the chair. Several screens on the wooden shelves showed oscillating displays that reminded Madeleine of medical monitors in a hospital room.

On the far side of the room, under a window, a broad leather couch with a standing lamp at one end offered comfortable seating and in front of the couch was a coffee table and two chairs.

Logan put his hand on her elbow and invited her to precede him into the room. She found the gesture pleasantly old-fashioned.

He walked around the desk, took a chair from beside the coffee table and rolled it up to the desk, motioning for Madeleine to be seated. He sat on the large desk chair and pulled a square box across the desk toward him. It looked like a small wireless phone charger but when he waved his hand over the box, the screens activated. Twisting in his chair, he flicked several switches on the shelving beside and behind him and, like tuning a radio, adjusted a knob alongside one of the small displays containing a wave pattern. A soft hum filled the room.

He saw Madeleine watching and said: 'We're now isolated from prying eyes and ears. More security.'

She swivelled her chair and looked around the room, noting that the window was protected by steel bars. It was a setup that belonged in the CIA Communications Centre at Langley rather than a small Venetian hotel.

'This is a very secure room. What do you keep in here? The passwords to Fort Knox?'

'Within these walls I keep a commodity that's more valuable than gold, the most valuable commodity of all, in fact – *information*. Inside these little beauties…' he patted one of the towers beside the desk, '…is the sum of my knowledge – everything I've learned about the power, including my own thoughts and deductions – its history, its use, its dangers, and its potential.'

He leaned back while the computers booted.

'Sir Brian Talbot is the director of a department of NATO Military Intelligence,' he said. 'I don't know his official title or that of his office but he's English and seems to have a tight connection with British Military Intelligence, plus access to a great deal of resources and an interest in most of the affairs of Europe. We've had some dealings in the past to our mutual benefit. I first met Sir Brian some time ago when… Ah, one moment…'

He reached out and touched an icon on the centre screen. The word '*authenticated*' briefly appeared alongside the icon and the screen resolved to show an office scene where a bearded man Madeleine estimated to be in his fifties was patiently staring at them across a desk. The two leftmost screens now showed a mosaic of scenes being recorded by cameras throughout the hotel and on the street. The right pair of screens displayed arrays of desktop icons.

Madeleine focused her attention on the man on the centre screen. His tie was loosened and his top two shirt buttons undone, revealing a thick neck and also a tuft of chest hair that was a reddish-orange colour to match his beard and hair. Beside the man sat a woman who placed a manila folder in front of him. Her hair was gathered and tied up in a bun and her face was set in a stern expression. In contrast to the man, her suit top was buttoned tight to her neck. She sat with a straight-backed posture. Madeleine thought her considerable natural beauty was marred by her attempt to appear overly strict and professional.

The man's face registered acknowledgement that he could now see them.

'Logan!' he said. 'Good to see you.' His eyes sharpened. 'Who do you have with you there – without wishing to pry too deeply, of course?' There was a grumble from his chest which Madeleine eventually recognised as an expression of humour.

'Good evening, Sir Brian. I see the evening is as hot in Brussels as it is here. Allow me to introduce Madeleine Galli, a new friend and colleague.' Logan inclined his head to Madeleine, who had widened her eyes at his reference to her as a colleague, then addressed the second person on the screen. 'And a good evening to you, Selene. So, once again, Sir Brian has persuaded you to work late into the evening.'

Madeleine caught a brief flash of annoyance on the woman's face but then, incongruously, she gave a warm smile and a nod.

'Damn you, Logan, you've done it again.' Sir Brian frowned briefly, then he, too, smiled. 'If that was a guess, you've been annoyingly accurate lately.'

Madeleine didn't understand his comment; something carried over from a previous meeting, perhaps, but she could see he was both irked and amused at the same time.

Sir Brian's eyes flicked to Madeleine. 'If you're in that room, Madam, Logan obviously vouches for you. Good evening to you.'

Without waiting for her reply, his face became serious. 'I'll get straight to the point. Something's come up that I'm sure will interest you, Logan. It's connected to the incidents we discussed last week, but there's a difference.'

He waited for Logan to indicate he was paying attention, then opened the manila folder and patted the top page.

'Yesterday, in the early hours of the morning, the Chief Information Officer of a Swiss bank, I'll call him Mr B, received a phone call. In front of his startled wife, he got out of bed, put a coat over his pyjamas, and left the house without a word. The security officer on duty reported that he arrived at the bank in the company of two people, described by the officer as 'an Oriental man and a very young girl with dark skin like an African'. Mr B greeted the officer cordially and did not appear to be under duress. He led the other two into his office, where the security man was surprised to see him switch off the security camera. This was sufficiently unusual for the officer to contact his superior, whereupon he was instructed to enter the office to ensure all was well. This he duly did. Mr B and the young girl were seated at Mr B's desk, with the Oriental gentleman also behind the desk but with his chair set back a little, observing but not participating.

The officer asked if everything was alright, and Mr B assured him all was fine, appearing to be surprised at the question. Unwilling to question him further, the officer withdrew. Twenty minutes later, the trio emerged from the office and, after Mr B had wished the officer a good night, they all drove away in Mr B's car.'

Sir Brian paused as a man entered into view behind him and handed him a message. He scanned the message then dismissed the man.

'Here's where things get a little bizarre,' he continued. At their reaction he held up his hand. 'I know… it's bizarre enough already.' He looked again at his notes. 'The next event occurs five minutes later and a kilometre from the bank. Mr B's car, heading in the direction of his house, suddenly swerved into the path of another car – which happened to be a *police* car – and the resulting collision caused significant damage to the Police car, disabling it. Mr B's car, a large and apparently new SUV, only received dents and scratches. Mr B and his companions were arrested – an action which they apparently all accepted with minimum fuss. As soon as the police discovered Mr B's identity, his state of dress and his demeanour caused suspicion. He acted – how did they describe it…?' He looked at the paper in front of him and read: '… *as if he were enjoying a day at the fair.*'

Sir Brian looked up at the screen and continued: 'They raised his deputy and made an immediate check of the bank but found absolutely nothing out of the ordinary. No imbalances. Nothing appeared to have been stolen. And now, two days later, a complete audit has been performed which confirmed there are no missing funds. Nothing untoward, it seems, has happened at the bank.'

Madeleine smiled at his upper-class English use of the word 'untoward'.

Logan said: 'You've referred to the bank manager as 'Mr B'. I presume you have a reason for concealing his name?'

Sir Brian gave another rumble of mirth and picked up the top paper. 'My reason is nothing sinister, I assure you. His surname is Banda-ra-kai-anan,' he said, sounding out the syllables. 'He's Sri Lankan.'

Logan and Madeleine shared a glance.

'I thought you might find that interesting,' said Sir Brian.

'Indeed. But how can I help? Is he still in custody?'

'The Swiss police have exercised their right to hold Mr B and the other man, who, I have just learned…' he held up the message he had been handed, '…is a Japanese national, for forty-eight hours on suspicion of a major crime. The girl is being held in a juvenile home.'

He leaned forward. 'I've saved the best till last. This is the part that made me think of you. When Mr B awoke in his cell the next day – that's yesterday morning – he professed he could not remember anything of the previous night past the time he had retired to bed. A complete blank. That's the same scenario we discussed last week involving the Chinese and Indian bankers.'

Madeleine's ears pricked up. Was Sir Brian the 'friend' Logan had talked about earlier? The one who was helping him investigate the events where Logan suspected Sapphire may be involved?

'Yes, it is,' agreed Logan. 'And because of that, I suspect the collision with the police car might not have been accidental.'

'Do you mean they wanted to be arrested?' asked Sir Brian, surprised.

'Not exactly,' replied Logan. 'Not all of them. When does the forty-eight-hour period expire?'

'At three am tomorrow morning. If the police do not charge these people with a crime, they must be released when the holding period expires.'

Logan glanced at his watch. 'Not enough time. Still, I appreciate you informing me of this new occurrence…'

'Not at all.' Sir Brian interrupted. 'If these events can be traced to your 'Italian Master' – I forget what you call him, some silly name – it's possible he has now widened his interest to include financial institutions in Europe, in which case my office may well need to open a more official investigation. It's a worrying escalation but also an opportunity, because this bank's in our back yard.'

Logan nodded. 'I call him Sapphire,' he said. 'And I don't believe for a moment that you forgot.'

Sir Brian emitted another grumble of humour. 'Yes, that's the name – Sapphire.'

Madeleine waited to see if Sir Brian had finished. She leaned to her right to be more in camera. 'Can you tell us anything more about the young girl? How old is she?' She realised she had said *us* and not *me*.

'Yes, in fact, as of a few moments ago, I can.' Sir Brian again consulted the message he had recently been handed. 'She's about fifteen, but they haven't identified her yet. Hmm, here's something unusual. Apparently, she was examined and diagnosed as extremely autistic, barely able to communicate.'

Logan said: 'I see.' He drew in a breath. 'I would have liked to talk with Mr Bandarakaianan….'

Madeleine nodded. 'And I would like to talk to that girl.'

'*Good!*' said Sir Brian emphatically. 'I hoped you'd say that. I have a plane ready to go at Marco Polo airport with a forty-five-minute flight plan to Zürich. Colonel Ritter, the commander of *StadtPolizei Zürich* has been asked to give you every co-operation. How soon can you be at Marco Polo?'

Logan stood up, smiling. 'In half an hour.' He wagged a finger at the screen. 'You wily old fox, you could have just *asked* me.' Sir Brian sounded his grumbling laugh.

Logan looked at Madeleine. "From what you've told me tonight, I'm sure you could help, especially with the girl. So, are you able to come to Zürich?'

'Well…' she hesitated, caught off guard. 'I'm not sure… It's late… I was only thinking aloud.'

'We can be back in Venice by midday tomorrow.' He glanced at the screen where Sir Brian nodded confirmation. 'You *would* like to talk to the girl, wouldn't you?'

Despite feeling that things were getting out of control, Madeleine was intrigued. It seemed she had entered a different life-stream – something more *international* than she was used to. She knew she would regret it if she backed away now.

'Yes,' she said. 'I would.'

Logan pushed a button on the console to his right and spoke into a microphone. 'We'll need the speedboat, Nico, and please ask Pietro to pack overnight bags for both of us and one for Madeleine.'

'By the way,' said Sir Brian, 'Serene will be piloting the plane, and…' his grumbling laugh sounded '…there's a surprise on board.'

He raised a hand in farewell.

Logan waved his hand over the box and the screens faded to black with Sir Brian still rumbling.

'I thought her name was *Selene*,' said Madeleine. 'If she's in Brussels now, how could she…?'

'Selene and Serene are identical twins,' explained Logan, flicking switches as he spoke. The hum in the room died. 'They, and Sir Brian too, think nobody can tell them apart. They think I'm guessing, and the twins, especially, get annoyed when I guess correctly almost all the time. Did you notice Selene's reaction, and then Sir Brian's, when I addressed Selene by name without hesitation?'

Madeleine nodded.

He turned to face her and touched the bottom of his left ear lobe. 'I've noticed Serene has a small brown pinprick mark right here. Of course, if I can't see it then I *do* have to guess because they do look exactly alike. I hope they never find out how I can identify them…' He grinned mischievously.

Logan pushed his chair out of the way. 'The twins are very efficient. They act as the right and left hand of Sir Brian. You should see them working together. It's a thing of beauty. They play on the fact that they're identical and they're extremely adept at both the honey and the trap.'

The relationship between Logan, Sir Brian, and his twin lieutenants seemed well-established; they were undoubtedly more than occasional or casual acquaintances. Their familiarity suggested a lengthy history.

Madeleine nodded, considering the possibilities, then said: 'You're packing bags. Are we expecting to stay somewhere?'

'A precaution only, in case we *do* need a change of clothes. Just catering for contingencies.'

Madeleine shook her head as she stood up. The pace of events was making it spin.

With an effort, she focussed on the fact that she would soon be flying to Zürich. She had no trouble accepting that the organisation surrounding Logan Milan could pack a bag for her, and she had no doubt that the contents would be perfect, but she had to ask the question.

'If you're packing a bag for me, how do you know my size?'

Logan just smiled. 'Try me,' he said, echoing the words she had used when they first met. 'You can change on the plane if you wish.'

CHAPTER FIVE

A night in Zürich…

Saturday 12:10 am

Serene was indeed a perfect physical match to the woman who had sat beside Sir Brian in Brussels; the identical facial beauty was evident, but her appearance was very different. Her hair was down, a wavy brunette cascade framing her face and bouncing off her shoulders, and she wore minimal makeup. Her casual jacket, tight jeans and leather calf-length boots presented her as efficiently professional yet distinctly feminine. Madeleine discreetly checked and noticed the small mark on her ear lobe that Logan had mentioned.

Serene smiled a warm welcome and greeted Logan at the top of the stairs with a two-cheek kiss which Logan returned with equal warmth and familiarity. He glanced over her shoulder and noticed someone standing behind Serene. His face broke into a broad smile and he moved past Serene to warmly embrace a young man.

'Archie! *You're* the surprise. So, you got your certification for this plane.'

'Three days ago,' Archie replied.

Serene repeated the kisses with Madeleine and also with Nico who was carrying the three overnight bags. He had refused with a smile Madeleine's offer to carry her own. Watching Nico accept Serene's greeting, she marvelled at how easily he carried the bags, as if they weighed nothing.

Serene introduced Archie to Madeleine. 'Meet my co-pilot,' she said. The young man looked barely out of his teens and his hair bore such a remarkable resemblance in colour to Sir Brian's that Madeleine suspected a family connection. Nico put down a bag and reached out to grasp Archie by the shoulder and then gave him a lusty pat on the arm.

'Well done,' he said, holding his fist up for Archie to bump.

Archie grinned, making his face seem even more boyish, and said: 'I'll get the APU running.' He disappeared into the cabin.

Serene laid a hand on Logan's arm. 'Welcome aboard, Charles,' she said. 'Make yourselves comfortable. We'll be lifting off in five or six minutes.'

Madeleine followed Logan into the aircraft cabin. She leaned forward and whispered just behind his ear: 'Charles?'

He turned to her, his face feigning frustration. 'She's referring to Charles Xavier, the X-Man with the power of mind control.' He tapped his forehead. 'Just her little running joke – of which she never seems to tire.'

Logan lowered himself into one of the luxurious seats and buckled his seatbelt. Madeleine noticed he carefully checked the buckle was secure, after which he took two deep breaths.

'Not keen on flying?' she said.

The plane's engines clicked and fired before settling into an audible but not intrusive rumble.

His smile contained a touch of embarrassment. 'I fly often. I know the stats, and I know we have a great pilot. What I'm not keen on is my destiny being so completely out of my hands when I'm thousands of feet above the earth's surface.'

The nearest seats were arranged in a group of four, two facing forward and two facing back. Madeleine chose the seat facing the same way as Logan across a small aisle. Further down the cabin were another two single seats and across the aisle from these was a long couch that could possibly be used as a bed. Nico stowed the bags and sat across from Logan, facing him. As she settled into her seat and buckled her belt, Madeleine was reminded of the last comfortable chair she had reclined in and the half-glass of brandy their hurried departure had forced her to leave behind. *A pity*, she thought. *It really was exceptional.*

They were silent while the plane lifted into the air but once they had levelled, Logan gestured to include Nico and leaned toward her, his face serious.

'Before we land, there are a few things we need to discuss.' She indicated she was listening.

'The convenient loss of memory by the bank manager is a classic symptom of use of the power and this, together with the link with Sri Lanka, makes the involvement of Sapphire very likely.'

He rested his elbows on his knees. 'We won't have much time before the forty-eight-hour limit expires, so, Madeleine, if you could interview the girl and I'll talk first with the manager. If she's autistic, then even getting her to talk may be difficult but from what you've told me, you're qualified and experienced in that area, so that's a bonus. Anything you can discover about her involvement would be worthwhile.'

She nodded and he continued: 'Why would anyone take a young girl to a bank in the middle of the night, especially one who's autistic? What help could she possibly provide in whatever they were doing? It's obvious that the Japanese man and the girl, and possibly Mr Bandarakaianan as well, were intending something illegal. But what? Not a simple robbery it seems. When we don't even know what crime was committed, we're starting a long way behind the eight ball. That's an American expression, isn't it? Am I using it correctly?'

She laughed. 'Yes, we *are* at a disadvantage.'

She realised her use of the word '*we*' again implied she was accepting her role as a 'colleague'. She took a sobering moment to reflect again on her situation. Flying in a private plane above the alps, heading for Zürich at the request of a NATO intelligence chief, where she was about to be involved in a criminal investigation. Or was it? As Logan had questioned, *had* a crime been committed?

He interrupted her thoughts. 'And it may be that I can arrange a surprise for you.' His smile this time was smug and his eyes were playful.

'What sort of surprise?'

She had automatically tensed. She was not a fan of arranged surprises, especially surprise parties, preferring to be prepared for every event. After a couple of seconds, she let out a breath and forced herself to relax. She could see he intended nothing more than to please her. She actually felt a tingle of anticipation.

'If I told you that,' he said, 'it wouldn't be a surprise.'

EXACTLY FORTY MINUTES LATER, they touched down at Kloten airport in Zürich.

Serene and Archie remained on board the plane while Logan, Madeleine and Nico descended the boarding ladder where a police car waited on the tarmac. Nico stowed their bags in the boot and joined Madeleine in the back seat. As soon as his door closed, the vehicle drove away from the airport, accelerating to an alarming speed with the siren blaring continuously to clear the road ahead, which, considering the late hour, was surprisingly congested.

A light rain started to fall, enough to require intermittent use of the wipers, causing the city to be artistically distorted through the rain-smeared windows. Madeleine watched the streetlights and the buildings flashing by – just like her life at the moment, going so fast.

When they entered the inner city, Logan leaned across and conversed with the driver but his face was turned away from her and under the shriek of the siren, Madeleine couldn't hear what was being said. The driver spoke briefly on his radio.

The car halted outside the *StadtPolizei Zürich* building on Bahnhofquai and it took several seconds before the echoes of the siren had departed from the surrounding buildings. Madeleine could still hear the remnants of the wailing as she followed Logan from the car, leaving Nico to collect their bags.

A rainy mist collected on her hair and shoulders in the few seconds it took to reach the shelter of a small canopy providing only minimal protection to two tall doors. Logan depressed the large brass handle and opened a door then theatrically stood to one side to reveal an enormous, brilliantly lit entrance hall.

The ceiling of the hall was breathtakingly beautiful. It was a mass of vaulted arches covered in a vivid yellow and red floral decoration and illuminated by hundreds of hidden lights, while the walls displayed a mixture of painted pastoral and spiritual scenes. The hall was so huge and the surroundings so colourful that Madeleine felt she had entered a cathedral rather than a police station.

'Magnificent, isn't it,' said Logan as Madeleine stared at the unexpected beauty. 'I asked the driver to bring us to the main entrance so you could see this. I thought if you were interested in the ceiling of the Sistine Chapel….'

'It's beautiful. Almost overwhelming.' She turned in a circle. 'Thank you,' she said earnestly. 'You knew this was here?'

'I've read of these murals, but I've never seen them.'

'Why would anyone decorate a police station like this?'

'It wasn't always a police station. This building was previously a nunnery and an orphanage. The entrance apparently was dark, so someone decided it needed painting. They did such an amazing job that it's now a tourist attraction.'

'Mr Milan, I presume.'

The commanding voice came from a short, uniformed man striding towards them, his heels clicking on the tiled floor.

'*Oberst* Herman Ritter at your service,' the man said, his English precise, '…and, according to my instructions, *that* is to be taken literally as well as figuratively.'

He gestured around the entrance hall. 'When your driver reported you wanted to come to the main entrance, I had the lights switched on for you.'

'Thank you. Very much appreciated,' said Logan.

Colonel Ritter looked up at Logan. The top of his head reached only to Logan's shoulders, but Madeleine could see he was unperturbed by the height difference and was well used to having his authority unquestioned. His bearing was not arrogant however, merely confident.

'So… You wish to question the people we are holding regarding the incident at the VCT Bank in Altstetten?'

'That's correct,' said Logan. He glanced at his watch. 'I understand they are due to be released at three. I apologise if our arrival in the middle of the night is inconvenient for you.'

Colonel Ritter smiled. 'No inconvenience, I assure you, and you can take your time. We can hold these people until morning. It would be…' he paused, searching for the correct word, '…*inconvenient* to turn anyone into the streets at three am.'

He glanced at Nico: 'You have some bags? You can leave your bags over there.' He smiled as Nico set them down against a wall in the vast hall. 'They will be *quite* safe. Now…' his eyes moved to include them all, '…please follow me.'

Madeleine took the opportunity to speak. 'There was a young girl involved who is apparently being held at another facility. I would like to talk with her if possible.'

There was a crash as the doors to the entrance hall were closed behind them, followed by the sound of heavy bolts being driven home.

'I had her woken and brought here, Miss Galli. She is waiting for you.'

A WOODEN TABLE AND four chairs were the only items of furniture in the room. The woman sitting beside the young girl stood up as Madeleine entered.

'English?'

Madeleine nodded.

'I'm a nurse. She has not spoken since she was arrested, nor has she acknowledged anyone's presence. She may be autistic or, at the least, very disturbed, possibly by something she experienced recently.'

'Thank you,' said Madeleine.

The woman smiled. 'I'll be outside if you need me.' She left, closing the door behind her.

Madeleine sat at the table opposite the girl. She saw a teenager with a flawless complexion, deep olive skin, full lips and large brown eyes with pronounced lashes. She looked younger than fifteen. Her hair was dark, parted in the middle and sweeping down to frame her face and rest upon her shoulders. Her downward gaze allowed Madeleine time to study her face without appearing impolite. *This one is going to grow into a very beautiful woman.* If she had to guess, Madeleine would have picked the girl to be North African, possibly Ethiopian or Somali. Her posture had not changed since Madeleine had entered the room; her eyes had remained focused on the table and had not so much as flickered. She seemed to be taking no interest in her surroundings. Madeleine said nothing and after thirty long seconds, the eyes moved slowly and looked at Madeleine.

'Hello,' said Madeleine. 'If you speak English, my name is Madeleine – what's yours?'

The girl said nothing. Her eyes held Madeleine's for a moment, then returned to the table.

'Yesterday morning,' said Madeleine, 'I was sitting in a café in Venice and now I'm in Zürich. Isn't that strange? Where were you yesterday?'

There was no reply from the girl. Madeleine checked her clothing. She wore a blue dress with a white floral pattern, gathered at the waist by a thin white leather belt. White lace decorated the hem and neckline. She sat with her hands clasped before her, resting on the table. Her hands were finely boned with long fingers. A single plaited black leather band around her left wrist was the only other adornment. Madeleine's eye was drawn to a triangular piece of multi-coloured paper or cardboard fastened to the wristband by an inch-long piece of black string. The style of dress and the wristband with its strange attached triangle accentuated her youth.

After another long silence, the eyes again moved to stare at Madeleine. They unhurriedly rose and lowered once, before slowly returning to her eye level, where they stayed, unblinking for several more seconds.

'I'm tired. I want to sleep,' the girl said in a soft voice. Her 's' had a slight lisp to it. And was that a trace of an American accent?

'I know. It's late,' said Madeleine. She reached forward, extending her hand in greeting. 'I'm Madeleine,' she repeated. 'I'm pleased to meet you...' She left both her hand and the sentence hanging in front of the girl. This time, the eyes did not look away.

Ten more seconds passed. 'Tricola,' said the girl. She made no effort to take the hand.

'Tricola? Is that your name?' Madeleine extended her hand further and pointedly looked down at the clasped hands of the girl.

The girl's gaze moved along Madeleine's arm towards her hand, the journey taking several seconds. It did not stop when it reached Madeleine's hand but continued smoothly to rest on her own hands, where it paused and then returned to the centre of the table.

'My name is Tricola.' Again, the slight lisp on the 's'. 'I can tell you that much.' Yes, there was an American touch to that accent.

This girl was not autistic, but it did seem that she had been somehow traumatised. Every movement was slowed as if she were moving in a thick liquid.

'Are there some things you cannot tell me?' asked Madeleine.

She saw the girl's eyes widen a tiny fraction, an almost unnoticeable movement. For some reason, she was scared. Her head turned, still slowly but faster than before.

'I cannot tell you…' Her soft voice faltered and she gave an almost imperceptible shake of her head.

She breathed deeply. 'I cannot tell you…' Again, she stopped and lowered her head to look down at the table. She squeezed her eyes shut.

When she raised her head again, Madeleine saw her big round eyes were misty with tears. She was attempting to say something but she was having some difficulty.

'I cannot,' she said with finality. The sadness in her voice and in her eyes made Madeleine catch her breath.

Then Tricola pursed her lips and the tiny lines of a frown appeared on her forehead. Madeleine could see the signs of her internal struggle.

'Are you…?' Tricola opened her mouth and breathed hard. '…a good…' Her face took on a pained look, but there was determination there also. She forced the last word out: '… person?'

'Yes,' said Madeleine firmly. 'I *am* a good person. I want to help you.'

Tricola's hand suddenly reached out and clasped Madeleine on the forearm. Compared to her previous movements, it was done very quickly.

'Tanaka is a bad man,' Tricola squeezed the words between her teeth, her effort mirrored on her face. 'He likes to hurt people. I don't want to go with him.' Her voice was still soft but the words were said with urgency, her eyes pleading.

'Please….' She started, then she gave a loud cry of pain and brought her hands to her head, rocking in her chair. Choking cries came from deep within her. 'No, no, no, no…'

Madeleine jumped up, rounded the table and slid into the chair beside Tricola, gathering the writhing girl in her arms. The sounds from her throat were now just uncontrolled grunts of pain. Her hands each formed into a claw shape with the fingers pressed into the side of her head, her body rigid.

Suddenly, her eyes rolled back and she went limp in Madeleine's arms.

The door burst open and the woman rushed in, followed by a policeman.

'*Was ist los?* What happened?'

'She's had some sort of severe pain attack, and her body thankfully decided that unconsciousness was the best defence. Is there somewhere she can rest until she recovers?'

'Are you a Doctor?'

I've had some medical training. I'm a Psychologist.'

The woman spoke to the policeman in German. He left the room.

The woman took Tricola from Madeleine, lifting her gently.

'I've called for the Doctor. He may want to talk to you. I'll see she is comfortable.'

'Her name is Tricola.'

'She spoke to you?' asked the woman incredulously. 'She did not even move when I was with her.'

'Yes, she spoke. Where is Logan, the man I came with? I need to see him.'

THROUGH THE ONE-WAY WINDOW, Madeleine saw a man, fifty or sixty, dark-skinned, white-haired and balding. He was dressed in a baggy one-piece tan-coloured overall, probably police issue, and he was genuinely distressed. Madeleine could see it was not an act. Logan sat opposite the man, across a table identical to the one in the room Madeleine had just left. The only entrance into the interview room was through a door alongside the window. The door had a keypad lock. Beside Madeleine, Colonel Ritter stood with his hands clasped behind his back.

When she had entered the room, moments ago, Colonel Ritter had said softly: 'In two days, we have been unable to get anything from this man; he just didn't remember. In ten minutes, Mr Milan has apparently restored the man's memory. If I hadn't seen it myself, I would not have believed it. The man's name is Sami Bandarakaianan; he's been an employee of the bank for nine years. Exemplary record.'

'Sammy? That's a strange name for a Sri Lankan, isn't it?' observed Madeleine.

'It's spelt S-a-m-i. It may be an abbreviation of a longer name.'

'I see.'

In the adjoining room, Logan leaned forward and touched the man's hand. 'I assure you, Sami, this was all completely out of your control.'

Madeleine heard Logan's voice through speakers positioned on the wall. The quality of sound was surprisingly authentic as if Logan was in the room, not at all the tinny and artificial sound she remembered from the movies.

The man shook his head. 'It's unbelievable,' he said, his voice wavering. 'What have I done?'

'That's what we'd like to find out,' said Logan. He whispered some words and the man visibly calmed. While Logan continued to whisper, the man's head came up and he nodded. Logan patted his hand.

'When the girl was sitting at your desk, what did she do?'

'That's it, I'm sorry to say – I don't know. She was working on my computer, but for some reason I wasn't watching. I remember just gazing about the room. Then I was dragged away from my desk by that Japanese man. I don't understand…'

'That's normal. Don't worry about it.'

Logan paused, then said: 'Sami, I'd like to enhance your memory. You may have seen something which you can't consciously recall. Is that OK?'

'Yes, of course,' the man said eagerly. 'I'll do anything I can to help.'

'Good. Just relax, and listen to what I'm saying.'

Logan again reached out to touch his hand. He said some words, again too softly to be heard in the next room. Sami's head slowly fell to his chest.

'You are in your office at the bank,' said Logan. 'You've turned off the security camera and…'

'What? Turned off the camera? No! That's not… Why…?' Sami's head jerked up and he stared at Logan who calmly spoke again and his head drooped. 'Yes, I have…' he said slowly. 'I've turned off the camera.'

Logan continued in the same even tone as if there had been no interruption: 'You're sitting at your desk and the girl is sitting beside you….'

'Yes. She asks me to log on to my computer, and I press my thumb on the pad. Then she asks for my password. I won't tell her that. She says a strange word to me. I will never… Oh, yes, I do. I *tell* her. Oh… I've told her my password.' Sami's voice has grown alarmed, but Logan again calmed him with a few words.

'What happens next?'

'The security guard enters the room and immediately I feel good. I have just told this girl my password, but I'm *happy*. I assure him I'm happy. I assure him that all is well. He leaves.'

'What is the girl doing?'

'She inserts a USB drive. I can hear her typing very fast.'

'Can you see the screen?'

'Yes, I can see the screen. It's displaying a diagram.'

'What sort of diagram? Do you recognise it?'

'It's a *network* diagram. I look away. Why am I looking up at the ceiling?' Sami taps the table irritably for a few seconds. 'Now I can see it again; the screen is full of lines of words and symbols, she's searching through the lines….'

'Is there a title at the top of the screen?' Logan interrupted him. 'Anything to indicate what she's looking at?'

Sami frowns. 'No, only the lines.'

'What are these lines? A document?'

'Not a document. Just a mixture of characters. It's a computer language, I think; it must be a program. Now I've turned away from the screen. I'm looking around the room.'

'What is the Japanese man doing?'

'He is sitting next to the girl. He is watching everything she does. His face is calm but he seems tense, ready to jump out of the chair at any moment. He's watching the screen but he's also watching me. Every time I look at him, his eyes flick to me. Now the girl is typing again. Very fast.'

'Has she said anything?'

'No.' He furrowed his brow, thinking. 'She doesn't speak again after asking for my password.'

'Can you see what she's typing?'

'She's making some changes to the lines on the screen. It doesn't make sense to me. Uh… Oh, No!' Sami sat back in his chair, his eyes wide and raised one arm above his head.

'What's happened?'

'The Japanese man has taken me by the arm. He makes me stand up. His grip is strong and he's hurting me! He pulls me away from the desk. I can't see the screen.'

Logan sat back in his chair.

'Tell me what you hear.'

'The girl has stopped typing. She says: 'Don't hurt him.' She means *me*. She's asking him not to hurt me. The Japanese man slams his hand on the desk, the noise is very loud and he points at her. I hear her start typing again.'

Sami falls silent but Logan doesn't prompt him. After thirty seconds, Sami says: 'My computer is shutting down. The lid has been closed.'

'Thank you, Sami. You've done well.' Logan reaches across the table to touch Sami's hand, whispering to him. Sami takes several deep breaths.

'Now, just a few general questions, if I may?'

'Of course.'

'Has anything unusual happened in, say, the last two or three weeks? Have you met anyone new, for instance?'

'Unusual? No, nothing unusual. But, in fact, two weeks ago, I met many new people. You see, I've only been back a week from leave, and while I was away, I joined a golf club.'

'Did you holiday outside Switzerland?'

Madeleine said quietly: 'He's been to Sri Lanka.'

Colonel Ritter looked at her just as Sami said: 'Yes, my wife and I went back to my home town in Sri Lanka. I've been meaning to go back for years, but my recent promotion….'

'You've been recently promoted?' interrupted Logan.

'Yes,' said Sami proudly. 'To CIO of the bank.'

'Chief Information Officer?' said Logan, and Sami nodded. Logan paused, thinking.

'Tell me about the people you met at the golf club. Was there anyone you spent some time with? Anyone you also saw outside the club?'

'Why, yes,' said Sami eagerly. 'Mr… uh… Mr…' his face tightened, trying to remember. 'Oh no…' he said. 'I can't…' He put his hands up to his head and groaned.

Madeleine said urgently. 'I need to talk to Logan *now*. Can you let me into the room?'

The Colonel punched a code into the keypad, and Logan looked around as the door opened.

Speaking quickly, Madeleine said: 'The girl had a similar attack when she tried to speak about certain things. If you persist, it may become so painful he could lose consciousness.'

Sami appeared not to have noticed Madeleine's entrance. He was staring at the table, concentrating on one spot, his face strained and anxious, his hands rubbing his head. He moaned again.

Logan immediately spoke several words that were nonsense to Madeleine. Sami sighed heavily and closed his eyes. He remained still for several seconds, then opened his eyes and blinked rapidly.

'I'm sorry, what did you ask?' he said.

'I haven't any more questions, Sami. You've been very helpful. Thank you.'

Sami smiled, then noticed Madeleine.

'Oh,' he said. 'Hello. How did you…?'

'This is Madeleine,' said Logan. 'She's….'

'…a colleague,' finished Madeleine. 'Nice to meet you, Mr Bandarakaianan.'

Sami smiled. 'Most people cannot say my name the first time.' He stretched his arms out to the sides and looked around the room. 'That's funny,' he said. 'I know they woke me to bring me here, but I feel quite refreshed.'

Madeleine returned his smile.

IN THE NEXT ROOM, Logan looked through the window at Sami Bandarakaianan and watched him thankfully accept a cup of coffee and a sandwich from a policeman.

'Did you find a USB Drive on the girl?'

'No,' Colonel Ritter replied. 'She was carrying nothing. We are very experienced – I assure you she was searched… thoroughly.'

'In Sami's car?'

'Searched from top to bottom. We weren't looking for a USB drive, but if one was there, it would have been found.'

'Could someone have swallowed it?' asked Madeleine.

'It would have been found,' insisted the Colonel.

'It was probably disposable, broken and tossed from the car window,' said Logan.

'The route will be searched this morning.'

Colonel Ritter waved a hand towards the window and asked: 'What else can you tell me about *this* man?'

'I would expect his rise in the bank has been rapid, and his corresponding salary increases have enabled him to mix in new circles, including a Sri Lankan golf club where the fees must be astronomical,' said Logan.

'I'll have that checked,' said Colonel Ritter.

'He's been hypnotised and he's been instructed to lose all memory of the events inside the bank on Thursday morning. It seems there are also some strong suppression commands in place protecting important information with painful consequences should he try to reference that information.'

The Colonel's eyes widened but he said nothing.

'Can you do anything about those commands?' asked Madeleine.

'Yes, I could. But it would take some time. One thing I'd like to know is the name of Mr Bandarakaianan's new friend.' He glanced at Madeleine.

She understood. Logan thought this may be the man he called Sapphire.

'I think the girl has also been hypnotised,' she said. 'She's not autistic but she's very uncommunicative, and that's not her natural state. It's as if she's been instructed not to talk. She told me she couldn't speak of some things and had a severe pain attack when she tried to do so.'

'Did she manage to say anything?' asked Logan.

'She said the Japanese man, she called him Tanaka, is a bad man who hurts people. It was immediately after telling me this that she experienced such pain that she lost consciousness.'

Logan nodded. 'She wasn't supposed to talk about him.'

Colonel Ritter looked between Logan and Madeleine. 'You two make quite a team,' he said. 'We're not amateurs and we've questioned these people over the last day or so and we were unable to get anything useful from any of them. The girl and the Japanese man wouldn't even speak, and this man simply couldn't remember. You've been here only an hour and already made significant progress.'

'There's still a lot we don't know,' said Logan. 'Speaking of Tanaka, I'd like to talk with him, if possible. What do you know about him?'

'Nothing. His fingerprints are not in our database nor at Interpol. He doesn't seem to understand German or English. I arranged for a Japanese interpreter to be here in case you wanted to try to talk with him.'

'That makes his role in this affair even more strange. If you want to rob a bank, what use is a man who does not speak the language?'

'You think that robbery is the motive for these unusual events?' asked the Colonel.

'Robbery of some kind. Funds or information. If they disposed of the USB drive, they probably weren't after a large amount of information. Maybe just something short that could be remembered, like a name or an account number. Why else would you kidnap a bank manager and take him to his bank in the middle of the night?'

'Why else, indeed. At least, thanks to you, we may now be able to charge someone. Previously, Mr Bandarakaianan claimed he went to the bank willingly, but from what I've seen, he's now likely to realise he was kidnapped, which means we can charge Tanaka with abduction.'

'Maybe Tanaka was the girl's protector – like a bodyguard,' said Madeleine.

Logan looked at her appreciatively. 'That makes sense,' he said. 'She's young; she'd need someone to watch out for her. He was there to see she got what someone wanted, or…' he thought for a moment, '…or did what she needed to do. Sami said Tanaka watched the computer screen. He could have been making sure she didn't stray from her path. It's likely Sami's new friend from the golf club is involved and it would be useful to get that name from Sami but, for now, I think the girl is the key to this affair.'

Colonel Ritter nodded.

'Her name is Tricola,' Madeleine said. 'What will happen to her? Will she be charged?'

'She's almost certainly underage and likely to have been coerced to play her part.'

'Whatever part that is. What will happen to her?'

'If we can hold her – and that will rely on coercion being strongly indicated – she'll be made a ward of the court until we can find some next-of-kin. After that…'

'Could she be released into our care?' asked Madeleine. 'What do you call it – in our recognisance?'

'No. That's not possible at this stage….'

'Colonel,' said Logan, 'it's a good idea. We may be able to find out a lot more if I can talk to her in a different setting. We still don't know exactly what she's done, and she may know who's behind this.'

'I'm sorry, Mr Milan, I'd like to help you, but….'

'Colonel…' said Logan again. He took Colonel Ritter by the shoulder and bent down to talk quietly into his ear. The Colonel frowned at the initial touch but the frown quickly disappeared and he nodded as Logan spoke.

A few moments later, Logan straightened and patted the Colonel's shoulder.

'Very well,' Colonel Ritter said. 'I agree, but she must be returned here if required.'

'Of course,' said Logan. 'I'll inform you of anything we find.' He glanced at his watch. 'Now, let's see what Tanaka can tell us.'

'If he's likely to be violent,' said Colonel Ritter, 'I can have some policemen in the room.'

'Thank you, but Nico will be sufficient.'

———— ❧ ————

THE MAN BARELY GLANCED at the people entering the room until Nico entered. Tanaka's eyes locked on him and remained there for several seconds, looking him up and down. Madeleine noticed that Nico, in a similar way, made a careful assessment of the Japanese man. As the two stared at each other, the tension level in the room rose palpably. Madeleine was reminded of two wild animals circling each other. She glanced at the one-way glass behind which Colonel Ritter stood with two big policemen. Maybe his caution was warranted.

The interpreter, a girl in her twenties who had been introduced as Keiko, stood to one side of the table. Logan sat at the table across from Tanaka with Madeleine beside him. Nico relaxed and lounged against the wall, arms folded. Madeleine glanced at him uneasily. Tanaka was solidly built with broad shoulders and his arms filled the sleeves of his jacket. She knew that Logan considered Nico to be competent but if there was a chance Tanaka could react violently, she would have preferred Nico to be closer and not so relaxed.

'Please ask Tanaka why he was at the bank,' said Logan. At the use of his name, Tanaka's eyes flashed briefly to Logan, but then he stared down at the table. *He's wondering how we know his name*, thought Madeleine, but there was more behind his eyes in that brief look. He was hiding something. Madeleine concentrated on the man.

Keiko spoke in Japanese. Tanaka replied with a short sentence.

'He says he has nothing to say,' Keiko translated.

'Tell him if he cannot explain his actions, he may be charged with abduction.'

As Keiko started to speak, Madeleine leaned across and whispered in Logan's ear: 'Tanaka understands English.'

Logan looked at her in surprise, then smiled. He interrupted Keiko. 'Tanaka, this will be easier if you talk to me directly. I know you can understand me.'

Tanaka's eyes slowly rose to look at Logan. He took some time to consider Logan's words. Madeleine watched his face reflect his decision.

'You not charge me,' he said. He spoke English with a strong accent. 'I do nothing. The man came with me no problem, you ask him. You release me and girl soon.'

His hands betrayed his tension by forming into fists and then relaxing again. Madeleine tensed. Tanaka was indicating he was building up to some action. What was it? Would he refuse to answer or get angry and thump the table?

Madeline heard a rustle of movement from behind. Nico moving away from the wall?

'Mr Bandarakaianan now remembers what happened in his office,' said Logan. 'He knows he was abducted from his home. You're not going anywhere. You'll be charged and the girl will…'

Madeleine uttered a short cry of alarm.

With incredible strength and speed, Tanaka thrust the table aside, slamming Keiko into the wall. Ignoring Logan and Madeleine, he launched himself at Nico. He moved blindingly fast, crossing the room with his closed fist already swinging at Nico's head before Madeleine could react. As fast as he was, Nico's response was faster. A forearm knocked the punch aside and in the same movement, the fingers of Nico's right hand stabbed at Tanaka's throat. Tanaka twisted his head and Nico's stiff fingers found the side of the neck rather than the front, which forced a grunt from the Japanese man but he was still able to strike with his other hand again at Nico's head, at the same time bringing his knee up towards Nico's groin. Nico twisted his hand to push Tanaka's head down sharply, causing the blow Tanaka had thrown to land with reduced force on his shoulder. In the same movement, he turned his hip to meet Tanaka's knee. Nico moved as if he had all the time in the world, like an actor deliberately performing in slow motion. He reached around Tanaka's back and grasped the shoulder of his jacket, using the man's own momentum to spin him around so he now faced away from Nico, who dropped to one knee, forcing Tanaka to the floor. His free arm curled around Tanaka's neck, and all action ceased with the Japanese man forcefully immobilised in a chokehold.

Nico's actions had occupied less than five seconds and were accomplished so smoothly it could have been a choreographed dance.

The door burst open and the two policemen ran in, stopping when they saw they were not required. Colonel Ritter followed them into the room.

Madeleine pushed her chair away from the table and stepped around it to help Keiko to her feet. Keiko rubbed her arm but said: 'I'm OK, thank you.' She smiled a weak smile. Shaken but not hurt.

The Colonel spoke to his men in German. They pulled Tanaka up from the floor. Nico rose easily with him and released his hold. Tanaka eased his jacket around his shoulders with a shrug.

'Who are you?' he said to Nico. 'I not know you.'

Nico didn't reply and Logan said: 'Did you think you could escape from here?'

Tanaka sniffed. 'Maybe. More chance now than later, I think.'

'Who planned this robbery? If you give us some information, it may go better for you.'

Tanaka smiled. 'What robbery?' He looked at the Colonel. 'Even you charge me, I not be here long.'

Colonel Ritter ignored him. He inclined his head towards Nico and said to Logan: 'Your confidence was well justified.'

He nodded to his men and they escorted Tanaka from the room.

CHAPTER SIX

Vatican City…

'Your Eminence, I'm afraid I have bad news.'

The old man sat up in his bed, annoyed at being woken. He yawned, taking a moment to clear his head, then said: 'Well, speak up, Bartoch. Tell me your news.'

'Milan has the girl.'

'What girl? The woman in his hotel? You told me about that last night.'

'No. The Somali girl. He took her from the police in Zürich.'

'What? Impossible! How could he know about her?'

'He left the hotel in Venice last night with the woman and that man of his. Our man followed them to the airport where he discovered they had filed a flight plan for Zürich. They went immediately to the police headquarters on Bahnhofquai.'

'But how…?' The old man's face twisted in frustration. 'Oh, never mind. Where are they now?'

'They are in the air *en route* back to Venice.'

'Why would the police allow him to take the girl? She should have been released this morning.'

Bartoch started to speak but the man waved him to silence. 'He persuaded them to release her into his custody, that's clear. It will need to be dealt with.' His eyes narrowed. 'Is that all…?'

'Tanaka has been charged. Shall I arrange for his release?'

'Has he indeed? No, I'll handle that problem.' The man thought for a moment. 'Do you know the details of what happened in the police station, after Milan arrived?'

'Not yet. I expect a report in a few hours.'

'Good. I want to know exactly what he did. See that I'm informed immediately. This Milan is proving to be more troublesome than I thought.'

'Yes, Your Eminence.' He turned to leave.

'Bartoch!' the man barked. 'The woman! What did you discover about the woman Milan is with?'

'Of course, Your Eminence. My apologies. Her name is Madeleine Galli, and she is from Virginia, USA, where she works with her father for their firm, Galli and Galli. She is a forensic psychologist, well-respected, and also a professor of psychology at the University of Virginia. I don't yet know why she's in Venice, but she doesn't seem to have had any previous connection with Logan Milan.'

'Doesn't *seem* to have any previous connection. I expect more precision than that.'

'I haven't discovered her connection to him.'

The man grunted. 'A forensic psychologist…' he mused. 'Is she now?'

'It's a psychologist who works with law enforcement agencies. She has done work for the FBI as a profiler.'

The man's voice was ice. 'I *know* what a forensic psychologist does, thank you, Bartoch. Find out what her connection is with Milan. That's important. And Bartoch…'

'Yes, Your Eminence.'

'Do you know Mr Bowers?'

'Yes, I know him.'

'Tell him to come to my chambers in fifteen minutes.'

CHAPTER SEVEN

Excursion into the Dolomites…

Saturday 3:20 am

'If we hadn't involved ourselves,' Logan said, 'Tanaka would be walking away from the police station in a few hours from now, dragging Tricola with him.'

Ten minutes after arriving back at the airport, the Citation's wheels had departed the runway and begun to climb into the night sky above the city of Zürich. Madeleine heard the soft chatter of Serene's conversation with air traffic control from the cockpit.

Logan looked at Tricola, seated beside Madeleine on the cabin couch. She had a tight hold on Madeleine's hand and every few minutes she slowly lifted her gaze from her lap and looked at Madeleine with her big eyes to confirm she was still there. He could see she was exhausted but trying to stay awake as if she was worried that if she slept, it would all have been just a dream.

When she had realised that she would be leaving the police station with Madeleine and not with Tanaka, big tears had welled in Tricola's eyes and coursed down her cheeks and she had sobbed her relief. She had clasped Madeleine's hand and, from that moment, not let go. But, mixed with the relief, Madeleine could see that Tricola was still afraid. While they were preparing to leave the police station, she kept muttering the same words, like a mantra: 'We should leave here *now*. We *must* go quickly.' When the airport was mentioned, Tricola had said: 'The airport? Are we flying far away?' When Madeleine nodded, Tricola gasped and said: 'Yes, yes, that's good. But we must hurry.' Even on the way to the airport, she remained apprehensive, continually looking behind and up into the sky from the car window and saying under her breath: 'Hurry, hurry.'

Madeleine nodded her agreement with Logan's remark. She was happy that they'd been able to rescue Tricola from an unhealthy situation – she was just unsure about what that situation *was* exactly. She thought back over what she had learned about the incident at the bank, starting with the call from Sir Brian. She turned to Logan.

'One thing I don't understand,' she said, 'is the business about the collision with the police car. Fortuitous for us, undoubtedly, but that must have been the last thing they wanted to happen.'

'It's understandable,' said Logan. 'Even when someone is instructed to cooperate and appear happy, as Mr Bandarakaianan was, his subconscious, if it's strong enough, can rebel and initiate an action that he has no control over, especially if the role being forced on him goes against his deep beliefs about right and wrong. What happened, I think, is that Sami knew what he was doing was wrong, or his subconscious did, and the sight of a police car triggered a deep-seated and drastic response to escape from his situation.'

'He subconsciously swerved into the police car so they *would* be arrested?'

'It would have been at a more basic level than that. The police in that car represented safety, and the collision was a way to get their attention. But the interesting thing is that even the eventuality they may be arrested seems to have been foreseen. According to Sir Brian's report, none of them were dismayed by their arrest, even Sami. As Tanaka told us, he expected to be released once the police were unable to charge them with anything, presuming that the collision could be passed off as an accident. All indications showed that Sami had gone with Tanaka willingly and no crime appears to have been committed at the bank.'

'What does that mean?' asked Madeleine. 'Are you saying the plan was so meticulous it catered for every eventuality?'

'Or…' Logan said, thinking. 'Maybe this is not the first time…'

Madeleine thought about that. 'In any case, it was bad luck for...' she paused, '...*whoever*, that you were able to make Sami and the police understand that he had *not* freely taken a ride to his bank in the middle of the night.'

'Yes. We certainly disrupted somebody's plans tonight.'

Logan saw that Tricola had, at last, succumbed to her tiredness. Her eyes were closed and her head rested against Madeleine's shoulder. He lowered his voice and gestured for Nico to change seats so he could join the conversation. Madeleine eased Tricola's head from her shoulder and laid her down so she was reclining comfortably on the couch.

'From what I've learned already,' said Logan, 'the person behind what happened in Zürich is highly skilled in the use of the power, particularly coercion and memory manipulation. I'll know more when I can spend some time with Tricola.' He thought for a moment. 'If we assume that person is Sapphire and that his scheme, whatever it is, involves the gathering of money and precious stones and encompasses several Asian banks as well as this Zürich bank – it's building into a major worldwide operation.'

He lowered his voice further so it became a whisper and motioned them to lean closer.

'Tricola knows some information that he's taken considerable pains to protect, so he's going to be desperate to get her back, or...' he paused, '...if he's ruthless enough, to *silence* her. If Sapphire is aware that I may be able to circumvent the protection he's put in place, and we must assume he is – she's in real danger.'

Nico nodded. 'I like that little girl,' he said. 'They'll need to go through me to get to her.'

Logan unbuckled his belt and stood up.

'And me,' he said. 'Excuse me a moment. Now that we're flying level, Serene can patch me through to Sir Brian so I can brief him.' He headed towards the cockpit.

Madeleine made Tricola more comfortable with a pillow under her head and a blanket to cover her.

When Nico sat beside her and asked what she had discovered about Tricola, Madeleine related what had happened in the room. During the conversation, the first time they had spoken more than a few words, Madeleine marvelled at Nico's voice. Even while speaking it had a melodious quality, as if at any moment he could burst into song.

Logan returned ten minutes later and sat down again across from Madeleine.

'I've explained the situation to Sir Brian and asked him if he could provide extra security when we reach Venice.'

'Extra security?' enquired Madeleine. 'Is that really necessary? How could anyone know where we've taken Tricola? You didn't even tell Colonel Ritter.'

'Hopefully, it *will* be a waste of time,' replied Logan. 'But I've learned to use Sir Brian's help whenever there's a possibility it may be needed.'

Madeleine raised her hands in an 'OK' gesture of acceptance.

Logan continued: 'Sir Brian has asked Serene to accompany us. She can get things done in his name without us needing his direct authorisation, and she's highly skilled in other ways.'

Madeleine raised her eyebrows at his last statement, but he didn't elaborate.

Logan gazed out of the window into the night sky.

'By the way,' he said after a few seconds, turning his head to look at Madeleine. 'How did you know that Tanaka spoke English?' Nico raised his eyes, obviously interested in her reply.

'He was following the conversation.' In response to Logan's questioning look, she added: 'There are many indicators on the face, like eye movement and focus, that show understanding, or, conversely, the lack of it.'

'I'd only said a few words…'

'It was enough.'

'That's very impressive. Is this something you've developed through training?'

'In part. My father says I have a unique talent.'

Logan tilted his head. 'In what way are you talented?'

'I really don't….'

'Madeleine…' said Logan, reaching across and taking hold of her arm. 'Things may soon get serious. I think we've stepped into something big and, unfortunately, we may not have the option to just step out again. As I've just said, Tricola is in danger – in all likelihood, we all are.' His voice softened. 'I appreciate, of course, all you've done tonight and, at the same time, I'm sorry for dragging you into this situation.'

Madeleine looked at him soberly. 'I'm here of my own free will.'

She waited a few seconds, thinking about what he'd said, then observed: 'But you knew you were raising the level of risk when you decided to persuade the Colonel to let Tricola come with us, didn't you?'

'It was your idea, and it was a good one…' he took his hand from her arm and held it up against her protest. 'But I know you had no idea of the likely consequences if we *did* take Tricola with us.'

'But *you* did.'

'Yes. Everything we've learned so far tells us the stakes are high. Sapphire is expanding his operation – he's planning and preparing for something big. But we had no choice. You've heard how Nico feels about this girl; I suspect you feel the same, and there's no way I was going to abandon her to the wolves.' He paused, leaning forward. 'In any case, the deed is done. We'll certainly need all of the resources at our disposal to face whatever comes our way as a result. I need to know your capabilities. So, please, tell us about your talent.'

Madeleine took a deep breath. 'I have very acute sight and hearing. Better than ninety-nine point several more nines per cent of the general population. I'm able to notice activity on a person's face, hands, or body that only lasts for a few milliseconds, including changes in breathing or voice, and I've trained myself to recognise the meaning of these movements and their combinations. I call them *micro-movements*.'

'Like the 'tells' that poker players use,' suggested Nico.

'Not really. They're the macro version because they're usually obvious. I'm talking about the mini… no, the *micro* version.'

Logan said: 'Was this something you were born with or have you developed it?'

'I was born with the abilities and I've developed the interpretation and understanding over time. I thought everyone could see as I can and it was a surprise to learn that no one can, or, that is, no one I've ever met. It's like being able to compare two adjacent frames of a movie in real-time, using both sight and sound, and know what's changed. It got me into a lot of trouble when I was young. Adults don't like a child telling them they're lying or that *they* don't believe the words they're saying.'

'So, you're a human polygraph,' said Nico with a smile.

'No.' Madeleine made a derisive hand gesture. 'Much more accurate than a polygraph.'

'What can you deduce from the changes you see?' asked Logan.

'A lot. Is the person telling the truth or bluffing? Does he believe the words he or someone else is saying? Those are all the same thing, really – a measure of sincerity. I know if actions or words are genuine or just an act. If you know what to look for, people are quite transparent. I can tell how someone is feeling; if they're ill or in pain, or experiencing any of a hundred emotions. Also, I can sense what people are about to do before they do it – before *they* know in fact, that they are going to do anything – if that makes sense.'

She gave a short laugh and, in response to Logan's raised eyebrows, said: 'My father says it's the closest thing he's ever seen to being able to read someone's mind. He often accuses me of reading *his* thoughts.'

Logan wagged a finger at her. 'You knew Tanaka was going to attack Nico. I remember you cried out *before* he moved.'

'Yes, I knew he was going to try something a few seconds earlier, but I didn't think he would attack anyone. I should have warned you, but then he moved too fast to do anything about it.'

'Can you read everyone as easily and quickly as you did Tanaka?'

Madeleine smiled. 'Meaning – can I read you?'

He returned the smile.

'I wouldn't be here if you had any secret agendas or hidden motives or if any of the words you have uttered in my presence were…' she paused, choosing her words. '…ones you did not believe and, therefore, less than the truth.'

Logan shared a glance with Nico. 'That's worth knowing,' he said with a wry smile. He studied her.

'If someone knew about your ability,' he asked slowly, 'could they disguise their responses or give you a false reading?'

She shook her head. 'The micro-movements happen on a subconscious level. They can't be consciously controlled. People don't even know they're happening. As I said, there are some actions that occur *before* people know they're about to say or do anything. And, of course, just as much is revealed by the act of trying to hide true feelings.'

She leaned forward, using a smile to lighten her words. 'For instance, when Sir Brian called you in Venice, you told me many things about him and your relationship before I saw him on the screen.'

His raised eyebrows revealed his interest.

'His interruption made you both apprehensive and excited at the same time, like a...' she thought of an analogy, '...like a mountaineer about to attempt a difficult but rewarding climb. I could see he was a friend but not an *old* friend from your school days. I also knew he was older than you – you were respectful as with a relative like an uncle. I could go on...'

Logan nodded thoughtfully while Nico shook his head appreciatively.

'I talk about micro-movements and subsequent reactions in the paper I'm presenting at the symposium on Tuesday.' Madeleine stopped as a thought occurred to her. 'Will I still be able to attend...?'

'At this stage, I don't see any reason why not.'

She breathed a sigh of relief.

'Wouldn't these micro-movements, as you call them, be highly individualised?' continued Logan.

'I call that the eighty-twenty rule, with the twenty being the individual proportion. There's a set of actions or changes that happen with everyone, and some people add others. So, part of what they do might depend on the individual, but everyone does something similar before they are about to, for example, tell a lie. *Everyone.*'

'Fascinating. So, in your professional world, you make those sorts of assessments for clients.'

'Yes.'

'I can see how that ability would be a tremendous advantage in corporate negotiations.'

'And interviews with suspects or witnesses.' She smiled. 'And in everyday life. But, yes, it's what they pay me for.'

Logan leaned back in his seat and regarded Madeleine intently. His gaze lingered so long she said: 'What…?'

He shook his head. 'Sorry for the stare. You've just told me you have acute hearing, which means a wider than normal range of sounds reaches your conscious mind. On the face of it, that would make your ability to resist the power even more incredible. I know the power works at the conscious *and* the subconscious level, which means you must have a mechanism providing resistance at both levels. As I said before, I've made a particular study of resistance, and I've never met or even heard of anyone approaching your ability. I'd like to test it sometime – with your agreement, of course. It just reaffirms to me that you're a very special person.'

She bowed her head. 'Why, thank you, kind sir.'

Serene's voice came into the cabin. 'Please fasten your seatbelts, Ladies and Gentlemen. I'm beginning our descent to Marco Polo airport. You'll soon be back in Venice.'

Madeleine looked at her watch. 'We've only been in the air just over half an hour, from Zürich to Venice. That seems very fast.'

'This plane is a Citation Ten. It can fly at nine-tenths the speed of sound,' said Logan. 'Sir Brian only uses the best.'

Madeleine made an appreciative face and reached down to buckle a seatbelt around Tricola.

THEY WERE MET ON the tarmac by an officious man in a military uniform who introduced himself as Major Karel Lutyens of NATO Intelligence, assigned as their support, courtesy of Sir Brian Talbot. He talked to Serene and she called Logan over. Logan listened for a few moments then replied with hand movements that seemed to be giving directions. Major Lutyens nodded his understanding and ushered the plane's passengers into a large vehicle resembling a Hum-vee with several extra protuberances and antennas. Inside were three men dressed in similar gear, all armed with automatic rifles.

Madeleine glanced back at the plane. She could see Archie's red hair illuminated by the cockpit lighting.

'Will the plane just wait here?' she asked Serene.

'Yes. Archie will keep it ready for us.'

Ready for a quick getaway? Madeleine shook her head. A little too melodramatic.

She helped Tricola into the vehicle and Serene climbed in behind her.

The obviously military nature of their escort made Madeleine feel both reassured and uneasy at the same time.

'I expected a couple of men in suits, maybe with bulges in their armpits, not a troop of soldiers – Sir Brian is taking this seriously,' she commented, taking a seat alongside Tricola in the back of the vehicle. It was a tight fit with barely room for her knees and she regretted not taking up Logan's offer to change her clothes during the flight.

'As am I,' said Logan, seated in the same row across a small aisle. He turned so that Nico and Serene were included in the conversation.

'Major Lutyens just told us that a man asked about our flight plan when we left Marco Polo airport for Zürich, so it seems someone was taking an interest in us even at that stage. Accordingly, I think we should begin doing the unexpected. We won't be returning to the hotel. My mother has a ski villa high in the Dolomites. It's a two-hour drive and it's secluded and peaceful and it will be a perfect place to talk with Tricola. You said your aunt is returning to Venice on Monday, Madeleine. Do you have anywhere you need to be before then?'

Madeleine wondered why Logan referred to the villa as his mother's rather than calling it family property. Major Lutyens climbed in beside the driver and the door slammed shut. The engine fired and, with a jerk, the vehicle headed across the tarmac, away from the lights of the airport and into the night.

'Well, no… not really,' she said, realising that her expectation of spending a few hours in the company of Logan Milan for an evening meal may now stretch into days. 'Apart from the meeting with Claudia, I planned to take a few days to relax before the symposium.'

'Good, because this young lady needs to feel safe and I don't think she'd be happy if you were to leave us.' He pulled a phone from his pocket. 'I'll inform the staff to expect us.'

The staff? thought Madeleine. Logan owned several hotels. His mother kept a villa in the Dolomites with *staff*. That sounded like the lifestyle of the rich and famous.

When she looked at Tricola, she found her big eyes staring back.

Madeleine shared Logan's concern regarding Tricola. She was feeling frightened and vulnerable and that was only natural after her experience. She smiled, trying to show her support and compassion. For a fleeting moment, something else showed on the girl's face.

Madeleine turned quickly to Logan as if she had just remembered something.

'I hope Pietro will save my half-glass of Armagnac,' she said. Her voice was light-hearted, but her mind was racing.

The frightened, shy, defenceless girl image that Tricola projected was a façade. She was good, very good. So good that there had been no cause to suspect anything before now. What Madeleine had just seen was a calculating intelligence behind those big brown eyes that was definitely at odds with the exterior.

Logan laughed. 'That's not necessary. The cellar is well stocked.'

Tricola drew Madeleine's attention by tugging at her sleeve. 'You should not use your phones,' she said in her soft lisping voice. 'You must remove the battery from your phones. They will track you.'

Was it this thought that Madeleine had seen? Or was it something more? Who did Tricola think would try to track them through their phones, and how did she know that? Madeleine knew that lost phones could be tracked, but… remove the batteries? That seemed to be an extreme reaction.

Logan paused in the act of calling a number and looked at Tricola. He started to say: 'Who…' but stopped. She probably wouldn't be able to say a name.

'Anybody's phone can be tracked,' Tricola said. 'It's not difficult. If they know your name, your phone number can be found.'

There's something more, something she's not saying, thought Madeleine. Tricola was looking at Logan but noticed Madeleine watching her and glanced her way, confirming to Madeleine that she was feeling guilty for some reason.

Serene nodded her agreement to Logan and said: 'If someone is, as you say, taking an interest in you – even before Zürich, then it's possible.'

He gave a grim smile. 'I should have thought of it. It seems we've all got some adjustments to make. Thank you, Tricola. Let's get these batteries out.' He turned his phone over and removed the back with his thumbnail.

'But…' Madeleine objected. Surely, they wouldn't know *her* name. 'What if someone needs to contact me?'

She was suddenly feeling very much out of her depth. She was still adjusting to travelling with a military escort, and now she was being asked to make her phone inoperable?

'My father, or Claudia, might…' Madeleine stopped, realising her objection was selfish.

'There's a landline at the villa,' said Logan. 'You can call and let them know where you are.'

Tricola shook her head. 'You must not let *anyone* know where you are,' she said in a whisper.

Logan looked at her. 'What is it that you're afraid of?' he said, almost to himself. 'What do you know? I think there's more to you, young lady, than meets the eye.'

And I agree with that, thought Madeleine, as she reluctantly prised the battery from her phone. She needed to tell Logan what she had noticed at the first opportunity.

Serene paused in the action of taking off the back of her phone. Logan noticed her hesitation and said: 'Yes, I agree *your* phone shouldn't be at risk. You've only just decided to join us. But… to be sure…' He glanced at Madeleine as he said this, showing his sympathy for the inconvenience of disabling her phone, too.

Serene shrugged her shoulders and flipped off the back.

Logan turned in his seat and made himself comfortable.

'I suggest we all get some sleep if we can. We should arrive at the villa just after sunrise, and that's a very beautiful time in the mountains.'

THE EARLY MORNING SUN bathed the villa in a warm yellow glow. The building was nestled at the foot of a small grass-covered hill in the centre of a wide river valley bordered on both sides by the towering Dolomite mountains. It was indeed a beautiful setting, and Madeleine could easily imagine how even more magical the scene would be when the valley was covered in snow.

The huge mountain ranges appeared blue in the still morning haze, providing a stark contrast to the varied green and yellow colours of the grass and trees and the exposed bleached-white outcrops of Dolomite rock that dotted the hillsides and the valley floor.

Logan had pointed out the villa when it first came into view, far up the valley.

'The hill behind the villa blocks the bitter northerlies when they blast out of the mountains in winter,' he said. 'It can be cosy even in a full storm.'

The villa was large, the size of a tourist ski lodge. It was two-storeyed with a wide fenced deck extending around three sides of the top level. Four chimneys sprouting from the roof supported Logan's assertion of interior warmth.

The Major insisted his men exit from the vehicle first, and they did so in a state of alertness, facing in all directions, weapons at the ready. *Were they really expecting an ambush?* thought Madeleine, amused. But she had to admit Major Lutyens was efficient as he ordered his men to check out the building and the surrounding land. The driver extracted two large metal cases from behind his seat and set them on the ground beside the Major. *More equipment? First looking for an ambush and now readying for a siege!*

While the 'civilians' were slowly extricating themselves from their tight fit, Madeleine took Logan's elbow and guided him a short distance from the others as if to admire the spectacular view.

'A word of warning,' she said quietly. 'Tricola's appearance as a confused, innocent little girl isn't real. She's playing a part. I'm not sure why yet, but we should be careful around her. And, even aside from whatever it is that she can't talk about, she definitely knows much more than she's telling us.'

Logan appraised her words thoughtfully. He nodded.

Madeleine stopped him with a hand on his arm as he turned back to the villa. 'One more thing. Did you notice she has a wrist band? Do you think that's…?'

Logan covered her hand with his. His skin was surprisingly soft.

'Yes,' he said. 'I've noticed, and, yes, it's almost certainly working as a talisman.'

MADELEINE MET MAY-LIN, her husband Jai, and their daughter, Maia, a teenager with a beaming smile, who looked to be a little older than Tricola but Madeleine was pleased to see that the two made an instant connection as the only 'youngsters' in the group.

The unexpected guests were quickly made welcome, May-Lin fussing over Logan.

'Mr Logan, we no see you for such long time. Very nice surprise. Is one of these ladies your wife – or soon to be wife?' She raised her eyes and nodded knowingly when Logan said Madeleine and Serene were colleagues. It was not difficult to understand what she was thinking: *If Mr Logan wants to introduce these ladies as 'colleagues', that's OK with me.*

'You need food? You want some coffee?'

May-Lin hovered like a honey bee while Jai calmly stood and bowed to each person as they came through the entrance to the lounge. Madeleine waited just inside the door to take her bag from Nico and she watched him walking with his fluid grace from the vehicle to the villa. Behind Nico, Madeleine saw the Hum-vee drive around the corner of the building – *putting it out of sight?*

The lounge had the appearance of a large hotel bar complete with tables and chairs in the centre of the room and leather-covered sofas spaced around the varnished wooden plank walls, but a closer examination revealed that the 'bar' was in fact an impressive kitchen and serving area, which was plainly capable of catering for large numbers of visitors. As she gazed around the room, Madeleine's eye caught the paintings on the wall and she realised immediately that these were not prints but originals.

'We've all had a long night and the journey was not particularly restful,' Logan said. 'We may be here a while so, again, I suggest we all catch up on sleep for a few hours, and we can gather on the deck at around midday for some refreshment.'

Madeleine took up her bag and May-Lin despatched Maia to show Madeleine and Tricola to the upstairs bedrooms. During the journey from the entrance lounge to the top floor, Madeleine discovered that Maia was on a summer break from the University of Verona, where she was studying medicine. Maia's English was good, but in a short time, Maia and Tricola were conversing in Italian which was too fast for Madeleine to follow.

She was happy to be excluded and realised how tired she was as soon as she lay on a bed.

CHAPTER EIGHT

A villa in the mountains, beautiful scenery, Tricola's secret…

Saturday 12:30 pm

The sound was subdued. It was noticeable only because it did not belong in the rural scene that Madeleine was surveying. She held a fresh cup of coffee and rested her elbows on the wide decking rail.

For some minutes, she had been watching Nico in a small grassy area at the side of the villa, practising a series of actions that may have been Tai Chi but could have been another martial discipline. His movements were so smooth and coordinated and his balance rock solid even when he leaned so far that she thought he must topple at any moment, that she found herself transfixed. One movement led seamlessly into another in an increasingly complex dance. Eventually, Nico gracefully lowered himself until he sat cross-legged on the ground. After five minutes he hadn't moved and she had transferred her gaze to the long valley which stretched several miles until it terminated when the mountain ranges on both sides converged.

When she looked back, the grassy area was empty.

She had woken twenty minutes ago and was pleased to find that it was still morning and she hadn't overslept. She showered quickly and dressed in calf-length jeans and a light shirt she had discovered in the bag Pietro had prepared the night before. She was not surprised when the clothes and even the slip-on shoes fitted perfectly.

There was no one else on the deck yet and she relished the scent of the fresh country air and welcomed the peaceful perfection of the scene that was occasionally and beautifully augmented by bursts of birdsong.

The unusual sound lasted for only a few seconds, virtually disappearing as soon as it appeared, and it took a few more seconds for her to register the discord. She straightened. What *was* that sound? She listened but it was not repeated. Then she recognised it. A helicopter – no, *two* helicopters.

Footsteps approached and she turned to see Logan and Serene. He had a coffee pot in one hand and a jug of iced water topped with slices of lemon in the other, and Serene was carrying a large platter filled with fruit, sliced meats, tomatoes, olives, cheese, and bread.

Logan, too, had changed his clothes, his evening suit swapped for jeans and a white T-shirt. Serene had moved in the opposite direction, her jacket and jeans replaced by a blouse over a short colourful red and yellow summer skirt. She placed the platter on the nearest of the deck's solid wooden tables and slid herself into a chair.

Madeleine noticed that their tops both bore the same embroidered logo – *Insieme* – which Madeleine knew could mean 'together' in the sense of a relationship. Maybe May-Lin's instincts were accurate. Were Logan and Serene…? The word seemed familiar to Madeleine in another context but she couldn't place it. She wondered about Serene's change of clothing. Did Logan's mother, like Logan, keep a feminine wardrobe in multiple sizes? Or was Serene the same size as Logan's mother? She smiled to herself. A feminine mystery.

'May-Lin told me you were up,' Logan said, his blue eyes squinting against the bright sunlight. 'Where's Tricola?'

'She's still sleeping. I thought it best not to wake her.'

Logan nodded. 'I see you already have coffee.' He indicated the food platter. 'May-Lin's food is legendary. She cures the meat herself. I can recommend the prosciutto.'

'Shouldn't we wait for Nico?'

'He's showering after his morning exercises. He'll join us when he's ready.'

'OK. By the way, did you hear that sound a few minutes ago?'

Logan looked at her. 'What sound?'

'I heard the distinctive beat of two helicopters. Very faint and only for a few seconds. They were somewhere over there.' She waved a hand to the west, reaching with her other hand for a piece of bread and brushing her hair aside as she brought it to her mouth.

Logan and Serene shared a glance.

'It could be the Mountain Rescue Service,' said Serene. 'But they would not normally use two....'

Logan looked back at Madeleine. Before he could ask, she swallowed and said: 'Yes, I'm *sure*. I heard *two* helicopters.'

Logan offered her the cheese plate then picked up a piece of bread and placed a slice each of cheese and meat on it. He took a bite. Through his mouthful, he said: 'I'll alert Major Lutyens, but it's probably nothing.'

Serene nodded in agreement. 'How could anyone find us here? Unless they can track us through our phones even without the batteries.'

A crash of breaking glass caused everyone to turn. Tricola stood at the entrance to the deck, a pool of milk spreading from the pieces of jagged glass scattered at her feet. She looked as though she'd just woken. Her hair was tousled and she still wore the pyjamas that Maia had given her. Her expression was miserable, on the verge of tears.

'Not through your phone,' she said, her voice a moan of despair. 'Through *me*.'

Madeleine was closest. She went to her, guiding Tricola around the puddle of milk and into a chair. She turned back just as May-Lin arrived with a mop and bucket. May-Lin waved her away, saying: 'No problem. No problem.'

Madeleine sat beside Tricola. 'What do you mean?' she asked gently.

'I'm so sorry,' Tricola said, the sibilant words accentuating her lisp. 'I should have told you. They've tracked me before when I've tried to run away. If they find me now, they'll hurt me. They'll hurt everybody.' She shook her head, her eyes brimming with tears.

Madeleine put her arm around the girl. She could feel her body shaking.

'It'll be alright. You've seen the soldiers. No-one will hurt us. Take a deep breath and calm yourself. Just tell us what you mean. How can they track you without a phone?'

Madeleine caught Logan's inquiring glance. This didn't sound like someone putting on an act. Madeleine agreed. The girl was genuinely frightened.

Tricola took several deep breaths, looking at each of them in turn. In a soft voice she said: 'I've tried to run away from these people many times. The house where I was kept is built on the top of a hill and has huge grounds like a park and there are lots of places to hide, but I am always found and punished.'

Tricola drew the letter 'T' in the air, then quickly shut her eyes and her brow crinkled. A small pain in her head observed Madeleine. She can't even think of Tanaka without being affected.

Logan said to Serene: 'Tricola is talking about the Japanese man who accompanied her to the bank.'

Tricola nodded. She breathed deeply then continued, speaking slowly in halting phrases, testing to see what reaction her words or thoughts would produce in her head.

'One time, I escaped into the grounds and found a perfect hiding place. I wormed my way into a thicket of brambles. The thorns scratched me but I kept going. The mass of brambles was thickest in the middle and I thought I could hide in there. I could hear a humming. Right in the middle of the thicket I discovered a metal tunnel with a whirring fan inside. I couldn't believe my luck. I was bleeding in many places. I crawled into the tunnel and stopped the fan with a stick, got behind it and removed the stick. I was safe there. No-one would think to look in the brambles, let alone search them and, even if they did, I couldn't be seen behind the fan. I had some food with me and water and I was prepared to wait for days. I watched though the fan. Hours later, I saw… this man…' she drew the 'T' again, and winced at the pain that caused. 'He walked up to the brambles… he listened on his ear-phone… and he came straight towards where I am, pushing through the brambles, cursing when the thorns scratched him.' She paused. 'I know he can't see me.' Another wait. 'Someone is telling him where I am.'

She closed her eyes to shut out the memories, or perhaps thankful that she'd successfully completed what she wanted to say.

Softly, she said: 'That time, the punishment was bad.'

Madeleine felt the pain this young girl had suffered. She wanted to reach out and hold her but she saw that Tricola wasn't finished. Madeleine also wanted to ask about the person directing Tanaka, but that would surely cause Tricola more pain. She glanced at Logan and saw that he too was holding that question back.

Tricola lifted her head and said firmly: 'I think I have a transmitter inside me.'

Her eyes indicated that she was surprised that she could talk about her suspicion. 'I hoped this time I am too far away but… I've searched but I can't find it.' She took hold of Madeleine's arm. 'You *must* find this horrible thing and take it out of me.' She gasped with the relief of being able to get the words out.

Madeleine put her hand gently on Tricola's.

'I see you're as surprised as I am you were able to tell us all that,' Madeleine said.

'I know what I can talk about and what I can't. If I can think about it without any reaction, I can talk about it. I can't even think about… the *other*.' Tricola shook her head. Her micro-movements told Madeleine her words were the truth. She thought how difficult and wretched Tricola's life must have been.

Logan stood up. 'Will the Major have anything that can locate a transmitter?' he asked Serene.

'Perhaps. I'll ask him,' said Serene. She placed the bread in her hand onto the table and used a napkin to wipe her mouth. Logan put a hand on her arm.

'Thankfully, Madeleine's sensitive hearing has given us plenty of warning. *If* these are the people we talked about earlier, they obviously landed some distance away so they wouldn't be heard, and they hope to surprise us. Maybe they intend to wait until tonight. Whatever their plans, if they've put the helicopters down in the western hills and intend to walk here, that will take a few hours. You have time to eat a bite or two.'

Serene smiled at him and picked up the bread, then she put her face close to his and took a bite.

'Is that OK?' she said, mimicking a petulant teenager. 'Can I go now?'

Logan laughed. 'You may now leave the table.' He waved her away and addressed Tricola. 'You should eat something too, and then Madeleine can check you over.'

Tricola looked at the food, her eyes checking each item on offer. She calmed herself with a visible effort and reached for a piece of cheese which she pushed into her mouth and followed it with three olives, her cheeks bulging as she chewed. Before she had finished the mouthful, several slivers of prosciutto joined the cheese and olives. She took a piece of bread in one hand and a peach in the other and said something as she looked around the table, her words muffled by the food in her mouth. The only intelligible word was '… water?'

Madeleine and Logan exchanged another glance. Maybe she was just hungry, or simply greedy, but to Madeleine, she looked more like someone who had learned to make the most of food when it was available.

While Logan poured Tricola a glass of iced water from the jug, Madeleine said: 'If the helicopters are carrying people looking for Tricola, why don't they just swoop in and land in the carpark?'

'I can only assume they want to retrieve Tricola using stealth rather than a direct assault which might allow us time to call the police and would then risk a confrontation with the Italian authorities.'

'Then shouldn't we call the police now?'

Logan looked at her with raised eyebrows and although he didn't speak, she understood what he would have said: 'And tell them what? We heard helicopters a long way away and we think some people are coming to take this girl away.'

She smiled. 'Sorry,' she said.

SERENE RETURNED WITH Major Lutyens and one of his men in tow. The Major had a device in his hand, the size and shape of a pack of cigarettes.

'We use this to check for bugs or transmitters in a room,' the Major said in his crisp English. 'It should detect transmitters under the skin but it may depend on the type of transmitter.'

He handed it to Madeleine and said: 'Switch it on here. If green bars show in this window, there is a transmitter nearby. The number of bars will increase as you get closer to the transmitter.'

Madeleine stood up but the Major held up his hand.

'Did you *see* the helicopters?' he asked.

'No. I only heard them.'

'Was the rotor sound deep and throbbing or light and fast?'

'It was light, I suppose, just normal. It took me a few seconds to identify it.'

'Thank you,' said the Major. He turned to the man standing behind him. 'Probably not transports. Two medium choppers would mean ten to twenty personnel. I want a radio check from each man, sergeant. One man on top of the hill. One on the roof, the other two patrolling. Two hour shifts and then change. Report *anything.*'

'Sir!' The sergeant turned and his boots clattered across the deck.

'Major,' Serene said, 'I'm qualified with the weapons you're carrying. How can I help?'

Major Lutyens looked her up and down. 'Sir Brian told me about you,' he said. 'Heckler and Koch G28 Sniper rifle?' She nodded. 'Come with me,' he said. He led her away and Madeleine heard him say: 'I think *you* might be best on the roof…'

'On the *roof?*' Serene said in mock alarm. She looked down at her dress. 'I'd better change first.'

'I'll need to contact you via your phone,' said Major Lutyens. 'I don't have a spare radio.'

'In that case I'll replace my battery,' said Serene, glancing at Logan who nodded his agreement.

Serene and the Major left the deck, following in the footsteps of the sergeant.

Logan watched them go. 'Removing and destroying the transmitter is the first priority,' he said. 'Then…' he paused, '…logically, the best move would be to leave here, but if we have a few hours, I'd like to take some time to talk with Tricola…' he smiled at her, '…if that's OK with you, Tricola.'

Tricola swallowed her mouthful of water and looked alarmed. 'I cannot tell you….'

'I know to talk of some things is painful. I can help with that.'

Tricola looked doubtful and turned to Madeleine who gave her a nod of encouragement.

'I'd better find Nico and bring him up to date,' said Logan.

IN THE BEDROOM, Madeleine and Maia examined Tricola who stood beside her discarded pyjamas with a towel clutched at her neck. Even though she had invited the inspection, Tricola had, at the last moment, been reluctant to undress. Madeleine initially thought she was just being modest, but now she knew better.

They had been unable to locate the transmitter by visual check, but not because there was no evidence of a cut on Tricola's skin – rather, there was too much evidence. Madeleine had expected to look for an insertion point that would be revealed by a small scar but, when Tricola's back was bared, she was alarmed to see it was covered by a dozen or more scars from minor cuts and round puncture wounds, some old, some recent, as well as many bruises. Some of the bruises formed lines across Tricola's back as if she had been whipped, with the backs of her legs and buttocks displaying similar bruising. Maia gasped in shock, a hand going to her mouth as her eyes stared at the evidence of the abuse Tricola had suffered. At the gasp, Tricola looked over her shoulder and noticed Madeleine's expression.

'I'm sorry you have seen me like this,' she lisped.

'Was this the form that your punishment took?'

'Yes, not only when I run away. I do many things wrong. I try to do what they ask, but I don't understand… sometimes I'm too slow.' She was the picture of a vulnerable and confused little girl.

Madeleine again saw a flicker behind the eyes.

'Tricola,' she said firmly, 'you don't need to keep this up.'

Tricola stared at the floor. 'What do you mean?'

'Your frightened little girl act. I know that's not who you are.'

Tricola's eyes widened in surprise. Maia also looked at Madeleine, puzzled by her words.

'Why are you acting like this?' asked Madeleine. 'It's not you.' She made sure it was not an accusation, just a question.

Tricola's closed her eyes. She said nothing and Madeleine waited.

When Tricola started talking, her lisp was gone and her voice had lost its husky tone.

'When you talked to me at the police station,' she said, 'you gave me hope that I could escape, that I could *finally* get away from those people. You were different, not part of the police, so you may not be in their control. That's why I tried to talk to you, even though I knew it would hurt….'

She looked up directly into Madeleine's eyes. Her own eyes were clear. Madeleine was startled by the raw intelligence that shone there.

'They told me how to act,' Tricola continued. 'I had to practice it many times, and… I was also given some…' She searched for the word. 'Some… *instructions*.' Her face registered disgust. 'And I had to drink a horrible soup.' She shook her head. 'I felt I was being manipulated, like a puppet, but I couldn't do anything about it. Anyway, if the police interfered, I was to be a robot, saying nothing, moving slowly. If I didn't do that, my head hurt.'

She drew in a long breath and let it out.

'I suspect your misunderstanding and the slowness you were punished for were deliberate,' Madeleine said. 'I don't think you're ever slow at anything.'

Her suspicion was confirmed by the brief look that crossed Tricola's face.

The girl hesitated but then continued. 'The other part,' Tricola said, '…what you called the frightened little girl – that's natural for me. I've played that part my whole life. It kept me alive through bad times.' She paused and Madeleine felt the depth of her burden. 'It makes people want to protect me rather than hurt me.'

Tricola looked at Madeleine, checking her reaction.

'I'm sorry,' she continued, a frown briefly marring her unblemished brow. 'It's another thing I should have told you earlier. It was just easier and safer to continue. I know you're a good person, and you're all trying to help me. You are my friends.'

Tricola desperately wanted that last statement to be true. Madeleine said: 'But you've thought that before and been betrayed, so you find it hard to trust anyone.'

Tricola's eyes flicked up. 'Yes,' she whispered. 'But how do you know that?'

Madeleine smiled. 'You're shouting it with your whole body.'

Tricola studied Madeleine, a moistness coming to her eyes. She returned the smile. 'I've always been able to hide myself and my thoughts from everyone. I don't seem to be able to hide anything from you. You, too, have a gift.'

Me too? thought Madeleine. *Tricola seemed to be gifted with electronic equipment, computers, and phones. Was that the gift that Tricola was acknowledging she had? Or… was it her intelligence?*

Tricola brought her hand up to dab at her eyes, and Madeleine noticed the leather strap around Tricola's wrist with the triangular piece of cardboard attached. Logan had said it was a talisman.

'What's that?' she asked. 'Could the transmitter be in that strap? Shall I check it?'

Tricola moved her other hand to cover the strap, tightening her elbows quickly to her sides when the towel threatened to slip.

'No!' she cried out, alarmed. 'The transmitter is not there. I'm sorry…' she was immediately contrite, '…I don't mean to be rude. But this *cannot* be removed.'

'That's OK,' Madeleine said, patting her arm to calm the girl. 'We won't worry about that now. Just relax.'

During the conversation, Maia's astonished gaze had flicked between them, her face alternately showing surprise, puzzlement, and concern.

Madeleine beckoned to her. 'Turn on the Major's device, and let's see what we can find.'

THE TRANSMITTER WAS LOCATED behind Tricola's left shoulder blade. Maia probed the spot indicated by the location device with her finger and confirmed she could feel a lump. She cleaned the area with some alcohol and apologised that they had no anaesthetic. Maia paused, holding a scalpel from her medical kit close to Tricola's skin.

Tricola, waiting calmly, said quietly: 'Don't worry. This is physical pain. I'm used to that. Just get it out.'

Madeleine reached out to hold her hand.

Maia made a shallow cut parallel to the already existing scar. Tricola flinched and her eyes pinched shut, but she didn't cry out. A trickle of blood flowed from the wound. With tweezers, Maia reached just below the skin and extracted a metal object the size and shape of a hearing-aid battery, which she dropped into a cup as more small beads of blood escaped. Madeleine handed the cup to Tricola while Maia wiped the cut and applied a pad, using some sticky gauze strips to cover Tricola's most recent injury.

'Thank you,' said Tricola, staring into the cup. 'I'd like a bird to take this far away.'

Maia handed Tricola a pile of clothes, jeans, and a cream top.

'These should fit you. They'll be more comfortable than that dress.'

She exchanged the clothes for the cup containing the transmitter. 'There's an old well outside that hasn't been used for years. There's water at the bottom. It's deep, I think. I'll drop this in there.'

Madeleine's head jerked up.

'Motorbikes,' she said.

CHAPTER NINE

Visitors to the villa and Occhio di Ra…

Saturday 1:20 pm

'The safest place is here in this room,' said Logan. 'We'll leave the reception to the Major and his men. How many are there, Nico?'

Major Lutyens had his radio to one ear and a phone held in front of him, set on speaker. Madeleine could hear the reports arriving from his men. She heard Serene's voice from the phone say there were four motorcyclists riding 'dirt bikes'. Madeleine had a view of the carpark from where she and Tricola stood but couldn't see the approaching road. Behind her, in the kitchen area, May-Lin, Jai, and Maia were huddled next to the serving counter.

Nico was standing at the window beside the Major. He echoed Serene: 'Four. Could be a group out for a ride, but…'

The sound of a helicopter echoed up the valley and Nico's gaze lifted. He searched the sky and watched as the helicopter came into view, heading directly for the villa.

'Time for the police?' reminded Madeleine.

Logan nodded. He pulled his phone from one pocket and a battery from another. He flipped off the back. 'I'll make the call the moment that helicopter starts to descend,' he said.

The motorcycles were loud, but the helicopter overpowered them as it approached the villa. Together, the noise was deafening.

Two surprises followed.

The first was that the helicopter didn't pause in its flight but continued over the villa and up the valley, its distinctive sound quickly fading once it had passed overhead.

The second was that the four motorcyclists pulled into the carpark in front of the villa and stopped in the centre with their idling motors producing irregular loud popping noises. One pulled out a map and spread it over his handlebars. They talked amongst themselves, looking around at the villa and the countryside. The man with the map pointed at the hill behind the villa then folded the map and tucked it inside his jacket. He bent down and turned off his motor, the popping noises gradually ceasing as the others followed suit. The silence was like a cleansing wind.

One by one, they dismounted and removed their helmets. Someone said something which resulted in a burst of laughter. The man with the map reached again into his jacket and took out a cell phone. While the others milled about, stretching, he put it up to his ear and spoke briefly.

Nico said: 'One of them is a woman. They don't seem to be in any hurry.'

The man with the cell phone motioned for the others to group together in front of the villa and then he stepped back and raised the phone to his eyes.

'My God,' said Nico, 'Now he's taking a photo.' Frowning, he looked at Logan. 'Perhaps these are not the people we thought they were.'

'I'll talk with them,' said the Major. He spoke into his radio, letting his men and Serene know what he was about to do. 'Keep a careful watch. If anything looks out of the ordinary….' He clipped the radio onto his belt and spoke into the phone: 'Serene, do you have a clear view?'

Madeleine heard Serene's answer: 'I'm out of sight. Clear view.'

The Major slipped the phone into his pocket and walked to the door.

'Do you want some company?' asked Nico.

'No, thank you. Keep back from the windows, just in case.'

He opened the door and walked briskly down the steps and into the carpark. At the sound of his footsteps, the man holding the cell phone looked up and registered surprise, possibly at the Major's uniform. He walked forward to join his companions, waiting for the Major's approach. The group was perhaps fifty feet from the villa, so Madeleine couldn't see details, but there was nothing to indicate that these people were not just friends taking a bike ride in the country.

Major Lutyens reached the group and spoke to the man who had taken the photo. The man turned and pointed down the valley, then moved his arm to indicate their route. They conversed for a few moments. The man looked embarrassed, and the Major nodded at something the man said. The woman spoke up and pointed to the villa. Major Lutyens nodded again. He lifted his radio from his belt and spoke into it, then turned and waved to the bikers to accompany him.

'The Major seems to think they're legitimate,' said Logan. Madeleine relaxed and smiled reassuringly at Tricola.

'Funny though…' said Nico. 'That photo he took….'

The Major came through the door. 'The young lady has asked if she could use a toilet. Tricola, would you…?'

Madeleine watched the first biker enter. He politely smiled and nodded to the people in the room. That his smile lacked warmth was not unusual – nobody intended to make lasting friendships here. When the woman came through the door she was nervous but maybe she was embarrassed at needing to ask for the toilet.

'It's OK, Tricola,' said Madeleine, 'I'll show her.' She beckoned to the girl – close up she looked to be only about eighteen – and walked toward the hall leading to the bathrooms.

'Wow, this is a great place you have here,' the girl said, turning her head to look around. Madeleine heard an east-European accent, maybe Russian. 'This is better than our hotel.' Her voice was insincere, just making small-talk.

Behind Madeleine, May-Lin said: 'You want cold drink?'

Any reply to May-Lin's question was lost as Madeleine turned from the lounge and led the girl down the gently curving hallway. When the bathroom door came into sight, she stopped and indicated the sign with her hand. The girl murmured: 'Thank you' and moved past her. Madeleine hesitated, unsure whether she should stay and wait or return to the lounge.

As the girl opened the door, she looked back at Madeleine and smiled. Madeleine returned her smile then turned away. If the Major thought these people were not a threat....

She realised with a start there had been something in the girl's eyes just now. She began to turn back....

An arm circled Madeleine's throat from behind and something cold touched her neck. There was an electrical buzz and Madeleine slumped to the floor, her body involuntarily rigid with a searing pain in every muscle.

She watched in helpless horror as the girl bent over her and the buzz sounded again.

MADELEINE OPENED HER EYES. She felt disoriented and found it difficult to concentrate or even focus. What had happened? She was looking at the ceiling. The grooves in the stained-wood ceiling were all beautifully aligned – she hadn't noticed that before. She turned her head, wincing at the stiffness in her neck, and saw people. Who were these people? There was the soft feel of leather under her hand. She was lying on a couch. Had she been asleep? Her body ached with tiredness.

Words came to her.

'That's number four, Mr Bowers.' The voice was high-pitched, almost childlike. Like the girl, the accent was east-European.

'Tie him like the others.' The one called Bowers was standing behind Major Lutyens, holding a gun at his back. 'So, there were only four men, Major? If you're lying, someone will die.'

He spoke with a distinctive rounded-vowel south-English accent, but his voice had a hard edge, and his light-blue eyes were cold. *Like ice,* she thought. Another thought followed: *professional – he's done this before.* Madeleine blinked her eyes, trying to clear her head. She wondered how he knew Major Lutyen's rank.

'Four men.' That was Major Lutyens. His voice betrayed his anger and frustration but also admitted defeat.

'Good. Dopey, when you've tied him, search them all carefully. They have stuff hidden in all sorts of places.'

Dopey? Had she heard that name correctly?

The man gave Major Lutyens a push towards the wall. 'Please take a seat, Major.'

Madeleine stared at the man Bowers had addressed as 'Dopey'. He was massive – in bulk as well as height – closer to being seven feet tall than six, his obviously muscular body straining against his clothing. Madeleine did not think she had ever seen a bigger man.

He had a huge hand clamped around the arm of one of Major Lutyen's soldiers and was being unnecessarily rough with his searching, his face openly displaying a sadistic enjoyment. He gave a high-pitched giggle when the man grunted in pain.

'Oh, Dopey,' called Bowers, 'one more thing….' He tossed a two-way radio to the big man, who released the soldier to catch it. It looked like the radio Major Lutyens used.

'Disable that, will you.'

Dopey caught the radio and smiled. It was a sturdy military-standard piece of field equipment designed to survive rough handling. Dopey slapped the radio twice into his palm to test its construction, then held the radio in his two massive hands and twisted. The solid casing bent and cracked and finally separated, the radio simply coming apart in the middle. The big man gave a final tug to snap the wires that were all that remained connecting the two halves. He held his hands apart and gave a grunt of satisfaction, then dramatically opened his fingers and let the broken pieces fall to the ground. It was an impressive display of raw strength.

Bowers glanced around, making sure everyone had witnessed the radio's destruction. Dopey bent to continue his searching.

'Dax…' Bowers addressed the third man. 'Do you have all their phones?' At the man's nod, he said: 'Good. Check that one's gag.' He pointed at Logan.

'I've already…'

'I've told you, it's important. Check it *again.*'

Bowers stood with his pistol held loosely at his side. Beside him stood the girl, also armed with a pistol. She had hers pointed at Nico, but she was also covering the Major and the soldiers. Her stance was casual but her arm was steady and Madeleine could see she was attentive.

Bowers let his eyes travel around the room. He nodded, seemingly satisfied, then with his free hand he reached into a side pocket and retrieved a phone. He thumbed a button and spoke into it. His voice was soft but she caught the phrase 'come on down'. He finished the conversation and pointed at Tricola.

'Siska, tie her and the Chin girl, then take them outside and put them in the helicopter when it arrives. Keep your gun to the Chin's head. If anyone interferes, shoot her.' He paused to ensure Siska understood him, then said: 'I hope you heard that, Major.'

Major Lutyens grunted.

Siska flicked a glance at Bowers. Madeleine was surprised by the anger as well as the fear she saw in that glance.

When she understood that Maia would be taken away at gunpoint, May-Lin began an unintelligible wailing and pleading, probably unaware she wasn't speaking English.

'*You!*' Bowers shouted with surprising force. He moved his pointing finger to Jai. 'Shut her up, or *I will.*' His finger wavered between them both. 'Understand this. You even *think* of calling the police and this little one will not be coming back to you.'

Jai's eyes betrayed his feelings but outwardly he was calm. He put his arm around May-Lin and whispered in her ear then helped her to a chair. May-Lin's face was twisted into a mask of despair.

Madeleine's mind was becoming more focussed and she gasped when she recognised Logan slumped against the wall, his eyes closed. Silver tape was wound around his head, covering his mouth and jaw, leaving just his nose free. Nico sat beside him with his hands bound behind his back. Despite his predicament, he looked alert. Madeleine had seen Nico fight. She couldn't image how he could have been overpowered.

Her gaze moved past Nico. The Major was now sitting with his men lined up along the wall. With a start, Madeleine realised that Serene wasn't there.

At the sound of her gasp, Bower's head tuned towards her.

'So, the Sleeping Beauty is awake at last,' he said. 'I think Siska gave you a little too much juice.' He walked over and stood beside her. Almost to himself, he said: 'Some people are very interested in you, Madeleine Galli.'

How on earth did he know her name…? Of course… a simple explanation was that someone had given him that information while she had been unconscious. But why would he want to know her name? How long had she been unconscious?

Madeleine heard the sound before anyone else seemed to register it. Gradually, the insistent beat of the approaching helicopter filled the room.

Bowers checked the soldiers, making sure they had been immobilised.

'Tie her too,' he said, indicating Madeleine, 'and then the old Chins. Tie them both to a chair. Tie them good. I don't want them getting free for a while.'

The one called Dax walked towards Madeleine. He motioned her to sit up and put her hands behind her back. Madeleine saw no benefit in resisting so, with some difficulty, she pushed herself into a sitting position, her stiff muscles protesting the movement. There was a moment of dizziness that thankfully cleared quickly. She watched Dax take a plastic cable tie from his pocket then turned away and felt him roughly take hold of her wrists. He zipped the tie tight and the plastic bit painfully into her skin. He straightened and crossed the room to Jai and May-Lin.

Bowers pushed his pistol into his jacket and slipped his phone back into his side pocket. Madeleine was astonished to see him rub his hands together with childish glee.

'A good day's work,' he said in a gloating tone. 'No, a *great* day's work. We have some very valuable prizes here which will be seriously lucrative for us, gentlemen.' He bowed toward Siska, '…and lady.'

Siska smiled at Bowers and walked through the door, driving Tricola and Maia in front of her, their hands tied behind their backs. The smile was cold; she was angry about something, and it had to do with Bowers. As ordered, she raised her pistol and placed it against the back of Maia's head. At the last moment, Tricola threw a despairing look at Madeleine, then stepped outside.

The helicopter noise increased and quickly became deafening. This time, it was definitely landing.

'This will be a tight fit,' said Bowers. 'Dax, we'll take the weapons with us – trash the phones and radios. Get them on their feet, Dopey. Once we have everyone else in the chopper, you can come back and carry *him*.' He flicked a finger at Logan.

'Siska!' he called out the door, '…remember they're all to be blindfolded.'

STANDING BEFORE THE GAPING door to the helicopter, a tingling across her neck and shoulders made Madeleine uncomfortably aware that behind her, on the roof of the villa, Serene was probably observing the scene in the carpark through the telescopic sight of a sniper rifle. Was their assault and abduction sufficient reason for Serene to use lethal force? Was she waiting for just the right moment? Would she try to somehow disable the helicopter? Madeleine's logic said no, but the tingling persisted as her body tensed in anticipation of the explosive crash of bullets disturbing the calm afternoon air.

A blindfold was slipped over her head and she felt a bizarre relief when she was roughly bundled into the helicopter. A minute later, they rose into the air without a shot being fired.

MADELEINE FOUND IT HARD to believe she was actually chained to a stone wall.

From the time it had taken to walk to their current location she knew this was a large building. They had descended several sets of stairs rather than using an elevator and, apart from the carpet she felt briefly underfoot at the entrance, she had walked the entire journey over wood and stone. She had also *smelt* stone around her, reinforcing her idea that this was perhaps an old castle. She knew Italy had plenty of castles, many in private ownership.

They had been transported by vehicle from wherever the helicopter landed and drove for about thirty minutes over windy roads. Their blindfolds made the transfer from the aircraft awkward; Madeleine had to feel for each step. Major Lutyens and his men had been taken in a separate vehicle. At one time, Madeleine heard the clanging of railway crossing bells and, at the end of their journey, they paused while gates were opened.

Before her blindfold had been removed, handcuffs had been placed on her wrists, and the plastic tie had been cut. A chain attached her handcuffs to an iron ring set into the wall. Thankfully, the chain was long enough to let her sit comfortably.

Siska was gathering the blindfolds from the others in the room, her face expressionless. Tricola and Maia sat on the cold stone floor beside Madeleine along one of the walls. Maia was distraught, sniffling her distress, her cheeks streaked with tears. Tricola in contrast was stoically calm and she smiled at Madeleine when her blindfold was removed, then moved to comfort Maia. Tricola gave the impression this treatment was not novel for her.

On the opposite wall sat Nico and Logan, similarly chained but set further apart. Logan regained consciousness during the flight. There was a large bruise on the side of his face and the skin had split beside his left eye. He was still gagged with silver tape. A third chain hung limply between Nico and Logan.

A prison built for six, thought Madeleine wryly – *and almost full.*

Set into the wall on Madeleine's right was a solid wooden door with a narrow, barred viewing slot and large iron hinges. To her left, the fourth wall featured a single small high window which allowed only a dim light into the room even though it was mid-afternoon. If the window had also contained iron bars instead of glass, it would have completed her picture of a medieval dungeon.

Siska was the only other person in the room. She removed Logan's blindfold and bent to check his gag. Madeleine saw a querying glance from Nico, which Logan answered with an almost imperceptible shake of his head. What was that about? Was Nico asking if he should try something while Siska was turned away? He was handcuffed and chained to the wall, but he could probably reach her with his feet. Madeleine was glad Logan had replied negatively. Unless they were sure that Siska had the keys to their handcuffs, disabling her wouldn't achieve much.

Siska stood up. Madeleine thought she may not get a better chance. In a conversational tone, she said: 'Where are we, Siska? Where are the Major and his men?'

Siska did not acknowledge that Madeleine had spoken.

'You don't like Mr Bowers, do you?'

That got a reaction. Siska spun around in her crouch. 'What do you mean? What do *you* know?'

'He sent you outside first to confirm if the Major was telling the truth about the number of men he had. He sent you as a guinea pig. You knew that but you went anyway.'

Siska grunted. She stood up and moved to the door, muttering under her breath. She probably didn't intend her words to be heard, but they were audible to Madeleine.

'Bastard. Always the expendable one. What choice? Obayadai.'

The last word didn't make sense. Was it Russian? Someone's name? Then Siska repeated the word and Madeleine realised she was saying 'Obey or die' with the words rolled together like a slogan.

The girl turned with her hand on the door latch and hissed to Madeleine: 'You know *nothing*.'

Logan groaned, and his back slid down the wall until he rested on one elbow. He breathed heavily through his nose, sucking in the air. He seemed to be having difficulty breathing. Siska looked at him for a moment then turned away. She hauled the heavy door open, walked through and slammed it shut. From the outside, there was the unmistakable sound of a bolt sliding into place.

Madeleine heard Siska greet someone outside the door. She urgently made a shushing sound, asking for silence from the people in the room. Maia held her breath to silence her sobs and Logan's laboured breathing quieted.

A man replied to Siska. He talked softly but Madeleine heard him say: 'Bowers said not to speak to them.' From the voice, she knew it was the one called Dax.

Siska reacted defensively. 'She talked about Mr Bowers and I told her to be quiet.'

'Did you check the gag?'

'Yes. It's secure. Why does he have to stay gagged?'

'No idea. Because Bowers says so.'

Their footsteps moved slowly away from the door.

Siska's voice again. 'What's Bowers going to do with them, do you know?'

'What do you care?'

'I don't – as long as I get my money.'

Madeleine closed her eyes and opened her mouth – a trick her father had taught her to improve her hearing – and concentrated on the sounds.

'The African girl will be given back to the Magician,' Dax said, his voice growing softer with distance. 'And I think he'll want the one who's been gagged. The others…' Madeleine could not hear the rest of the sentence.

She opened her eyes and looked across the room at Logan.

'Can you breathe OK?' she asked anxiously. Logan nodded. His breathing did seem easier. 'Are you badly hurt?'

Logan shook his head.

'And you, Nico?'

Nico also shook his head. 'Could you hear what they were talking about?' he asked. 'I couldn't pick up anything.'

Madeleine related what she had heard.

'You heard all that? You do have a good set of ears.'

Nico turned to Logan and said: 'How do you want to play this?'

To Madeleine's surprise, Logan turned his back to Nico and his hands moved rapidly in what was obviously a sign language. He had some difficulty because of the restriction imposed by the handcuffs, but he persisted for about twenty seconds.

Nico's response didn't make sense. He said: 'There's nothing in the room or outside the door.'

Logan signed again. Another twenty second burst.

Nico didn't respond immediately, then he said: 'Are you sure?'

Logan nodded and indicated Madeleine and the girls with a tilt of his head.

'Logan asked first if there were any listening devices nearby,' Nico explained. 'Then he told me that in a few minutes, he will slow his heartbeat until he appears to lapse into a coma. We must call for help and when someone comes in, we must get them to remove the tape.'

'That was sign language,' said Madeleine.

'Yes. Very useful for occasions when we can't talk.'

Madeleine addressed Logan. 'How long can you safely stay in that state?'

She realised she had not questioned his ability to slow his heartbeat. She glanced at the girls, who were both staring wide-eyed at Logan. Maia was now more astonished than distressed.

Nico answered for Logan: 'Hours.'

Madeleine nodded. If Logan had plans beyond the removal of his gag, she didn't need to know them now. If possible, obviously, they would locate and free the Major and his men, if they were in the same building…

She stopped herself there. That was getting way too far ahead. But thinking of the Major prompted a question that had been on her mind for some time.

Despite Nico's assertion that there were no listening devices, she whispered to him: 'What about Serene?'

Logan's hands replied. Nico watched, then said: 'Our ace in the hole. She'll be waiting close to where the helicopter landed for communication from us.'

'What?' Madeleine couldn't help saying the word out loud. 'How could she possibly know where…?' She was interrupted by Logan's hands.

'He says he'll explain later.'

Logan settled himself, lying on his side on the floor and making his arms as comfortable as possible. His head was against the wall and he faced away from Nico so his hands were visible.

LOGAN LAY STILL for about thirty seconds. Then his body began to convulse, his limbs moving erratically. It really looked like he was struggling for breath. Despite her forewarning, Madeleine was alarmed. He hadn't mentioned convulsions. Had something gone wrong? It didn't require any acting to cry out: 'Help! Somebody help. We need *help*!'

Tricola surprised her by shrieking even louder: 'He can't breathe. Somethings wrong. He can't breathe! He's *suffocating*!'

There were running footsteps in the corridor. There was a pause as someone stood outside, probably looking through the viewing slot. Then the bolt was withdrawn and the door swung open but nobody entered. Madeleine could not see past the door into the corridor. She cried out again.

'He's dying! *Do* something! Hurry! He needs help.'

Dax entered the room, his pistol drawn. He spun to check behind the door, then covered and checked each person in turn before looking at Logan. Siska followed behind him, her gun also in her hand.

'He can't breathe through that mask,' said Tricola urgently. 'He's not getting any air!'

Logan stopped convulsing and lay still. Dax hesitated. He took a step towards Logan and stood over him.

'Get that tape off him, or he'll die!' Madeleine shouted.

Siska said: 'He was having some trouble breathing before, I think.'

Dax shoved the pistol into his belt.

'Keep them covered,' he said to Siska. 'And don't watch me, watch *them*.'

Tricola said again: 'He can't breathe. He needs to breathe.'

Dax bent to feel for a pulse on Logan's neck. After a few seconds, he said: 'There's no pulse. He's dead.'

'It's only been a few seconds,' said Nico. 'I can revive him with CPR. Unlock my handcuffs.'

'You can't let him die,' implored Madeleine. 'There's still time. You *can* save him.'

Dax leaned back, concerned and frustrated but still cautious.

'Put your gun against that one's head,' he said to Siska, pointing at Nico. 'We don't need him. If he tries anything, shoot him.'

'Are you *sure* about this?' asked Siska. She moved up to Nico and raised her pistol.

'Bowers said this one's important,' said Dax, but his face displayed his indecision.

'*Hurry!*' Madeleine cried.

Dax swore loudly, reaching out with his hands. He checked that Siska was ready. 'You *watch* them all, y'hear! I don't want any surprises.'

He started to pull off the tape that was covering Logan's mouth.

Logan's face was turned away from Siska and Nico, but Madeleine saw his lips move as soon as the corner of his mouth was uncovered, whispering to Dax. Dax didn't pause, unwinding the tape as if nothing unusual was happening. Logan continued to talk to Dax while his jaw was freed, then he took two huge convulsive breaths and began to cough violently. He raised himself onto his elbow as the coughing seemed to take him over. His hands moved involuntarily, in time with the coughs. Nico's face wore a concerned look, but his eyes were following the hands.

'Thank you,' Madeleine said to Dax and was surprised when he smiled and nodded at her. He stood up.

'We're here now,' he said, addressing Siska, 'so we may as well move them early.'

'*Move* them?' Siska asked, puzzled. 'Move them where?'

'For now, into the corridor.'

'But we don't have any plastic ties… What's going on?'

Dax said, as if instructing a small child: 'We have guns, don't we? That's enough, isn't it? *We* have guns, and *they* don't.'

He reached into his pocket and pulled out a ring of keys, handing them to Siska and pointing at Nico. 'Free him first and get him on his feet. I'll cover you.'

'I wasn't told they would be moved so soon.' Siska's voice was petulant.

'You don't get told everything. I'm in charge while Bowers is away.'

Madeleine saw Logan and Nico share a glance at that news.

'I know, but are you sure about freeing them? Shall I call Dopey?'

'We don't need that big ape for this. Just do as you're told.' He raised his gun towards Nico.

Siska sighed. She tucked the gun into her belt and pulled on Nico's hands to reach his handcuffs. There was a click of a lock and Nico brought his hands from behind his back and massaged his wrists. His hands blurred into motion and his fingers stabbed into Siska's neck, one on each side. Siska's knees buckled. Nico caught her and lowered her unconscious body to the floor.

Madeleine's gaze snapped to Dax. His behaviour was odd. He still had his gun pointed at Nico but he seemed unconcerned about what had just happened. He watched calmly as Nico collected Siska's gun then picked up the keys and unlocked Logan's handcuffs. Dax noticed his outstretched arm and looked at the gun as if something strange and unexpected was in his hand. Logan reached out and gently took the gun from him, checked that the safety was on and slipped it into his belt in the small of his back. He patted Dax on the shoulder and said something in his ear.

'Thank you,' Dax said. He smiled.

Logan took the keys from Nico and walked over to Madeleine. He unlocked her handcuffs.

'*Damn you*,' Madeleine said, hitting him on the shoulder as soon as her hands were free. 'I thought you were dead!'

'It had to be convincing,' Logan said quietly. 'Now smile and join in. The scene is not yet over.' More loudly, he said: 'And Dax is playing his part very well, don't you think?'

'What?' she exclaimed. Logan squeezed her arm, softly but insistently. 'Oh, yes,' she said. Was that what Logan wanted her to say? 'Yes, of course — quite brilliant.'

Dax bowed. Despite the circumstances, Madeleine had to stifle a giggle. What was going on?

Logan moved to free the girls. They were both wide-eyed, alternately looking at each person in the room. Like Madeleine, they were struggling to understand what had happened – what *was* happening.

Madeleine stood up, crossing the room to kneel beside Siska. 'Will she be OK?'

Nico answered. 'She'll be asleep for a while, but she'll be fine. It's all part of the play.'

'All part of the…?'

'The *play*.' Nico put particular emphasis on the word.

'Oh, the *play*.' Madeleine finally understood. This whole charade had been planned by Logan and Nico, with Dax as a star player. With sudden insight, she saw that Logan's previous episode of laboured breathing while Siska was in the room had also been part of the setup.

'On to the next scene,' said Logan. Dax glanced at Siska and Logan said quickly: 'She won't be required for this scene. She can rest here.' He took Dax by the arm and led him out of the room, beckoning everyone to follow him.

Madeleine checked the girls and saw the relief on their faces. They smiled back at her, Maia hopeful but wary and Tricola trusting and confident. Madeleine hoped her trust would turn out to be justified. She gathered them to walk in front of her.

'Dax, where would Dopey be right now?' Logan asked.

'In the kitchen, of course.'

'Of course,' echoed Logan. 'And, apart from us and Dopey, how many other people are here?'

'Two.'

'Is anyone stationed at the main door?'

'Christus is there. Marcus is at the rear.'

'Good. Do they speak English?'

'Yes. Mr Bowers insists on it.'

'I understand. And Major Lutyens, where would he be.'

'Lutyens…?'

'The soldiers. Which room are they in?'

'They're not here. They were taken to the asylum.'

'Remind me where the asylum is.' Logan's tone was conversational.

'In the village of Cortese, by the church.' Dax spoke as if Logan should know this information.

'Right. How far would you say that was from here?'

'Twenty kilometres.'

'Thank you. That was very good.'

Dax was so pleased he almost clapped his hands.

'OK, please lead the way to the main entrance,' said Logan. 'Nico, you take the rear.'

DAX LED, BUT LOGAN stopped him whenever they came to a corner and peered around before allowing him to proceed. They walked along corridors, past many rooms with closed doors, and up several stairs without meeting anyone. The aged rough stone walls confirmed the building to be an old castle, but the flooring and lighting indicated considerable modernisation. Madeleine wondered at the age of the original construction and would have loved to explore, but she forcefully brought her thoughts back to the present.

Logan stopped before an open doorway which Dax confirmed led to the castle's entrance hall. Logan took a quick look into the hall.

'There's a man standing by the main door; that would be Christus?' he asked. Dax nodded. 'Can you call him over for a chat, please?'

Dax walked through the doorway and called out. Logan said quietly: 'Hopefully, even if he was here earlier, he won't recognise me without my blindfold, but, just in case, Nico…'

Nico moved up to the door, Siska's gun in his hand. 'Keep the left side of your face turned away,' he said. 'Hide those bruises if you can.' Logan grunted acknowledgement. He touched one of his bracelets and stepped into the hall.

Madeleine heard Logan speaking to the man, saying his name several times. The words he said were a mixture of English words and others she didn't know. Put together, they seemed nonsensical. The man's footsteps moved away.

'Let's go,' said Logan's voice.

Madeleine entered with the girls. The hall was vast. An arched stone roof towered over her head, forming a buttressed dome and other arches to the left and right led to two more corridors. She reluctantly dropped her gaze. She would have liked to examine the stonework more closely but this wasn't the time.

The man Logan had been speaking to reached for the main door and opened it before turning about and standing stiffly alongside the opening, resuming his post. He seemed not to notice them, staring straight ahead. She looked questioningly at Logan, who held out a hand inviting her to walk through the door and out of the castle.

'I simply convinced him that nobody came this way. He will believe that until the day he dies.'

'Unless someone regresses him, like you did to Sami.' She instantly regretted her words. They sounded ungrateful.

'Sorry,' she said, 'I didn't mean….'

Logan looked at her. 'That's a possibility,' he admitted, 'but his state is sufficient for the moment.'

He turned to Dax. 'Is anyone likely to be outside at this time of day? A groundsman? Someone patrolling outside?'

Dax shook his head.

Nico leaned in and whispered in Logan's ear.

'Ah yes, of course,' said Logan. 'We'll need a suitable vehicle. Do you have a car?'

Dax pulled a set of keys from his pocket and described a car parked around the corner of the exterior wall.

'Thank you, Dax. And the last thing I require is your phone.'

Madeleine frowned. Why would Logan want Dax's phone? *Of course… to contact Serene.* She reminded herself to find out how Serene could be nearby as Logan expected.

Dax obligingly dug into his pocket again and handed over his phone.

'Anything else we should know?' said Logan.

Dax gave the question serious thought, then answered: 'No.'

'Then here we must say goodbye to you. You've done well.'

Dax's face beamed. *He really overreacts to praise*, thought Madeleine, then realised it was probably part of Logan's… she hesitated a second over the word… Logan's *spell.*

Logan continued to talk to Dax whose face became calm then blank. Logan handed him back the gun he had taken earlier, which Dax solemnly accepted. He pushed it into his belt, silently turned, and left the room.

'Why did you give him his gun?' whispered Madeleine.

'Just to confuse the situation. How could we have forced him to help us escape when he still has his gun?'

'He won't remember, will he?'

'No. Only Siska will remember what happened but she'll have some difficulty convincing Dax – even when he can't find his car keys and phone.'

'A pity,' said Madeleine. 'I suspect her involvement in this is not entirely her own choice.'

Logan threw her a querying glance but said nothing.

CHAPTER TEN

Escape to a refuge for the night…

Saturday 5:45 pm

Madeleine emerged into the bright, clear sunlight of late afternoon. A glance over her shoulder confirmed that the castle was a substantial structure, probably fifteenth or sixteenth century from the architecture. She saw circular towers and solid battlements thirty feet high with three large multi-storeyed square buildings in the centre. The castle stood on the peak of a hill with a more extensive range looming behind, and commanded an unobstructed view of the countryside in all directions. In front, a narrow road curved down a gently sloping grassy incline and disappeared into a forested valley.

Fifty yards away was a bizarre sight. The road passed through a purely decorative ornamental gate that stood alone, straddling the road but allowing free passage on either side to anyone willing to step a few paces off the road.

Logan handed the keys to Nico who disappeared around the curve of the wall to retrieve the car. Despite Dax's assurance that no other people would be encountered, Madeleine felt apprehensive and exposed while they stood and waited for Nico in front of the castle walls. She felt sure they would be discovered at any moment.

A hand touched her shoulder and she jumped involuntarily.

'Sorry, I didn't mean to…' said Logan. She smiled, embarrassed.

'Do you regret accepting my invitation to dinner?' The casual question calmed her, which was probably Logan's intention.

She thought about it.

'Not at all,' she replied. 'It's been quite an experience. I wouldn't have missed it for the world.'

'Good.' He nodded, his hand moving down her arm – almost a caress, but probably just a contact to help her confidence.

There was the rattle of an engine starting from around the corner.

'Ah,' said Logan, striking a theatrical pose. 'Our chariot approaches.'

If Dax was well paid for his efforts, it certainly wasn't evident in his choice of car but Logan didn't seem fazed with the compact, well-worn, faded-paint sedan that pulled up.

'All aboard,' he said. 'And Nico, I don't think we'll bother opening the gate.'

Since leaving Marco Polo airport and the luxury of Sir Brian's plane, each vehicle they had occupied had been constricted and uncomfortable – Dax's car was no exception.

Madeleine squirmed into the middle of a back seat that was clearly built for two, with Tricola on one side and Maia on the other. For the first time in many hours, Madeleine was pleased to see the girls were in a good mood despite their discomfort, and she got a smile from both when she warned: 'No comments about the size of my hips, please.'

Madeleine smiled back at them, but when she glanced at Logan, he was staring at Dax's phone with a worried frown.

The car lurched into motion. It was immediately apparent that the vehicle had such poor or possibly broken suspension that, in the back seat, they felt every bump and undulation of the road as if they were riding on the rims of the wheels.

Nico deliberately drove off the road onto the grass and steered around the strange gates, which brought more smiles and a cheer from Maia. Madeleine looked back through the rear window as a final check that no one was following and saw the tracks their wheels had left in the grass. She also saw, carved into the stonework above the gates, the words *OCCHIO DI RA*. *Occhio*, she knew, was Italian for Eye but she didn't know what the Italian word *Ra* meant. Short words were usually common words in most languages, so it was strange she hadn't heard of that word. She felt a jolt as the car re-joined the road.

Their off-road escapade had not lightened Logan's worried look. He gave a frustrated grunt.

'What is it? Is the battery low?' asked Madeleine.

Logan looked at her apologetically. 'Worse than that. First, I foolishly forgot to ask Dax for his sign-in code. Second, I don't know Serene's number, so I can't contact her anyway. I thought I could do something using GPS, but if I can't even get into the phone….'

Tricola leaned forward. 'The battery could be a problem but probably not,' she said. 'Or his remaining data allowance may be low, but I can work around that. Getting her number and location is definitely not a problem at all. Can I have the phone?'

Her voice was confident and in complete contrast to the almost catatonic, lisping little girl that Madeleine had first met.

Madeleine watched as Tricola inspected the phone, turning it over in her hands. The screen lit up, and she rapidly pushed the buttons on the side and top of the phone in a particular sequence.

Noticing Madeleine's interest, she explained: 'First, I'll revert it back to factory settings, then make it recognise my fingerprint… we have plenty of data, that's good… then get Serene's number…' She raised her voice to ask Logan: 'What's her surname?' While she talked, her thumbs danced rapidly and fluidly across the phone's face, unimpeded by the swaying and bumping of the car.

'Forbes-Madsen,' replied Logan, also watching Tricola. He spelt the name, including the hyphen.

'Okay. Unusual. That makes it easy.' Tricola continued talking while her thumbs typed and her fingers swiped the screen, moving, it seemed to Madeleine, at somewhere near the speed of thought.

'So, the obvious first, I think… OK, her number's not there… It'll be in the Vault, though… Yes, here it is – Forbes-Madsen…' Tricola gave a grunt of satisfaction. 'Now, I'll download a GPS tracker… Installing… OK…' She brought the phone to her mouth. 'Dial Serene…'

She handed the phone back to Logan, 'Her phone is ringing. Her location will appear on this map when she answers.' She pointed at the bottom of the screen. 'This red dot shows where we are.'

Madeleine realised her mouth was agape. The whole process had taken Tricola less than a minute. She had the disquieting thought that the reason this young girl had been taken to the bank had something to do with the expertise she had just witnessed.

'After you've talked to her, you should destroy the phone.' Tricola sat back and regarded the faces staring at her. She smiled and shrugged her shoulders.

From Dax's phone, Madeleine heard a soft: 'Hello? Who is this?'

'Charles,' replied Logan. 'We're about twenty minutes away from you. I hope you haven't been waiting long. Two things I need your immediate help with…' Logan related the information Dax had provided regarding the location of Major Lutyens and his men. 'I presume you have men you can send…? Good. Secondly, have you been able to arrange transport suitable for six?' Serene replied, and Logan said: 'Excellent.'

He listened, then said: 'Yes, Maia's with us. We're all well. No injuries.'

Logan tapped the phone to finish the call.

'Thank you, Tricola, you certainly saved the day there.'

Tricola looked embarrassed. 'But I didn't do anything, really….'

Madeleine added her thanks by way of a pat on Tricola's knee. She wondered why Logan had specifically mentioned Maia, but she also wanted to ask a question she had been thinking about for some time.

'How did you know Serene would be nearby? We flew for about an hour. How could she know where we went?'

'Every aircraft flying in Italian airspace must have its transponder switched on at all times, broadcasting its position. Bowers could, of course, have switched the transponder off, but that would breach regulations and risk unwelcome attention. I knew Serene would have made note of the registration letters of the helicopter and it would be an easy task for her or Sir Brian to track it. Bowers had no reason to believe there was anyone left on the ground who could do that.'

'Not quite true,' said Tricola. 'Several apps can do it. Today, anyone can track aircraft in real-time on their phone. You can see all the aircraft flying in the air above you if you want to.'

Logan laughed. 'I didn't know that,' he said. 'And, luckily for us, neither did Bowers.'

He wound down his window then prised the back from Dax's phone and tossed it from the car. The battery followed. He then crashed the phone against the dashboard with such force that it shattered, throwing what was left in his hand out the window.

Madeleine's eyes widened. That had been a surprisingly powerful blow. She wondered if he had somehow enhanced his strength using his power.

'Your performance back in the dungeon was impressive,' she said to Logan. 'I've heard of people slowing their heartbeat but never seen it. Can you also enhance your strength?'

Logan turned in his seat to look at her. 'To a certain extent, yes, but only for a very short time,' he said. 'It can take its toll on my muscles and joints.'

'What else can you control?' She thought of the Hypnotists she had seen. 'Pain?'

He smiled. 'Yes, but I've learned that pain control should also be used sparingly. Pain is an important message.'

Bells and red flashing lights announced the imminent arrival of a train at a railway crossing ahead. Madeleine was pleased and relieved when they pulled to a halt, both for the temporary respite from the jostling ride and because she remembered hearing the bells of a rail crossing on the inward journey.

THE PASSING TRAIN prevented conversation, even with the window rewound, but after Dax's car had bumped across the railway tracks, Madeleine first tried to adjust her body into a more comfortable position which she only partially managed, then, in the lull that followed the noise of the train, she took the opportunity to ask what had happened while she'd been unconscious and how Bowers' team had managed to capture everybody.

'I blame *you*,' said Logan, looking back at her with a straight face.

Madeleine was dumbfounded. How could she possibly be to blame?

'Me?' she said, incredulous. 'I wasn't even *there*.' Something was wrong. There was a mismatch between his eyes and his words.

'Exactly. I blame you *because* you weren't there.'

She frowned and studied him. His words were shallow. He believed them, but there was another message underneath. She realised it was some sort of joke. She wagged her finger at him. His face softened and he winked.

'If you *had* been there, instead of electing to wander off with Siska, you may have been able to warn us of what was about to happen. You could have warned *me* I was about to be knocked unconscious.'

'Oh…' said Madeleine. She screwed her nose at him. 'I see. So, what *did* happen?'

'For that,' said Logan, 'you'll need to ask Nico because, for most of the time, I was in the same out-of-action state as you.'

Nico flicked a glance over his shoulder at Madeleine before returning his eyes to the road. 'Well…' he said, 'I guess I could start with the girl following you to the hallway….'

NICO WATCHED MADELEINE lead the way across the lounge. The girl following her seemed the odd one out in the group of visitors. She was much younger than any of the men and she didn't seem attached to anyone. Why was she with them? He smiled wryly. Was he really trying to make relationship judgements? Madeleine would be the one to have an opinion on that. He would try to remember to ask her after they'd gone.

He was still thinking about the photo the man had taken. The position of the sun would have placed the faces of his subjects in shadow – a basic error, which made Nico wonder if the photo was a photo of the villa instead. But why would anyone want to photograph the villa while pretending to photograph his friends?

He had checked the three men as they entered the room. The photographer had entered first. He strode confidently to the centre of the room, his eyes deliberately flicking to each person, pausing, and finally scanning the room. Nico felt a tingle at the back of his neck, a warning he had learned to heed, a sign that something wasn't right. Had this man just professionally assessed the room and the people in it?

May-Lin asked: 'You want cold drink?'

'Thank you, but no, we have plenty of water.' The man's voice was friendly and he spread out his hands apologetically. 'We appreciate your hospitality,' he said with a smile. 'We've been riding for three hours without a break. We wanted to see how far up this valley we could get, but...' he shrugged. 'Nature calls, and I'm sure your facilities are better than anything the mountains have to offer.' He laughed at his joke.

Nico relaxed. The man sounded genuine. He checked the other two men.

One man immediately stood out. He was huge. He had to duck his head to enter the door, so he was several centimetres taller than the two-metre frame, with enormous shoulders and massively muscled arms and legs. Nico assessed the man as he would a competitive opponent. He was an impressive physical specimen, but those bulging, overdeveloped muscles would actually impede the man's movement. Very strong but slow and awkward. He would tire quickly.

The big man came to a halt beside the photographer, standing close to him as if waiting to be told what to do. His face was friendly but his smile was forced. Again, a slight tingle on Nico's neck. By itself, the artificial smile was nothing – some people simply acted that way in new social situations. But, added to his other tingle…? Nico had been resting his weight on one of the wide windowsills. He slowly straightened, stretching the muscles in his hands.

The final man through the door had also entered confidently. He walked casually around the room, looking at the walls and the ceiling as if admiring the architecture.

'Very nice,' he said, his tone casual, interested. 'Very nice indeed. This style was common for ski lodges in the nineties. Would that be when this was built?'

He addressed his question to Logan, who thought for a moment, then said: 'Yes, I think it's about twenty years old. My mother…'

A gun appeared in the man's hand and the butt slammed against Logan's head with a dull thud. Logan collapsed to the floor. As he fell, the man moved to stand over him, placing the barrel of the gun against Logan's temple. There was a stifled cry from May-Lin.

Nico narrowed his eyes and resisted the urge to move until he could determine the measure of the man holding the gun. He looked competent and relaxed. Nico tensed to launch himself at the gunman the instant he moved the gun away from Logan's head or if his concentration faltered for a split second.

'Nobody move!' ordered the photographer, as if reading Nico's mind, drawing a gun from his jacket and covering Nico and the Major. 'Or he *dies!*'

He waited to be sure his command had been heeded.

'Dopey, search them for weapons.'

The huge man lumbered forward. He didn't seem to mind the derogatory name.

The focus of the man holding the gun against Logan's head remained steady, his eyes flicking between Nico and the Major. Nico glanced at Major Lutyens. Was he going to try anything? The Major looked at him and sighed, giving a small shake of his head. Nico slowly turned his gaze to look at Jai. Did Jai carry a weapon? Nico hadn't seen one. Jai was behind the leader and out of his direct sight but he was ten metres away. His eyebrows raised into a question and he rested his hands on the counter. Both hands slowly closed into fists. He would need to vault the counter and cross ten metres of open floor to get to the leader. In that time, could Nico stop the other man from pulling the trigger and sending a bullet into Logan's brain? Possibly. The man's attention would be drawn to Jai's charge, and that may be all the distraction Nico needed. But what could Jai do? He certainly looked willing, but his capabilities were unknown.

Nico returned his gaze to the gunman threatening Logan. The longer he waited to do something, the less the chances of success. Right now, he assessed the chances as no more than fifty-fifty. He drew in a breath and shook his head. That wasn't good enough. Jai's fists uncurled.

Nico relaxed as the huge man checked him for weapons, slapping his sides and legs harder than was necessary. Then, holding Nico's arm in a deliberately powerful vice-like grip intended to leave bruising and grinning at the grunt he elicited, he spun Nico around to check his back. Nico made a mental note: *if ever he got a chance…*

Nico was dragged over to where Logan was lying. The man with the gun to Logan's head hadn't moved, and his gun still rested against Logan's temple.

'Sit down here,' the big man said in a small, childlike voice, indicating a place three metres from where Logan was lying. Nico knew he could move fast, but once he was seated, it would be difficult to attack the man threatening Logan at this distance. He checked the man again. His eyes were watching Nico, aware that if Nico was going to try something, it would be just before he was seated. The risk was still too high.

Dopey placed a hand on Nico's shoulder. Anticipating a forceful shove to the ground, Nico let his legs fold so that he dropped instantly into a sitting position. The huge man had already begun to push on Nico's shoulder when it simply wasn't there anymore, causing him to overbalance and forcing him to take a stumbling step to awkwardly try to regain that balance. He growled angrily but with his tiny voice it sounded like a whimper.

He glared down at Nico who prepared himself for a retaliatory kick or hand strike, but instead there was a grunt from the leader. Dopey's eyes flicked up in response and the leader impatiently nodded at Nico.

'Tie him first, and then the soldier.'

Dopey blew out some air in frustration – a sound that reminded Nico of a horse's whinny. The man bent down and dragged Nico's arms behind him. Nico could see no gain from resisting, so he allowed a plastic tie to be slipped over his wrists. He tensed his wrists as the plastic bit into the skin, accepting the pain, and waited until Dopey was satisfied and stood up. Only then did Nico relax his wrists. The plastic was still tight, but it was not the circulation-stopping tightness that the giant had intended.

Nico checked that Logan, although unconscious, was breathing comfortably. He watched as Dopey stepped over to Major Lutyens and pushed him forcefully to the floor, this time making sure the Major felt his strength. He turned the Major face down and roughly pulled his arms behind him, wrapping a plastic tie around his wrists. The Major grunted in pain and Dopey laughed. Dopey hauled him upright by his collar and bent to take the radio and a knife that were attached to the Major's belt, then patted his pockets. He looked again at the leader who held out his hand for the radio just as the girl appeared out of the hallway.

She called: 'Someone will need to carry the woman.'

Dopey seemed to assume that anything to carry would be his job, and he shuffled in the direction of the hall without being asked. He tossed the Major's knife onto a chair.

The leader waited until the girl joined him. He reached inside his jacket and handed her another pistol, directing her attention to Nico. Then he

135

stepped up to Major Lutyens. In a smooth movement, he grabbed the Major by his jacket and dragged him to his feet, turning him around. He stood behind the Major, his gun pushed into his back.

'Now, Major… I presume from the crown on your shoulder, that's your rank?' Major Lutyens just grunted.

'I was very interested,' continued the man casually, 'to see a military presence here. Very interested indeed. Let's discuss your men, who are no doubt scattered about the countryside and perhaps even inside the building. What is this room called?'

Major Lutyens hesitated, not expecting the question.

'Ah… Here? The lounge, I suppose.'

'Good. Listen to me. Be very careful. Call your men in with these words: *Everybody stand down and report to the lounge.* Those words only, Major. Don't try to insert any extra code words. You will stand in front of me, right here. Don't turn around. As each man arrives, you will direct them to lay their weapons on that chair and sit along the wall. Is that clear?'

Major Lutyens nodded and the leader snapped at him: 'Out loud, Major, if you will, so there are no misunderstandings.'

'I understand.'

'Good. If anything goes astray, I'll put a hole in your back and my loyal comrade will kill your friend. I hope you understand that as well.'

He flicked a switch on the radio and held it beside Major Lutyen's mouth. The Major repeated the order as requested.

Dopey appeared, carrying the limp form of Madeleine. Nico was relieved to see she was breathing. The leader noticed his concern, smiled, and said: 'Stunned only. She'll recover.'

She was carried to a sofa and deposited with surprising gentleness. *Perhaps Dopey reserves his brutality for men only,* Nico thought. *Or maybe for people who are able to feel pain.*

One of the Major's soldiers came through the main door. He was relaxed but he tensed as soon as he comprehended the scene in the lounge. His rifle started to rise.

'Stand down, Curtis,' said the Major sharply. 'They have the advantage. Surrender your rifle.'

'Very good, Major,' said the leader as if congratulating a child. 'And quite correct. We do have the advantage. Sit him down, Dopey, against the wall. Tie his hands, then check him over. Drop his rifle and radio over there.'

As soon as the soldier was seated, the leader pulled a roll of tape from his jacket pocket. He pointed at Logan and said: 'Dax, gag that one and gag him well. I want tape around his head from below his nose to his jaw, so he can't possibly speak.'

Two more soldiers arrived and were directed to join the soldier against the wall.

'When the fourth of Major Lutyen's men came into the room, that's about the time, I think, that you woke up,' said Nico.

NICO SLOWED THE CAR as they approached the intersection indicated on the map as the location of Serene's phone.

The village street, in the stillness of early evening, was quiet; an elderly couple conversing on a doorstep; a baker closing the shutters on his shop window; a teenager cycling past in the opposite direction, her pony-tail waving; a small brown dog investigating something interesting in the gutter.

A large modern black all-terrain vehicle looked out of place among the older cars on the street. It sat menacingly on one corner of the intersection. Madeleine focussed apprehensively on the car and reached forward to alert Nico and Logan, but they were already looking in its direction. The doors of the vehicle opened and Madeleine tensed but then relaxed when Serene and Jai stepped out. Maia threw open the door and leapt from Dax's car the instant it stopped and ran past Serene into her father's arms. He held her tightly, his relief evident.

Serene was watching the two when Logan walked up to her. She was dressed again in the outfit she had worn when flying – a light leather jacket, jeans and boots. In this small village scene, Madeleine thought she just needed to turn her collar up to look like a secret agent from a TV series.

'Jai insisted on coming with me,' Serene said casually. 'He was quiet the whole journey and very focused. I would not like to be any of Maia's abductors if he caught up with them.'

Logan nodded. He glanced at the vehicle. She followed his glance and said: 'It's rented. Not in my name. Less conspicuous than the Hum-vee, I thought.'

'Only slightly,' said Logan with a grin.

'I was looking for something with comfort and versatility that would seat six,' replied Serene. 'I do remember a car you hired in Las Vegas that proved entirely unsuitable for the task.' Her return smile was wicked.

'On that occasion, I didn't expect to be driving in the desert, but I take your point.'

'Sir Brian also offered some more men, but, again, I thought it best not to be the talking point of everyone who noticed us.'

Serene turned to face him. 'My dear Charles…' she said, as if the previous conversation had not occurred and they had just met, '…so nice to see you again.' She looked closely at his face. 'Oh, I see you're wearing some reminders of your experience. I thought you told me 'no injuries'.'

He smiled as she embraced him and kissed his cheeks, being particularly tender with his left side.

'It's nothing,' said Logan. 'Good to see you too. Thanks for following up. Any news about Major Lutyens and his men?'

'They should be being gathered as we speak.'

'Good.' He looked around, checking that everyone could hear him. 'Now, we shouldn't waste time; we should keep moving. Where's the airport from here?'

'It's north, but we won't be going there.'

Logan raised an eyebrow.

'It's just a grass strip and there aren't any suitable aircraft available, not even for hire. If you want to return to Venice, I suggest we could return by car or train – there's a station nearby. But, if you want to return to the lodge…?' Serene left the question open.

'When our escape is discovered, the lodge will probably be under surveillance,' said Logan. 'A difficult task with all the open ground around, but not impossible.'

He motioned Jai and Maia closer.

'Jai, I think you and Maia should take Dax's car and head back to the lodge. Leave the car some distance away where it's well hidden.' Jai nodded. 'Even if the lodge is being watched,' Logan continued, 'they shouldn't bother you if Tricola's not there. However, it would be best, Maia, if you keep out of sight for a while.'

'Nobody will take her again,' said Jai. It was the first time Madeleine had heard him speak. His voice was surprisingly soft in tone, but his words had the hardness of steel.

Nico handed Jai the keys to Dax's car and they watched Jai and Maia walk towards it, Jai's arm protectively around his daughter's shoulders.

'We'll drive south and find a place to stay for the night,' Logan said. 'I'm keen to talk to Tricola as soon as possible. We've been working too much in the dark. We need to know more about what we're up against.'

Madeleine caught Tricola's eye and gave her a reassuring smile.

As they headed for Serene's vehicle, Serene stepped over to walk beside Madeleine. 'By the way,' she said. 'I thought you might need your bag, so I retrieved it from your room at the lodge. It's in the back seat.'

'Oh, *thank* you,' said Madeleine with feeling, amazed and thankful that Serene had taken the time to retrieve her bag with everything else she had to consider. Having her phone inactive was bad enough, but she shuddered to think how she would have existed without her credit card and the other essentials in her bag.

Putting on an atrocious New York accent, Serene said: 'Us goils gotta stick togethuh.'

Madeleine couldn't help it. In spite of their tense situation, Serene's humour was infectious. She laughed out loud, forming a new appreciation of the capabilities of this woman. It seemed Sir Brian chose his people carefully.

'First thing…' said Logan, '…we need to find a store where I can buy some new phones.'

'You'll need a burner app,' said Tricola, 'if you want the phones and the phone calls to be anonymous and untraceable.'

'Did you say a *burner app*? What's that?'

'It routes calls or texts through a new number each time.'

'I think we'll let *you* buy the phones,' said Logan.

THE APPROPRIATELY NAMED *Albergo Crocevia* – Hotel Crossroads – was set on a country intersection surrounded by beautiful shaded grassy woodlands. It shared the crossroads with a small café on the opposite corner that was closed and deserted for the night. Drawn to the neon lights of the hotel sign and also attracted by its relative isolation, Serene parked in the empty carpark, and Logan knocked on the door marked *Ricezione* – Reception. Seemingly in response to his knock, the hotel lights and the neon sign abruptly turned off, leaving them blinking in the sudden darkness until their eyes adjusted and the light of the moon peering through wispy clouds provided enough light to at least see each other. Serene uttered a grunt of annoyance, but Logan remarked that it could not be better, as anyone following them may not now recognise the building as a hotel.

Thankfully, his persistent knocking resulted in an overhead light being switched on, and a buxom middle-aged woman answered the door, introducing herself as *Signora* Palpete. She accepted them inside but made sure they were aware that it was now past closing time for her and she was therefore entitled to add a small premium to the tariff. It seemed that *Signora* Palpete was, at that moment, the sole occupant of her hotel.

Logan paid for five rooms and also negotiated the use of a small common lounge.

Once they had viewed their rooms and taken a short time to freshen up, they gathered in the lounge where a small platter of bread and cheese provided by *Signora* Palpete sat on a low side table. The cheese proved tasty but was soon devoured, leaving everyone still hungry. They had not eaten since lunchtime and then only sparingly, so there was no opposition when Nico suggested he should get some more substantial food. *Signora* Palpete was not in the least offended by Nico's suggestion – her reactions told Madeleine she was in fact relieved that she would not be obliged to feed five hungry guests herself.

She had heard them speaking English, so the *Signora* spoke in English to Nico. Her English was good but she spoke slowly, using extravagant hand gestures. She suggested he would be able to get everything he needed at a village restaurant owned by her cousin. She would telephone him.

Logan leaned close to Madeleine's ear and whispered: 'Nico's Italian is, in fact, excellent.'

'It is fifteen kilometres away, but the food is worth every step, *Signore*,' *Signora* Palpete continued and gave Nico precise directions.

She then spread her arms to include the others. 'But your room price does include breakfast,' she said, nodding to solicit their approval.

Nico held out his hand to Serene for the car keys. 'I'll be back as soon as I can,' he said.

LOGAN PLACED TRICOLA in a comfortable chair in the centre of the lounge and drew another up to face her.

'Can you two please wait over there for now,' Logan said to Madeleine and Serene, indicating two chairs just inside the door. 'We don't want any distractions, especially at the beginning. I'll call you over later.'

He escorted them toward the door and, quietly enough so that Tricola couldn't hear, he asked: 'Do either of you have a nail kit that includes a sharp knife or scissors?'

Serene nodded and produced a thin clear plastic container from an inside jacket pocket, snapped it open and took out a small pair of gold scissors.

'Thank you,' said Logan. 'That's perfect.'

He walked back to where Tricola was seated, pulled his chair a little closer and sat down. He leaned forward and asked if she was comfortable. She gave an apprehensive nod.

He said: 'I don't want to rush this, so we'll take our time. Just relax and listen to my voice. I assure you I'll be able to detect areas where suggestions have been inserted, and I'll try to remove them, especially the ones that cause you pain. I'll be careful.' He waited until she indicated she understood. 'Now, I'm going to be saying some words that will appear to be random, but I need to determine your reaction to them. I'll only be talking to you, so just listen to my voice. Close your eyes if you like. You shouldn't feel any discomfort but, if for any reason you want me to stop, just hold up your hand.'

Tricola didn't reply. Logan waited. Twenty seconds passed. Tricola nodded in response to something Madeleine hadn't heard. Logan then repeated: 'I'm only talking to you. If, for any reason, you want me to stop, just hold up your hand. Nod, if you understand?'

After a short interval, Tricola slowly nodded. Her face was relaxed. Her eyes were open, but they were unfocused, staring into space. *It's already begun*, thought Madeleine. She hadn't heard any of the strange words Logan had previously used. He must have spoken very quietly during that pause.

Logan leaned even closer. Madeleine concentrated and could hear him talking softly. After a while, he touched Tricola's hand, then rested a finger on the leather band around her wrist. Tricola watched him calmly. He spoke again, more of his fingers now touching the band. She nodded her head as if replying to something he had said. He was quiet for a few seconds, assessing her, and then, in a smooth movement, Serene's scissors appeared in his hand and he cut the string holding the small coloured piece of cardboard to the band around Tricola's wrist.

The cardboard triangle fluttered to the ground and Tricola gasped audibly, watching it fall, her eyes wide in alarm. Logan held her by the wrist and continued whispering to her. Tricola's other hand had started to rise. It stopped and hovered, then slowly lowered back down to her knee. Still talking, Logan slowly eased the plaited leather band over her hand. Watching her closely, he held it poised over her fingers for a moment, ready to replace it, but when she didn't react, he detached it completely from her hand and let it fall to the floor behind him, out of her sight. Tricola again drew a long breath but this time it was in relief rather than alarm.

She closed her eyes and let her head tilt back.

FIFTEEN MINUTES LATER, Logan rose from his chair and walked over to where Madeleine and Serene were sitting.

'I've removed all of the pain protection blocks. She should be able to talk freely now. Come and join us. She's not under any influence at the moment. She may seem a little strange, maybe a little reserved; she's still recovering from her experience.'

As they stood, Logan handed Serene her scissors.

'I'm going to ask her now about her time at the bank,' he said. 'Serene, you know more about banking than I do. If you have any questions, just ask.'

He turned to Madeleine: 'Let me know if you see or hear anything… unusual.'

'How?' asked Madeleine. 'If she lies, for instance, it may not be wise to let her know that we know it's a lie.'

'Good point. Make a tapping noise – two taps for something wrong like a lie, three for confirmation, if she's telling the truth.'

Looking from one to the other, Serene said: 'What on earth are you talking about?'

Logan put a hand on Serene's shoulder. 'It's a long story. I'll tell you later. Suffice to say that Madeleine has some unusual gifts, among which are acute sight and hearing and she's able to tell truth from lie.'

Serene raised her eyebrows but said nothing as Logan led them towards Tricola.

'Why did you leave out 'one tap'?' asked Madeleine.

Logan smiled. 'One tap could be accidental. We don't want the affairs of nations to depend on the misinterpretation of a finger knocking against a cup.'

Madeleine snorted. 'OK, but just to reiterate, it's more about whether she believes what she's saying – which may not necessarily be the truth.'

'Ah… what *is* truth? Very philosophical,' said Logan with another wry smile.

MADELEINE AND SERENE drew up two more chairs and Logan fetched the table that still had the cheese plate. He took his recently-purchased phone and activated a recording app, placing the phone on the table.

Tricola's eyes had been closed, but as Madeleine and Serene sat down, she opened them and smiled. Madeleine noted her breathing was slow and regular. She looked relaxed.

Logan said: 'Tricola, how are you feeling?'

Tears formed in her eyes. 'It's wonderful,' she said. 'I feel free, like I'm floating. That horrible tight feeling…' She circled her hand over her head, '…is *gone*.' She sniffed to control her emotion and straightened in her chair. Her voice was different. It was more mature, more confident.

'Good,' said Logan. 'Now, if you feel up to it, I want to ask you about your visit to the bank in Zürich. Is that OK?'

Tricola dabbed at the corners of her eyes with the back of her finger, stemming the tears that had started there.

'Yes, of course.'

'You went into the office with the manager and the Japanese man, Tanaka,' said Logan, speaking slowly and evenly. 'You sat at the desk with the manager. What did you do then?'

'I logged into the central application server using the man's thumbprint and his password.'

'How did you know his password?'

'I said the keyword *albatross* to him, and he replied, just as I'd been told he would, with his password and the name of the daily reconciliation job.'

'Who told you to say that word to the man?'

'Lucifer.'

Logan sat back in his chair and repeated the word softly. '*Lucifer?*'

'Yes.'

'Does Lucifer have any other name?'

'Some people call him the Magician, but not to his face. He likes people to call him Lucifer.'

Logan shared a glance with Madeleine and Serene. Madeleine tapped three times on the leg of her chair.

'A fallen archangel…' Logan said, thinking out loud. 'Cast out of heaven because of his contempt for humanity. A strange choice of name.'

He leaned forward again.

'Once you were logged into the server,' he said to Tricola, 'what did you do?'

'I checked the network, found the reconciliation job and added my code.'

'Your *code?* What do you mean by *code?*'

'I added my own computer program instructions to the reconciliation job.'

'I see. Was your code stored on the USB drive?'

'Yes.'

'So, you inserted some lines of code. Is that all you did?'

145

'Well… not quite. I had to modify some file names and addresses, but that didn't take long.'

Logan paused, then said carefully: 'What did your code do?'

'Stripped money from where it wouldn't be detected and performed an EFT.'

Logan glanced at Serene. 'Electronic Funds Transfer,' she said. Tricola nodded.

Serene touched Logan's arm. 'Can you be more precise?' she asked Tricola. 'Where was money taken from, and where was it sent?'

'Small amounts were withdrawn from floating mortgage interest allocations and transferred to accounts in Lucifer's banks.'

'Electronic transfers are checked and cleared at a central point, aren't they?'

'The transfers have legitimate credentials.'

'OK,' said Serene. 'But, wouldn't the bank's own security checks detect the difference between the amount due and the amount paid?'

'No.' Tricola shook her head. 'It's easy to bypass the security routines. The amounts are deducted at the point of allocation. The correct amount is still recorded in the reconciliation logs. The funds transfer is not recorded anywhere.'

Logan glanced at Madeleine. She tapped again three times. Tricola was speaking the truth.

Serene said: 'Wouldn't the account holder notice the deductions?'

'The amount of interest charged is always changing on this type of account, so the customer doesn't notice tiny differences.'

Serene nodded thoughtfully. 'But, when you added your code to the reconciliation job, *that* change would be recorded – the date-time stamp of the job would be updated.'

'I revert the date-time to the previous values. The change is never detected. The funds transfer is never detected.'

Serene sat back, her eyebrows raised.

Logan said, evenly: 'How many times have you added your code to a banking system?'

Tricola gave the question a few seconds of thought. 'Counting the VCT bank – nine times.'

Logan checked that the phone was recording. 'Can you tell us the names and locations of the other eight banks?'

Tricola recited a list of banks and cities. The first bank mentioned was the Maxim International Bank in Hyderabad, India. This bank was repeated three more times associated with different cities in India; Bangalore, Delhi, and Mumbai. Two banks were in China – one in Shanghai and one in Hong Kong. Singapore and Vavuniya, Sri Lanka, rounded out the list.

'So, the VCT bank was the first European bank,' whispered Serene.

'Yes,' said Tricola.

Serene continued: 'You said the amounts were transferred to Lucifer's accounts in other banks. Which banks are these?'

'Not to Lucifer's accounts. The amounts are transferred to Lucifer's private *banks*. He owns four banks in India and one in Sri Lanka, and the funds are split between them.'

'He *owns* five banks?' said Serene, incredulous.

'Yes.'

'Do you know the names of Lucifer's banks?' Serene pulled out her phone.

Tricola tested saying one of the bank's names, still not convinced that she was free of the expected accompanying pain. Relieved, she recited the names of four more banks. Although the names were being recorded by Logan, Serene also typed each name into her phone.

She rose from her chair. 'I need to update Sir Brian with this information immediately. We'll probably need Interpol involved. I imagine Lucifer will have his identity hidden in multi-layered companies regarding the ownership of these banks, but we can start digging.' She put the phone to her ear and walked away towards the hallway.

Logan nodded. To Tricola, he said: 'We'll also need you to identify the code you added so it can be removed.'

Tricola looked worried. 'Lucifer won't like that. He'll know it was me who told you.'

'That's true,' said Logan, 'but everyone here will protect you and, right now, Lucifer doesn't know where you are.'

Tricola's frown remained. She looked to Madeleine for support.

'We're all on your side,' Madeleine said. She moved her chair close to Tricola's and leaned over to hug her.

Tricola buried her head in Madeleine's shoulder. 'Thank you,' she said in a muffled voice.

Madeleine held her for a while, then she gently lifted Tricola's head and, taking her by the shoulders, asked: 'What was the role of the Japanese man, Tanaka?'

Tricola's body tensed, her face registering disgust. 'He makes sure I get to the bank and when I'm there that I follow the plan. I have my *instructions…*' she tapped her forehead forcefully, her anger evident, '…but Lucifer still doesn't trust me. Tanaka knows a little about computers. He's an ignorant fool, but he knows enough to be able to check that I'm only doing what's expected and no more. He's a cruel man who hurts me. But I think he does it on Lucifer's orders.'

After a moment, Logan said: 'Tricola… what's your relationship to Lucifer. Why were you working for him?'

Tricola sat up and sniffed, blinking away some moistness in her eyes. She drew in a long breath. 'I think Lucifer *owns* me,' she said slowly. 'He told me he bought me from the Sultan. He says I belong to him, and I'll never be free. If I don't do what he wants, I'll be punished.'

There was a silence while Logan and Madeleine processed Tricola's information. Madeleine tapped slowly three times on her chair.

Logan said: 'What's the Sultan's…?' just as Madeleine said: 'Well, you're free…'

They stopped together. Logan indicated that Madeleine should continue.

Madeleine said: 'You're safe and free from the influence of both Lucifer and Tanaka now.' She leaned forward, resting her elbows on her knees. 'Tricola… where are you from? What country?'

'Somalia.'

Madeleine nodded and took the opportunity to pursue something she'd been thinking about while Tricola had been talking.

'You're a teenager…' she said with a gentle voice, '…yet you're obviously well-educated and an expert with computers and computer code and phones as well. Somalia is not a country known to be….'

She paused, and Tricola continued her sentence with a smile '…a world leader in electronics.'

Madeleine nodded.

'*One* person is responsible for that,' said Tricola, '…although he certainly didn't intend it – the man who killed my family and took me as a slave when I was nine years old. Sultan Abdullah Ahmed Assan.'

Logan sat back in his chair, letting a breath out between rounded lips. 'I still have some questions,' he said, 'but that's a story I'd like to hear.'

'So would I,' said a voice from the hallway. 'But, maybe after dinner.'

Nico entered the lounge carrying a large bag from which emanated the aroma of spiced meat and herbs.

'I'm reliably informed this is the best veal saltimbocca in all of Italy,' he said, carefully moving the empty cheese plate to one side and placing the bag on the table. 'Please excuse the plastic plates.'

He looked up as Serene re-entered the room, pocketing her phone.

'What on earth is producing that delicious smell?' she asked. 'I'm suddenly hungry.'

THE ROLLED PIECES of veal were each secured with a substantial wooden skewer which invited the use of the fingers for eating. The meat was exquisitely tender, melting in the mouth, and the delicious filling of prosciutto, spinach, cheese, and herbs, did indeed give weight to Nico's claim. Madeleine's main concern was preventing the cheese and juices from escaping from the corners of her mouth. She found it continually necessary to dab her lips and wipe her fingers with a paper napkin.

Twenty minutes later, the only remnant of the meal was a pile of clean skewers.

Madeleine said: 'I'll tell you one thing. Since I've met you all, I've had experiences I never thought would come my way. But… I've certainly eaten well.'

Nico laughed. 'We do our best with what we have,' he said. He stood and cleared the remnants of the meal from the table and took the bag and cheese plate to a kitchen at the end of the hall.

Logan indicated the comfortable couch and armchairs by the window.

'Let's sit over there,' he said to Tricola. 'When Nico returns, can you tell us your story? I think it may be important that we know it.'

Tricola sighed and nodded. Madeleine glanced uneasily at Logan. She could tell there were parts of her past that Tricola would rather not recall.

They were seated when Nico returned. He was carrying a jug of iced water and some glasses. He placed these on a side table then drew over a chair to join them. Logan quickly updated him with a summary of Tricola's story so far. When he had finished, Nico stood, walked to Tricola, bent down, and embraced her.

Tears sprang again to Tricola's eyes. She answered Nico's hug by holding his arms.

'Thank you,' she whispered. Nico released her but cupped her face with his hand before sitting down.

Madeleine offered Tricola a napkin and she used it to dry her tears. She took a deep breath and looked at each of them.

'Thank you all,' she said earnestly.

She turned her eyes to Madeleine, who smiled encouragingly and prompted her: 'You are nine years old….'

'I was nine,' Tricola said, nodding. 'On a Sunday, I went with my aunt and some other women to the well….'

CHAPTER ELEVEN

Vatican City…

'I'm *extremely* disappointed.'

'Your Eminence, I wasn't there at the time. I…'

'*Another* cause for disappointment.'

Bowers had the sense to remain silent.

'Where are they? Have you lost them?'

'Not at all. That imp of yours, Bartoch, is an electronic wizard; he's given us a solid lead.'

'Is that so? I was told he would be useful. It's why I acquired him. So… *solid* is it? How solid?'

Bowers hesitated a second. 'Ninety per cent.'

'*Explain* the ten per cent uncertainty.'

'We are tracking only one of them. We're not sure the group is still together.'

The man stared at him, then said: 'One will be enough. Where does your solid lead point?'

'To a hotel in the countryside near Verona. I have men on their way.'

'Call them off.'

'What? Your Eminence…'

'Call them off.' The eyes were piercing. '*This* time, I'll use someone more *reliable*.'

CHAPTER TWELVE

Tricola Sandantisa…

Saturday 9:20 pm

'I lived in a small village near the town of Baji in the north of Somalia. We shared a well with two other villages. My aunt and I took our water jars and walked with some other women to the well on *Axad*, which is Sunday. I waved goodbye to my sister Calaso, and she waved back to me. She was too young yet to make the journey to the well. I have not seen her since that day. There are many people I haven't seen since that day.

We met several other women from the other villages at the well and stayed to talk for a while. It was a happy time. The women talked about their husbands. They were laughing and behaving like young girls. I wasn't supposed to hear or understand, but I did.

We put the water jars on our heads and headed back to the village, but we'd only gone a short way when we saw, in the hills, there was smoke coming from our village – a lot of smoke, rising high in the air. My aunt said put the jars down, but I said if there is fire, we will need the water, so we ran as best we could, balancing the jars.

Then trucks came racing down the valley from the direction of the village. We knew what they were. We hadn't seen much of the war – that was mainly in the south, but we had heard of it. The trucks were spread out across the valley in a line. There was nowhere for us to run, so we just stopped and stood there, trying not to be noticed, hoping they would pass us by. One swerved toward us and stopped beside us in a cloud of dust. We held the cloth of our *guntiino* over our mouths as the dust whirled around us. There were five of us, including me.

Three men were standing on the back of the truck. One of them shouted in Arabic, ordering us to get on the truck. I didn't know what to do. There was still a lot of dust in the air – maybe I could run and get away. But what about the others? He pointed a gun at us. We still hesitated – did they want the water as well? He fired his gun at the ground. Big puffs of dirt flew up in our faces. The noise was very frightening. I put my jar down, making sure it didn't spill – maybe someone could still use the water – and climbed onto the truck. Then I helped my aunt to climb on board.

One of the women was Jamila, the sister of the head man of our village. She was old, and when she tried to climb up, the man kicked her away. He kicked her in the head with his boot. She fell to the ground, shrieking with her arms around her head. He banged his hand on the cab of the truck, the engine roared loudly, and we moved away from Jamila, leaving her curled up in the dirt with our jars standing beside her like the pillars of a miniature temple.

We four sat on the back of that truck with our arms around each other, and we wept.

The trucks caught up with the other women who had been at the well and they were also forced to climb onto one. Then there was a shouted conversation between the men on the trucks that turned into an argument with men gesticulating in different directions. Some trucks continued down the valley, but the two containing the women from the well turned west towards Ethiopia.

After we had spent all our tears, we sat in silence for a long time as the trucks jolted across the rough ground, until my aunt said: 'At least Jamila will be able to tell them we've been taken.'

She spoke in Somali, but the man overheard her. He laughed and said, mockingly, in a strange accent: 'Huh. Who she tell? Everybody dead.'

He raised his gun above his head. 'Assan!' he shouted. 'Assan!' The other two took up the name and shouted it too.

I shut my eyes and put my hands over my ears, trying to force his words out of my head.'

Tricola stopped talking. Her eyes were unfocused, staring into the distance. *She's back there, experiencing it again,* thought Madeleine. They sat in silence, waiting for her. Madeleine took the opportunity to tap three times on her chair.

After a while, Tricola's eyes returned to the room. She looked at each face before speaking again.

'I became the companion of the son of Sultan Assan,' she said, 'in his palace in Ethiopia. The Sultan had instructed that a boy about his son's age be brought back from the raid, but I was the best his men could provide. I was the *only* child they brought back, the rest were women, and they all disappeared. I never saw them again, including my aunt.

They asked me my name and I told them my name was Tricola, although that's not my real name. A Somali name contains the names of our fathers. It's a family history. I'll never use my old Somali name again because that name died with my family. The Sultan chose my second name, 'Sandantisa', which in Somali means 'Sandan's gift'.

Sandan was a spoiled little boy. He was a year or so older, but I was taller. He had everything and he had nothing. He had a room full of arcade games and pinball machines and another room that contained an electric race track for miniature cars. For me, it was like entering a magic world.

Sandan had tutors who came to him at regular times during each day. One for languages; Somali, Arabic, and English. One for history and politics. One for mathematics and philosophy. And one for technology – computer studies. His father thought this subject was very important. Of course, one of Sandan's rooms was packed with computer equipment. And he had games – lots of computer games – all new, the latest version.

We all talked in a mixture of Somali, which is my language, and Arabic, which was also spoken in our area. I didn't speak Arabic every day but I understood it. The exception was the Computing Tutor, Max, who was American. He spoke no Somali and only very poor Arabic.

Sandan didn't want to learn. His father had said he must stay in the room while his tutors were here, and so he did, but he didn't listen to them. He said he would be Sultan anyway, after his father, so why bother. He would rather draw with his pencils. He was very good; he could draw anything. I sat with him and I watched him drawing as scenes appeared on his page: desert scenes, dunes with rippling sand, camels and close-up scorpions, Berbers and hill tribesmen – he drew wonderful pictures. I asked him where these ideas came from and he said from television and from his memory. His father sometimes took him into the desert. I think that was the only part of his 'education' that he enjoyed.

While Sandan drew, *I* listened to the tutors. Sandan didn't mind if I asked questions, and the tutors were eager to discuss anything with me. They were happy to teach *someone*, to justify their position. It made them feel they were at last doing their job instead of talking to deaf ears. I'm sure they all reported to the Sultan, but I'm equally sure they told him what they thought he wanted to know and would have left out any mention of their inability to teach Sandan.'

'I presume you learned your computer skills from Max then?' asked Logan.

'Yes, that's partly true. I hadn't even seen a computer, so it was strange at first, and I was a little afraid of the machines and their coloured lights, especially when Max made one speak to me. But my fear soon turned to fascination when he talked about the theory of computing and how computers work. The mystery disappeared when I learned about operating systems and file systems and computer languages from him. Our own language difficulties forced him to take everything slowly and, maybe because of that, it all made sense and I understood it.

Then he introduced me to the internet, and I felt like a door to the whole world had opened wide. Everything I could think of was at my fingertips. I had just to reach out and touch it. I'll never forget that feeling. My head buzzed with excitement, and I spent all my spare time exploring the world – no, the *universe* – through that keyboard, mouse, and screen.

In spite of the fact that my life had been taken from me along with everyone I knew, I was *consumed*. I had no time to mourn, no time to think about my past life – I had fallen into a new world, a world I never knew existed, but a world I was part of. I fitted perfectly. It seemed to awaken something in me, a thirst I didn't know I had.

I still talked with the other tutors every day, and I looked forward to our discussions, but I spent hours, days, with Max. After a few weeks, it became easier if we talked in English because while my English improved quickly, Max's Arabic never did.'

Now I know where the touch of American in Tricola's speech came from, thought Madeleine.

'Soon, I was asking Max questions he had to think hard about. I could see possibilities – ways to do things – that he found hard to follow. I saw that I could take this piece of information and that piece, put them together, and a door that had been closed would open.

Months slipped by, two or even three years. I lost track of time; it passed so quickly. I slept only when I was so exhausted my eyes wouldn't focus and my fingers hurt. Sometimes, I slept all morning but I was always ready when the first tutor arrived after the midday meal.

IT WOULD HAVE BEEN Max who told the Sultan about my ability. One day, the Sultan came to Sandan's rooms, appearing unannounced at the door just after the Language Tutor had arrived while the kitchen girl was still clearing our plates. I think Sandan almost had a heart attack, if that was possible for a young boy. He leapt to his feet but then stood paralysed and staring at his father. He had some pencils in his hand, which he let fall to the ground. They made a tinkling sound on the tiles.

I had only ever seen the Sultan from the window while he walked in the gardens surrounded by a retinue of people. He visited his son every

Monday at noon, and ate with him, but I had to go to my own room during this time, and I never saw him. He had never before come unannounced.

He was responsible for the death of my family, and I hated him for that, but I could see he was detached from the people who did the killing. He may not have been a bad man; his raids into Somalia were no more than a way of life. It was how things were done. I'm not sure he knew that his men killed indiscriminately. They brought him slaves because it was his right as Sultan, and he was expected to demonstrate his authority.

The Language Tutor and I walked quickly to the door to leave the Sultan with his son, but he looked at me and told me to stay. My first thought was that I had done something wrong, but he didn't look angry. He told Sandan he would talk to him later, and he beckoned me to follow him.

In another part of the palace, he stopped and looked at me for a long while, up and down – an assessment of some sort.

'Mr Gronholm tells me…' the Sultan's nose wrinkled, and I knew that was a reference to Max's bad Arabic, '…that you may be able to achieve what so far he has not.' He stared at me again.

'We shall see,' he said. He walked away and I turned to see Max standing in a doorway.

My relationship with Sandan and the other tutors ended that day, and my education immediately became more specialised.

It was from Sultan Assan's chancellor that I learned about finance and banking. Max continued his formal teaching but now he talked about audit logs, security routines, operating system loopholes, cryptography, and breaking passwords.

'Get in,' he used to say, 'get the data, and get out.'

It was fun; it was a game. Solve the problems, get around the obstacles, leave no trace – I did what they asked of me. To me, it wasn't money; it was just numbers – reduce here, increase there, keep the balance. Again, it didn't take long before I was able to find paths and work out simpler and more efficient procedures that Max hadn't seen. At first, I tried to hide from him that I could see a better way or that I had already seen the answer to a problem. I was worried he would be jealous or feel stupid or maybe lose his position if he wasn't needed anymore. Max was nice. He was always kind to me. He was like a big brother who treated me as a friend, not a child. I liked him and I didn't want to hurt him. But when he realised what I could do – he was *pleased*, pleased for *me*. He told me he was happy that his protégé was leaving him behind, growing into something he couldn't be. 'My little pony…' he used to call me '…galloping higher into the sky'.

We worked together for a long while, from a summer to a summer – so more than a year. The chancellor told us what he wanted us to do, and we did it.'

Tricola paused. She gestured to the water jug. 'Can I please…?'

While Nico picked up the jug and filled a glass, Madeleine took advantage of the break to ask: 'How did Max, an American, find himself in the court of an Ethiopian Sultan? Do you know?'

Tricola's smile contained a trace of embarrassment. 'I think he was hiding from someone, maybe the law – I didn't ask him. He was certainly overqualified for the job of tutoring the Sultan's son in basic computing.'

Nico handed her a glass of water and she gratefully took some.

'Thank you,' she said. She placed the glass beside her and took a breath before continuing.

'One morning, Sultan Assan came into the room where I was working. Max was sleeping on the bed in the corner because we'd been up all night. The Sultan had his chancellor with him and also a man I hadn't seen before.

It was the man I would later know as Lucifer.

Sultan Assan usually only talked to Max, even with his bad Arabic, and I could see that he considered waking Max but, instead, he talked to me.

'Have you done it?' he asked me in Somali. He was referring to the task we had been set the previous evening. There was a message contained in the slow, deliberate way he asked the question. 'No' was not an acceptable answer.

'Yes, your Majesty,' I replied. 'We have the information you wanted. We broke through the last firewall this morning.' Actually, I had done that while Max was asleep.

The Sultan surprised me by saying: '*Hambalyo!*' which means 'Well done.' He clapped his hands in a rare display of delight and turned to Lucifer, switching to English.

'She said she has broken into the database, just like I told you she would. Things should now progress nicely for you. The bank is as good as yours.'

'Thank you, your Majesty,' Lucifer said. 'The emeralds will be delivered today.' His black eyes stared at me. He waved his hand. 'And who is this delicate little flower?'

'I would not describe this one as a 'flower'. She is more like a flaming torch and worth her weight in gold,' the Sultan said proudly. 'I found her in the desert and nurtured the spark I saw within until it grew into a blazing fire, burning bright. With the skills of this little one, there are no doors that are barred to me – as you have just witnessed.'

'Indeed. I was told that system was impossible to breach. Can you please ask her how long it took her?'

Of course, I understood his question and almost answered immediately, but to interrupt the Sultan would have been a major breach of etiquette. I bit my lip.

'Ask her yourself,' Sultan Assan said, in a good mood now. 'She speaks English. I taught her that as well.'

The Sultan had given permission for me to speak, and I didn't need Lucifer to repeat the question. 'It took about eight hours…' I said, then paused; I wasn't sure how to address him. 'There were many layers with good encryption. The most difficult part…'

'That's enough. He doesn't need to know the details,' the Sultan said in Somali. His tone indicated my involvement in the discussion was over.'

Tricola turned her palms up and shrugged.

'Four days later, I flew in an aeroplane for the first time in my life, eventually landing in Rome.'

'*Rome?*' That wasn't the destination Madeleine expected to hear. She looked at Logan, who was regarding Tricola with similar surprise. Logan had suspected that Sapphire, or to use Tricola's name, Lucifer, was based near Venice.

'Do you know which airport you landed at?' Logan asked. 'Fiumicino on the coast or maybe Ciampino?'

Tricola shrugged.

'Where did you go from the airport?'

'I didn't notice the direction. It wasn't a long journey, fifteen or thirty minutes. We didn't go through the city of Rome. I was taken to a huge house with a swimming pool and fountains and many other buildings, where I've lived ever since. The grounds were vast, like I said before at the villa. A hundred acres, I think or maybe more. Lots of trees and hedges and hills and wide grassy areas with streams.'

'And Lucifer was there? At the big house?'

'Yes, he met me there on the first day. But he's not there in person very often. Only once or twice a month. Tanaka takes care of me – watches over me. He gets instructions from the earpiece he always wears. There are some other staff – a cook and some gardeners and another man who was called Tiru, a secretary of some sort – he ran the house and the housekeepers.'

'Can you describe Lucifer?'

'Ah… he's not as tall as you; much older, a bit thicker; long white hair. He's very intense, and his eyes are piercing – they stare at me all the time.'

'Anything unusual about him? You said his eyes were black?'

'Unusual? No, I don't think so. Oh, one thing, I suppose… he brushes his hair over his ears, but I saw them once and they're very small.' She stopped and thought. 'I'm not sure about his eyes. They *are* dark – they seem black. Oh…' She stifled a yawn and looked up at Logan. 'Sorry… I'm tired. If you want to know any more, can we please continue in the morning?'

Logan opened his mouth, but Madeleine interrupted him. 'Of course,' she said. 'There'll be time enough tomorrow.'

Logan looked at his watch and conceded. 'OK, we'll continue fresh in the morning. The route to the big house will be in your memory, so we should retrieve that first.'

As Tricola stood up, she shook her head. 'I still don't understand why Sultan Assan would sell me. The Sultan valued me very highly; I know that. I was very sad when I had to say goodbye to Max, and even to Sandan, who wasn't a bad person, just lazy. What price could Lucifer possibly have paid to a man who has everything and needs nothing?'

Logan and Madeleine exchanged glances.

It was not payment but *persuasion* that had allowed Lucifer to pluck his flower from the Sultan's garden.

CHAPTER THIRTEEN

A visit from the Carabinieri…

Sunday 7:40 am

Madeleine woke.

She let her eyes roam around her room, seeing it for the first time in daylight. It was cosily furnished and featured a bright colourful décor. The sun was streaming through her window, and she could see leafy trees shimmering in the breeze.

She stretched then let her arms fall back to the bed, taking a deep breath. The new day seemed just like a typical sunny day, inviting her to push all her worries aside and offering a promise that her life would now begin moving back toward normal.

A knock sounded on her door. Madeleine expected it would be Logan, but *Signora* Papete's voice called: 'The Carabinieri are here for an identity check. Please bring your papers to Reception.'

A few seconds later, Madeleine heard her knocking and calling again at another door.

She reluctantly tossed back the covers, jumped from her warm bed and dressed hurriedly. She hoped she would be able to shower later. She took a moment to splash some water on her face, rinse her mouth, and push a comb through her hair. Searching in her bag to confirm her passport was there, she touched an unfamiliar object which, after a moment, she recognised as one of the phones Tricola had purchased. She slipped her bag over her shoulder and was ready to go. She smiled, satisfied. There were some benefits to travelling light, a fast exit being one.

A sudden thought: *Tricola! She won't have any papers.*

Madeleine calmed herself. Logan would deal with it. He would talk to the Carabinieri and they would believe that they had checked Tricola's papers. She smiled wryly to herself. Two nights ago, she would have placed Logan's power firmly in the realm of fantasy. Now she fully accepted it and, furthermore – it was *really* useful at times.

A last glance in the mirror and she stepped from her room just as Nico passed by on his way to the stairs. He greeted her with his broad smile and a '*Buongiorno*' and indicated she should go first. He said the word slowly, savouring the syllables, and, with his rich voice, it sounded wonderfully melodic, reminding her of the beautiful *Santa Lucia* he had sung when they first met. On impulse, she slipped her arm around his waist and kissed him on the cheek.

'Good Morning, Nico,' she said. 'And what a wonderful morning it is.'

He laughed happily at her gay mood. The opposite door opened and Tricola emerged. She was dressed but her hair was tousled and her eyes looked frightened.

'The police…?' she said.

Madeleine put a hand on her arm.

'It's just an identity check. I'm sure Logan will explain if they ask for your papers. They'll be looking for illegal refugees or something similar. It'll just take a few minutes and then we can check out the breakfast that *Signora* Papete promised last night. I don't know about you, but *I'm* hungry.'

Tricola smiled, but she was still apprehensive as Madeleine led her to the stairs ahead of Nico. Another door closed behind her in the hallway, and Madeleine glanced back to see Serene was following.

THREE UNIFORMED CARABINIERI, one of them a woman, stood at the hotel entrance and a fourth, an officer, was talking to Logan by the reception desk. Madeleine knew the Carabinieri were a military police force operating alongside the civilian *Polizia*. As far as she understood, the *Polizia* tended to concentrate on the larger cities, and the countryside was generally policed by the Carabinieri, who also handled more serious cases of national significance. Given their military status, she was not surprised that these Carabinieri were well armed, although she was thankful, as one would expect for an identity check, that their weapons were securely holstered.

Logan stood easily, his hands behind his back. The *Signora* was behind the Reception desk with her ledger open in front of her.

At the sound of their footsteps on the stairs, Logan's hands started moving. Madeleine felt Nico touch her shoulder, stopping her at the foot of the stairway. He stepped past her and halted Tricola in the same way. With a soft but insistent pressure, he indicated they should stand back against the wall. He waited until Logan's hands also came to a halt, then stepped up to stand beside Logan. Serene appeared and also stopped at the foot of the stairs.

'Is there a problem?' Nico asked, addressing the officer, his American accent loud and belligerent. 'Why have I been disturbed?'

'Just a routine check,' the officer said in good English. He motioned for Nico to move back. 'Please wait a moment, *Signore,* and have your papers ready.'

His head was turned towards Nico, away from Madeleine, so she was unable to assess his statement, but his words were immediately betrayed by his eyes as they scanned the new arrivals. At Tricola, they widened imperceptibly in recognition. He knew who she was by sight. Did the Carabinieri have her photo? Surely, the Swiss police wouldn't have issued her *photo.*

Madeleine tapped twice against the wall just as the officer addressed Logan. 'Now, *Signore,* you say you do not have your papers? Why is that?'

Had Logan heard her taps? – the officer's words may have masked them. She tapped twice again, using her fingernail to sharpen the sound. Behind his back, Logan's middle finger and thumb met in the universal OK sign. He understood.

Instead of moving back, Nico stepped forward, moving between the officer and the three others at the door.

'A pity,' he said. 'One a woman and these two just boys. Serene, keep them back.'

His words made no sense to Madeleine, but she felt Serene take hold of her arm and pull her to one side, away from the group of men. Automatically, Madeleine pulled Tricola with her.

In a fluid motion, Nico took a step toward the closest man and his hand blurred to strike him in his chest, below the ribs, in the area Madeleine knew as the celiac or solar plexus. The man gasped in pain, his body doubling up, his hands moving involuntarily to his stomach. His legs buckled and he fell to land on his knees. At the sound, the officer turned just as Nico stabbed at the second man's neck, his hand extended flat like a knife. The man's hands had started to rise in a defensive motion but had barely passed his waist when Nico's stiffened fingers made contact with his neck. The man toppled backwards and Nico reached an arm behind his back to catch him, breaking his fall. This gave the woman time to draw back a step, reaching for and freeing a long wooden baton at her side. She raised the weapon. Her movements were practised and fast, but before she could draw back her arm enough to strike, Nico stood up, smoothly moved inside her arms and hit the woman on both sides of her neck, the same double strike Madeleine had seen before. The woman collapsed just as Siska had done in the castle, her baton clattering onto the floor. Again, Nico took the time to ensure she would not be injured by her fall.

The officer, recovering from his initial stare of disbelief, scrambled with his holster, trying to draw his gun. Nico rose and twisted toward him, taking hold of his elbow, his thumb pressing into the flesh of the officer's arm. To Madeleine, his movement from a crouch, holding the woman, to rising, turning, and grasping the officer's arm was unerringly precise and so graceful it was balletic. The officer's hand seemed to lose feeling and flopped open, dropping away from his holster to hang uselessly at his side. Nico drew back his right arm and moved it forward, again at an impossible speed, the heel of his palm striking the officer in the centre of his chest. Or – *seeming* to strike him. It looked as though Nico's hand didn't actually make contact before the officer was pushed violently backwards, landing in an unconscious heap against the wall.

In the silence that followed the explosion of action, Nico bent and checked each of the Carabinieri, removing their holstered guns as he did so. He replaced the baton in the woman's belt and helped the one kneeling, desperately gasping for breath, into a sitting position.

Madeleine regarded the aftermath of Nico's aggression open-mouthed, staring at the four Carabinieri sprawled on the Reception floor.

'Couldn't you just have talked to them, like you did with Colonel Ritter in Zürich?' she asked from behind Logan. 'Was this violence necessary?'

'To answer that question properly would take some time,' Logan said over his shoulder. 'For now, the answer is no; that wasn't an option because I can't influence more than one person at a time. I need to touch them or be close enough so they know I'm speaking to them. Very soon, if all goes well when we get back to Venice and I find what I'm looking for, I hope to be able to change that.'

'I see,' she said, moving to stand at his side. 'Well, in that case, why didn't you try to help Nico?' Her tone wasn't critical, just curious. 'There were four of them.'

'There was no need.' Logan replied. 'As you say, there were only four. I would almost certainly have been in his way.'

'What if the officer had been able to draw his gun?' Madeleine persisted. 'If he hadn't hesitated, he may have had time.'

Logan turned to her. 'In that case, Nico would probably have attended to the gun before the wooden baton. As you saw, best to just stand back and let him handle it.'

He saw that she was unconvinced. 'Don't worry,' he acknowledged, 'if he *had* needed me, I was ready.'

Nico checked the officer, easing his half-drawn gun from its holster. He stood up, breathing normally and showing no sign of his recent exertion.

'Non-lethal like you asked…' he said, '… although this one will be out for a few minutes.'

Nico dropped the four guns he'd collected onto the Reception desk in front of the wide-eyed *Signora* who had frozen in shock. As the police weapons clattered onto the wooden desktop, she recovered from that state and recoiled back from the firearms as if they were snakes, her hands raised.

'What… have you… done?' she breathed.

'I assure you, *Signora* Palpete, this will not be a problem for you,' said Logan. With quick steps, he rounded the Reception desk. Taking her by the arm, he said a few soft words. The woman visibly relaxed, and her hands fell to her sides. Logan assisted her onto a stool, where she sat breathing heavily.

Noticing Madeleine also eyeing the firearms, he said: 'We'll return those to their owners when it's safe to do so.' He turned away from her: 'Nico, the men will have plastic cable ties on them to use as restraints.'

Nico nodded. Logan said: 'Immobilise these four and let's get them out of Reception.'

To Serene, he said: 'Check outside for any activity, and check their vehicle… it would be good to know if anyone is trying to contact them.'

He calmly surveyed the room as Serene headed for the door.

Madeleine asked: 'What did you signal to Nico? How did you know they were not just doing an identity check, as they said?'

He smiled at her. She realised she *had* asked a lot of questions. She shrugged apologetically and his smile broadened.

'I'm not discouraging your questions,' he said. 'Quite the contrary. It's good that you want to know.' He pointed at the officer. 'A full Colonel in the Carabinieri does not concern himself with identity checks. I signed to Nico to disable them – *non*-lethally – so we can determine what they know, who ordered this search, and how they found us.'

He started forward to help Nico.

'Mr Milan…' Tricola held up a hand. 'I think I know the answer to your last question.'

Logan stopped. 'Please call me Logan,' he said, inviting her to continue.

'In the car, we called Serene on Dax's phone. That call could have been traced and Serene's phone could have been followed to here.'

Once Tricola said it, it was obvious. *But that would mean there must be a connection between…*

Madeleine gasped. 'Logan…' she said, 'Lucifer must have considerable influence with the Carabinieri if he was able to request their help to get Tricola back.'

Logan slowly nodded his head. 'It seems so,' he said. 'But they can't have been sure that we were with Serene, with explains the identity check instead of a raid on the hotel in force.'

Madeleine looked again at the Carabinieri officer, a Colonel according to Logan, lying on the floor. 'A full Colonel…' she mused. 'That was all you had before you decided to attack *policemen*? There could be a reason why a Colonel is doing identity checks.'

'You know what I think about coincidence. If something seems out of place, it probably is.'

She nodded. 'Anyway, you were obviously right. He recognised Tricola instantly, and he didn't need to think about it, so he's probably seen a photo of her.'

Logan took the legs of the man Nico was dragging out of the Reception area. Madeleine and Tricola picked up the woman.

LOGAN AND NICO had returned to Reception and were lifting the last of the Carabinieri, the Colonel, when Serene came through the door, quickly walking to Logan.

'All quiet outside,' she said. 'There *was* a request for an update on their radio. It wasn't urgent; just checking up. I let them repeat it a few times, then I answered. I cried out in my best panicked German that I was a tourist and there had been a terrible accident. Some policemen are hurt. Please send an ambulance. The location was, of course, some distance away.'

'Good.' Logan smiled. 'That buys us a little time, but I want to be away from here in less than thirty minutes.' He signalled Nico he was ready to lift.

'There's something you need to do when we leave, Serene,' he said. 'It concerns your phone…'

'NOW, COLONEL…' Logan said in a friendly voice, '…we're going to have a little talk.'

'Are you *mad?* We only wanted to check your papers. Free us immediately. I'm placing you under arrest for an assault on officers of the law.'

They were seated in the dining room, next to Reception. The woman and the two young men were at one table under Nico's watchful eye and Logan sat across from the Colonel at a second table. Madeleine, Serene, and Tricola had drawn up chairs a short distance from the Colonel's table. After some more reassurances from Logan, during which Madeleine noticed he again touched her arm, *Signora* Palpete had agreed to go about her normal business.

Madeleine tapped twice, although Logan already knew the Colonel was lying.

'You're in no position to arrest anyone,' Logan replied. 'But we *are* going to talk.'

The Colonel lowered his head and muttered something which Logan appeared not to have heard, but Madeleine caught the words: '… *tuoi trucchi a Occhio di Ra non funzioneranno con me.*'

She gave a start of recognition and before Logan could speak, she said: 'Logan, he just said: *Your tricks at Occhio di Ra won't work with me.* Those words, *Occhio di Ra,* were carved above those strange gates at the castle where we were held. Eye of something. I don't know what a '*Ra*' is. Sorry, I didn't think it was worth mentioning at the time.'

The Colonel stared at her in disbelief. He did not think it possible his words could have been heard.

'So that castle was called *Occhio di Ra.*' said Logan. 'The Eye of Ra.' Then he softly said one word: '*Sekhmet.*'

Madeleine had thought 'Ra' was an Italian word, but when Logan said the phrase, she realised that Ra referred to the Egyptian god of that name. She had an uneasy feeling that she had not heard the last of these ancient gods.

The Colonel raised his head. 'I have a strong mind,' he said angrily, knowing his pretence of an identity check was now useless. 'You cannot hypnotise me against my will if I'm prepared for it. Try your tricks if you must – you will just waste your breath.' His chin jutted forward defiantly.

'I agree with you,' said Logan. The Colonel frowned. He hadn't expected agreement. 'This will *not* be like *Occhio di Ra,*' Logan continued. 'In this case, *we* are not the ones restrained.'

'This action is futile,' the Colonel persisted. 'You are foolish to try to detain us. We reported that we were entering the hotel. It won't be long before someone tries to contact us, and when we don't answer reinforcements will be sent. You have committed a serious crime. You will all soon be in jail.'

'I doubt that jail was ever our intended destination,' Logan replied. 'But that's no longer relevant. As for your resistance... I've made the overcoming of such resistance my speciality.'

As he said this, he touched the gold ring on his finger. It looked like an absent-minded gesture, but Madeleine suspected it was more than that. Was his ring, and whatever was engraved on it, a talisman to be used against resistance? Logan glanced at Madeleine, saw she was watching his hands, and gave a hint of a smile. She realised he was confirming her thoughts and telling her: *Yes, the ring overcomes resistance; with one exception — you!*

Logan continued to lightly rub the engraving on his ring and whispered some words — or, more accurately, made some sounds, as Madeleine couldn't make out anything meaningful. Were they Egyptian words? He continued whispering for several seconds then he touched the Colonel on his arm. The Colonel did not appear to notice the touch.

Logan stood up and crossed to where the other Carabinieri were seated with Nico. The two men were sitting together and the woman slightly apart. He stood before the men, talked to each for a moment and touched them one after the other on the shoulder. Both men's eyes closed instantly and their heads dropped in unison to their chests. When Logan stepped over to the woman, she recoiled in horror.

'No!' she cried in English. 'What have you done to them? What are you — *un Diavolo*? Keep away from me.'

She held her hands up to block him. Logan stopped his whispering and said clearly: 'Time to sleep.' He touched her raised arm and, like her colleagues, her eyes closed and her head dropped as her neck muscles relaxed.

Nico took a knife from the table and bent to cut the ties he had placed around their wrists.

Logan turned back to the Colonel. He repeated his words to the woman: 'Time to sleep.'

'I warn you,' the Colonel said. 'I will not be so easily… so easily… ah…' He looked about in bewilderment. 'I'm not sure… I don't…' He lapsed into Italian, but his words slowed and eventually stopped. He stared forward, his eyes at first vacant, then his lids closed and his chin lowered to rest on his chest.

Logan resumed his seat in front of the Colonel. He crossed his legs and leaned back.

'How are you feeling?' he asked.

The Colonel's head rose and his eyes opened. *'Molto bene, grazie,'* he said. His lips moved but his face remained still and expressionless. Madeleine found the effect eerie.

'Can you please speak in English?'

'Of course.'

'Can you tell us your name?'

'Colonel Allessandro Bertoli.'

'Thank you, Colonel. Would you like something to drink?'

'No, thank you. We stopped for a coffee before we came here.'

Madeleine was surprised at the Colonel's tone. It was friendly and conversational. She had expected him to be cooperative but in a forced manner. Logan also seemed to be treating their interaction as a conversation.

'Why did you come to this hotel today?'

'To find a woman and to see if a girl who is of interest to us was with her.'

'So, you hoped to find a girl. Do you know her name?'

'Her name is Tricola Sandantisa.'

'What were your orders regarding the girl?'

'Take her to the station. She would be picked up.'

'And the rest of us?'

'If you were here, I was to arrest all of you for kidnapping.'

'Kidnapping? But Tricola is with us willingly.'

'That's not important. She's underage, and her father wants her returned.'

Despite listening intently to every word, Madeleine was amused because the Colonel obviously wanted to use his hands as an aid to his speech but, each time he tried, the ties at his wrist held his hands back. He was unable to solve this puzzle, and every sentence started with a wriggling of his shoulders as he sought to bring his hands forward to join in the conversation.

'Her father?' said Logan. 'She was being held prisoner by her so-called father and treated as a slave.'

'That's absurd. She is his legally adopted daughter.'

Logan paused to consider that statement and looked at Tricola. She shook her head in denial.

'Have you seen proof of that?' Logan asked.

'Her age?'

'No, her legal status.'

'Of course. It was an important point for the charge. When I was told she was adopted, I requested a copy of the papers. They were delivered to me last night.'

Tricola's hand went to her mouth.

Logan leaned forward. 'Whose daughter is she? What is her father's name?'

Madeleine held her breath. Finally, they would know Lucifer's real name.

The Colonel said: 'I don't know.'

'But… you saw the adoption papers.'

'Yes, and they were authentic, but the parent's names were considered confidential and were obscured on the papers I received, by order of General Mastricht, the regional commander.'

'I understand. Was it the General who ordered you to visit this hotel?'

'He *asked* me personally. We are good friends, and he trusts my discretion.'

Logan sat back, thinking. He glanced at his watch.

'How do you know about *Occhio di Ra*?'

'I heard that name at my briefing.'

'What were you told?'

'I was informed that you were a dangerous group of fugitives who evaded capture yesterday at a place called *Occhio di Ra.*'

'We were abducted and held at *Occhio di* Ra against our will. That's undoubtedly a crime, isn't it?'

'I was told you were fugitives who had kidnapped a girl.'

Madeleine could see Logan debating whether to pursue the point.

'So, you were ordered to arrest us. Did you have any special instructions regarding me?'

'I have seen your photo, Logan Milan. The General said you had used hypnosis to trick the people holding you. I don't think that's possible. I was told that you may try to hypnotise me but that you would not be able to if I was strong and resisted. As you can see, the General was correct.'

'Yes, I can see that.'

Logan looked in turn at each of the others. Was there anything they wanted to ask? Each person shook their head but Madeleine stood up and beckoning to Logan, she moved a short distance away. He joined her.

She said quietly: 'Are you going to make them forget they saw us? We don't want an assault charge added to the kidnapping one.'

'They won't remember an assault. They will report that there were some guests at the hotel, but they weren't the ones they were seeking.'

'And their bruises?'

Logan put on an innocent face. 'I wonder how they happened?'

'What about the *Signora? S*he saw the fight.'

'Yes, I've given her a little adjustment.' He smiled. 'It can quickly get messy, can't it?'

She gave a return smile and nodded.

He looked at his watch again. 'Time to go.'

He walked over to the other sleeping Carabinieri, checking each one and talking softly to them, touching a shoulder or an arm. He returned with Nico and bending over the Colonel, he laid a hand on his shoulder and whispered in his ear. When Logan finished speaking, the Colonel's head relaxed and fell forward. Nico reached down and cut his wrist tie.

'Thank you, Colonel,' Logan said. 'Actually, you *were* reasonably resistant.'

He regarded all of his sleepers. 'They'll all wake together in just under an hour at exactly nine o'clock and feel quite refreshed.'

Nico left the room and returned carrying the guns he had removed from the Carabinieri. He placed each one back in a holster and fastened the straps.

While he worked, Madeleine asked: 'When they wake, they'll find themselves in the hotel dining room. How will that be explained?'

'They've just finished interviewing the guests here,' said Logan. 'For them, only a couple of minutes will have passed. If the time discrepancy ever gets noticed, it'll just be a puzzle they can't explain.'

'Neat,' said Madeleine. Logan bowed theatrically.

'Now,' he said. 'Let's wrap this up. Serene's phone was here when they arrived — we'll presume they checked that, so if they haven't found the people they're looking for, they'll check again and find it can't be located. That should confuse them for a while.'

To Serene, he said: 'Time to remove your battery. We'll need to change to a new vehicle quickly in case they reported ours when they arrived. If they did, then your phone and that vehicle were here at the same time, and they'll make that connection. Use one of our new phones to contact Sir Brian and get his help with a vehicle. I don't think we should rent again. Also…' he paused, glancing at Tricola, '…tell him what we know about Tricola and see what he can do about the kidnapping charge. It would be best if we didn't have to avoid every policeman we saw.'

Serene pulled out her phone and removed the back.

'Just a moment,' said Madeleine. To Tricola, she said: 'Can you wipe everything off Serene's phone?'

'Of course, but if we're taking out the battery….'

'If we leave Serene's phone here, intact,' explained Madeleine, 'they'll search the hotel thinking she's hiding or for some reason didn't present herself as requested. That search will take more time, and when they find only the phone, they won't know when she left. It could have been anytime last night or early this morning.' Madeleine paused. 'If we take out the battery now, they'll know that Serene was here up until this time, and so she was in the hotel *after* the Carabinieri arrived.'

Logan nodded. 'Yes, I see what you mean. If Serene could have left the hotel *before* they arrived, that's a better fit with the facts as they know them. Good idea.' He studied Madeleine. 'You're quite an asset,' he said.

'An *asset?*' she said indignantly. 'Like a piece of furniture?'

No,' he protested. 'I mean, you're proving indispensable.'

'So, you'd like me on a leash?' Her smile was wicked.

'What? No, I didn't mean… It was a compliment.' He realised he was being teased and turned to Serene for support. Madeleine was amused to see him momentarily off balance, possibly for the first time since they had met.

Serene, wearing her own amused smile, ignored Logan's plea. She snapped the back onto the phone and used her fingerprint to turn it on.

She regarded the screen, her smile fading to a frown. 'A pity,' she said. 'It's taken me years to build up my contacts.'

'I can save them,' said Tricola, accepting the phone. 'I'll copy all your data first and hide it in the Vault. If you want to call a number, let me know, and I can retrieve it for you.'

'What is the Vault,' Madeleine asked. 'That's the second time you've mentioned it.'

'It's a place Max set up,' said Tricola. 'He's stored a ton of really useful information there. Completely safe and untraceable.' She looked down, and her fingers started their rapid dance on the face of the phone.

Serene, in turn, held her hand out to Madeleine. 'Can I borrow *your* phone?' Madeleine reached into her bag and handed over her 'untraceable' phone. Serene dialled a number and, with the phone to her ear, headed out the door.

'Once we leave Serene's phone behind, we've removed the last means they have of tracking us,' Logan said. 'We should be able to… what's the term they use in the spy world? Go black?'

'In the movies I've watched, I think the term is 'go *dark*',' said Madeleine.

Logan smiled. 'Yes, well, whatever they say, we disappear.' He held up his hands. 'OK, Let's quickly gather our meagre belongings and depart.'

'For where?' asked Nico.

'We'll decide that on the road.'

CHAPTER FOURTEEN

Gabrielle and the General…

Sunday 10:10 am

Four coffee cups and a glass of milk formed a circle on the round ceramic-tile-topped table. Madeleine reached for her cup, brought it to her lips and, finding the temperature was perfect, savoured the flavour in her mouth a while before swallowing. Leaning back in her comfortable chair, her eyes shaded by a large brightly-coloured sun umbrella, she surveyed the busy scene.

Logan had suggested a refreshment stop, and they had left the autostrada and driven to a small picturesque village nestled between two low hills. The square was bustling with people coming and going from the market stalls that filled the centre of the town square, and the air hummed with market trading exchanges combined with the muted conversation drifting from nearby customers of the cafés that surrounded the market; a hum that was punctuated only briefly by louder sounds – a car horn from an adjacent street or a shriek of greeting as friends met.

'OK,' Logan's voice interrupted her reverie. 'Can you spell the word 'roughly'?'

Smiling, she replaced her cup on the table and leaned forward. Using her hands, she spelt out each letter of the word in the sign language alphabet that Logan had just taught her. Beside her, Tricola also spelt the word with her fingers. She was so fast that Madeleine deliberately spelt slowly to avoid being caught up in a race.

'You chose that word because it contains 'G', 'H', and 'Y' – unusual letters,' Madeleine accused him.

Logan laughed. 'True,' he said. 'Now, there are a couple of easy shortcuts you can use. Let me show you.'

Madeleine concentrated on his hands as he demonstrated the signs for some common words.

'With those and the ability to spell, you can communicate anything, given time,' he said.

Tricola lowered her hands so Logan couldn't see them and spelt to Madeleine:

H-e v h-a-n-d-s-o-m-e. U l-i-k-e?

Madeleine put her hands beneath the table where only Tricola could see and replied:

T-h-a-t m-y b-u-s-i-n-e-s-s u l-i-t-t-l-e i-m-p

Tricola laughed happily.

LOGAN SAT IN A RELAXED pose, his gaze moving lazily over the market square. One hand encircled his coffee cup but it was his other hand that drew Madeleine's attention and she stared at it, fascinated. The heel of this hand was also resting on the surface of the table, but that was where the similarity ended. A moment ago, Logan had placed a coin on the back of his hand and now he was absentmindedly running it smoothly across his knuckles. His fingers moved up and down rhythmically to pass the coin over each finger in turn. When it reached the last knuckle, the coin was caught by the thumb and passed under the hand to once again resume its journey across the top.

Madeleine found it hard to take her eyes off this demonstration of dexterity. She pulled her eyes away to share a glance with Tricola who was also watching with an approving smile. Serene and Nico were obviously used to the sight, treating the display as nothing out of the ordinary. Madeleine waited for a fumble or a moment of awkwardness but when, after a few minutes, it didn't happen, the pleasant and relaxed atmosphere finally induced her mind to wander.

Her thoughts drifted away from the coin and the market and her recent dramatic experiences and settled on the upcoming symposium. She was concerned about her lack of preparation for the event she had travelled half the world to attend. Two days out from the symposium, she would normally be fine-tuning her speech and revisiting background research. Since meeting Logan, she now had some new ideas she'd like to investigate, and that would need time.

She was also keen to have time to deal with Aunt Claudia's request for help. When Madeleine had called Claudia to let her know she would be in Venice for a month, Claudia had been happy, but she had also expressed relief and had asked for Madeleine's help. She recalled Claudia's voice…

'Madeleine, we've been told my apartment building has a subsidence problem, and the tenants have had to move out! The Council sent me a letter requesting a meeting with each of the current occupants. They said they have an offer to present to me. I'm worried. Can you meet them with me? I know it's what you do, dear. Tomas says you're very good at it. They're so *insistent,* you see. Everything has to be done *right now*. It just worries and confuses me.'

Claudia had said the letter warned of an imminent danger of the building collapsing. The Council owned the apartment building, and they intended to demolish it, strengthen the foundations and rebuild.

Madeleine needed to return to Venice as soon as possible and it seemed that now that they could no longer be tracked, they were free to do so. Did Logan agree that they could return? She opened her eyes to ask him just as Logan said the word: 'Mastricht.'

'I'm sorry,' said Madeleine, 'what did you say?'

Logan had been talking to Nico and Serene. The coin was nowhere to be seen. He looked at her. 'Ah… you were in your own world for a while. Back with us now?'

'Yes. I was thinking about the symposium on Tuesday. I really need to do some work before then.' She paused. She was curious about what was being discussed but also wanted to ask about returning to Venice. Her curiosity won.

'Did you say something about Mastricht, the Carabinieri General?'

'Yes. I was saying that, apart from Tricola, there are two people who know useful information about Lucifer,' said Logan. 'That's Sami Bandarakaianan and General Mastricht. Sami's in Zürich, but Tricola has just found the General's home address…' Tricola waggled a phone at Madeleine, '…and today, being a Sunday, he may well be at home. Funny thing, chance, isn't it?' Logan's face wore an exaggerated look of surprise. 'Since we left the autostrada, we've actually been travelling directly toward his home town without realising it. His house is only thirty minutes away. I think we should pay him a visit.'

'Logan, I…' began Madeleine.

'And we'll have you back in Venice by tonight.'

She grimaced. 'I'm sure you said something similar on Friday evening.'

Logan's expression became serious. 'I need you. *We* need you.' He gestured around the group. 'The five of us make quite a team, you must agree. The visit to the General will only take a couple of hours and may give us important information regarding the person who requested our capture by the Carabinieri. If that was Lucifer, we may get a lead to him.'

He leaned forward to emphasise his sincerity. 'I have business in Venice too, so after the General has told us what he knows, we'll head back there for a few days to regroup. You can do your preparation and attend your symposium – and you're meeting with your aunt, aren't you?'

Madeleine nodded.

Logan's voice took on a more serious tone. 'You'll need to check out of the Moresco, and we should be careful about how you do that because the hotel may be watched. We can't stay in *my* hotel – if we were followed to the airport on Friday night, the *Magari* is almost certainly known to Lucifer. However, my mother has an apartment above her newly opened store on the *Calle Salvadago,* just off St Mark's Square, which shouldn't be associated with me because I've never stayed there. And if you're thinking an apartment might not be big enough for the five of us, let me assure you it *will* be. My mother does not do anything on a small scale.'

Logan's reference to another building owned by his mother intrigued Madeleine. Without thinking about it, she said: 'Your mother sounds interesting. I'd like to know more about her.'

Logan frowned at her change of subject but realised she was not objecting to his plan. He stood up.

'Interesting? She's definitely that,' he said, 'and I'll talk about her if you wish, but let's have that conversation on the way.'

THE AUDI WAS A NOTICEABLE step-up in luxury from the car Serene had rented and light-years ahead of Dax's decrepit vehicle. The pendulum of transport comfort was definitely on the upward swing.

The swap had taken place at Verona's Villafranca airport; the Audi was waiting in a carpark location communicated to Serene by Sir Brian. Madeleine wondered briefly how such vehicle exchanges were organised but decided she didn't need to know.

Nico drove, with Serene in the front passenger seat. Logan and Madeleine occupied the rear seats with Tricola between them.

Open countryside of blurred greens and browns sped past the window. It was a wine-growing region and the road wound between terraced hillsides covered in parallel lines of twisted leafy vines with large sprawling mansions crowning the hilltops.

The café table was five kilometres and ten minutes behind them when Madeleine considered enough time had elapsed. She leaned forward and looked meaningfully at Logan.

'What do you want to know?' Logan's voice carried a hint of resignation.

'Tell me about this mother of yours who owns so much property. What's your relationship with her?' Madeleine had decided to be forthright.

'My mother is Gabrielle Lind, and she owns an international cosmetics company – *Insieme* – *this* company…' he touched the logo embroidered on his T-shirt, '…you may have heard of it. She inherited the company from my grandmother. It's concentrated in Europe, but it also has a presence in the States.'

Madeleine suddenly realised she *did* know the brand. It wasn't one she used, but she now understood why the name had seemed familiar when she first saw it embroidered on the clothes Logan and Serene had worn when they had lunched on the deck of the villa in the Dolomites.

'She's an extremely rich and powerful woman,' continued Logan, 'and she controlled my life completely – what to wear, where to go, what to say – until my father took me to England. She tried to control my life there too – enrolling me in schools, art classes, gymnasiums, sending clothes, tickets to concerts, arranging skiing holidays in Austria….'

He took in Madeleine's puzzled look. '…all without any consultation with me or my father,' he explained. 'The tickets or the acceptance forms would just arrive.'

He paused, looked directly at Madeleine and smiled. 'I hadn't realised until now how difficult it would be to tell you anything and know I can't lie… not even a white lie?' She shook her head.

He drew in a breath, organising his thoughts. 'Well, then. We have a complicated relationship. I admire her. I like her… but love… yes, I love my mother.'

He looked at her for confirmation. He was asking *her* if he was telling the truth.

Madeleine laughed. 'Love is difficult to define,' she said.

Logan nodded his agreement. 'She has many good features. She's very generous. Extremely intelligent. In some ways, I find her amazing. But… unfortunately, there's always a 'but'…'

He stopped and then, more slowly, he said: 'I could easily have lived a rich and idle lifestyle if I could accept her controlling manner. She behaves with the best of intentions, but she knows without doubt that her way is the best way – the *only* way. I couldn't live like that. I needed independence and I wanted to be able to pursue my interests and investigations freely and that would have been impossible under her rule. She considers my areas of interest to be a complete waste of time.'

'So, I rebelled, I suppose. I was young. I resolved to not accept anything from her, not a *sou*, because everything came with conditions. I cut myself off and kept my own affairs completely separate from hers, much to her annoyance.'

He spread his hands. 'I would characterise our relationship, especially lately, as cordial and respectful… Actually, we had a good time the last time we were together, so maybe we're evolving…' He shrugged.

He'd been truthful; he wasn't attempting to hide anything, but Madeleine was confused. Logan was the owner of several hotels and obviously wealthy. When he had revealed who his mother was, his wealth was instantly explained. Question satisfactorily answered. But now he was saying he had distanced himself from her, so the question of his wealth was back on the table. Should she ask about that? *It's really none of my business*, she thought.

As if she had read her mind, Serene, looking back from the front seat, said: 'Tell her about your fund.'

'That has no connection to my mother,' Logan said, but he was defensive, and a glance at Madeleine confirmed she knew that.

He sighed. 'It's an example of life pushing in one direction despite all your efforts.' She retained a questioning look on her face.

'I was prepared to live by my own wits and devices, and I did just that for a few years, but when I turned twenty-one, I was informed of a fund of investments and shares that my *grandmother* had set up for me on the day I was born, which, I must admit, does prove… handy… at times.'

'Tell her how much your fund is worth,' Serene said in a silky voice.

'That's not relevant. Now you're just being mischievous.'

Serene shrugged. 'You just said we're a team. She should know. It's public knowledge if you know where to look. I'm sure Tricola could find out in two minutes…'

Logan wagged a finger at her. 'Serene…'

Serene drew with her finger on the leather console between the seats. She traced the numbers 6-5-0, followed by 'M-I-L-L', then 'E-U'.

Mill Eu? Did that mean six hundred and fifty million euros?

Both Madeleine's and Tricola's eyes went wide.

'Wow…' said Tricola.

'THE GENERAL'S HOUSE is just around the corner up ahead.' Tricola pointed, checking the display on her phone. 'Turn left here.'

'We don't want to alarm the General by crowding his doorway,' said Logan. 'So Madeleine and I will knock on the door while you three wait in the car. Keep an eye out.'

'Are you OK with that?' he asked Madeleine. She nodded.

Nico slowed for the corner, but as soon as he rounded it, he pulled immediately into the curb.

Up ahead, a small group of a dozen people had gathered in the street, together with four parked vehicles. Two of the vehicles displayed the word 'Carabinieri' across the doors in large white letters; another was an ambulance, its back door gaping wide, and the last vehicle, parked in the middle of the road, was a bright orange van with a satellite dish and several

187

antennas on the roof. The name *Telenotizoggi* – which Madeleine translated roughly as 'Telenews Today' – was painted on the side.

'Nico, your Italian is best,' said Logan. 'See if you can find out what's happening. With the ambulance here, I don't think this is about us – but be careful.'

Nico opened his door and sauntered towards the crowd with his easy stride. He stood in the road, checking the vehicles and the people. Madeleine couldn't see any Carabinieri; the police cars were empty. They must all be inside the house. The ambulance was also empty. Nico bent to talk with a woman who answered him enthusiastically, gesticulating and wide-eyed, her head bobbing up and down. The man beside her joined in the conversation, and soon there was a group of four or five around Nico, all trying to talk at the same time. He listened to them, nodding and asking questions, then extricated himself and returned unhurriedly to the car, leaving the group still talking excitedly amongst themselves.

Nico folded himself into the driver's seat.

'It seems Abel Mastricht was found dead this morning. He was discovered hanging from a beam in the bedroom thirty minutes ago by his cleaner. The ambulance has just arrived. Apparently, the Carabinieri have already told the neighbours that it's been confirmed as a suicide.'

They sat in silence, digesting the news. Questions whirled in Madeleine's head. Why would the General hang himself? Surely not because he had failed to capture them? Such failures must happen all the time.

She glanced at Logan, her thoughts exploring more extreme avenues. Could Lucifer have anticipated they would seek out the General and decided drastic action was necessary? Was it conceivable that Lucifer was tying up loose ends? It was a tragedy but also a pity that with the ending of the General's life, a promising lead had also been extinguished. She decided to give voice to her thoughts.

'Logan… it's an extraordinary coincidence that he dies just as we are about to visit him. Could he have been *compelled* to kill himself? Is that possible?'

'Normally, I would say no,' said Logan. 'This talisman I wear…' he held up his hand to show his ring '…will help to overcome resistance to the power, but there's a big difference between prevailing over resistance and forcing someone to do something that is directly opposed to their will or beliefs. Self-preservation is a powerful force. But…' He broke off and thought for a moment. 'Lucifer has already shown himself to be extremely adept at coercion spells – Sami and the other bankers are examples, and wresting Tricola away from Sultan Assan is another – so, in this case, I have to say it *is* possible; it would depend on the person, but Lucifer *may* be able to compel some people to overcome their self-preservation drive.'

'Which makes him extremely dangerous,' said Serene.

'Indeed.' Logan tapped Nico's shoulder. 'Get us out of here.'

Nico started the engine and swung the car into a U-turn.

'Can I borrow a phone,' asked Serene. 'I'd like to update Sir Brian.'

Madeleine handed hers over: 'Why don't you keep it.'

Serene smiled her thanks and glanced at Tricola. 'It's alright,' she said, 'no need to retrieve Sir Brian's number from your Vault; it's one number I know.'

Nico turned the corner and the Audi picked up speed, heading back in the direction they'd come. Madeleine heard Serene contact Sir Brian and listened to her report the General's death and their suspicion that it may not have been suicide. She remembered Logan saying that there were two people, the General and Sami Bandarakaianan, who had information about Lucifer, and now only Sami remained from that pair. If Logan felt the need to head to Zürich in case something similar happened to Sami, that would further postpone her return to Venice. Her brow furrowed and she grimaced, turning away from that line of thought. Making sure Sami was safe and stopping Lucifer were more important than a symposium or the domestic worries of her aunt.

Her mind was brought back to the present when she heard Serene exclaim: 'Oh No! When?' then: 'Just a moment, I'll put you on speaker. Can you repeat that?'

Sir Brian's voice sounded thinly from the phone. 'I said that Sami B from the VCT bank was told to take some immediate stress leave, so when he didn't turn up at his office on Saturday, that was expected – but now both he and his wife have disappeared. A colleague visited and learned they're not at their house and no one, including their neighbours, knows where they've gone or when they left. The *StadtPolizei* informed us. We're assisting in the search for Sami and his wife.'

'Thank you, Sir Brian,' said Logan. 'Is his car missing?' He received an affirmative reply and said: 'I suggest you check his phone records.'

'Yes, I thought the same thing. We're doing that now.'

'Good,' said Logan. He briefly glanced at everyone in the vehicle. 'I think it's best if we head back to Venice and wait for an update there. With the General's death, it's important that I speak with Sami as soon as you find him.'

'Very well,' said Sir Brian, 'I'll let you know any developments.'

'Thanks,' Logan said again.

He signalled to Serene, who picked up the phone, turning the speaker off and saying to Sir Brian: 'What would you like *me* to do?' Madeleine heard Sir Brian's reply even without the speaker: 'This is quickly turning into a major incident. Stay with Logan for now. Because of your one-call phone, *I* can't contact *you,* so stay in touch....'

She heard Logan say *'Damn'* with feeling and turned her attention away from the phone conversation.

'I should have suggested Sir Brian put a tap on Sami's phone,' he said. 'I thought about it, but at the time it seemed a long shot that Lucifer would contact Sami again.'

'You think Lucifer has lured Sami somewhere? And his wife?'

'Yes. I do.'

They rode in silence for a time which Madeleine broke by saying: 'Should we go to Zürich and wait *there* for news?'

Logan shook his head. 'Sir Brian is vastly more able to track Sami down than we are, and we can be in Zürich in an hour once he finds him – assuming the Citation is still available, and if not, well, we can still be there quickly.' Logan's eyes revealed his unspoken thought: *If Sami is still alive.*

He sat back in his seat. 'You and I both have pressing business in Venice; that's where it makes sense to be right now.'

Looking at Tricola, he said: 'We can also talk to this young lady about her trip from the airport to the big house when we get to my mother's apartment. Maybe a visit to this 'big house' and a discussion with the staff there will turn up something useful.'

He waited for acknowledgement from Madeleine and Tricola, then pulled a phone from his jeans pocket. 'I need to call my mother. And I'll let Pietro know our plans.'

'Pietro's phone and the phones at the *Magari* may be being monitored,' said Serene.

Logan smiled. 'I have my ways,' he said. He typed a number and put the phone to his ear.

Madeleine could hear the phone ringing.

'Driver...' Logan said, '...to Venice, if you would be so kind.'

CHAPTER FIFTEEN

An Insieme hideaway…

Sunday 5:45 pm

When Logan had mentioned his mother's 'store', he hadn't prepared Madeleine for the scene that greeted her holding Logan's hand for balance and stepping off the water taxi onto the stone steps of *Calle Salvadago*. She loved the familiar beauty that was everywhere in Venice, but this was breathtakingly intimate and old-worldly. She could imagine this scene would have changed very little over the last hundred years.

Linking the *Basino Orseolo* canal and St Mark's Square, *Calle Salvadago* was a short, covered dual walkway of timeworn stone pillars and arches. The lights of the stores lining each side of the walkway – admittedly, today, electric, but the effect would have been similar then – bathed the stonework in a soft yellow glow that contrasted with the harsh glare of late-afternoon sunlight emanating from the open square visible at the far end of the covered street.

At the point where they had landed, the *calle* bent at a right-angle to follow the edge of the canal basin where, twenty yards away, the ancient architecture was jolted into the present by the presence of a Hard Rock Café. Passing alongside the Café, the street quickly reverted to its older heritage, becoming a narrow cobbled alleyway that quickly disappeared between the tall buildings.

The old and the new side by side.

Insieme was a new store, Logan had said, but the exterior was not new. The store was directly across the *calle* from the steps on which they stood, and the façade they faced was in keeping with adjacent stores – small windows cut into thick stone walls, allowing the passer-by a reluctant glimpse of the treasures inside. Through these windows, Madeleine could see small glimpses of display stands and wall shelves filled with brightly coloured bottles and boxes similar to those gracing cosmetic outlets in major cities throughout the world. The *Insieme* brand name was prominent throughout the interior. It was also written in gold-painted bold stone letters across the arched entranceway to the store, which was situated at the start of the dual walkway leading to St Mark's Square. Here, at the shopfront, a large curved modern display window showcased the full range of *Insieme's* wares.

Logan led the way between the stone pillars of the store entrance. Madeleine found it difficult not to slow her walk, her eyes swinging from side to side, trying to take in the variety of perfumes, creams, powders, and accessories on offer. It was pricy, high-quality merchandise aimed at the top end of the market. She would have loved to linger and examine the fragrances emanating from the display shelving around her more closely. Hopefully, she would get a chance later.

Logan approached a woman in a severe black dress with her hair tied in a bun and thick-rimmed glasses perched on a prominent nose.

'Edith Montforte?' he asked.

She had obviously been warned of his arrival. She nodded formally, took a quick stock of him and his companions and led the way to an elevator at the rear of the store, where she produced a key, inserted it into a lock beside the elevator doors and stood back.

'That key is for you, *M'sieu,*' she said.

THE APARTMENT WAS MUCH larger than Madeleine had expected, encompassing the entire floor of the building above the *Insieme* store. It offered four bedrooms – Madeleine said she would share with Tricola – each with an adjoining private bathroom and a large open central area featuring, in one half, opulently decorated black leather couches and easy chairs, all filled with pink cushions. As with the villa in the Dolomites, original paintings hung on the walls, a mixture of modern and classical art. The other half of the room was occupied by an ebony-black dining table separated from a spacious bright stainless steel and glass kitchen by a long free-standing curved marble-topped bench. Above the dark furniture, an enormous chandelier with hundreds of hanging crystal teardrops seemed to crawl over the ceiling. The vast room was also lit from recessed, concealed sources along the top of each wall.

Just as the transport had improved markedly, so, it seemed, had the accommodation.

While Logan talked with Tricola about her journey from the airport to the place she called the big house, Madeleine paid her bill and checked out of the Hotel Moresco by phone. At Logan's request, she arranged for her bags and briefcase to be collected and delivered to a café in St Mark's Square, where Nico retrieved them.

When Logan had pinpointed the location of the 'big house', which only took twenty minutes, he announced that was enough 'work' for the night and took them all shopping for a change of clothes. Madeleine and Serene ushered a giggling Tricola in and out of several 'chic' fashion stores catering for the 'young and beautiful' – '*and frustratingly skinny*' commented Madeleine. Logan and Nico visited a men's store described by Logan as 'old-school and old-fashioned but knowledgeable and more than satisfactory in every respect'.

TRICOLA SHOWERED FIRST. She took an elaborately long time to choose from her new clothes, asking Madeleine's opinion on several combinations before Madeleine insisted Tricola wear what she had on *right now* so that *she* could also shower, rather than stand a moment longer in a towel wrap.

The bedroom shared by Madeleine and Tricola was the main bedroom. Even so, the bathroom was still surprisingly large and luxuriously appointed. The marble walls were fitted with two huge mirrors surrounded by light bulbs; an oval bathtub that could possibly accommodate four people was partially sunk into the floor, and an open shower was appropriately decorated with Egyptian-themed mosaic tiles. A tier of wall shelves offered a variety of soaps, creams and perfumes, all *Insieme* products, of course. Madeleine recognised fragrances from the store and felt like a child in a candy shop.

After a shower that thankfully featured both ample water pressure and sufficient heat maintained at a near-scolding level, Madeleine chose a perfume, dressed in the outfit she had purchased with the aim of being casual and comfortable yet topically *fashionable*, and strolled from the bedroom toward a hum of conversation in the big lounge.

Serene was facing the window, gazing into a darkening sky, with her phone to her ear, while Logan chatted with Tricola in one corner of a couch that looked as if it could easily seat six.

Logan and Tricola looked up when Madeleine entered the room. He stood up, gave a low whistle, and spread his hands.

'*Mama Mia,*' he said appreciatively, 'you certainly scrub up well, Miss Galli.'

'Thank you, *Signore,*' she replied, pleased with the effect she'd produced. 'Does that mean I looked particularly terrible before?'

Tricola giggled, and he wagged his finger at her. 'Don't start that again. Just accept the compliment.'

She smiled and surveyed the room and the kitchen. 'Is Nico still changing?'

'Nico has decided he will cook for us tonight,' said Logan. 'He's out acquiring his ingredients.'

'You told me he was a good cook,' Madeleine said.

'Better than good,' said Logan. 'He puts a lot of effort and flair into his dishes, but he enjoys it. Always very tasty and very… artistic.'

He put his hand on her arm to guide her towards the window, which overlooked the canal. His hand felt pleasantly firm, inviting but not insistent, directing her to the window but also gently pulling her close. She leant her shoulder against his.

When they reached the window, he said: 'Sir Brian has reported to Serene that although they haven't been able to trace Sami's movements yet, they have made some progress toward tracking the funds flow between the banks Tricola identified.'

The pressure of his hand lessened, but he left it on her arm. She looked down on the *Basino Orseolo,* where the canal widened in front of the steps to the *Calle Salvadago.* It was dusk, and the street lights and shop lights illuminated the rows of gondolas moored in the basin and reflected brightly in the calm water. A particularly ornate gondola, its dark woodwork elaborately carved, with its own lamp shining atop a short pole like an inviting beacon, waited at the steps for customers. *Not long to wait,* thought Madeleine, eyeing the young couple in deep discussion at the top of the steps, casting frequent glances at the black gondola. The boy extended one hand in a dramatic gesture towards the water, and their hands came together as they started down the steps.

'But there has been resistance,' Logan continued. 'Some of the banks that have been 'hacked' for want of a better word, including the VCT in Zürich, are reluctant to admit that their security could have been compromised and, even with the information that Sir Brian was able to supply, are insisting on an internal investigation before allowing an external one. So, the flow has been slowed but not stopped.'

He seemed to realise that his hold on her arm was no longer needed and let his hand fall.

'Unsurprisingly, the Indian banks that Tricola said are owned by Lucifer are flatly refusing any 'interference', as they're calling it, in their affairs and won't allow any access to their files without a warrant. That process is urgently underway, but Sir Brian expects a protracted legal battle.'

'And, in the meantime, Lucifer will be making other arrangements.'

'Indeed. We've staggered him but unfortunately, for now, he's still upright.'

They stood quietly, looking through the window into the gathering darkness. The black gondola pushed away from the steps, and the young man slipped his arm around the girl's shoulders and pulled her close.

Watching the gondola slide into the basin, Madeleine asked: 'What about the big house where Tricola was kept, now that you know where it is? Is it far away? What will you do?'

'The house is near Tivoli, about thirty kilometres east of Rome – the area where the Roman emperors, as well as renaissance popes and cardinals, built their luxury villas. Serene has put the house under surveillance already. I'll visit it as soon as I can. Probably tomorrow.'

'Alone?'

'No,' he said with a smile. 'I'll ask Nico if he'd like to accompany me.'

'Nico....' A thought came to her. 'Why haven't you taught Nico to use the power?'

'Firstly, it takes a dedication of time, effort, and study for several years. Nico would be quite capable, but he's not interested. His interests lie elsewhere.'

He looked at her with a question in his eyes. She held up her hands.

'No thanks.' She smiled. 'I also have other interests.'

THE VIEW OVER THE *Basino Orseolo* contained continual movement; walkers and shoppers filled the narrow street; people in groups, in pairs or alone, slow strollers, quick travellers hurrying to a distant destination, dawdling tourists; gondolas arriving, people alighting or boarding – a popular drop-off and pickup point. A hub of the city.

'When we last arrived in Venice,' Madeleine commented, 'you thought it worthwhile to arrange some protection. Now you don't seem so worried.'

'Tricola was in real danger then. Maybe I was being paranoid, but I thought it was possible Lucifer might want to silence her before she talked. At that time, we were vulnerable, firstly when we landed at the airport and then until I had a chance to talk with her. But she's been with us now for a day or so. He must know we've broken the defences he installed, and she's talked to us – Sir Brian's activities will confirm that – so there's no longer any reason to do her harm. He may still want her back, but he has to find us first.'

THIRTY MINUTES LATER, Nico appeared from the elevator, laden with cartons under his arms and bags in his hands.

He politely refused offers of assistance, deposited his burdens on the bench and immediately bent to his preparations, which he accompanied, to Madeleine's great enjoyment, with snippets of song, moving seamlessly from one tune to another. Madeleine stood by the marble bench with her eyes closed, listening to his smooth voice, which in her judgement was truly worthy of an operatic stage, or any stage. It wasn't just the quality of his voice that was so attractive. His phrasing, pitch, and sense of the song were nothing short of perfect.

She was mildly annoyed at the interruption when Logan announced his presence beside her with a soft cough. He held two glasses containing a liquid of similar hue to the Armagnac she had enjoyed at the *Magari*.

'Surely not?' she said, her eyes widening.

'Not the same, but in the same league,' he replied. 'Definitely one area where my mother and I are in complete agreement.'

He handed a glass to her and indicated the couch by the window where they had stood earlier. They walked slowly across the room, Madeleine thankful, when they reached the couch, that she could still hear Nico's singing.

As they sat down, Logan said: 'I've something to ask you.'

She nodded.

'I have a hunch I'd like to follow. You mentioned that your aunt had a problem with the foundations of her building. Where does she live?'

Madeleine took a sip of the brandy and made an appreciative face. 'Very nice, indeed.' She looked up at him.

'Claudia's moved out of her apartment, but the building is in a wonderful location with a great outlook in the Castello district, on a square at the entrance to the *Arsenale,* the old naval shipyard.'

Logan arched an eyebrow. 'Really?'

'Yes. Why?'

'I'm also interested in that shipyard.' He stared at her, then said slowly: '*Could* it be?'

'Could it be… what?'

'Is her apartment building close to the large towers at the canal entrance to the *Arsenale*?'

'Yes, it is. It's virtually next door to a tower. Actually, I think it's been built where part of the entrance fortifications used to be.' She leaned back and crossed her legs. 'Now you have me intrigued.'

Logan leaned back with her. He laid an arm along the back of the couch, bending it so he didn't quite touch her shoulder. He regarded her, thinking for a moment.

'You asked once before,' he said, 'if our mutual interest in Venetian foundations might be more than coincidence. I now think it's much more.'

Logan raised his glass to his lips. He sipped and slowly swallowed.

'I think I mentioned that I'm in Venice because I'm looking for an object buried in the city's mud beneath our feet. It's one of the artefacts I said had been hidden to prevent its misuse.'

'I remember. You said it was a container. What sort of container?'

'A cylinder…' he said, '…a cylinder made of gold.'

He paused before continuing. 'If my source is correct, the cylinder contains a manuscript I've been seeking for many years, called the True Book of Thoth. The mud will have prevented the air from reaching the cylinder and being made of gold, it should be preserved intact. Hopefully, the interior material, which I believe is parchment rather than the more fragile papyrus, is also preserved. There may be an associated talisman inside the cylinder. I hope so, because I've collected a host of information about this talisman.'

'So, the manuscript contains a spell? One that could be misused?'

'Not one spell; a collection of spells.' Logan twisted his body so he faced her more squarely. 'In the myths, Thoth was the god of writing and knowledge. In the time of turmoil, when the gods were at war, he preserved the most important spells. If you look up Thoth today on the internet, you'll only be told that he recorded a spell to be able to talk to animals and one to recognise the gods, both fanciful nonsense probably designed to divert more serious study. That's why I call this book the *True* Book of Thoth. It contains many spells which have a dark side to them, spells that can be used to influence others without their consent, including one very powerful spell that allows other spells to have a mass effect. By itself, not necessarily bad, but when combined with such power of control as Lucifer has already demonstrated....' He allowed her to finish the sentence herself.

'You believe this manuscript was written by an ancient Egyptian god?'

'No. I believe it was written by a man, and that the stories of those times, when amazing almost unbelievable *god-like* events happened, have been handed down through the generations as tales or myths of the actions of gods.'

When she said nothing, he continued: 'My reference says the Book of Thoth was placed in a cylinder made of *the metal of the Pharaohs*. The location of the cylinder was encoded using a mixture of ancient languages and, so far, I've managed to uncover that it was buried, to quote: *'at a depth twice the height of a man in the liquid earth beneath the entrance to the Arsenale of Venice'.* There's another short passage that I haven't yet decoded.'

He waited until he saw she had made the connection.

'The document I'm quoting from is ancient, but it was only recently re-discovered in France. A few months after the well-known Parisian antique dealer Maurice Clerveaux died, his daughter, Elena, found an underground storeroom on land her father owned in Picardy. Stored inside this room was a trove of Egyptian treasures, apparently the result of several centuries of tomb looting. Among the golden statues, masks, jewellery, weapons, and musical instruments Maurice had 'collected', were drawers of ancient documents and manuscripts. There was even a complete war chariot in the store. Elena promptly arranged for the bulk of the treasures to be returned to Egypt, which really annoyed the French government. The affair caused a sensation in archaeological circles; you may have read about it?'

Madeleine shook her head.

'I managed to obtain copies of several of the documents from the Clerveaux storeroom,' Logan continued. 'The document I'm talking about dates from the late thirteen hundreds, but the cylinder and its contents are much older than that. Venice was in the process of becoming the greatest naval power in the world, and around this time, the construction of the massive towers at the entrance to the *Arsenale* began. That's when the cylinder was retrieved from another location and re-hidden beneath the *Arsenale* fortifications.'

'Retrieved and re-hidden by whom? And why?'

Logan hesitated. 'That's a long story. For the moment, I'll just say that a group used to exist called the Shining Ones, a reference to their worship of the stars, an ancient secret society charged with keeping the forbidden knowledge hidden. As to why it was moved — I suspect that the previous location was in danger of discovery.'

'Just like this one is now.'

'Yes, but the Shining Ones have not been heard of for seven hundred years. The burying of the cylinder seems to have been their last activity. Times are different now. The cylinder would have been considered safe until just a few months ago when the Clerveaux papers came to light, and even then, right up until today, the mighty towers of the *Arsenale* entrance would still have been considered an impenetrable barrier to discovery.'

Madeleine nodded. She thought for a moment. 'If you find the cylinder, do you anticipate any problems with the law? Is there an 'archaeological finds' law?'

'There are excavation restrictions for historical objects of *Italian* origin, and they must be reported. However, this object is not of Italian origin.'

He waited to see if she had any more questions.

'But back to the present,' he said. 'You've told me that the Council – or someone *influencing* the Council – is about to demolish a building *beside* one of the *Arsenale* towers. I thought the cylinder would be beneath a *tower* because the twin towers are the predominant feature of the entrance. But I now suspect that someone else has also read the Clerveaux papers and *has* completed the decoding of the cylinder's hiding place, thereby discovering a more precise location. This person obviously commands considerable resources and wants the cylinder very badly, and…' he leaned forward. '…*that* means we're in a race to retrieve it.'

He was speaking of Lucifer, and that thought chilled her. She placed her glass on a side table and thought about another implication of his words.

She tried to imagine how meeting a man by chance in a café could possibly lead to the object that man was seeking being buried beneath – of all the buildings in Venice – the building her *aunt* occupied. It stretched the bounds of coincidence. That thought jogged her memory. There had been something else recently that had seemed impossibly coincidental. Something that had happened on the night they first met. She struggled to remember. Yes, it was her unusual middle name, Kimi. She had never heard of anyone else having that name until she saw it written on Logan's paper. The name of his fellow Master in America, 'Algonquin' Kimi.

Once again, she had the distinct feeling she had left her old world and entered a different world, where the cosmic laws she knew and trusted had been twisted and replaced by a new set. Things that had seemed impossible before were becoming commonplace. Outside of her control, and in an increasingly mysterious way, her fate was becoming entangled with that of Logan Milan.

Her thoughts were interrupted by Logan.

'Madeleine,' he said, 'I've decided to postpone my visit to Lucifer's big house. I'd like to accompany you and your aunt Claudia to your meeting with the Council tomorrow, if I may. I think that meeting may prove to be very informative, and it will certainly be interesting.'

ON THE PLATE IN FRONT of Madeleine sat a piece of glistening fish. A thin crispy golden-brown layer sat atop a cube of velvety soft pure-white flesh, wrapped like a gift in a wreath of woven long-leaf parsley with the base washed by a sea of thick red sauce. According to the introduction to the dish provided by Nico, the fish was prime cod, lightly fried; the pigmented sauce was a Spanish garlic and red pepper *Romesco*; and the dressing providing the beautiful shine to the fish was made from olives, almonds, and anchovies.

The effect was amazing, a wonderful contrast of colour presented on a pure white plate, and it fully deserved the word Logan had used to describe Nico's cooking: *artistic*.

Although her hunger had been advanced to a disturbing level by the delicious aromas emanating from the kitchen, Madeleine was reluctant to disrupt the tableau Nico had prepared; her knife and fork were held ready but poised motionless above the plate. A glance around the table showed a similar reluctance to be the first to destroy these superb works of art.

Nico laughed and plunged a knife into his fish. 'Don't let it get cold!' he said jovially, lifting a full fork to his mouth.

He paused while tasting, his face registering his analysis of each of the components of the dish he'd created and then his satisfaction as he nodded his head and swallowed. As if the dam had been broken, everybody moved at once, and the only sounds for several minutes were of chewing mixed with murmurs and sighs of appreciation.

MADELEINE STOOD UP and taking her plate in hand, she walked to stand beside Nico. Bending down, she kissed him on the cheek.

'Absolutely fabulous,' she said. 'A meal fit for a Queen and one I'll remember for a long time.'

'I echo that,' said Serene. 'You are still surprising me, Nico.' She was sitting beside Nico and she rose to kiss him on the other cheek.

'The pleasure was mine,' said Nico. He smiled broadly, his voice confirming that he meant the words.

Madeleine also collected Serene's and Tricola's plates and cutlery, stacked them on top of hers, and took the pile to the kitchen.

She thought about Serene's remark. It reminded her of a question she still had to ask Logan.

'I REMEMBER SAYING THAT, and it's true,' said Logan.

Logan and Madeleine shared one of a pair of two-seater couches set on either side of a low but broad dark mahogany coffee table sitting in the centre of the lounge area. Two steaming coffee cups waited within hand's reach.

Madeleine had reminded Logan of the remark he had made when she expressed surprise at Nico's American accent as they stepped from the gondola in front of Logan's hotel, the *Magari*. He had said that Nico had also surprised *him* when they first met.

She was half-turned towards him, legs crossed, waiting patiently for him to explain.

'I met Nico in Naples,' Logan said. 'He was a tourist at the time, I think…' He called across the room to where Nico sat with Tricola and Serene in front of an electronic game console. 'Nico, were you in Naples as a tourist when we first met that evening on the docks?'

Serene and Tricola had gamepads in their hands, thumbs and fingers flying, staring at a TV screen on the wall where strange creatures duelled among brightly coloured flashes of light with explosions, beeps, and squeals emanating from the speakers.

Nico was observing. He looked up, rose from his seat, collected his coffee cup, and crossed to join them at the coffee table. Again, Madeleine marvelled at his effortless grace.

'Tricola's a natural,' Nico said, sitting on the opposite couch. 'Amazing coordination. I'm sure she could make a living as a professional gamer.'

'Madeleine has asked how we met,' said Logan. 'I said it was in Naples, which you were visiting as a tourist, I thought.'

'A homeless destitute would be more accurate,' said Nico. 'I'd just stepped off a bus from the airport.'

'Destitute? How come?' asked Madeleine.

Madeleine saw Nico tense a little, uncomfortable with the question. She said: 'If you'd rather not....'

'No, it's OK,' said Nico. 'There's no reason you shouldn't know. It's somewhat in your line of work, actually. My mother has DID – you probably know what that is.'

Madeleine said: 'Dissociative Identity Disorder. Yes, I do.'

'I'd flown to Naples with my mother, Paula. It was a holiday we'd planned for some time. She was born in Naples and wanted to show me the neighbourhood where she grew up. I'm named after her father. But, at the airport, she had an episode of being Marion, her alternate self.'

'Did that happen often?'

'At the time, her switches to being Marion were occurring only about once or twice a year.'

'How does she cope? How do *you* cope?'

'She's fully functional in both of her identities. It's just that Marion doesn't know me and wouldn't allow me to stay in the house we normally shared. Whenever Marion appeared, I moved out for a few weeks.'

'Your father…?'

'Couldn't handle it. He wanted her – 'put away' was his term. He left when I was fifteen and lives in Portland. We have a good relationship but from afar.'

'Oh, I'm sorry. Is your mother receiving treatment?'

Nico gave a wry grin. 'Yes, *Paula* has been in treatment for years. I've met her psychiatrist – he's an OK guy. Marion refuses treatment. It's ironic, really, because we had planned the trip at a time when it was most unlikely Marion would surface.'

'I'm sorry to hear that. It's unfortunate. If there's anything…?'

'Thank you,' said Nico. 'I've kept in touch with the psychiatrist, and he says she's shown real progress over the last few years – whatever that means.' He smiled. 'They've begun a relationship actually… I know that may not be strictly ethical, but she's very happy when she's Paula, and she apparently tolerates him when she's Marion.'

Madeleine couldn't suppress a smile.

Nico smiled also and breathed deeply, relieved, Madeleine could see, to have the explanation over.

'So…' she prompted, '…you're in the airport at Naples….'

'We had just picked up our bags after landing when Marion appeared. She ignored me as a stranger, expressed surprise at being in Italy, and immediately arranged for a return flight to Los Angeles. Apart from physically restraining her, I couldn't stop her. My attempts to talk to her resulted in a threat to call the police.'

'Why didn't you return with her?'

'I didn't really have a choice. She claimed my suitcase as hers, and I wasn't able to convince her otherwise without making a scene which, from experience, I knew would have been very detrimental to her state. I was left standing in the airport with a few hundred American dollars and my passport.' He shrugged his shoulders. 'Even back in the States, I'd need to find accommodation, so I thought I may as well do that in Italy and maybe see something of Europe. It was time to strike out on my own. I had no worries about my mother making it safely home – as I've said, she's extremely capable.'

'It sounds awful, and it sounds exciting,' said Madeleine. 'How old were you?'

'Nineteen.'

There was a moment of silence, then Nico continued: 'When the bus from the airport entered the city, it was evening. I got off close to the docks where I thought I might find a place to spend the night. I'd been looking for no more than five minutes when a group of men approached me. I stepped aside to let them pass, but they spread out and surrounded me. I presume my clothing, which was clean and good quality, gave a false impression of my impoverished status. Luckily, I was saved by the intervention of Logan and Mr ShangWu.'

'Hardly!' protested Logan.

He turned to Madeleine.

'You remember ShangWu, my chef?'

'Yes. At the *Magari.*'

'Seven years ago, ShangWu and I were on the Naples docks to buy fish and were strolling back to my hotel when we came across the scene Nico has described. A young man was being harassed by five others, obviously intent on doing him some harm with robbery in mind. We stopped walking just as they moved apart and surrounded him.

I started forward to help, but ShangWu put a hand on my arm and told me to wait. All he said was: 'He holds himself well', which didn't make sense at the time. I knew ShangWu was no coward, in fact he's an accomplished martial artist – which becomes important later – so I didn't understand why he wanted to wait rather than help immediately, but he obviously saw something I didn't. We stood in the shadows and watched the scene play out.

'I told you that Nico surprised me when we first met, and that was before I'd heard his voice. The surprise for me was in the way he acted. It wasn't how I expected a man to act in those circumstances.

'Firstly, I noted that he didn't seem frightened or even worried. He stood calmly, waiting for someone to move, his hands held loosely at his side. That, I think, made his opponents wary, none of them wanting to make the first move, but I could see that, backed by their simple weight of numbers, their attack would not be delayed much longer.'

Madeleine stole a look at Nico. He was listening to Logan, his eyes down, remembering the occasion. He wasn't embarrassed by Logan's reference to his lack of fear; to him it was the simple truth.

'In fact,' continued Logan, 'the first move, when it came, was made by the young man. He danced backwards without looking, and his back-kick made solid contact with the chest of one of the muggers. He didn't stop there, continuing to move back, stepping over the fallen body as if he had eyes in the back of his head so that he neatly exited the circle through the gap he'd made. Before his next victims could get over their surprise and react, he turned to each side and threw a heavy punch into the face of the man standing there, one with his left hand, one with his right. In the space of five seconds, three men were on the ground.

'ShangWu then surprised me by saying: 'Very good. I've seen enough. Now we go.'

He walked forward and shouted in a loud voice: '*Polizia*'.

'The two men still standing didn't hesitate. They turned and ran in different directions. The two who had been punched staggered to their feet and also ran – one limping and one wiping blood from his damaged nose. The one who had suffered the first kick got to his feet with difficulty. He was bent over, clutching his chest. The young man, Nico, went to him and took his elbow, offering support, but the man shrugged him off with a curse and, still bent double, stumbled away, disappearing behind a warehouse.

'I followed ShangWu as he approached Nico.

'Your kick was good,' ShangWu said, 'but your punch was all wrong. Show me your hands.' He took Nico's hands in his own and turned them over. Nico didn't resist.

'If you continue to punch like that, you will break your hands.'

Nico shrugged. 'Thank you for your help,' he said.

'I did not come to save *you*,' ShangWu replied. 'I came to save the others. *They* were going to get hurt.' He inspected Nico's fingers. 'And your knuckles were in danger, too.'

ShangWu looked Nico up and down. He dropped Nico's hands and used his fingertips to feel Nico's chest and stomach through his shirt, then his shoulders and forearms. I was surprised that Nico let him do that, but he stood there with just a puzzled frown on his forehead.

'What training have you done?' ShangWu asked.

'Training?' said Nico. 'None.'

Logan laughed and said to Nico: '*Training? None.* Do you remember saying that…? It was the equivalent of saying: Training – what's that?'

'I remember,' said Nico, smiling.

'ShangWu was as incredulous as I was,' Logan continued. 'He asked: 'Where did you learn your back-kick technique?' and the young man replied…'

Logan looked at Nico, who took his cue and said softly: 'It seemed to be a good idea at the time.'

'Yes… it was simply a good idea at the time.' Logan shook his head and regarded Nico with a half-smile on his face.

After a moment, he said to Madeleine: 'I realised that if Nico hadn't drawn their attention, ShangWu and myself may have been the victims of those muggers, so when we learned he was looking for a place to stay, the least I could do was offer the young man a bed.'

'Why do you insist on calling me the 'young man'?' asked Nico. 'You would have only been mid-twenties yourself.'

'Those few years make all the difference,' Logan said, his grin broader this time.

'On that first night, when Nico had gone to bed and I was catching up on some research, ShangWu came to me. He bowed formally and waited. I knew he had something important to say, but didn't want to interrupt me. I put down my work and nodded to him.

'I have some money saved,' he said. 'I want to give it to you so you can make arrangements. This man *must* go to my uncle in China. He has a solid centre like an oak and excellent reflexes, very fast, and perfect muscle type. This man can be trained and moulded into something special. Very special. He also has a high combat sense and awareness of ground and space. I know these things. It would be a crime if he was not trained; a waste of talent; a corruption that cannot be allowed to....'

Logan laughed. 'I had to hold up my hand to stop him before he progressed to talking about causing tears in the fabric of space-time. But I understood what he was saying. It was amazing that someone without training had performed as Nico so effortlessly had against five opponents.

ShangWu explained that his uncle was a Kung Fu Master, a famous teacher, who refused to teach anyone who was not worthy, who had not taken any new pupils for two years and who definitely did not teach Westerners. But ShangWu said: 'He will accept this one.'

We talked long into the night and after he had fully explained his proposition, I agreed, but I insisted he did not need to use his own savings.

'It would be a complete change of lifestyle,' I said. 'We know nothing about this young man, including why he's in Naples. He probably has other commitments, but we can at least make the offer. Of course, he must agree to undergo the training.'

'Of course,' said ShangWu in a tone that asked why anyone would *not* take up such an opportunity.

'In the morning, I put a proposal to Nico. An all-expenses-paid trip to China to train at the Shaolin Wing Chun Kung Fu school of ShangWu's uncle, where, I felt compelled to add, he was sure to be the only Westerner.

'No conditions. Stay only if you want to and stay as long as you like,' I said to him. I didn't expect him to accept, but it seems we had caught him at a crossroads.

'He stayed three and a half years, at the end of which he spoke fluent Mandarin and was a Wing Chun Master, an extraordinary achievement in such a short time.' He turned to Nico. 'Then you spent a year in Okinawa, didn't you?'

'Yes, a year,' said Nico, 'courtesy of Mr Akihiro.'

'Adding aspects of Karate to your repertoire.'

Nico nodded. 'Interestingly, the more things seemed initially different between the disciplines, the more they turned out to be the same.'

Madeleine smiled. 'It seems you also picked up some Zen teachings,' she joked.

'Yes,' agreed Nico. He returned her smile, but he wasn't joking.

CHAPTER SIXTEEN

Vatican City…

'I'm afraid so, Your Eminence,' said Bartoch. 'At this moment, I don't know where they are. We're watching known locations, but they haven't appeared yet.'

Bartoch waited. The man sitting at the desk held several papers in his hand while his eyes scanned a pile of documents on the desk in front of him. Although the room was well-lit, a reading lamp on the desk further illuminated the documents with a bright circle of light.

The man didn't look up or reply.

Bartoch went on: 'I have some more information about the woman, she….'

He was waved to silence. 'I've more important considerations at the moment than Mr Milan's mysterious companion.'

Bartoch hesitated a moment. He said: 'But…' The hand gave a quick movement, warning against continuing the sentence.

After a pause, Bartoch decided on a different tack: 'Something I can help you with?' he asked.

The tone was curt. 'Your willingness to help is admirable, Bartoch, but someone is attempting to seize my financial assets, so unless you have financial and legal skills to match your considerable electronic talents, I think not.'

There was a silence. Bartoch stood for a moment, unsure whether to leave or try to speak again. Before he could make his decision, the man said: 'I want Mount Sinai closed down.'

'Closed down? What do you mean? Locked up?'

'Closed down! Send the staff to their homes, wherever they are.'

'Why?'

The man's head jerked around to stare at Bartoch with narrowed eyes. '*Why?*' he mocked in an icy tone.

Bartoch did not move.

The man lowered the papers he held to the desk and placed both hands flat on the desktop. He drew a breath in through his teeth.

'Bartoch, I don't like to be questioned, and my reasons are not your concern. However, just this once, I'll indulge you.' He paused. 'By now, Milan will have talked with the Somali girl and extracted from her everything she knows, including the existence and location of Mount Sinai. He'll go there. I want him to find nothing.'

'Would you like the place guarded or watched?'

'No. I don't want anybody there or nearby.'

Bartoch's brow creased, but he decided against asking 'why' again. Instead, he ventured: 'If he knows what the Somali girl knows, then there's no reason to continue to try to get her back, is there?'

The girl worried him. He knew he was highly skilled with electronic devices, but her talent was freakish.

A derisive snort. 'There are many reasons. Firstly, she's mine, and secondly, while I appreciate your efforts, Bartoch, in our world of electronic commerce and communication, she's gifted in a particularly useful and valuable way. I would like to use those gifts again. Also, *for your information...*' the last phrase dripped with sarcasm, '...I do *not* like interference in my plans, and I make a point of *punishing* any such attempt.'

He returned his concentration to his documents, his dismissal obvious.

Bartoch swallowed. 'The staff at Mount Sinai…' he said, '…do you want them fired?'

The man looked up. Irritation glared in his face, but he forced himself to answer with a firm but calm voice.

'No, of course not. As I said, send them home for a while. Just for a few days, a week at the most. I want them all gone by early tomorrow.' His head raised as if a thought had presented itself. 'Except…' he said, '…except for Tanaka.'

'The Japanese? What shall I tell him?'

'I want him here. Tonight. I have a task for him. If Mr Milan is avoiding his hotel, we are presented with an opportunity.'

Bartoch did not even consider seeking more information about the 'opportunity'.

'And our guests?' he asked instead.

The man paused. 'Hmm, yes, the guests. They can stay – Milan will not be able to find *them*. See that they have enough provisions for a week.'

'You're going to leave them alone?'

His answer was an imperious stare. Bartoch lowered his head but then, after a moment, he raised it as if to speak again.

The man held up his hand.

'Bartoch… do *not* ask any more questions. Just get it done. *Immediately.*'

Bartoch bowed his head. 'Yes, Your Eminence.'

Ten seconds passed. The man's head had lowered to his papers, now it slowly rose.

A heavy sigh. 'Bartoch, you are still here. Why?'

'I'm very sorry to continue to disturb you further, Your Eminence,' Bartoch said quickly, 'but you will want to hear the information I have.'

The man swung his chair around.

'Really?' he said. 'You *think* you know what I want. This is very interesting, Bartoch. Maybe you have more metal in you than I thought.' He gazed at

Bartoch, re-assessing him. 'Very well,' he said, 'tell me this important information.'

'Firstly… from her American firm, I've discovered that Madeleine Galli is in Venice to attend a medical symposium.' Bartoch paused to allow the man to express his appreciation of this news, but when there was no observable reaction, he cleared his throat and continued. 'Secondly, one of the tenants evicted from the *Arsenale* building in Venice is named Claudia Galli. She is Madeleine Galli's aunt, her father's sister.'

The man leaned back in his chair. He was silent for a long while, his face expressionless.

Finally, he said: 'So… the aunt is linked to the *Arsenale,* and that creates… at last… a connection between Madeleine Galli and Logan Milan. A connection that is somewhat… unclear… at the moment, but a connection, nonetheless. I'm sure it will be understood in time.'

He rose from his chair, his manner suddenly friendly and buoyant. He took a step forward and clasped Bartoch by the shoulders. Bartoch winced.

'Thank you,' the man said. 'Well done. You're correct. Those two pieces of information *are* of interest to me.'

One hand relaxed its grip and patted Bartoch's shoulder, a gesture of appreciation if not quite affection.

'Now, let me think… The Council is meeting with the tenants soon, aren't they? When is that?'

'Tomorrow.'

The man took a step back and slowly folded his arms. He stared at Bartoch.

'I'm travelling to Venice early tomorrow for another matter which has suddenly gained significance,' he said. 'I'll be taking Tanaka with me.'

He turned, took two paces to one side and clasped his hands together. 'This is coming together nicely.'

Turning sharply to face Bartoch, he pointed at him.

'*You* will take care of Mount Sinai this evening and accompany me in the morning. I'll give you some documents to read, and I'll arrange for you to attend the meeting with the aunt. Find out what she knows, if anything, about the object we seek. Find out if she's a player or a pawn.'

'*Me*, Your Eminence? I don't usually leave the Vatican… Surely, Mr Bowers…'

'*You*, Bartoch. You are one of the few people I can trust who know enough about this matter and the people involved to be able to do what I ask. I would certainly not trust Mr Bowers with such information.'

'Of course, Your Eminence,' Bartoch conceded, but he still hesitated.

'Something more?' The man's face hardened and his good humour faded.

'Do you want me to try to discover the whereabouts of Madeleine Galli and the others through her aunt?'

'No. That would be clumsy and unnecessary.'

The man smiled, which took Bartoch by surprise. It was not one of his common expressions.

'*You* may not know where these people are right now,' the man said, 'but, thanks to you, I know where one of them *will* be and, as I've said before – if I have *one*, the others will follow.'

CHAPTER SEVENTEEN

Meeting the Council of Venice…

Monday 10:20 am

The Council offices where the tenant meetings were to be held were on the fifth floor of a building in the San Polo district across the Rialto Bridge.

Madeleine and Claudia had arranged to meet Logan in the foyer. As he had when he had picked her up from the Hotel Moresco on Friday evening, Logan arrived precisely at the agreed time of ten-twenty.

Madeleine introduced her aunt to Logan, and Claudia's eyes flicked between the pair, trying to deduce the actual relationship. It took her some time to accept Madeleine's assurances that Logan was just 'a friend' she had met on Friday who may be able to help when dealing with the representatives of the Council of Venice.

Logan saw a woman whose age was difficult to determine. Claudia's face retained a youthful appearance, fortyish, but that was betrayed somewhat by a touch of white in the hair at her temples, so maybe closer to fifty. The familial resemblance to Madeleine was unmistakable, especially her bright sparkling eyes which were the same striking emerald colour. Crinkle lines at the corners of her eyes and mouth provided physical evidence of an ordinarily bubbly, jovial nature, which, today, was understandably subdued.

'Thank you for supporting me,' Claudia said to Logan, '…for taking the time out from your busy day.'

'You may be helping me as much as I'm helping you,' replied Logan.

Claudia smiled, thinking he was just being gracious. 'Thank you, dear.'

Logan returned the smile. 'Do you know when your building is due to be demolished?' he asked.

'Oh, they've already started,' said Claudia.

Logan looked at her in surprise.

'I went to the apartment this morning,' she said, 'just to see my home one more time, and there were two big excavators in the square and a crew of people in bright orange vests. A man told me that the site will be cleared today.'

Logan and Madeleine shared a glance.

'They aren't wasting any time,' said Logan. He checked his watch. 'Speaking of time…' he said.

They started walking across the foyer.

'Madeleine told me the Council said in a letter to you they were going to present an offer at this meeting,' said Logan. 'Do you know what it is?'

'No,' said Claudia, shrugging her shoulders, her features tense now that the meeting was imminent. 'I've no idea.'

Madeleine gave Claudia a concerned glance, noticing her worried look. Her aunt caught the glance and put on a brave face, taking them both firmly by the elbows and directing them toward the elevators.

'Into the lion's den then, shall we?' she said.

THE TWO MEN looked like clones, at least as far as their attire was concerned. They wore a similar shade of grey suit, white shirt, and blue tie and had identical thick-rimmed glasses. But there was one startling difference, and that was height. One man, the only one who had spoken so far, was taller than the other by a head. It wasn't that he was particularly tall, rather that his companion was exceedingly short. Madeleine estimated that the man would be under five feet. She would be surprised if his shoes were touching the floor.

When Madeleine entered the room, the two men were already seated. They both registered surprise when three people walked through the door, the short man especially so. They must have been expecting only Claudia to attend the meeting.

The tall man stood to greet them and, with a wave of his hand, indicated the chairs opposite. He introduced himself as *Signore* Machiavi, which sounded uncomfortably close to 'Machiavelli'. Madeleine responded by introducing herself and Claudia, but when she mentioned Logan's name, he stopped her before she could say his surname and said: 'Just Logan will be fine.' His smile was friendly, an attempt to be informal, but Madeleine saw there was a deeper reason.

Signore Machiavi did not bother to introduce the other man. When Madeleine glanced at the unnamed man, she was puzzled by his expression. She captured it in her mind and considered it as she sat down. The man had not recognised them when they entered, of that she was sure, but now he was pleased, almost smug as if he'd won a bet. Had he heard one of their names before?

Once they were all seated, *Signore* Machiavi stated that the meeting was to answer any questions the occupants of the building may have, and to present a generous offer from the Council. He indicated a folder on the table in front of Madeleine, which he said contained information for the tenant. He made a specific reference to the fact that the building was owned by the Council and was on Council land.

At Madeleine's request, he agreed to conduct the meeting in English.

'Before we start,' said Madeleine, 'can I ask why you requested this meeting with only my aunt and not with all of the tenants?'

'We consider these meetings private and confidential. Each tenant needs to make their own choices.'

Signore Machiavi's English was precise, his words clipped, but his eyes betrayed that he didn't believe those words. The statement was plausible, thought Madeleine, but a more likely reason was to divide and conquer. Or was she being cynical?

Facing Madeleine, Claudia, and Logan across a long boardroom table that could easily have accommodated twenty people, the two officials from the Council were seated in the centre of the table. The room was opulent, almost gaudy, with wood-panelled walls, the floor covered in a thick red carpet, tall glass windows featuring red velvet drapes, and three ornate matching chandeliers. The table was wide, too wide to comfortably shake hands across, and was made of an intricately-grained wood varnished to such a high sheen that Madeleine was worried that if she touched it, she would leave a mark.

The setup was deliberately confrontational and designed to intimidate. To Madeleine, however, it was a commonplace scene, one she had encountered during innumerable inter-company negotiations. She was as comfortable at this table as at her kitchen table at home. She smiled reassuringly at Claudia and received a trusting smile in return.

'Very well,' said Madeleine. 'We do have a few questions.' She looked directly at *Signore* Machiavi and was rewarded by a momentarily uncomfortable reaction which reinforced her interpretation that he had expected a meeting with one person, a mild and compliant tenant, and not three people willing to ask questions.

'My aunt says she saw no cracks or any other evidence of subsidence,' Madeleine continued. 'Do you have a report detailing the extent of the alleged subsidence and, specifically, the location?'

Machiavi reacted to the word 'alleged' but chose not to challenge it.

'The location is unimportant now,' he said. 'The building is being demolished as we speak because it is unsafe. The safety of our tenants is very important.'

'I understand that, but is there a report available that details the original problem?'

'A report? Yes, an engineer's report was prepared, and it should be in the folder in front of you. You can take the folder when you leave.'

That was a lie. He knew there was no such report in the folder. He was hoping she wouldn't bother to look. Madeleine tapped twice on the wooden arm of her chair with her finger.

'Good,' said Madeleine. 'Please allow me a moment while I find the report.'

Madeleine opened the manila folder. Machiavi flicked his eyes at his companion but did not receive a response.

There were several documents in the folder. Madeleine found two copies of the notice of intention to demolish the building, both the public notice and the one sent privately to the four occupants. There was a report of the subsidence problem facing Venice – a magazine article, not a scientific paper. There was no engineer's report.

Madeleine looked up at him, the unspoken question on her face.

'Somebody has made a mistake,' Machiavi said, matter-of-factly, not in the least perturbed by the fact that the report was not in the folder. 'It should have been included. I'll have a copy mailed to you.'

Another lie. The report didn't exist. Either he would make one up, or he would forget he offered to send it. His evasion confirmed that the subsidence was just an excuse to demolish the building.

Madeleine said: 'Thank you, I'd appreciate that.'

She decided to push the point a little further and said: 'In the absence of the report, do *you* know where subsidence has been detected?'

'Unfortunately, not.' His smile was cold. 'I'm not an engineer.'

Under the guise of fiddling with her pen while taking a moment to think, Madeleine spelt out 'L-i-e N-o R-e-p-o-r-t' to Logan with her fingers.

She looked at Machiavi. 'Your letter said the Council intends to rebuild at that location.'

'Yes,' said Machiavi. 'A new and modern block will be built with the latest amenities. The present tenants will be offered a new apartment in the building. What's more, each tenant will be able to choose their apartment décor. This is the offer I spoke of earlier. I think you'll agree; it's very generous.'

Madeleine leaned forward. 'Of course, as compensation for the considerable inconvenience they will suffer, I trust the tenants will also be offered an unchanged rental with a guarantee of no increase for a reasonable period.'

Machiavi looked uncomfortable. 'I'm not sure about that. We would need to discuss any such arrangement with…'

A knock on the table interrupted Machiavi. The man beside him nodded.

So, thought Madeleine, the small man *is* in charge.

Machiavi swallowed. 'What period did you have in mind?' he asked.

'Five years seems reasonable to me,' said Madeleine.

The man laid three fingers on the table.

Before Machiavi could speak, Madeleine said: 'Yes, three years would be acceptable.'

A frown betrayed Machiavi's momentary anger at being a bystander in the exchange, but he swallowed and forced himself to smile.

'*Signora* Galli will be offered the apartment at her current rental, guaranteed for three years.'

'And that would of course apply to the other tenants as well.'

Machiavi's eyes narrowed and his body tensed. He was ready to resist any further off-the-cuff concessions.

'Of course,' he said. The phrase 'through gritted teeth' came to Madeleine's mind.

In the following pause, Logan said: 'Have you engaged a builder or developer to do the rebuild?'

Machiavi glanced to his left at the man sitting beside him. He received a nod from the man.

'Yes, we have,' he said.

'Can you tell me the name of the company involved?'

Again, a glance. This time, there was a hesitation, then, again, a nod.

'The company is *Stella di Mattino Construzione* – Morning Star Construction,' said Machiavi.

From the corner of her eye, Madeleine saw Logan's eyes, which had been gazing straight ahead while he listened, flick to look at Machiavi.

Machiavi didn't notice. He continued: 'The company has proven experience and a solid reputation, and, once the foundations have been inspected and strengthened, Morning Star is prepared to finance the re-construction in return for an interest in the building ownership.' He smiled to himself. 'That's the reason we were able to get this project underway without delay. The Council alone would have taken…'

He broke off as the man on his left turned his head sharply to look up at Machiavi, a frown on his face. Machiavi had evidently divulged too much information. Madeleine wondered if the short man was from Morning Star Construction.

Logan continued as if he hadn't noticed. 'Can you tell me the name of the principal of Morning Star Construction?'

'That information is not available,' said Machiavi curtly.

'I see.' Logan changed tack. 'The inspection and strengthening of the site,' he said, 'who will be doing that – the same engineers who detected the subsidence? If so, can you tell us *their* name?'

'That work will be done under Council supervision, and we will ensure it fully complies with our building code. Who is contracted for this work is of concern to the Council only.'

Logan nodded as if he had expected this answer. When he sat back, Claudia spoke up. 'I've lived in my apartment now for twenty years. It's my home, which I was forced to leave. What if I don't like the new apartment?'

'*Signora* Galli, your building was eighty years old – it was showing its age. Your new apartment will be modern. A modern bathroom, a larger kitchen, new carpets, drapes, and light fittings, most of which you can choose. I'm sure you will like it.'

'I liked my old apartment,' said Claudia stubbornly, folding her arms.

Machiavi was unmoved. He waited a moment and said: 'Do you have any more questions?'

'I have three,' said Madeleine. 'Firstly, I understand demolition has already begun. How long will it take to demolish the building, and how long will the rebuilding take?'

'The last of the tenants was relocated over the weekend. I understand your possessions have been stored *Signora* Galli – satisfactorily, I hope – and you are staying with a friend, is that correct?'

Claudia nodded.

'Good. The demolition began this morning, and it will take most of the day. The new building will be ready for occupancy in five months. We will keep you fully informed.'

'You've moved very quickly, haven't you?' said Madeleine. 'Claudia couldn't see any evidence of the subsidence, no cracks or tilting; there seemed to be no imminent danger. So that leads me to my third question – why the rush?'

'Rush?' said Machiavi, a little flustered by the question, 'Ah… there's no reason to wait… Morning Star wants access…'

The short man interrupted him.

'Sometimes, it's what you *can't* see that's important,' he said in a soft voice. 'We're not rushing. We're simply being efficient.'

OUTSIDE THE COUNCIL BUILDING, Claudia couldn't wait to tell her neighbours the 'good news'.

'I'll call *Signora* Messini, and she'll tell the others. Thank you so much, my dear, I could never have done that myself. I said we were walking into the lion's den, but I didn't think I was bringing a lioness with me.' Claudia giggled. 'I'm sure they were about to increase our rent just before this affair started. It's such a relief to be certain of no increase now for three years. Pity he didn't accept five, but no matter. And a new apartment! I didn't say anything in *there*, but my old apartment *was* looking tired – it needed new curtains and the carpet was quite worn. Oh, I can't thank you enough, but I must go. I've got so much to do now. I'll call you later, dear.'

'No. Remember, I lost my phone,' said Madeleine. 'I'll call you.'

'OK, call me tomorrow and tell me how the… the…'

'The symposium?'

'Yes, the symposium. I'm sure you'll do fine. But call me and tell me how it went.'

Madeleine nodded and Logan said: 'Claudia, did your building have a basement?'

Claudia frowned at the unexpected question. 'Yes. Why do you ask?'

'Were there any seepage problems, at high tide perhaps?'

'Oh, it was nothing. You got used to it.' Claudia said. She waited for him to elaborate, but Logan just smiled.

'Thank you,' he said.

Claudia dismissed the thought with a shake of her head. Resuming her interrupted air of happiness, she said to Madeleine: 'We'll arrange for a time for you to visit me in Ravenna.'

Madeleine nodded and leaned in to give her aunt a kiss on the cheek. Claudia turned and walked away with a purposeful stride. Logan and Madeleine watched her cross the street. She glanced back and waved gaily.

'I'm glad she's happy with the arrangements,' said Logan, 'but five months is a long time to wait.'

'She'll enjoy being with her friend in Ravenna. They get on well. It'll be like a holiday, and she should be in the apartment before the worst of winter.'

They started walking back towards the Rialto bridge.

'When I applied to the Council for permission to explore the foundations of the *Arsenale*,' Logan said, 'I presented my reasons as archaeological. In the meeting, I stopped you before you mentioned my surname because I didn't want it to ring any alarm bells. I was hoping Machiavi and the other man were only involved in the demolition and reconstruction of Claudia's building and weren't aware of my interest in what's underneath. In essence, I hoped the left hand of the Council didn't know what the right hand was doing.' He shrugged light-heartedly, then became serious. 'But the other man's last remark makes me now think otherwise. Is he aware that something may be buried beneath Claudia's building? What could you tell from his words?'

'The sentence about 'what you can't see' was deliberately ambiguous, and he was pleased with his guile. He didn't expect us to understand the hidden meaning. Machiavi didn't show any understanding of another meaning, though, so he's not in the picture.' She paused. 'But there may be more to it. The small man *knew* us. Or he recognised one of our names, at least. So, I would say there's a good chance he's aware of your interest.'

'Very well,' said Logan. 'We should assume he is. If they're already knocking down the building, my application is academic anyway. I won't get approval to explore beneath the foundations now.'

He walked a few steps in silence, then said: 'I need to talk to the people doing the demolition. I want to ensure they finish clearing the debris from the site late enough in the day so that any official inspection of the foundations cannot happen before tomorrow. Meanwhile, we can explore the site tonight.'

'If you're thinking of using the power to achieve that, wouldn't that be close to using it for self-interest?'

'I'm not against using the power for self-interest, just against using it to manipulate or disadvantage innocents. I will certainly promote my own self-interest when others are trying to do harm to me or mine.'

He smiled at her. 'However, I may not need to use the power. The towers and the old fortifications are part of the historical heritage of Venice. There could be many reasons why a cautious approach to this demolition might be warranted. If a delay is necessary, I may just suggest one or two.'

'Your suggestions are sometimes more than suggestions.'

'Sometimes,' he said enigmatically, 'and sometimes not.'

'By the way,' she said, 'you reacted when Machiavi mentioned the name of the construction company. Have you heard of Morning Star before?'

'No,' replied Logan. 'But I suspect I know who runs that company.'

'From the company name?'

'Yes. It may be another coincidence, but the Latin name for the planet Venus, also known as the Morning Star, is *Lucifer*.'

He nodded as Madeleine stared at him.

'I'll go to the site this afternoon. In the meantime, I'll ask Serene to get me some items I'll need tonight.'

'What do you need? Can I get them?'

'Thank you, but obtaining some of the equipment will require assistance from Sir Brian,' said Logan. 'I'll need night vision goggles, specialised digging equipment, and a top-of-the-range metal detector.' He thought for a moment. 'And we should be prepared to work in water, so we'll need appropriate clothing.' He saw her frown and added: 'I'm not talking about underwater gear, but we may be standing in waist-deep water.'

He took Madeleine's arm to move her in front of him to pass a large group of chattering tourists taking up most of the narrow street.

'Also,' he continued, when they could walk side-by-side again, 'I think it will be a worthwhile investment to buy a good laptop for Tricola.'

He pointed to an open-air café on the street beside the Rialto Bridge.

'Let's get a coffee, and I'll call the apartment.'

It was a popular location and they had to wait ten minutes before being served. Madeleine led the way into the crowded courtyard, saying: 'I'll find a table. I'm good at this.'

Logan laughed. 'The best I've ever seen.'

Madeleine sipped her espresso while Logan conveyed his requirements to Serene. After completing the list, he listened for a while and then finished the call.

'That's interesting…' he said.

'What is?'

'Serene's man watching Lucifer's big house has reported that he thinks everyone left last night. The place has been locked up. He hasn't seen any movement around the house or grounds this morning. He thinks the house is empty.'

'Closed down for a summer break?'

'Perhaps, but rather coincidental, isn't it. It's abandoned just as we learn its whereabouts. Someone – is it Lucifer? – always seems to be one step ahead of us.'

CHAPTER EIGHTEEN

Theatre Minerva, Venice…

Bartoch did not like this huge, sprawling building.

The inadequate lighting, often only a single bulb located sparingly, surrounded him with dark corners. It felt like a cave, a cold place that smelled of stale air and dust – he wouldn't have been surprised to hear the sound of dripping water – an entirely alien environment compared to the clean, brightly-lit interiors to which he was accustomed. The bare floorboards amplified his footsteps which were accompanied by occasional echoes of creaking wood and, just then, the muffled but startling bang of a closing door somewhere in the distance. The corridors in this part of the building had unusual dimensions, the ceiling too high and the walls too close. They twisted and turned unnaturally, without a clear purpose, confusing his sense of direction.

Not normally claustrophobic, he nonetheless felt restricted and confined.

He hurried on, following the directions he'd been given, until he rounded a thick floor-to-ceiling curtain and, without warning, found himself standing on a large stage with neat, orderly rows of seating extending from the stage front, rising swiftly in a broadening arc until terminated by two huge balconies.

As theatres went, the auditorium was medium-sized, but the open space seemed vast after the maze of narrow corridors he had just traversed. The stage had been set up for a lecture or a speech with a large rostrum at the centre front. Bartoch stared over the empty seats, thankful he had not intruded on a lecture in progress. On impulse, he clapped his hands, but the noise was swallowed by the silence.

Bartoch turned on his heel. He knew he was now close to the room he sought, which, he'd been told, was behind the stage.

Twenty seconds later, he knocked on a door and was asked to enter.

'So the meeting is concluded,' the man stated before Bartoch had closed the door. 'Good. What did you discover about *Signora* Galli?'

'The *Signora* was accompanied by her niece, Madeleine Galli, and…' Bartoch left a dramatic pause, '…by Logan Milan.'

He was disappointed when his news produced only a slight rise of one eyebrow. He hurriedly continued: 'I agreed to some concessions regarding the rent and Milan asked about Morning Star Construction. It may have been an innocent enquiry or it may be more.'

Bartoch waited, but when the man only nodded, he continued: 'Also, progress in clearing the site is slower than planned. It will be completed today but probably around dusk.'

'So,' the man said quietly, 'we won't be able to inspect the site until the morning.'

'Yes, Your Eminence.'

'That is unfortunate, and… it leaves the area vulnerable.'

'Vulnerable?'

'Yes, Bartoch. The building no longer provides the protection it once did, and the site will therefore be exposed during the night. I think some contingency is warranted. Get Mr Bowers and his team here as soon as possible. Send the plane.'

'At once, Your Eminence. Do you think Milan will interfere?'

'I've told you before I'm not a patient man. Mr Milan's interference already deserves retribution, and I will attend to that in due course. My mind is focused on another task at the moment, but let me be clear – if Mr Milan intends to make a nuisance of himself at the eleventh hour by feebly trying to prevent me from retrieving the object I have invested so much time, expense, and effort to obtain – *that* I will not abide. My response will be extreme and final.'

CHAPTER NINETEEN

Race for the prize…

Tuesday 03:30 am

Four figures walked unhurriedly along the street that bordered the canal leading to the two towers guarding the entrance to the *Arsenale*.

At first glance, they could have been two couples returning from an evening at a restaurant or bar. The two men were carrying bags that looked like large sports bags, but that was not unusual. Perhaps they had been to a gymnasium. One oddity, however, was that the contents of these bags seemed to weigh more than mere sports clothing, but many sports required equipment as well as clothing. Another was that all four wore heavy boots, those of the men extending up to their calves, but even that choice was not unknown among partygoers of both sexes while frequenting the nightspots of this city.

Even after a second glance, therefore, a casual observer may have turned away and continued on to his destination, curiosity satisfied and coat pulled tight against the light rain that had been falling since late afternoon.

But there was one who did not.

From a shadowed position between two buildings, a pair of eyes stared fixedly at the quartet through binoculars that cast a soft green glow around the edges. A phone was brought out from a pocket and, with the screen shielded behind a jacket lapel from the rain and unwanted observation, a number was entered, and the call button was pressed.

LOGAN HAD SUGGESTED that he, Nico, and Serene undertake the search of the apartment site with Madeleine and Tricola remaining in the *Insieme* apartment.

'You're giving your speech tomorrow,' he said to Madeleine. 'You'll want to be prepared and rested.'

But Madeleine had insisted that she be included.

'I'm prepared as I can be,' she argued, 'and I'm the only one with a legitimate claim to be at the site. My aunt lived in the building and if someone happens to question what we're doing, I can say we're searching for... a lost item of jewellery.'

Logan raised his eyebrows. 'In the dark?'

'Yes. Before rebuilding begins tomorrow.'

When he made no further comment, she quickly continued: 'Well... it's *just* plausible and better than nothing. Another set of eyes must be helpful, and surely I can at least be a lookout.'

Madeleine found herself amazed at her own words. She never thought she'd be suggesting she be the lookout for a semi-nefarious nocturnal activity. She hoped Logan didn't ask: '...looking out for what?'

Logan turned to Nico, who shrugged, then Serene, who nodded. 'It makes sense,' she said. 'And it's probably better if we appear to be two couples.' She winked at Madeleine. 'We can be lookouts together and let the men do the work.'

Tricola assured everyone she would be fine alone. 'I'll set up the laptop and start the search for the information you want. The structure of companies and their principals is a long way from the financial databases I'm used to, but I'll see what I can find. I don't expect company databases to be as well protected.'

'We need to be discreet,' said Logan.

Tricola pretended to be indignant. 'No one will know I've been looking.'

'Good,' said Logan. 'Find out who's at the top of Morning Star Construction, if you can. I'd like to confirm my suspicion. You'll probably find some attempt to hide that information.'

He smiled at Tricola's derisory snort, then glanced around. 'I suggest we four get a few hours sleep. I'd like to set out for the *Arsenale* entrance in the dead of night at three am.'

Resting a hand on Tricola's shoulder, he said: 'Don't stay up too late. While we're gone, don't answer the intercom or let anyone in. We should be back before morning. When you wake, don't go outside. We'll call you when we return and identify ourselves.'

FIVE STEPS UP FROM street level, Madeleine huddled with Serene on a red-tiled landing that formed the entranceway to the building adjacent to where Claudia's apartment had once stood. All that now remained of her aunt's apartment building was a hole in the ground that already resembled a muddy swimming pool. As soon as the solid basement walls had been removed, the ever-present water that Venice eternally tried to repel would have begun seeping into the unprotected vacant space. A small shelf of hardened earth surrounded the depression in the mud that defined the former basement of Claudia's apartment building.

The absence of the street light that had previously been attached to the missing building meant that the now vacant lot was cast in shadow and, with the rain becoming heavier, the two men standing in the excavated basement would be almost invisible to anyone crossing the square.

The covered entrance where they stood afforded an unobstructed view across the square to the canal and good protection from the rain. Logan and Nico were exposed to the rain, but they were unaffected by it, covered as they were from head to toe in one-piece wet-weather overalls, including a jacket and hood.

With their night-vision goggles, they looked to Madeleine like the frogmen from the black lagoon.

At that hour of the morning, there was no movement in the square. Other street lamps illuminated the square, but the rain fused the light they emitted into a hazy yellow glow which the surface water reflected, rendering all objects indistinct.

Nico and Logan waded, as Logan had foreseen, through water that alternated between knee-deep near the walls to thigh-deep in the centre, methodically traversing the ground from side to side with the metal detector. Logan was swinging the detector, his earphones protected from the elements by his hood, while Nico carried a spade in one hand and, in the other, a long rod sharpened at one end. Four small arms could be extended from the sharp end of the rod by the touch of a switch. A grappling rod, Logan had called it.

He explained that the rod could be pushed into the earth and the arms mechanically expanded to grasp small to medium-sized objects. It should be powerful enough to operate in the water-logged muddy soil that supported the city of Venice.

FORTY MINUTES LATER, they had crisscrossed the whole basement area, obviously without locating the object they sought. They put their heads close together for a brief discussion and then waded back to the centre of the hole. Logan began to turn in circles, moving outwards in a careful spiral one step at a time, pausing periodically when he and Nico would huddle over the display screen to check a variation in the signal from the detector.

As Madeleine peered into the gloom of the misty night, they stopped again. Both men were bent over the detector, focusing intently on the dial. Logan's hand was pressed against his head, tightening the headphone against his ear. He waved his hand, indicating a direction.

They moved a half-step.

Behind Madeleine, there was the sound of a door opening.

'I'm sorry,' she said, automatically apologising, stepping to one side and turning. Two people stood framed in the open door with another man behind them. A big man. 'We were just sheltering…'

She stopped because she realised she was speaking in English, which might not be understood.

Then she remained silent because she recognised the men.

A small movement, and Madeleine heard an electrical buzzing sound that was terrifyingly familiar. She automatically tried to twist away from the door but felt an intense pain radiating from her shoulder that stopped her breath. Her body arched backwards in a spasm, her hands clenching. She heard the buzzing sound repeated. Her legs collapsed. One shoulder hit the wall of the entrance, and she slid down the wall onto the tiled landing, her limbs rigid. There was a scuffling sound behind her, out of sight; the sound of another body falling. Serene.

A gag was being wrapped around her mouth. Immensely powerful rough hands pulled her arms behind her, and she felt a plastic tie once again pull her wrists together. Her legs were similarly bound. She tried to resist, but her head felt dazed and fuzzy and her muscles would not respond to her commands.

There was a cry of pain from Serene and a giggle from the man Madeleine now knew to be Dopey.

Although her sprawled body was still on the landing, Madeleine's head and shoulders extended beyond the shelter provided by the building entrance. She could feel raindrops falling onto her face and spatting onto her open eyes. She couldn't blink – nothing seemed to be under her control. She stared into the night. Three-quarters of the water-filled basement was visible to her rain-washed eyes, and she watched in helpless horror as Dopey lowered himself into the pool and waded slowly and purposefully toward Logan and Nico, who were still hunched over the detector. They had their heads close together, probably discussing something the device had located. Madeleine could hear the different sounds the patter of the rain made on her face, on the steps, on the surface of the pool, and on the cobbled stone of the square. Within that rhythm, she could also hear the swish of Dopey's legs parting the water – surely Logan could hear that, too?

'You ladies will wait here…' said a voice Madeleine recognised as belonging to the man called Bowers '…and be thankful we have no instructions regarding *you* tonight.'

Two sets of legs came into view – Dax and Bowers, descending the steps. They walked to the edge of the hole and waited there, one with folded arms and one with hands on hips, obviously trusting that Dopey could achieve whatever was planned without their help. Madeleine wanted to cry a warning, but she doubted she could raise more than a croak even if she wasn't gagged. There was the sound of movement behind her. A body scraping on the tiles. Trying to move. Serene. Madeleine couldn't turn her head, couldn't move a limb. She marvelled that Serene was able to move at all after being zapped.

Dopey slowly but relentlessly advanced on Logan and Nico. He was five yards away when Logan and Nico acted strangely. Nico thrust his rod and spade into the ground, and they both straightened from their normal bent stance, each placing a hand on the other's shoulder as if providing mutual support. Were they just taking a rest? Was it possible they knew Dopey was behind them and this was a planned move? Madeleine had seen Nico in action and knew how capable he was, but against this giant of a man, she wondered if even he could prevail.

Logan lifted his hands to remove his night-vision goggles just as the huge man reached them. Shockingly, Madeleine knew then that Logan and Nico were completely unaware of his presence. They were still facing away from him when Dopey reached out, and, with his huge hands, he cupped their heads and cracked them together. The sickening sound reminded Madeleine of a watermelon being broken by a mallet.

Dopey lowered his hands so that one encircled Logan's neck and the other Nico's, catching them before they could fall, holding them both easily despite their bulky wet-weather clothing. He leaned forward and, with his massive weight, bore both men down, thrusting their heads under the water, moving his legs apart and steadying himself to hold them in that position.

Madeleine screamed, but she heard nothing more than a gurgle. Bowers and Dax exchanged a few words and then watched impassively from the edge of the basement hole as the seconds ticked past.

Madeleine felt a tug on her legs from behind, then a sawing motion rocked her bound feet back and forth. Serene was somehow working at the tie around Madeleine's legs.

Madeleine focussed intently on the scene in the pool, her eyes piercing through the dim light. Horrified, she saw the water around Dopey was churning, evidence of both men struggling beneath the surface. After only a few seconds, the water above Logan's position went alarmingly still. Surely, he hadn't succumbed so quickly. Nico's hand briefly rose out of the water, twisting around behind his neck to try and pry a finger loose, but his purchase must have been poor, and the giant was too strong. He didn't seem affected. There was a flurry of splashes around Dopey's legs, Nico was trying to kick him, but the attack had no effect; Dopey simply adopted a wider stance and the splashing ceased.

Madeleine screamed again, trying to distract Dopey. Her body contorted with the effort. Suddenly, her legs were free, and one leg slipped off the top step of the landing. She teetered on the edge for a moment, her body threatening to tumble down the steps before she used her other leg to pull herself back from the brink. She twisted her hips and drew her legs up. Could she stand? With that movement, she felt a sharp pain at the back of her leg. Had she pulled a muscle? No, she realised… Serene had kicked her! Of course. Stop moving.

With her legs free, Madeleine wanted to get up and run at Dopey, distract him somehow. Or run for help. Both options were probably futile, but she had to do *something*. Against all her instincts, she obeyed Serene and kept still, her eyes riveted on the struggle in the middle of the pool. She felt her hands now being tugged as if something was working at that tie.

A full minute that seemed like an hour passed before Nico's struggles also ceased and the water was menacingly still. Dopey waited, continuing to bear his weight down into the water. Then he slowly stood up. He stretched his back and stared down, searching the surface of the water. For what? Movement, perhaps, or for bubbles?

Madeleine felt drained, exhausted, unable to move even if she wanted to, her tears mixing freely with the rain on her face. The tie binding her hands was still being worked on and she felt a series of sharp pains as something scratched her skin; Serene had not given up her efforts, but Madeleine no longer cared. It was all too late.

Satisfied, Dopey turned away from the watery gravesite and waded quickly to where Bowers and Dax were standing. They both leaned forward to help him out of the pool. There was a short conversation. Even over the noise of the rain and the sobs coming from her own throat, Madeleine heard their words. Dax asked Bowers if they should now search the pool, but Bowers replied that wasn't their job. He'd waited long enough, he said, for Milan to find the object, but Milan had failed. It was up to the Magician now. Dopey pointed towards Madeleine and Serene, and Madeleine's heartbeat quickened, but Bowers shook his head.

'We've stopped Milan, so we've done what we came to do. Without Milan they're no threat. Best we leave quickly.'

Madeleine watched them hurry across the square. As they reached the corner of the square, she thought she saw a movement in a doorway. She blinked but when she looked again all was still. She let her eyes close. Until now, she didn't think she had blinked once since she'd been stunned and the relief to have her eyes closed and protected was intense. She felt the tension and stiffness draining from her body which became unusually warm. Probably a similar reaction to shock, she thought distractedly.

Suddenly, her hands were free and with that freedom she was immediately energised. Her fingers tugged at her gag, twisting it back and forth until she worked it out of her mouth. She turned to face Serene, reaching out for the tie around Serene's wrists.

Serene screamed, a hoarse sound through her gag, her eyes wide with urgency, and Madeleine roughly pulled the gag from Serene's mouth.

'No!' Serene shouted. 'Leave me. Get them out of the water! Logan will have slowed his heart rate. He may still be alive. Get him out first. Nico… I'm afraid… will not…'

Madeleine didn't wait to hear more. She leapt down the steps and splashed into the pool, heedless of any danger hidden beneath the surface. She gasped at the chill of the water. Flailing her arms and legs, she pushed her way through, fighting against the drag of her clothing. She reached the centre and thrust her hands into the muddy liquid. A moment of panic when she couldn't feel anything, widening her search area, and then she touched an arm, grasped hold of the rough clothing, and with all her strength, hauled it upwards. Nico's head broke the surface, his goggles still covering his eyes, the water streaming from his ashen face. His hood had fallen from his head and it was filled with water, adding to his weight. She remembered Serene's words: 'Get Logan first. He has a chance.' But she couldn't just drop Nico back into that foul water. Desperately, she started to drag him towards the edge. She got him moving but, even with the buoyancy afforded by the water, his body felt like it was weighed down with stones.

She reached the edge of the pool and cast frantically around for someone to help her. She cried into the night, an unintelligible sound, but she was alone. Alone, dragging a dead body and another that she had probably condemned to drown by choosing to take Nico first.

Miss Emily, I need your strength now, thought Madeleine, bending down to pull Nico's arm across her back. With all the strength of her arms, she clamped onto Nico's cold hand as she straightened her legs and twisted her back to raise him out of the water and manoeuvre him onto the earthen rim of the hole. She wasn't sure she could do it, but her determination drove her. His body slumped onto the edge and threatened to fall back, but she arrested that movement, pushing against him and screaming at him: 'No, no, *no!*' — heaving until he rolled onto his back and was stable.

He needed someone to start CPR on him immediately, but Logan's need was greater. Logically, she knew there was a better chance of one living if she concentrated on just one. By trying to save both, she may lose both. The logic was undeniable, but she couldn't follow it. She simply could not abandon either man.

Madeleine turned back to the dark pool and was momentarily disoriented. She wasn't viewing the basement hole from the same perspective and she took a second or two to locate the place where Logan should be. Her heart almost stopped when she saw the shape of a man standing in the pool.

Dopey had come back!

She took an involuntary step back before she realised it was the rod and spade Nico had placed there, calling like a beacon, marking Logan's location.

She frantically pushed through the water to the spot and reached into the depths, twisting about as her hands found nothing, but then, as before, she brushed clothing. Her fingers fastened onto the jacket and she hauled with all her strength but the clothing slipped from her grip and she lurched backwards. Her feet went from under her and she tumbled into the water, which eagerly closed over her head. She felt the slimy filth entering her nose, her boots scrambling in the muddy earth, her arms waving desperately to find purchase in the murky water and push her head back to the surface.

She burst into the air with a gasp, spluttering and coughing, blowing the water from her nose and shaking her hair. She resisted a desire to pause and gather her wits and forced herself to stand up and move forward. She deliberately steadied her feet before again reaching beneath the surface. Her fingers recoiled as they brushed the hair on Logan's head but she recovered and grabbed for the hood of his jacket, hauling him up. Holding the hood high so his head was out of the water, she backed towards the edge, dragging his lifeless body behind her.

When her heels hit the edge of the hole, her breath was coming in painful gasps that she could feel rasping in her throat and lungs. Her legs felt like lead, and her arms were quivering with fatigue. She knew she would not be able to get Logan out of the hole alone. She twisted her head, scanning the square. Was there anybody who could help? Since the time they had arrived, she had not seen a single person cross the square, but perhaps…

The empty square mocked her. Madeleine glanced towards the building where they had sheltered and was amazed to see a shape on the ground, a shape that was moving, inching across the pavings of the square. It was Serene, still bound, squirming like a trussed worm towards her.

Should she go to Serene and free her so they could both get Logan out of the water? How long would that take? Too long. She knew that seconds counted.

Also, just as with Nico, Madeleine could not let Logan's body drop back into the water while she went to Serene. She had no choice. She had to give it her best shot.

With that sober realisation, she felt her determination return like a second wind. She moved her grip from his hood to his shoulder and lifted Logan, bending to get her back under his arm. He should have been lighter than Nico, but if anything he felt heavier, or maybe she was wearier. She knew she only had the strength for one attempt, so she'd better make it good.

With a scream worthy of an Irish Banshee, she put every ounce of effort she had into straightening her legs and twisting her shoulders to literally throw Logan onto the bank. She felt the muscles of her neck tighten and cramp. When his body hit the bank, she gathered his legs and thrust them upwards, screaming again, her desperation lending her the extra ounce of strength she needed. She leaned against him to prevent him from falling back, gasping for air and spitting out the water that entered her mouth with every breath – so weak from the effort that her trembling legs threatened to crumble at any moment. Her arms couldn't maintain the pressure of trying to hold him on the edge; she could feel the strength ebbing from them. She fell forward onto her elbows, but Logan didn't move and she realised he was safe.

No time to lose. The next step was to start CPR. Madeleine summoned a reserve of energy from somewhere, clambered up the bank and collapsed on the edge, her body heaving as lungs and heart struggled to get oxygen to her starved muscles. She cannot rest. No time to rest. She closed her eyes and lurched herself onto her knees with an effort that left her dizzy just as a strange sound came from nearby. A cough.

Logan had coughed. He coughed again.

Madeleine's eyes snapped open. Logan was on his side, on the edge of the pool, in imminent danger of falling back into the water. She reached out and dragged at his jacket, pulling him a few more inches toward safety.

'Nico…' he croaked. 'Help him. Please…'

Madeleine stifled a cry in her throat and, scrambling to where Nico lay, she wrenched the grotesque night-vision goggles from his face. He wasn't breathing. His face was a ghostly white in the lamplight but, with a silent thank-you to her acute eyesight, she noted his lips were not yet blue. She felt at his neck. There was no pulse. With muddy fingers, she opened his mouth and checked that he had nothing inside, then tilted his head back, pinched his nose and pushed two quick breaths into his lungs, feeling his chest rise and fall. His lips were wet and startlingly cold. There was mud and dirt in her own mouth, and she tried to generate saliva to spit it out. Madeleine ripped open his jacket and placed the heel of one dirt-caked hand on his sternum above the heart. She placed the other hand on top and began chest compressions, counting aloud: 'One, two, three….'

When her count reached thirty, she again gave him two breaths, then resumed the count from one.

Time stopped. All the world consisted of thirty compressions followed by two breaths; repeat.

Her actions became automatic and, despite her concentration on the rhythm, other thoughts entered her mind. She pictured their magical voyage along the canals with Nico singing *Santa Lucia,* a song that will always be *his* song. She remembered his grace of movement. Twenty-nine, thirty. Time for two breaths.

Her fatigue hovered over her, pressing like a heavy weight from above, but she refused to let it take over. She'd locked her arms straight to do the compressions, and she knew if she relaxed them now, relaxed any part of her, she would collapse.

Serene was at her shoulder. Logan had freed her. 'Madeleine, I can't help you. That big bastard dislocated my thumb. I'm sorry.'

Madeleine nodded her head. 'That's OK.' She wasn't sure whether she said the words aloud or just thought them.

Thirty and two. Repeat. Thirty and two.

She heard Serene's voice again, but the message didn't register until it was repeated.

'Madeleine… Can you hear me? It's been ten minutes. I think….'

She tuned out the rest. Ten minutes? No, it had only been two or three, surely.

Thirty and two.

ShangWu's words came to her. 'It would be a crime and a waste if Nico wasn't trained.' *Well*, she thought, *it would certainly be a waste if he didn't live.* She looked down at his face, so pale. It jerked slightly with each of her compressions. She really did want to hear his voice again.

Thirty and two.

She was no longer counting aloud, just counting to herself. It didn't matter if the outside world knew what number she was up to. Only she needed to know.

There was silence now. There had been silence for a long time. The rain had stopped. When had that happened? Madeleine didn't know – couldn't spare the time to think about it.

'Huh!' She barked a grunt of amusement. Some lookout she'd turned out to be. First time on the job, and look what had happened. What was the count?

Thirty and two. Thirty and two.

Serene's voice again. Softly in her ear, a hand on her shoulder. Caring. 'Madeleine, it's over. It's been too long. He's gone. You're wasting your time. We've called for a water ambulance.'

In time with her counting, so she didn't lose the count, Madeleine said: 'Serene, you *don't* under*stand*. I have *all* the *time* in the *world*. And I *won't* give *up* on *him*. I *won't* give *up* on *him*.'

Two breaths. Start again at one.

Serene had asked her to stop, but why? Had she given a reason why? Madeleine couldn't remember the actual words Serene had said. She tried to focus on the question but still could not think of a reason to stop. Her counting kept interrupting her thinking. It was so arbitrary, choosing a time to stop. From a deep recess of her mind, something told her that her thoughts were becoming irrational.

Twenty-nine, thirty.

She was continually flicking her head to keep water out of her eyes. Was it raining again? No, not rain. Although the night was cool, the sting of salt told her it was sweat from her forehead.

'Damn you, Nico,' she said to him, bending to give him the breaths that were due, trying to push the life back into him, from her mouth to his. 'Don't you *dare* leave us. You come *back*, you hear me!'

She leaned on his chest with renewed vigour, her shoulders protesting with red-hot pain.

'*Damn* you *two*,' she cried out loud. '*Damn* you *four*, *damn* you *six*…' She worried about breaking a rib. But what did that matter now? She felt the tears on her face mixing with the sweat and her voice broke. '*Damn* you *eight*,' she said, through a sob. '*Damn* you…'

Nico's chest moved. Against her push. Resisting. He coughed. From a long way away, Madeleine heard Serene's voice. 'Oh, my God…' Then she was there, rolling Nico onto his side as Madeleine fell back on her heels, exhaustion washing over her in physical waves, her arms and shoulders on fire and her body shaking uncontrollably.

Nico coughed again, violently, water oozing from his mouth and nose. He shuddered and sucked in air.

THE GREEN GLOW increased momentarily as the glasses were lowered and held by one hand while the other fumbled for the phone. Again, the screen was shielded while numbers were entered, but the thumb paused before entering the last digit. Siska knew her news would not be received well. In her experience, the bearer of bad news sometimes bore the brunt of the blame, and she seemed to attract blame like a jam jar attracts wasps. Reluctantly, she hit the last digit. Not to report what she had seen would undoubtedly result in a worse outcome. Much worse.

She waited for the call to be picked up. She hoped she would not be asked to do something drastic. What could she do? She had no gun. Her task had been to observe and report if anyone showed an interest in the demolition site. She'd done that, and Mr. Bowers had taken over.

Wait and watch, she'd been told. Then, one of the women had somehow freed herself.

Her call was answered.

'What is it?' The voice was curt. The message clear: Why am I being disturbed?

She reported what she had seen.

Siska took the phone away from her ear and quickly covered the speaker with her finger as the tirade that issued from the phone was easily audible in the alleyway.

The sound of an approaching motorboat filled the ensuing silence, and Siska whispered urgently into the phone: 'Someone's coming,' shutting the phone off, pressing her body against the wall where the shadow was darkest as a searchlight illuminated the canal. She turned her face away from the water ambulance passing twenty feet from where she stood.

TWO PARAMEDICS ATTENDED to Nico, checking his responses, measuring his statistics and giving an opinion that his chest was only bruised, with no broken ribs. They announced he should recover fully and suffer no adverse lasting effects from his ordeal, the story of which had been considerably sanitised by Logan.

They insisted, however, that Nico and Serene be taken by the ambulance to the hospital to be assessed. Nico's chest and Serene's dislocation would need to be X-rayed.

WHILE WAITING FOR THE ambulance, Serene recounted their ambush by Bowers and the rescue of Logan and Nico by Madeleine. To Madeleine, Serene made her retrieval of the two men from the water sound much more heroic than it was.

Serene finished by saying to Logan: 'I thought it was just possible that *you* might survive. I know you can almost die at will, but… I honestly didn't think Nico had any chance.'

Madeleine thought of Serene as always in control and was surprised to see her eyes were wet with tears.

Logan reached out and put a hand on Serene's shoulder. 'I was dazed by the head knock when I was pushed underwater,' he said. 'After a few seconds, I knew I wouldn't be able to free myself from the grip on my neck, so I relaxed and slowed my heartbeat to use less oxygen. I can go without breathing in that state for around five minutes.'

He turned to Madeleine and touched her on the arm. He held the touch there for a moment, then said: 'However, it seems I was unconscious when you pulled me from the water. It took me a while to recover, and I'm sorry I wasn't able to help you. I owe you my life and also that of Nico. If I can ever repay that debt, I will.'

Nico stood up painfully, clutching his bruised chest. He laid an arm on Serene's shoulders and touched his head to hers. Then he crouched down beside Madeleine and gently enfolded her hands in his. He held them for a long moment.

'I was dead,' he said. 'You brought me back. I owe you my life. I thank you, and I won't forget.'

'There's no debt to pay,' Madeleine protested. 'What I did, any of you would have done and, anyway, I didn't do it alone. If Serene hadn't freed me….' She turned to Serene. 'How did you do that, by the way? You were as immobilised as I was, with one hand out of action.'

By way of answer, Serene moved her tongue in her mouth. A moment later, a small piece of dark metal protruded from her lips. It looked like a tiny razor blade.

Madeleine stared at her, incredulous. 'Are you telling me you always have that in your mouth?'

Serene nodded. With a flick of her tongue, the blade disappeared.

'But you were gagged… How did you manage…?'

'With difficulty,' Serene said.

Madeleine continued to stare. What sort of woman carried a blade in her mouth? For what profession would that be thought a good idea – a necessary item? She remembered Logan's description of Serene and her twin sister Selene as members of Sir Brian's organisation, probably some sort of intelligence operatives.

As much as she had learned over the past few days, she really didn't know the world in which Serene lived.

'And, for the record…' Serene said, 'I watched you and I didn't believe what I saw. You *did* do what you did alone. Your perseverance was simply incredible. You just would not quit. And I echo Logan – if I can repay you for your actions tonight….'

'Oh, please…' Madeleine pleaded. She looked toward the canal.

A second or so later, the others also turned as the sound of an approaching motorboat reached them.

'That'll be the water ambulance.'

TWENTY MINUTES LATER, Madeleine watched the ambulance disappear around the curve of the canal, the blue flashing light still visible for a few seconds, reflecting on the buildings bordering the canal and on the water surface. For a brief snatch of time, a moment before it disappeared completely, the revolving light caught on a piece of glass. Madeleine narrowed her eyes, but the area was now completely dark. Probably a window pane.

She stood up, her legs feeling shaky. She wasn't looking forward to the walk back to the apartment.

Logan said: 'Before we go, we need to collect what we've left in the hole.'

'Your digging tools?' asked Madeleine, frowning. 'Don't go back in there. Leave them. They'll only remind you of the night you nearly died.'

'I'm not speaking of the tools.'

'Oh, of course… the metal detector.'

'Not the detector either.'

Logan looked at Madeleine. In the dim light from the streetlamps, Madeleine saw an extra sparkle in his eye.

'We found it,' he said simply. 'The cylinder.' He smiled at her widening eyes and nodded. 'The detector confirmed it's made of gold. Nico has marked the spot with his rod. It's about two metres down. We just need to pluck it out.' He smiled. 'I know you're exhausted, and there'll be too much for two of us to carry. Once we've extracted our prize, I'll call for a water taxi.'

Madeleine took a moment to get her breath. Her relief that their struggle had not been in vain was briefly overwhelming.

'Good,' she said. 'I'll be happy to get away from this place. I need a shower desperately.'

SISKA WATCHED A MAN emerge from the water-filled hole carrying a strange-looking item.

Just as well she hadn't reported the two men dead when they'd been brought from the water. She'd been about to, but the woman who had dragged them out had tried to resuscitate one of them…

She focused on the item and recognised it as a metal detector. The man placed it on the edge of the hole beside the woman. Siska took a moment to check out the woman. She recognised her now; it was the tall one, the one Siska had stunned at the villa in the Dolomites. Her name was… she thought for a moment. Her name was Madeleine.

A moment ago, she was sure the woman called Madeleine had looked straight at her.

The man re-entered the water-filled hole and spent some time in the middle working with a long pole, then he bent to lift another object out of the water and slowly waded to the side. Siska peered at his face through the glasses. That was the man Mr Bowers had wanted covered in tape so he couldn't talk. Bowers referred to him as Milan. Somehow, Milan had tricked Dax, that idiot, and escaped from the castle. Siska hadn't received all of the blame for that, thank God. In fact, she'd derived considerable satisfaction from seeing Bowers so angry he could hardly speak.

Milan struggled up the bank with something cradled in his arms. Something that glinted in the yellow light. The woman rushed to help him with the object, which seemed heavy.

Siska lowered her glasses and cursed. She had no idea what the object was, but it looked important.

She had more bad news to report.

CHAPTER TWENTY

A cylinder of gold and an Egyptian myth…

Tuesday 8:00 am

Madeleine stood so the needles of scalding hot water streaming from the shower head were concentrated directly onto the knotted muscles of her right shoulder, attempting to ease the constant cramping she felt there. With a twist of her back, she gave similar relief to her neck and then to the other shoulder. She groaned with the pleasure and the pain of coaxing her body back to normal function.

She was tired but it was a physical fatigue, an ache that she knew would disappear with time. Mentally, she buzzed with an elation resulting from the tremendous challenge that had been overcome with everyone emerging alive and well… *reasonably* well. She wasn't ready for sleep.

She dried herself slowly but thoroughly, then curled her hair up and twisted the towel to form a turban on her head. She dressed just as slowly, her legs feeling stiff and the muscles of her arms and back protesting any extended movement, but her skin luxuriated in the feel of the smooth, clean garments. When she had finished dressing but still in bare feet, she padded from the bathroom into the bedroom, removing the turban and patting her hair dry as she walked. She sat at the mirror and brushed her hair in long smooth strokes, feeling the tightness in her body being relieved with each stroke.

Nico and Serene had arrived back from the hospital only minutes after Logan and Madeleine had entered the apartment. Nico had been ordered to rest, so Madeleine was surprised when she entered the hallway at the same time as Nico came from his room, struggling to get his arms into a shirt. She was about to say they must stop meeting in hallways like this, but her hand came to her mouth when she saw the extent of the bruising she had inflicted on his chest.

She started to apologise. 'Oh, my God! Nico, I'm so…'

He immediately stopped her.

'Please don't apologise for saving my life. You did what you had to do, and I'm grateful. These marks…' he looked down at the blue and purple welts, '…are a reminder of your dedication and, from my point of view, they will be far too temporary.'

ON ONE END OF THE dining table, a basket of bread rolls and a plate of salami and cheese shared a circular tablecloth with a large bowl of green grapes and an ornate silver coffee jug.

The gold cylinder, cleaned of mud and polished to a shine, lay, cushioned by a towel, in the centre of the dining table. The ends were symmetrically rounded giving it a double-ended bullet shape. The lights in the room reflected on its surface so that it seemed to glow of its own accord. It was much bigger than Madeleine had expected. Logan had announced it to be one and a half metres long and thirty centimetres in diameter, and if it was solid gold, it would be worth a fortune by itself. It seemed the wrong shape to house a manuscript, although she supposed the papyrus, or whatever the manuscript was written on, would be rolled into a scroll. She recalled the images she had seen of the interior of Ptolemy's Great Library of Alexandria. Ancient manuscripts were always rolled. Even so, the cylinder was still far too large to be just a repository for a manuscript or even a collection of writings such as the True Book of Thoth that Logan had described. He'd mentioned a talisman that he hoped might also be inside. Maybe that took up the bulk of the interior.

Madeleine was pleased the cylinder hadn't been opened yet.

Madeleine and Nico were the last to enter the room. Logan was talking with Serene on the oversized couch. He was holding his phone as if he had just finished a call. Serene's left hand was bandaged. Tricola lay on the floor in the pose Madeleine recognised as typical of teenagers, lying on her stomach with the laptop in front of her, typing quickly – a position that would be decidedly uncomfortable for anyone over twenty.

Madeleine caught the word 'Sami'.

'Good morning…' she said. 'Is there news of Sami?'

Serene and Logan both registered surprise that she had heard their conversation. Logan said: 'No. Sir Brian has a witness reporting some people being forced onto a plane at a rural airfield near Wädenswil, thirty kilometres from Zürich, but we've had no confirmation.'

'Let's hope it wasn't Sami and his wife,' said Madeleine. When Logan agreed by nodding, Madeleine walked towards the table and said: 'Thanks for waiting for us.'

She looked eagerly at Logan. When he didn't move, she inclined her head towards the table and the object lying on it whose attempted retrieval had so nearly had a fatal outcome.

'Are we going to see what's inside?'

Logan smiled and shook his head. 'I'm afraid we can't do that just yet. The cylinder should be opened in a controlled environment.' He held up his phone. 'Fortunately, the National Archaeological Museum is located close by on St Mark's Square. With Sir Brian's help, I've just arranged an appointment with Dr. Sciazori, an eminent Egyptologist at the museum. I'll deliver the cylinder to him this afternoon and it will be securely stored while he makes some preparations, then he'll examine the cylinder and X-ray it and, finally, open it and preserve any manuscripts or other objects found inside. He's excited by the opportunity and happy to have us present at the opening, which should be tomorrow about midday.'

Madeleine feigned disappointment. She walked to the table.

'Can I touch it?'

Nico stopped beside the food, picking up a bread roll and pulling the bread apart.

'Of course,' said Logan's voice behind her.

She reached out and rested her fingers on the cylinder. It was smooth and surprisingly warm.

'How does it open?'

'I couldn't see how to open it at first,' said Logan. 'But there's a hairline crack near the end by your left hand. You'll need to look carefully. I think that end will detach like a lid. But I'm sure Dr. Sciazori will know what to do.'

Madeleine ran her hands along the cylinder, marvelling that she was touching something possibly thousands of years old. The surface was unblemished, showing no sign of wear or deterioration.

'Why is it so big?'

Madeleine nodded her thanks to Nico when he handed her a fresh bread roll filled with cheese and salami. She was hungry. He indicated the grapes. Did she want some? She shook her head.

'I can only presume it's big enough to house whatever's inside,' Logan replied.

She turned to look at him. His expression said: *Well… you did ask.'*

She wrinkled her nose at him, took a bite of the roll and turned back to the cylinder.

'You said you hoped there was a talisman inside. What does this talisman do?'

Logan stood up and approached the table. Serene followed him. Tricola looked up from the floor but continued to type on the laptop's keyboard.

'Inside here...' Logan said, spreading his hand over the cylinder, his voice soft, almost reverent, '...as well as the True Book of Thoth, I hope to find the was-sceptre of Sekhmet.'

'The *what* of Sekhmet? – Sorry...' She apologised for talking with food in her mouth.

'The was-sceptre. It's spelt w-a-s.'

When she still looked puzzled, he said: '*Was* is the Ancient Egyptian word for power or dominion. So, a was-sceptre is a sceptre that both symbolised power and was itself a source of power. Many hieroglyphs of the gods feature them carrying was-sceptres. This particular sceptre should take the form of a staff with two prongs at the bottom and a canine head at the top. It will look like a walking stick.'

'What does it do, this was-sceptre?'

'It's possibly the most powerful talisman of them all. It augments the power of the spells in the Book of Thoth.'

'OK. I hope I'm not asking too many questions, but why is it called the was-sceptre of Sekhmet then and not the was-sceptre of Thoth?' She raised her hand as a memory came to her. 'Actually, at the hotel, when you were questioning the Colonel, you mentioned the name of Sekhmet when I told you about *Occhio di Ra*. You said it almost as if it were a curse.'

'Thoth just recorded the spells that Sekhmet used. The was-sceptre *belonged* to Sekhmet, who was also known as the Eye of Ra, specifically the Right Eye of Ra. And yes...' he nodded to Madeleine, 'I felt Sekhmet's influence at that moment.'

Madeleine furrowed her brow. That was a strange statement. Did Logan believe an ancient Egyptian goddess was influencing affairs today?

Logan regarded the people gathered at the table. Serene was looking as puzzled as Madeleine.

'All of this may become clearer,' he said, 'if I tell you an Egyptian myth.'

He waved towards the couch. Madeleine ran her finger along the cylinder one more time. What would it say if it were able to talk? Would it be the same story Logan was about to tell? She followed Nico to the couch.

'Does anyone want coffee?' said Logan, turning to sit down, crossing his legs. 'This won't take long, but we may as well be comfortable.'

'I'd like one,' said Madeleine, raising her hand like a schoolgirl. She turned back toward the table but Nico's hand on her shoulder stopped her.

'Have a seat,' he said to her. 'I know most of this story, so I can be the waiter.' *And I recall you are a fine waiter,* thought Madeleine. Nico called over his shoulder: 'Anyone else?'

Serene frowned at him and said: 'You should be still in bed, resting, not working.'

He turned his head to see how serious she was. 'I'm sure I can carry some cups of coffee,' he said, 'without risking permanent damage.'

'SO... A STORY FROM Egyptian Mythology,' Logan said when they were all seated. He lowered his voice theatrically, '...reaching across the ages from the dawn of recorded time.'

His mood caught Tricola's attention. She unfolded herself from the floor and rose to sit beside Madeleine on the couch. Madeleine noted she now had the laptop in its proper place – on her lap.

'You've probably heard of the Egyptian god of the sun and creation, the falcon-headed Ra,' Logan began, 'or to give him his later name, Amun-Ra. Ra had two daughters – they may have been twins – called Sekhmet and Bast.'

Madeleine raised her eyebrows at the daughter's names. It took her back to their first meeting in the café when Bastia the cat had jumped on her lap.

Logan was watching her and smiled at her reaction. 'Madeleine has already heard of the twins, especially Bast,' he told the others. He paused, thinking. 'And, if I remember correctly, at the *Magari,* I also introduced you to the third person of the trio I'll be talking about, Pharaoh Menes.'

Madeleine nodded.

Logan uncrossed his legs and leaned forward, his voice taking on a more serious tone.

'Bast is sometimes referred to by Egyptologists as *Bast't* or *Bastet* but, in Egyptian writing, the second 't' was used to signify a feminine ending to a word and wasn't pronounced. I like to refer to her as simply *Bast*.'

'At first,' continued Logan, 'Bast was the more important…' He hesitated. '…I have to choose whether to say 'god' or 'person' next. In the myth, she's a god. In my view, she was originally a person – a very powerful person. But, for the moment, let's keep this part of the story in the realm of mythology. As I said, Bast was the more important. She was the goddess of the sun and of war, which were two dominant influences in Egypt at the time, but, ironically perhaps, she was a friendly goddess, her enemies more likely to experience forgiveness rather than wrath. Sekhmet was the goddess of healing and justice, but, again ironically, she was known as a 'harsh' goddess apt to punish her enemies with plagues and destruction.'

'The temperament of these two goddesses was reflected in the sites chosen for their temples. The temple to Bast was built at Bubastis, in Lower Egypt, on an island in the fertile Nile River, whereas the temple of Sekhmet was built at Memphis, far to the south in Upper Egypt, in the scorching heat of the barren desert.'

'The myth says that Ra became angry that man was not following his laws. He decided punishment was necessary and sent Sekhmet, the right eye of Ra, to correct the behaviour. She roared out of the desert and rampaged across the land, where the streets and the fields ran red with blood. Bast was aghast and pleaded with her father to stop Sekhmet, which he finally did, but only with great difficulty, for she had drunk of the blood and her power had increased.'

'That story is the myth as recorded and handed down through the generations.'

'However, I have other writings, and these tell a different story.'

'This story is about two sisters who, together with Menes, the first Pharaoh, were integral to the development of the power. Bast saw the power as an instrument to be used for the betterment of mankind.

257

Sekhmet saw the power as a means to achieve domination *over* mankind and to rule both Upper and Lower Egypt. At that time, there were people who were immune or resistant to the power. Sekhmet planned to rid the land of these people to achieve the ultimate control she desired. To put it simply, she proceeded to put to death all those able to resist the power. Today, it would be called evolutionary cleansing. This was the 'rampage' of the myth, and a great number of innocent people were slaughtered.'

'Bast, together with Menes, tried to oppose Sekhmet, and the struggle was long and bitter, but Sekhmet was the stronger in that battle, emerging as the victor. She blamed the massacre on her sister Bast, who became known as the Lady of Dread or the Lady of Slaughter. In the myths, this result is reflected by Sekhmet replacing Bast as goddess of the sun and war and Bast's demotion to become the moon goddess of fertility. Menes was also a winner, becoming the first ruler of both Upper and Lower Egypt, acknowledged even in the myths as being the living god Horus. He seems to have switched sides and joined Sekhmet, but I suspect he was a puppet ruler as Sekhmet was certainly the power behind the throne.'

'But if Sekhmet won the battle, Bast eventually won the war. The writings say she embarked on a process to *hide* the spells that were the basis of the power, and she charged a particular sect of her followers – the Shining Ones – and their children, and their children's children…' he waved his hand, '…with keeping them hidden.'

He paused a few seconds, then continued.

'It's certain that the word *hide* in these writings has more meaning than mere concealment. Somehow, the act of hiding affected the spell, perhaps even removing it from use – I don't understand this fully yet. The writings also say she *broke* the talismans but include the phrase *as much as she could*, which may mean they were not physically broken but rather that their power was nullified or lessened. Those that I've found have been effective but of course I've no way of knowing if they were even more effective originally and, if so, by how much.'

He pointed at the cylinder. 'I'm hoping the size and shape of that cylinder indicate it contains the physically complete was-sceptre of Sekhmet. This talisman was a primary factor in Sekhmet's power and may have been the item that tipped the scales in her victory over Bast.'

For a moment all eyes stared at the golden cylinder.

'One thing I don't understand…' said Serene, '…is how talismans work.'

'I've no idea,' admitted Logan. 'But I know they do. They are somehow infused by the spell they augment and work as catalysts. I'm almost ashamed to say that talismans are a part of the power that really *does* seem magical.'

Madeleine leaned back against the seat, Logan's myths and stories resonating in her head. She had previously thought of the power as akin to hypnosis, which it was, but she had always considered hypnosis as something that was exercised on a small one-to-one scale, affecting one person at a time. Logan was saying that using the spells of Thoth and the was-sceptre of Sekhmet, the power could influence many people – hundreds, perhaps *thousands*.

'Logan…' she said slowly. 'Are you sure we *should* open the cylinder? It sounds as though whatever's inside could be dangerous. It was hidden for a reason.'

'That's true,' said Logan. 'But the writings consistently say it was hidden so that the contents could not be used with the wrong motives.'

'Enslavement rather than enlightenment,' murmured Serene.

'Yes,' agreed Logan. 'This cylinder *must* be kept out of Lucifer's hands. But before we work to ensure that, we must know that the contents are as we suspect them to be.'

Pointing again at the cylinder, he said: 'Once I have confirmed that inside that container lies the True Book of Thoth and, perhaps, the was-sceptre of Sekhmet, then my first instinct is to hide it again immediately.'

'Without opening the book?'

Logan let out a breath. 'Possibly,' he said.

'You know the old saying,' said Madeleine. 'Even the purest can be tainted with sufficient temptation.' She looked at him from the corner of her eye. 'That's not to say that *you*, of course…'

'I have all of you to keep me honest.' He inclined his head towards Madeleine. 'And *you* especially.'

At Serene's frown, he explained: 'I may not have told you this. Madeleine is immune to the power.'

Serene let out a breath and sat back in her seat. 'Really!'

'Sekhmet beware!' Tricola said in a dramatic voice.

Madeleine laughed, but then became serious. 'Speaking of keeping the cylinder out of Lucifer's hands…' she began, '…he must have had Bowers watching the demolition site from the very building where we took shelter…'

'Yes. Again, one step ahead. Something we should have foreseen…' interjected Logan ruefully.

'Maybe, but the point is that Dopey deliberately tried to kill you and Nico last night. He marched purposefully into the water with only one idea in his mind – almost certainly acting on Lucifer's orders. Thankfully, he failed in that objective but, instead, we've taken the object Lucifer had expended a great deal of time and effort to obtain right from under his nose. If he had sufficient reason to want you… us… dead before, then he has even more reason now. Is it time to ask Sir Brian again for protection?'

'I think our best protection at the moment is that Lucifer doesn't know where we are, and the presence of soldiers would just announce us to the world. We're safe here. But we're not being passive. Thanks to Serene, we're watching Lucifer's big house outside Rome, and some good people are searching for Bowers and his group as we speak.'

Madeleine remained uneasy. 'We may be safe here, but we can't stay indoors forever,' she argued. 'You're taking the cylinder to the museum later today, and I'm speaking at the symposium.'

'Yes, Serene and I were just talking about that…'

Madeleine looked up. Was Logan about to say that she shouldn't go to the symposium? Logan caught her concern and gave a little shake of his head.

'Serene's also going out. We've agreed she should get a weapon.' He brought his hands up to emphasise his point. 'But I *am* going to suggest we all change our appearance a little, outside of the apartment. No need to dye your hair, but maybe glasses and a hat or scarf?'

'In this heat?'

'Well, you know what I mean. It's important that we're not imprisoned here, fearful to tread outside. Lucifer can't have eyes on every street or canal in Venice, but at the same time, we should take due care.'

CHAPTER TWENTY-ONE

A Symposium Speech and a Sistine Invitation…

Tuesday 4:30 pm

Madeleine looked up at the audience and finished her sentence.

'…to improve our understanding in this exciting area and provide new directions for future research.'

Her fingers flipped closed the folder that contained her speech notes.

'Thank you,' she said.

Stepping back from the podium, she was pleased that the applause was considerably more than just polite. Her speech had gone well. No mistakes, no stumbling over words. Her eyes swept the auditorium of the Minerva Theatre. She could see there was genuine interest in the audience, with several people taking notes.

She walked to the side of the small stage where the symposium director was waiting to congratulate her. From the opposite side of the stage, she heard the footsteps of the next speaker approaching the podium.

'Well done, Madeleine,' the director said. 'Some very original ideas. That will give them something to think about.'

He took her arm and directed her toward one of the rooms behind the stage.

'I've a surprise for you,' he continued. 'Our patron is keen to meet you. He says he found your speech very interesting. Do you have a moment?'

'Of course.' She had not met the patron before, and she had to admit she was flattered that he found her speech interesting enough to want to talk to her.

The director led her to a door which he opened. He ushered Madeleine inside.

A pair of armchairs had been pulled up to a small central table with an opened bottle of champagne and two glasses. A man Madeleine estimated to be in his late sixties or early seventies, was seated in one of the armchairs, relaxed with his legs crossed. He had a full head of pure white hair brushed back from his forehead and a neat matching perfectly-trimmed beard. He was immaculately groomed, his long-fingered hands lay crossed on his knee, and white shirt cuffs adorned with gold cufflinks were visible under a well-tailored dark grey business suit. His shoes were dark and, to her glance, had a rough appearance like alligator hide.

She took a moment to study him professionally, an automatic reaction whenever she met someone new. Her first reaction was positive. The smile he gave her and his demeanour were friendly, showing no evidence of guile or underlying motives. He seemed to be exactly as he appeared.

The man stood up. He stepped around the table and extended a hand.

'Ms Galli,' he said in a voice that reminded Madeleine of a narrator of a wildlife documentary, deep and smooth. 'Thank you for agreeing to meet me.'

His voice confirmed his interest in her was sincere. He meant the words he said. Madeleine relaxed and reproached herself for treating him like a police suspect, but she knew her assessment was involuntary — she could no more stop that process than stop breathing.

'It's my honour,' she said.

The director gestured toward the man. 'Madeleine, allow me to present Giles Vitivelli, the patron of our organisation.'

Madeleine took his hand. His skin was unusually smooth.

The man bowed to her. 'The honour is all mine,' he said.

He gestured towards the table. 'I've opened a bottle of champagne. Would you like a glass?'

Madeleine felt more like kicking off her shoes and putting her feet up than drinking champagne, but to be polite, she said: 'Thank you.'

The director took a step backwards. 'I'll leave you to your discussion.'

Madeleine smiled at him.

Mr Vitivelli nodded to the director and said to Madeleine: 'I found your talk very interesting.' She heard the door close. 'It reinforced some research I'm doing.'

Again, he was sincere and speaking the truth.

He picked up the bottle and a glass. As the champagne flowed, the gulp of the liquid and the fizzy buzz of bubbles sounded overly loud to Madeleine in the small room.

The full glass was handed to her, and the bottle set back on the table. A wave of a hand indicated the second armchair. 'Please…'

Madeleine sat down. 'Are you not having one?'

'I don't drink alcohol,' he said, 'and, anyway, this is *your* celebration.'

Madeleine now wished she had refused his offer but she raised her glass and sipped the wine, feeling its tingle against her lips. Despite her initial reluctance, she found the champagne pleasantly refreshing.

The man sat back in his chair and crossed his legs again, looking at ease.

'One aspect of your talk particularly interested me,' he said. 'It was the segment where you mentioned electrical activity in the brain preceding acts of choice or so-called free will. You – deliberately, I suspect – didn't let your argument expand into the fields of religion or philosophy, but you must have a personal opinion. Do you think we are really in charge of our lives?'

Madeleine drew a breath. She was tired. Although she had rested during the day, her body was still recovering from the stress of her early morning activities, and the mental exertion of delivering her speech, as well as the physical strain of standing for thirty minutes, had added to her fatigue. From experience, this topic tended to result in a lengthy discussion that, today, she would rather have avoided. She'd try to keep it brief.

'The answer to that question,' she said, 'relies on a couple of important definitions and your point of view. When faced with a choice, a person makes a decision, from his viewpoint, solely by exercising his free will. But, as you said, experiments have shown that a build-up of electrical activity occurs in the brain well before that person makes a conscious decision to act. Many scientists say this proves there is no such thing as 'free will' because you are only reacting to decisions already made in your brain. But we need to define who 'this person' is. Does he exist separate from his brain, his consciousness, his subconsciousness; or are they one and the same? We need to define 'free' too because although our subject believes his choice to have been a free one, he could have been influenced by external forces of which he is unaware.'

She paused. 'Having said all that,' she said with a smile, 'I like to believe I'm in control.'

In the discussion that followed, Madeleine found Giles Vitivelli to be surprisingly well-informed and also well-educated, able to follow the more scientific points without the need for explanation. She sipped slowly at her glass while she talked and when it was empty, she took advantage of a pause in the conversation to place it on the table. As if that was a signal, Giles Vitivelli uncrossed his legs.

'Thank you for your time,' he said. 'As I said, your subject was interesting, and I've enjoyed meeting you and talking to you.'

He stood up, and she rose with him.

'I hope I haven't kept you from a presentation you wished to attend,' he said.

'No, I've finished for the day.'

'In that case, I trust you're able to take some time now to enjoy our city,' he said, moving slowly toward the door.

'Luckily, yes. I've already been here for a few days, and I'll be staying on for a while.'

'Do you have anything planned?' She caught an eagerness in his tone. He was anticipating something. His next appointment, perhaps?

Madeleine felt she was repeating a conversation she'd already had with Logan.

'I'd like to explore some of your historical art, if I can.'

'Oh? What aspect of Italian art interests you?'

'Well, I've never visited the Sistine Chapel…'

'Really?' He stopped and looked at her. 'Well, that's fortunate. I may be able to help you there.'

'How do you mean?'

'I know some people at the Vatican. I'm sure I could arrange a viewing for you. In fact, what would you say to a private viewing in the company of a Vatican historian?'

Madeleine was speechless. She re-checked his signs. It was not an empty boast. He believed he could arrange a private tour.

'Why, that would be *marvellous*,' she managed after a second or two. 'But it would surely be a lot of trouble…'

'No trouble at all. What's the good of having influence if one doesn't use it? Now, let me think. Are you free this evening? Not many people know this, but the chapel is best viewed at night. The lighting has been set up superbly. It really highlights the ceiling much better than in mere daylight.'

'This evening?' She felt a familiar unease that the pace of her life was once again quickening, but she knew she would be unlikely to get a better chance to see the world-renowned chapel. *A private tour!*

'Well, yes, I'd like that… If you're *sure* it's no trouble,' she said with a smile.

There was a flash of something in his eye that puzzled Madeleine. In another person, she would have thought it was triumph. But, as an obvious philanthropist, it was more likely he was just pleased to be able to help.

'Good, it's settled,' he said. 'I have some appointments this afternoon and then I'm flying back to Rome. You can accompany me in my plane. Let me have your phone number, and I'll call you when I've made the arrangements at the Vatican.' He reached inside his jacket and pulled out a phone.

Another private plane? I could get used to this lifestyle. Then she remembered. 'Oh, sorry… I lost my phone over the weekend. It's so inconvenient.'

'Where are you staying then?'

'I'm staying with friends. I don't know the number. But I can borrow a phone and call *you* Mr Vitivelli.'

'*Giles*, please,' he said, glancing at a gold watch on his wrist. 'Very well. I can make the necessary arrangements by six o'clock. Call me then and let me know where to pick you up, and I'll send a motorboat.'

A hand slipped into his breast pocket and emerged with a business card.

'Call this number.'

She glanced at the card. It contained only his name, *Giles Vitivelli*, and a mobile phone number. No indication of his profession.

'How can I thank you?' she said.

'By calling me at six.'

He bowed to her and reached out to open the door.

CHAPTER TWENTY-TWO

The Chapel tour begins well, ends not so…

Tuesday 6:20 pm

The familiar sounds of swords clashing and magic rending the air issued from the speakers surrounding the wall screen. Serene and Tricola sat side-by-side on two chairs pulled so close to the screen that any nearer and they would have been inside the game. Cries of anguish and triumph from the players mixed with the sounds of battle from the speakers.

Nico lounged on a settee, his head resting on the pillow he'd been ordered to use, a cup of hot chocolate steaming on a small table. He watched the game, not minding that his nurses had temporarily forgotten him.

'I don't think it's a good idea to go to Rome,' Logan said to Madeleine. 'We're trying to keep a low profile. It's an unnecessary risk.'

'I'm being picked up and transported to a private plane,' Madeleine replied. 'It's not as if I'm wandering the streets. And I've wanted to experience the Chapel for a long time.'

'I understand that, but it's also very short notice,' Logan argued. 'I would have preferred it if someone went with you.'

Madeleine didn't say anything.

Logan looked at her and sighed. 'It's your decision, of course. Do you feel up to it, physically?'

'I felt tired earlier, after my speech, but some of that may have been relief that it was over. I'm OK now. I'm sure I'll sleep well tonight, though.'

'Hopefully, we all will.'

Logan put his hand on the table, pulled a coin from his pocket and sent it on its way across his knuckles, the coin moving effortlessly from one finger to another.

'How long do you expect to be gone?' he asked.

Madeleine, sitting opposite, was fascinated once again by the seemingly useless but impressive skill. For a few moments she stared at the coin before recalling that she'd been asked a question.

'I'm not sure,' she replied. 'A few hours maybe – I haven't made arrangements for a return trip yet. I hope I'll be able to fly back the same way, but maybe I'll stay in Rome overnight. In any case, I'd like to be back for the opening of the cylinder.'

She pointed at a small bag beside a wide-brimmed summer fashion hat on the marble benchtop. 'Thanks to your mother, I've been able to prepare for a possible overnight stay, and I've included your suggested glasses and a hat.'

'Please take this with you…' He caught the coin between two fingers and held it there while he pulled his wallet from the inside breast pocket of his jacket and took out a business card. With a pen from the same pocket, he wrote on the back.

'It's the phone number of the apartment…' he indicated a phone standing on one end of the black marble bench. 'Call if you need anything. And…' he looked at her, '…be careful. Do you have enough cash if you need it for the return journey? Don't use a credit card.'

She touched his arm. 'I appreciate your concern, but it's such a wonderful opportunity. I can't let it slip.'

'It *is* an amazing offer,' Logan agreed. 'What do you know about the man who invited you?'

'He's the patron of the GHO, the Global Health Organisation, in Italy. The GHO organised today's symposium. He's obviously rich and well-connected. Apart from that, I know he's genuine. I only met him briefly, but he told me no lies.'

'Ah,' he said. 'Genuine. Yes, I understand. That gift of yours can be very useful.'

She smiled. 'He's not the sort of person who would abandon me in Rome but, to answer your question, if something unexpected happens, I have enough cash.'

He held out his card, which she accepted, briefly amused that it was similar to Giles' card, containing just the name *Logan Milan* and a phone number, presumably of the phone Logan had left behind in the Dolomites villa.

'Do you have *your* new phone?'

'No, I gave it to Serene.'

'Take this one. It was the one Tricola was carrying but she'll be staying here.'

'Thanks,' Madeleine said. 'I'll call if I need to.'

The coin resumed its passage.

'Talking of gifts…' she waved at his hand. 'Apart from showing extraordinary coordination, why did you train yourself to do that?'

He shrugged, and she marvelled that he could do that without disturbing the movement of the coin. He paraphrased a reply that Nico had given earlier.

'It seemed like a good idea at the time. I find it relaxing.'

'Of course…' She gave a nod of appreciation.

He looked up at her, the coin still moving. 'So, you'll be in Rome…' he said thoughtfully.

'Yes, why do you say it like that?'

'Oh, nothing. Not really. It just reminded me that I keep postponing my visit to Lucifer's big house. Unfortunately, we're not in the best of shape right now.'

'That's true,' she agreed, looking at her watch.

She stood up. 'I'm being picked up from the *Basino Orseolo* steps below in ten minutes. I'd better go.'

She stepped away from him, collected her bag and the hat from the bench and headed for the elevator. Her wave to the gaming trio was only noticed and returned by Nico.

'Oh, by the way…' Logan said, raising his voice a little so she could hear over the noise of the game, '…I didn't want to disturb your focus until the symposium was over, but Tricola traced the head of Morning Star Construction earlier. The *real* head, not the puppets recorded in the Company Register.'

She pushed the button, and the doors opened immediately.

'Ah… Good,' she said, stepping inside and turning. Her hair was still pinned up from her symposium presentation, and she now placed the bag on the floor and used both hands to pull the hat on firmly.

She looked at him with a playful smile on her face. 'I've thought of a use for that coin trick of yours.'

She picked up the bag and reached inside, fetching a pair of sunglasses.

'And what's that?' he asked warily.

The smile became wider. 'To prove that men can be more than one dimensional. *You* can talk and shrug and roll that coin – all at the same time.' She put the glasses on and pushed them back on her nose to emphasise her statement.

He laughed, and that action disturbed his concentration. The coin toppled from his hand, struck the edge of the table and rolled onto the floor.

'The head of Morning Star…' she said, pushing the button for the ground floor. 'Anyone we know? Do we have a name for Lucifer?'

'The name meant nothing to me,' he said. He bent down to fetch the coin. 'But Tricola's been searching for more information about him.'

The coin had rolled further away than he'd expected, and he had to reach for it.

'His name is Vitivelli, Giles Vitivelli,' he said, straightening up.

But he was talking to the closed doors of the elevator.

'PLEASE WAIT HERE, Madeleine.'

Giles Vitivelli indicated a row of six chairs lined up against the wall. The chairs looked like museum pieces, too ornate to be comfortable. Although he hadn't mentioned it, Madeleine wondered if wearing a hat could be a breach of protocol. She removed it as, tentatively, she sat down on one of the chairs, placing her bag on the floor beside the chair and laying her hat on top.

Giles had led her through a side entrance to the Vatican, past two Swiss Guards who had acknowledged him with familiarity. They had entered this corridor directly, again through a side door, and had then walked for some distance, about five minutes, to their present position without meeting anyone.

A little further down the corridor and on the opposite side was an open door, and through it Madeleine could see a richly decorated tile floor. Her pulse quickened. Was that the famous chapel?

'I'll fetch Monsieur Garnier, the historian,' he said. 'He knows you're coming, so he won't be far away. Monsieur Garnier will show you the chapel. I'll join you later.'

He smiled and walked briskly away from her, disappearing as the corridor curved in the distance.

Five minutes later, he was replaced by a short man looking exactly as she imagined Friar Tuck, Robin Hood's companion, would look, tubby with the bald crown of his head surrounded by a half-ring of white hair and, to cap off the image, he wore a brown robe that looked like a monk's cassock, tied at the middle with a white rope. Madeleine had the bizarre thought he had donned a costume just for her.

'I am Monsieur Garnier', he said from ten feet away. His voice was high-pitched. 'English, I presume?'

Madeleine thought he was enquiring about her country of origin but realised he was talking about language.

'Yes,' she said, standing and reaching for her hat and bag. 'Thank you so much for taking the time to escort me. I hope I haven't put you out at all.'

'Not at all. Not at all,' he muttered, beckoning her to follow him.

His gait was fast but his steps were small and his forward lean reminded her of a tumble toy about to fall over. He led her past the open door she had noticed earlier. When she looked inside, he nodded.

'Yes, that's the Chapel, but that door is the public entrance. We will enter down here.'

THE SISTINE CHAPEL was all she had expected and more. The colours were so vivid – as Giles had promised, the ceiling and wall frescos were wonderfully lit, highlighting the artwork without bathing it in too much light. Monsieur Garnier talked constantly, obviously a man in love with not only Michelangelo's work but that of the other great artists of the era, pointing out works by Botticelli and making a special mention of some tapestries by Raphael, not normally on view but displayed now to commemorate the Pope's birthday.

As they circled the room, Monsieur Garnier talked about each painted segment in turn. But it was to Michelangelo that he kept returning, bringing to life the Renaissance world of the great master during the four years it took him to convert the chapel ceiling into scenes from the Book of Genesis, including the famous Creation of Adam, where the hands of creator and created met with just the slightest touch.

Madeleine's eyes drank in the magnificent works of art. She learned that Michelangelo was reluctant when asked to paint the ceiling because he considered himself a sculptor, not a painter, and he had all the work he could handle. But Pope Julius had insisted. Madeleine was awed by the perfection of the work of someone who did not consider himself a painter.

All too soon, Monsieur Garnier was ushering her from the chapel.

Back in the corridor, she thanked him from her heart and looked about, expecting Giles to be waiting but, although she could see for some distance in both directions, the corridor was as empty as when she had arrived. Monsieur Garnier indicated the chairs where she had been sitting earlier.

'I'm sure he will be but a moment, *Madame*.' Monsieur Garnier bowed to her and toddled off with his strange gait.

Madeleine stood for a moment, then, when no one appeared, resumed her seat.

Ten minutes passed, and she began to feel uncomfortable. Had she been abandoned in the middle of the Vatican? If she was discovered now by a guard, sitting alone outside the Sistine Chapel, she could be arrested as an intruder. She stood up and walked a few steps across the corridor so she was able to see a little further around the bend. Her footsteps sounded loud on the hard floor. When she stopped walking, she heard with relief that other footsteps were approaching. She took her seat and picked up her hat and bag, placing them on her lap. The footsteps were quick and she wondered if Monsieur Garnier had returned but, instead, she was surprised to see a boy of around twelve years appear, dressed in a white gown featuring a large silver cross on the front. He looked like a choir boy from a church service. Well… this *was* the Vatican… He stopped in front of her.

'*Signora* Galli?'

'Yes.'

'Please follow me,' he said brusquely. He started along the corridor in the direction she had originally come.

'Where is *Signore* Vitivelli?' she asked.

The boy turned back to her. 'He trusts you enjoyed your visit to the Sistine Chapel, but he is engaged at the moment. He will join you soon.'

Madeleine stood up. 'Where are we going?'

'I am to take you to your car.'

'Where I'm to wait for him?'

'Where you are to wait.'

The boy spoke with an authority that belied his years. In the moment before he turned his head away, Madeleine noticed his eyes were strangely vacant and disinterested. The surprising thought crossed her mind that he acted as if he were drugged.

They exited the corridor through the same door Madeleine had entered with Giles. There was now a car waiting outside the gate. The pair of Swiss Guards, engaged in their own conversation, barely glanced at them.

In the United States, the car would have been called a limousine with dark paintwork and tinted windows. It looked similar to the vehicle that brought them from the airport, but it was not the same car; the upholstery was a darker shade of grey, and the driver was different; longer hair showed beneath his cap.

The boy opened a rear door and stood aside. Madeleine thanked him and seated herself, placing her bag beside her. She kept the hat on her lap, undecided whether to wear it.

'Did *Signore* Vitivelli say how long he would be?'

The boy closed the door. The closing door obscured his face for a moment. He may have shaken his head in a negative answer to her question, or he may have simply ignored it.

She watched him through the window as he walked quickly through the gate with his head lowered. For some reason, she had an uneasy feeling. She tried to ignore it and settled back in the seat, the hat still held in her hands.

The driver started the engine.

'I think we are supposed to wait for *Signore* Vitivelli,' said Madeleine.

A glass panel rose from the seats in front of her, isolating the rear passenger section. She heard a clunk as the driver selected a gear.

'Please stop!' she called loudly, reaching for the door handle and pulling on it.

The door was locked.

CHAPTER TWENTY-THREE

Invasion of the Hotel Magari…

Tuesday 9:30 pm

Pietro greeted Eli Rosenberg as he descended the stairs. Eli was portly, and his shape, a broad face, and a full white beard, made him appear like a modern-day Santa Claus. One thing marring that impression tonight was the lit cigar he held in his hand.

'I trust your meal was satisfactory, *Signore*?' Pietro asked.

'Better than satisfactory, thank you,' said Eli, descending the last two steps.

'And your wife also enjoyed the lobster?'

'She did indeed. Very much. It was delicious, as always.' He rested his hands on the reception desk, the cigar trailing a thin wisp of smoke.

Pietro inclined his head. 'Anything else I can help you with?'

Over Eli Rosenberg's shoulder, Pietro's attention was momentarily drawn to a man who appeared at the hotel entrance. This man was also broad but unlike Eli, he didn't move with the bearing of one who is overweight.

'Last time we stayed here, you managed to get me a copy of the New York Times,' Eli said. 'Is it possible to obtain one again?'

'Of course.' Pietro reached below his desk for the single newspaper he'd had delivered in the morning.

He waved his hand when Eli reached for his wallet. 'A complimentary copy,' he said.

'Why, thank you, Pietro,' said Eli, accepting the newspaper. 'That's mighty grand.' He glanced down to read the main headline and then back to Pietro. 'Eleanor will be down in a moment. She wants to go to that café on the corner for dessert.' He leaned in secretively. 'She can't wait to try their hot strawberry zabaglione again.' He chuckled and slapped his hand on the counter. 'Gotta keep the little woman happy.'

Pietro smiled with him. 'The zabaglione is excellent,' he said.

'Good. That's good,' said Eli. He waved the newspaper in the air. 'Thanks for this. OK then, I'll wait over here.'

He moved across the foyer to a pair of armchairs, carefully placed his cigar on the edge of an ashtray and sat down with an audible sigh of relief and comfort.

Pietro waited until Eli was settled before turning his attention to the newcomer.

Pietro noted that the man was Asian and so he spoke in English. 'Good evening, sir. Can I help you?'

'You are manager?'

'Yes.'

'Logan Milan,' said the man. He drew out the second syllable of Logan's names, making them rhyme with 'barn'.

'I'm afraid Mr Milan is not available,' said Pietro, correcting his pronunciation. He repeated his offer. 'Can *I* help you?'

'Where is Logan Milan?'

'I'm sorry, sir.' Pietro answered politely, declining to expand on the information already given. 'Mr Milan is not available.' He patiently waited for the man to speak again.

'How many people in hotel?'

Pietro frowned. 'If you're asking whether we have a room available, the answer is yes,' he said.

'No. How many guest?'

'I'm not able to give you that information,' Pietro said, his voice becoming firmer. '*Signore,* if you would like a room, we do have a single available. If not, I have some duties to attend to.'

Eli's voice piped up from the chair where he had settled himself. 'Plenty of room, friend. Only two elderly ladies joined us for dinner tonight. I can *personally* recommend this hotel. I stay here every time I'm in Venice. You won't find better service anywhere.' His gaze flicked to the stairs. 'Ah… there you are, my dear.'

There was the sound of footsteps on the stairs. Pietro looked up to see Eleanor Rosenberg descending the narrow steps slowly and gracefully. She was a petite woman, especially when seen next to Eli, but she had what Pietro would call 'a presence'. She was elegant. She smiled down at him.

The Asian man also raised his eyes, looking at Eleanor and then across to Eli sitting in the lounge chair.

Abruptly, the man turned away and headed for the door. Pietro stared after him, relieved that he was leaving but trying to understand what he could have wanted. His eyes widened in surprise when the man closed the door and snapped the lock.

'What are you doing?' asked Pietro. 'Please open that door.'

The man walked quickly back to the desk.

'You show me computer room of Logan Milan,' he said, his tone unchanged from his earlier questions.

'*Scuza?*' Pietro wasn't sure he had heard correctly.

The man's arm reached out quickly and grabbed the front of Pietro's shirt. Eleanor Rosenberg, on the last step, uttered a short squeal of surprise. The man dragged Pietro from behind the counter, at the same time waving for Eleanor to join Eli by the chairs.

Eli had risen from his chair. 'Here, just a moment….'

'*Sit!*' the man commanded. 'Both.' He pulled Pietro toward the chairs, staring hard at Eli. Pietro tried to resist by digging in his heels and struggled to release himself from the man's grip, but the man was too strong – his efforts had no effect and didn't even slow the man. Eli sat down. The man took Eleanor's arm and hastened her into the other chair. Eli started to stand again in protest but the man threw his hand out, hitting Eli in the chest. Eli fell back into the chair, spluttering.

'You two, sit, stay in chair!' the man said, glaring at the Rosenbergs. Eleanor was breathing hard, obviously frightened and distressed. Eli took hold of his wife's hand to comfort her.

The man pulled Pietro toward him until he was only a few centimetres away.

'You show me computer room,' he repeated. 'Now! – or I hurt.'

'I don't care what you do to me. I'll *never* do that,' said Pietro, trying not to let his voice waver.

'*Arigato!*' said the man triumphantly. 'So Milan *has* computer room.' He threw back his head, a fierce grin on his face. 'And I no hurt you; I hurt *her.*' He pointed forcefully at Eleanor Rosenberg, his finger close to her nose. She shrank back from him, pushing herself into the chair.

'I can't open the door. Only Mr Milan can open the door.'

'If you not open door, I break finger. If you still not open door, I cut finger off one by one until you open door. Then toe. You open door *now.*'

He opened his jacket with his free hand and withdrew a knife. At the flick of a switch, a wickedly curved blade sprang free, the steel gleaming in the foyer lights. Eleanor made a terrified sound in her throat, and Eli tried to calm her, patting her hand.

'Break finger take too long,' the man said. 'Maybe I just cut finger.'

Pietro presumed the man wanted to steal Logan's computer data. He knew that everything Logan had in his computer room was backed up in several places. It could be recovered easily. The data was also encrypted, and it would take an expert working with sophisticated software a long time to make any sense of it. He had told the man that only Logan could enter the room, but Pietro did have a key, a duplicate of the one Logan had, but set to Pietro's thumbprint. Nobody else knew of this key's existence apart from Logan and himself. Not even Nico knew. Should he try to insist he couldn't enter the room?

At Pietro's prolonged hesitation, the man shrugged. He replaced the knife inside his jacket, then in a fluid motion, he bent his arm and his fist crashed against Eli's jaw. It was a brutally efficient blow and Eli slumped in his chair. Eleanor screamed – a scream that was silenced immediately as the man's hand clamped over her mouth. The man bent close to her and shook his head. Slowly, he removed his hand and wagged his finger in her face to reinforce his demand that she should not make any sound. Eleanor tore her gaze away from the man and reached for her husband, cradling his head, tears springing to her eyes.

'Eli…' she whimpered.

Logan said the welfare of the guests was paramount. Pietro groaned. Whatever he chose to do, he would be letting Logan down.

'Next is the finger,' the man hissed. 'Computer room. Now.'

The man's eyes bore into Pietro's. Pietro lowered his head and sighed.

AS TANAKA LAID THE little manager's unconscious body on the floor, the key the man had just used to open the door fell from his hand. In Tanaka's opinion, it would be more efficient to kill this one and the two downstairs, leaving no witnesses, but he'd been explicitly ordered to leave the hotel manager alive. He had no such instructions about the old couple, both unconscious now, but it didn't make sense to kill witnesses if you didn't kill them all. Thinking about the manager reminded him, and he dug in his pocket, pulling out the folded piece of paper containing a note he had laboriously copied letter for letter as instructed on the phone call he'd received from Lucifer.

'Find the room containing Milan's computers,' Lucifer had said. 'Get in there and bring back anything useful. Laptops or Hard Drives. Look for manuscripts. I want to know what he knows. Now, listen carefully – this is important – I want you to write this message down and leave it with the manager.'

Tanaka tucked the note into the breast pocket of the manager's waistcoat, making sure it was visible and would be noticed.

He stood up and pushed open the door. It was heavy and he frowned when he saw the bars now withdrawn behind the door. He had considered breaking the door if the little man had held out. He saw now that would have been impossible.

The lights came on. He wasn't sure whether that was triggered by the door or his movement, but it saved him the search for a light switch.

He let his gaze roam the room. He recognised most of the equipment. Printers, modems. In the corner, a UPS box to ensure continuous power. There were some items on the shelving behind the chair that were not familiar. He ignored them; they could have been anything. He felt he should work fast, but his logic told him he had time. The old man had mentioned two old ladies – they wouldn't be a problem, even if they turned up unexpectedly. The locked front door should turn away any other prospective guests. The only problem he could foresee would be a current guest arriving back at the hotel, but the old man hadn't said anything about other guests.

He crossed the room to a row of file boxes under a bookshelf and opened one, reaching in and retrieving a handful of papers. He scanned them, reading the English words laboriously. Notes about brain functions. He dropped them on the floor. In another box, he found papers written in French. He couldn't read French. The first few papers from the next box were in German. He spoke some German, but these were technical notes he didn't understand. He flung them away in frustration. They weren't manuscripts. It wasn't what he came for. He didn't want to carry boxes of papers.

He ran his eyes over the books, but nothing was of interest. Books about Egyptian history. More medical volumes. Medieval witchcraft. A book about the Hittites, whoever they were.

He moved to the desk and opened the drawers, surprised they weren't locked. He gave a grunt of understanding. Milan obviously depended on the door for security. He searched for a USB drive or a standalone backup hard drive, but nothing in the drawers or on the main desk looked promising.

Tanaka noticed the three towers beside the desk. They were an unusual shape, but he knew what they must be. He smiled. Of course. Why look for backup devices when he could take the primary servers? He checked for cables and found that each one only had a power cable. They must be connected by Wi-Fi or maybe Bluetooth. The dwarf, Bartoch, would know all about them.

He unplugged the three towers and lifted one to assess its weight. Not heavy. He could carry two easily, but they were too bulky to take all three.

Tanaka took a moment to study the room again, this time more slowly. Was there anything he was overlooking? Should he take some of the papers? He decided it would take too long to find anything worthwhile. He checked the hardware on the metal shelves. One or more of those boxes could be a backup device, but he couldn't carry everything. Should he try to destroy some of the equipment? Or at least damage it? He dismissed the idea. Too noisy and too difficult. A waste of time. He had what he wanted.

He picked up two of the towers, tucking one under each arm. He'd return for the third.

CHAPTER TWENTY-FOUR

A kidnap, a ransom demand, and a response…

Tuesday 10:30 pm

The telephone rang.

Serene looked at Logan. She mouthed: 'Who?'

He frowned as he stood up and said: 'Madeleine, or my mother – they're the only people with the number.'

He picked up the phone. 'Hello?'

As Logan listened, his face became set like granite. After thirty seconds, he said: 'Thank you. I'll be there soon.'

He replaced the phone on its cradle and walked towards the hallway leading to the bedrooms.

'I'll ask Nico to join us. And Tricola, too,' he said calmly.

'Who was it? Was it Madeleine? Is she OK?'

'It was Pietro,' Logan said over his shoulder.

'Pietro? But you said…' She stopped. Logan hadn't stopped walking, and he was out of hearing.

WHEN EVERYONE WAS SEATED, Logan said: 'An hour ago, a man entered the *Magari*....'

Serene and Tricola sat facing him across the dining table. They were leaning forward, eager to hear what he had to say. Nico sat beside him but, in contrast, he was leaning back with his legs crossed, an arm hooked over the chair, relaxed. His laid-back attitude did not surprise Logan. He'd never seen Nico unruffled, let alone angry. He took everything as it came.

'From Pietro's description,' continued Logan, 'the man was Tanaka. He seriously assaulted two of my guests and forced Pietro to open my computer room, then he knocked Pietro unconscious. When he recovered, Pietro found a note in his waistcoat pocket.'

He paused, taking a moment to remember Pietro's words exactly.

'The note said: *I have Madeleine Galli. Bring the objects you took from the Arsenale to my villa in Tivoli tomorrow at noon. Bring my daughter.*'

Tricola gasped. Her eyes widened and her hand flew to her mouth. Beneath her hand, her long, drawn-out '*Nooo*' sounded like a wail. Serene put an arm around her shoulders.

Logan looked at Serene. 'Please inform Sir Brian. It seems I will soon be meeting Lucifer directly, so maybe I can discover what has happened to Sami as well as Madeleine.'

To Tricola, he said: 'No need to worry just yet. We still have a few tricks up our sleeve.'

Serene nodded. She patted Tricola's arm and pulled out her phone. 'I'll arrange for some men to be on standby,' she said.

'Thank you,' said Logan.

'Are you going to do as he demands?' asked Nico.

'At this point, I'm going to *seem* to do as he demands. Pietro also said the computer room has been searched and papers are over the floor, so my first action will be to check that out.'

'You'll return to the *Magari* tonight?'

'Yes. Lucifer won't try to harm me until I bring him the cylinder.' He rose and walked to Tricola. Crouching in front of her, he reached out to hold her hands in his.

'I'd like you to come with me to the hotel. Depending on what Tanaka has done to my equipment, and what he has taken, you may be able to help me.'

'Will you give me back to him?' Tears formed in Tricola's eyes, brimming on her lower lid.

Logan gripped her hands to give force to his words. 'Never. Not in a million years.'

'But Madeleine…' The tears coursed down her cheeks.

'…is safe for now, and we'll do everything in our power to make sure she stays that way,' said Logan.

The corners of her mouth twitched in a brief smile of gratitude. She pulled a hand away from his to wipe at her eyes. Serene handed her a napkin.

'I AM SO SORRY, *Signore*, with my heart. I have failed you.'

Logan had just unlocked the door to the computer room and pushed it open. Logan and Pietro stood on the threshold, looking in, with Tricola peering over Pietro's shoulder.

'On the contrary, Pietro, you prevented Eli and Eleanor Rosenberg from suffering further harm. This…' he swept his arm to encompass the room, '…is nothing compared to their welfare. You behaved correctly in extreme circumstances, and there will be extra in your pay to recognise that and compensate you for your experience.'

'I need no extras, *Signore*. You have given me a good life in this hotel. It is more than enough.'

Logan smiled at him. 'We shall see.' He inclined his head. 'The Rosenberg's stay will of course be complimentary and we will cover any medical bills.'

'I've already made those arrangements, *Signore.*'

Logan nodded. 'Of course.'

Pietro peered into the room. 'I have touched nothing,' he added. He looked back at Logan. 'Can I help in any way?'

'No, thank you. Please check on the Rosenbergs and convey my apology and best wishes for a quick recovery. I'll see them as soon as I've finished here.'

'Certainly, *Signore.*'

Logan stepped into the room, immediately noticing that the tall servers beside the chair were missing. His eyes scanned the other equipment. It looked intact and undamaged. He crossed to the bookcase, stooping to pick up some papers scattered across the floor. He glanced at them and stacked the papers on top of one of the file boxes before gathering more from the floor, checking each before adding it to the pile.

'Well,' he said, 'that's a bonus. None of the papers in these particular files are important, except for a few that have been taken out of the Clerveaux file, and they seem to be complete. I don't think any papers have been stolen. On the other hand…' he turned back to the desk, '…Tanaka *has* taken my primary towers.'

He looked around. He was talking to himself. Tricola was still standing at the door, her eyes darting around the room. He beckoned her to enter.

She stepped forward, walking immediately to the metal racks and running her fingers over the equipment as if greeting each item.

'Are these backup servers?' she asked.

Logan said: 'Yes – backup and archive servers. I can easily restore all the missing files, but I would not like Lucifer to have access to the information on the servers Tanaka has taken. That can only make him even more powerful.'

'Is the data on your servers encrypted?' she asked, matter-of-factly, as if she were asking if he'd had a good day.

'Yes, the servers have AES encryption.'

Tricola nodded approvingly.

'Do you know their IP addresses?' she asked. She continued to circle the shelving, checking and touching.

'Yes, of course.'

'Then if they are ever connected to the internet, which they would need to be to download decryption software, I can track them, and, given a few minutes, I can prevent access to the folders, or hide the files, or destroy the contents if you wish.'

'When switched on, the servers will automatically connect to the internet. But it's a secure connection.'

'Good. The security won't be a problem.'

Logan thought for a second. 'It's best if he's unaware that any important files are on the servers. Hide the files if you can. I'd like to retrieve the servers to save the hassle of re-creating them, but delete everything if that's not possible.'

'OK. I'll need a computer with the highest specification you can get as soon as you can get it.'

Logan was pleased that Tricola, in her element, had forgotten her worries. She seemed at once much more confident and self-assured.

'I have a reserve computer in that cupboard by the printers. It's top of the range in specifications and quality. It just needs power.'

He opened the cupboard doors and bent to pick up a computer tower which he carried to the desk and placed on the floor. It was wider than the previous towers but not as tall. He plugged in one of the leads discarded by Tanaka.

'I'll log you in,' he said, waving his hand over the pad on the desk.

He brought up a notepad on the screen and entered some numbers.

'These are the IP addresses to identify my machines,' he said. 'I'll get you a list of the file names.'

Tricola sat down on the chair.

Her fingers flashed over the keyboard. To Logan, she looked like a speed typist on double time. Her fingers seemed to move as fast as her thoughts. Screens that Logan recognised as displaying the computer's capabilities appeared and disappeared.

'This will do,' Tricola said. 'I'll download some tracking software. Is that OK?'

'Go ahead,' said Logan.

A download display box appeared. When a green bar started moving across the box, indicating the download was active, Tricola pointed at the side of the screen and said: 'This graphing app is known to have a memory leak. I'll uninstall it and get you a better one.'

This time, she didn't ask permission. He noticed she preferred to use the keyboard rather than the mouse. The screen contents changed so often that he barely had time to read what was being displayed.

Abruptly, she sat back. 'Your servers are not online yet.'

'It's likely that Tanaka is taking them to Rome,' said Logan. 'They may wait until tomorrow to try to access them.'

'Do you have a phone I can use? The tracking software can contact a phone when the servers come online, and then with a remote access app I can communicate with this computer through the phone.'

'I don't have a spare, and I'm picking our one-time phones won't be suitable,' he said with a frown. 'I can buy one, of course, but not until tomorrow.'

'That may be too late. No, I can't use the burner phones. It's best if the phone can't be traced to you anyway,' said Tricola.

'Wait…' his frown disappeared, '…Pietro has a box of phones that guests have left behind, and we've been unable to find the owner. Will one of those do?'

'Probably. If they're new. Can I see them?'

'Of course. But before that, I need you to get me some information on Lucifer's house and grounds.'

'Mount Sinai? What do you want to know?'

'*Mount Sinai*? Is that what it's called?'

Tricola looked up in surprise. 'Yes, why?'

'You didn't mention that before.'

'Tricola frowned. 'Sorry… I…'

Logan waved his hand. 'No need to apologise. It's just… an interesting name. The place where Moses and the Israelites received the commandments of God.' He paused, thinking, then said: 'I wonder if Lucifer equates himself with Moses in that respect… Anyway…' He focused on his request. 'I need topographical maps of the grounds, plans of the buildings, photos – aerial ones if possible – as detailed as you can get. I want to know Lucifer's villa as if I owned it.'

'That shouldn't be difficult. I'll see what I can find.'

She turned to face the screens, and her fingers began their flight.

THE CITATION TEN streaked through the morning sky at almost the speed of sound.

It had lifted off from Marco Polo airport at ten am, a few minutes after Logan, who was the last to arrive, had boarded carrying a long wooden case that looked like it contained a small torpedo. Serene met him in the passenger cabin.

She eyed the case. 'How…?'

'Don't ask,' said Logan. 'Let's just say I persuaded Dr Sciazori to change his plans.'

When he had deposited the case behind a seat, she handed him a small packet.

'This is your earpiece – Sir Brian's compliments. These are very new. *Seriously good kit.* Talk normally, and everyone on the network can hear you and anyone talking close to you. It fits invisibly right inside your ear – this thread is the antenna and also the on-off switch.' She smiled. 'Insert it like this with the antenna pointing to the outside. Here's the instruction sheet – read it!'

Logan took the sheet of paper she handed him. 'What's the range?'

Serene smiled. 'That's classified. I assure you it'll be enough.'

Logan raised his eyebrows.

'Who's on the network?'

Serene's wave of an arm encompassed Logan and Nico. 'Just the people in this cabin – including Tricola.'

'That's good. Thanks.'

They turned in different directions, and a few seconds later the engines started.

WHILE THE PLANE CLIMBED to its cruising altitude, Nico and Logan reclined their chairs and tried to get a few minutes rest. Logan had his eyes closed but he was alert. Nico had his eyes open but seemed the more relaxed. Tricola lay on the long seat, her head on a pillow. The phone she'd chosen from the abandoned ones Pietro had shown her was close to her face and her thumbs periodically danced on the screen. When Logan opened his eyes and gave her an enquiring glance, she shook her head. No sign of Logan's servers connecting to the internet.

Serene entered the passenger's cabin. She walked slowly up the aisle and sat beside Logan. She caught his glance at the pilot's door and said: 'We're in Archie's capable hands.' She saw he wasn't convinced and added: 'I'll notice if there's any change. He'll call if he needs me.'

Turning to include Nico, she said: 'The squad is in place. If we need firepower, I can call them in a few minutes. And…' she smiled at Logan, '…all the vehicles you requested are now confirmed.'

Logan nodded. 'Thanks. That's one less thing to worry about. And the camouflage gear for Nico?'

'Yes, also ready and waiting.' She took in a breath. 'I know I don't have to say this, but if it comes to a choice, Sir Brian wants Lucifer alive.'

He looked up at her. 'I understand.' He paused. 'Assuming we prevail.' She nodded slowly. A moment later, he said: 'How long until we land?'

'Fifteen minutes to Ciampino airport.'

Logan reached for a folder that lay on the seat beside him. He beckoned to Nico. 'Let's go over this one more time.'

Nico smiled and moved into the seat opposite Logan. Serene stood at his shoulder. Logan unfolded one of the maps Tricola had printed and placed it between him and Nico.

'Serene, your squad is here?' He pointed to a location.

Serene leaned forward to check and nodded. 'Yes. They're in a bus pretending to be a tour group.'

'Good. When we land, Nico will take you on the motorbike to join them. Should things go badly wrong, you're our ace in the hole. Nico, when you've dropped Serene, you'll ride to here and follow the farm road to this point, then you'll hike up to the top of this hill. From there you should get a good view of the surrounding countryside. Reconnoitre as much as you can. Let me know if there are any men in the villa's grounds. The Land Report in here…' he tapped the folder, '…states the size of the estate as eighty-five hectares which is over two hundred acres, so you won't be able to cover it all.'

He stopped and let his gaze rest on Nico.

'You have two tasks. First and foremost, our focus is to find Madeleine.' He rested his finger on the map. 'Here's the main house with one group of buildings around it and a second group over here. When you're able, make your way to the outbuildings and see if Madeleine is being held in one of those. If you find her, free her if you can. If you find her and there's a problem with getting to her or setting her free, we can mobilise Serene's troops at that point. If she's not in one of those buildings, try and get into the main house and search it.'

'If anyone gets in my way…?'

'That's your second task. We need to clear the field. If anyone is out there, disable them.'

He regarded Nico silently, fully aware of the size of each task he was asking of him. Logan didn't ask Nico if he thought he could do it. Nico was one of the few on the planet Logan would consider capable.

Nico returned his look impassively. He nodded. 'If she's there, I'll find her,' he said.

Serene said: 'It'll be difficult for one man to do both of those things. Maybe I should assist him?'

'I appreciate the offer, but no. I need someone I know and trust to bring the cavalry if and when it's needed.'

He waited a moment. Serene nodded.

'Meanwhile,' Logan continued, 'I'll wait until midday and go in the front door with the case.' He took in the concern on their faces. 'I'm aware of Lucifer's capabilities, and I've made some careful preparations for an encounter with him. As I told Tricola last night, I have a few tricks up my sleeve.'

Logan waited a few seconds. 'Any more questions?' Serene and Nico looked at each other then back to Logan.

'He asked you to bring Tricola to him,' said Serene. 'How much of a problem will it be when she's not with you?'

'I'm not going to carry all our negotiating eggs into the spider's lair,' said Logan, '…to mix a few metaphors. I'll be going in alone. I need Tricola to wait with the plane and ensure Lucifer does not get my data. She'll be ten minutes by fast car from the estate. I hope it won't come to it, but I'll call for her if she's needed, and Archie can drive her.'

Serene said: 'I don't like the idea of you going in there alone.'

'I must go in alone for the same reason Lucifer will be alone. If anyone goes with me, there's a risk he'll use them – and that includes Tricola.'

When no one spoke, Logan said: 'So, we're all happy?' He folded the map. 'One last thing… if I'm in trouble, I'll use the word *Pharaoh,* in which case…'

'We come running,' said Serene.

'Only if you think that's the right action. You do what you think is necessary. Remember,' he said, 'we need to keep each other informed about what's happening to each of us.'

He sat back in his chair. 'So, let's check these earpieces.' He looked at Serene. 'Does Tricola have hers in?'

'Yes, she does. I've already checked hers.'

Logan reached up to his ear as if he were scratching an itch and his fingernail touched a stiff thread inside his ear. Immediately, a female voice in his ear said quietly: '*Node active. Battery high.*' He could hear the same message repeated as first Serene's and then Nico's earpiece came online.

'OK. Testing… one, two…'

'One of your servers is online!' Tricola called.

She looked up as Logan stood quickly and walked toward her. 'It'll take me a few seconds to connect,' she said.

She bent towards the screen in concentration.

'Do you need my login user-id and password?' asked Logan.

'No,' she said. 'It won't take me long…'

They waited, and then Tricola said: 'Thread the needle and pull it tight…'

Logan didn't know if she was describing her actions or quoting a poem.

'I'm in!' she announced.

Looking over her shoulder, Logan saw a miniature image similar to what he would expect on a computer screen, but there were two mouse pointers visible, each moving in different directions. It looked confusing.

'The red pointer is me; the white one is… my opponent.'

The screen split into two, divided down the middle, the white pointer on the left and the red on the right. 'Now we're not getting in each other's way,' said Tricola.

'I thought that was the idea,' said Logan, 'that you should get in his way.'

'I'm not going to interfere with him or block him. I'm going to simply hide the folders that contain your files.'

Logan looked around. 'Do you have the list I gave you of the files I want to keep from Lucifer?'

Tricola tapped her forehead. 'Up here,' she said.

She was obviously enjoying herself. This 'duel' had the same ingredients as a computer game, and she seemed to be treating it as such. There were two opponents, each with a goal to achieve. Success was achieving your objective and denying your opponent his.

The phone in Tricola's hands was continually moving. At times, her thumbs alone fluttered across the screen, then the phone was rotated sideways and Tricola used the fingers of one hand to tap and swipe and scroll. Then it was twisted back to thumb control.

She began humming to herself. The tune was familiar.

'What?' The fingers stopped moving. 'How did he…? She peered at the screen. 'Of course…' she said, '…it's Bartoch!' She smiled. 'Oh, my funny little man, we'll put a stop to *that*.' Her hands blurred into action. She flicked her eyes up and noticed Logan's concerned look. 'It's no problem. I know him. He's good, but not *that* good. I've already hidden most of your folders. He won't know that they ever existed. He's searching blindly. Just a couple of minutes more…'

The humming resumed. Logan knew it was a well-known song but couldn't remember the title.

'There!' she exclaimed. 'Number one is done. I'll leave him stumbling around there and wait for the next one to come online. Then on we goo to number two.' Logan shook his head and smiled at her rhyme.

'I could leave him a calling card if you like. Something cryptic…'

'No. I don't want him to suspect what you've done. I'd like him to think Tanaka took the wrong servers.'

Tricola screwed up her nose. 'Awww…'

The name of the tune she'd been humming came to him. Queen's 'We are the Champions'. Logan smiled again and ruffled her hair.

'No calling card,' he said.

CHAPTER TWENTY-FIVE

Madeleine confined, meets an old acquaintance…

Wednesday 9:30 am

Madeleine woke on a bed. She was comfortable and her head was pillowed. When her eyes focused, she was in a small white-walled room lit by a single naked bulb. Madeleine blinked. Her head felt dizzy.

She was on her back, lying on top of the bedcovers. She started to sit up but lay down immediately, closing her eyes as the room moved in a nauseating way. She breathed heavily and her hands grasped the bedclothes to steady the swaying motion she was experiencing.

'It will take five minutes for your head to clear,' a voice said. She knew that voice. Was it Sami?

Another voice, a woman's, said: 'Get her some water.'

There was a shuffling of feet and Madeleine heard water running from a tap. More shuffling, and something cold touched her hand. She opened one eye to a slit and recognised a cup being offered to her.

'Thank you,' she whispered.

A hand pushed under her head and lifted it so she could drink. Her mouth was dry. The water was cool and refreshingly welcome. She swallowed with difficulty and choked as some liquid threatened to enter her lungs, squeezing her eyes tight as her head ached with the sudden movement.

'You've been injected with something just as we were,' the man said. 'I know how you feel. Try to relax. In five minutes, you'll be fine.'

Madeleine took another drink, then blindly held the cup out for it to be taken from her. Her head was lowered back to the pillow, and she let it fall to the side so she could see the person beside her.

It *was* Sami Bandarakaianan.

'Good morning,' Sami said.

Morning? Was it morning already? Her eyes moved under her narrowed lids, examining the room from this new perspective. She saw a large window in one wall, and through it she could see another room. An internal window?

'Sami…' she croaked. 'Where am I?'

'I wish I knew. But you should rest for a few more minutes. You'll feel much better soon. Then we can talk.'

THERE WERE TWO ROOMS with a connecting door. The door was unusual – a solid sheet of metal without any handle. Above the door were two lights, one red and the other green. The window in the wall allowed a view of the other room and Madeleine could see it was a big room, bare except for a table and six chairs. There were plates and cutlery on the table, set for three people.

Sami introduced Madeleine to his wife, Melda, who impressed Madeleine with her calm demeanour in the face of what had to be a stressful situation.

Sami explained that the connecting door could only be opened by a remotely controlled switch or a timer. When the red light came on, it announced that food would soon be brought to the table next door.

'Two men will come with our food,' Sami told her. 'While the red light is on, we must stand by the window and be visible. One of the men will watch at all times. If he can see us, the other man will set food on the table. If he cannot see us, they will leave immediately and we get no food. If they do leave food, then five minutes after they have left, the lights will change from red to green, the internal door will click open and we can eat. When we have finished eating, we must return to this room and close the door.'

Madeleine nodded. 'What is this place?'

'We think it's an old bomb shelter from the sixties, but all of the storage cupboards and equipment you'd expect in a shelter like this have been removed.'

'To make it a prison.'

'Yes.'

Madeleine scanned the room they were in; the bedroom. There were six beds in the room and some metal shelving, empty, attached to the wall. Her overnight bag and hat were nowhere to be seen, but her black shoulder bag was on the bed where she had woken. In the corner was a basin with one tap and a towel. A source of water, and she'd be able to wash and freshen up.

A noticeable feature was a square bulge set in the back wall between two of the beds. It was three feet wide, extended out three feet from the wall, and reached from the floor to three-quarters of the height of the wall. The top was covered with a sloping grill.

'What is that?' asked Madeleine. 'An air filter?'

'No, I don't think so,' said Sami. 'I think our air supply comes from next door. There's a grate in there set into the wall...' he pointed, '...do you see it? We've noticed there's a slight breeze coming from that grate.'

A metal square that looked the size and shape of an air conditioning vent was set high in the far wall against the ceiling.

'The small gaps above the window allow airflow between the rooms.'

Sami walked over to the wall bulge.

'I've looked inside. It's dark and difficult to see anything, but there are two cylinders encased in there. Perhaps they contain extra oxygen, for an emergency? There's a label on one of the cylinders, but the writing's faint; we've both tried, but we can't read the words.'

Madeleine looked at him. 'Let me try.'

She stepped onto one of the beds beside the bulge, thankful for her height, which enabled her to see inside the grill without needing to stretch. It *was* dark inside, but she could see the label Sami had mentioned. It was dusty, and the letters were red on a blue background – not high-contrast colours. The label had one word printed on it. Beside the word was a yellow triangle containing an exclamation mark – the international symbol for '*Warning*'. Probably not oxygen, then. She focussed on the letters and after a moment could make out part of the word. The first part was 'Halo'. She thought of angels. She moved her head to get a better view of the rest of the label. The second part of the word was 'thane'.

Halothane.

Madeleine stepped down from the bed.

'Could you read it?' asked Sami.

'Yes, it says Halothane.'

'Halothane? What's that? Do you know?'

'Halothane has been used as an anaesthetic,' said Madeleine. 'It puts you to sleep.'

'Puts you to sleep?' repeated Sami. 'Why?'

Nobody spoke until the silence was broken by Melda.

'In a nuclear bunker,' she said from an adjacent bed, 'I can think of a use for an anaesthetic gas.'

Sami frowned, then said slowly: 'Oh… if all hope is lost…you could go to sleep.'

Madeleine nodded. 'Yes. As long as you're breathing Halothane, you'll stay asleep. If you breathed it for too long…'

Melda stood up. 'But why would such a thing still be here when everything else has been removed?' she asked. 'Do you think it's still operational?'

'Operational?' answered Madeleine. 'I doubt it. Look at this place – as you said, it's old.' She touched the casing. 'It's been built into the wall, so it may have been too difficult to remove. I don't see any controls. Hopefully, the seals are good, but if the cylinders have been here for years, I don't think we need to worry today.'

The red light came on.

'Hurry,' said Sami. 'Stand by the window.'

A minute later, the door in the dining room opened and two men entered. Madeleine recognised both of them. One was Tanaka and the other Dax. It seemed strange to see these two together. She stared at Dax. The last time she had seen him, he had calmly watched while Dopey tried to kill Nico and Logan.

Tanaka came immediately to the window while Dax, carrying two cloth bags, waited by the door. Tanaka studied the people through the glass. He seemed satisfied. He took a phone from his back pocket, pointed it directly at Madeleine and snapped a photo; then he waved to Dax and took up a position facing the window with his arms folded. Behind him, Dax transferred the contents of the bags onto the table. There was bread, cheese, apples, milk, and three plastic cups. *No coffee,* thought Madeleine. She would have liked a coffee to wake her up.

MADELEINE WAS HUNGRY, possibly an after-effect of her injection. She didn't stop eating until all the food was gone. The last piece of bread was washed down by a swallow of milk.

As she sat back on her chair, her stomach satisfied, Sami spread his hands apologetically and said: 'We now must go back to the other room. We can rest there.'

'At least we don't have to do the dishes,' said Madeleine.

Melda patted her arm. 'Good,' she said. 'Stay positive.'

A SHORT TIME AFTER Madeleine had made herself comfortable on a bed, Sami came to sit beside her. He asked what had happened to her, and Madeleine related how she had been offered a tour of the Sistine Chapel in the Vatican. She finished by telling Sami that she had been enticed into the wrong car, and that was all she remembered until she woke up here.

'The man who brought you to the Vatican…' said Sami, '…could he have something to do with your kidnapping?'

'No, that doesn't make sense,' said Madeleine. 'Why would he bother to arrange a tour of the Sistine Chapel? Why take me to the Vatican at all? When that boy reports that he delivered me to the car, or…'

A thought struck her. Could the *choir boy* have been part of the kidnap plot? She remembered thinking he was drugged. Could he have been under the influence of the power?

She threw her hands up in frustration. 'I don't even know *why* I've been kidnapped. I don't know anything that's of use to anyone.'

'It just seems more unlikely…' Sami persisted, '…that someone took advantage of a random opportunity to kidnap you from outside the Vatican. They would have had to be extremely well-informed. Perhaps your Vatican tour was to keep you occupied while arrangements were made. Do you know your benefactor well?'

'We only met yesterday, but he's a respected patron of a medical organisation and well-known at the Vatican. How much further from being a kidnapper can a person get?' She gave a small laugh.

'In any case,' she continued, 'when Giles finds that I've disappeared, I'm sure he'll start a search for me – and he's a powerful man, probably with connections to the…' She stopped. She was going to say 'police', but to complete that sentence would acknowledge the similarity of Giles' connection with the police to Lucifer's with the Carabinieri.

'Did you say his name was…' Sami hesitated, '…*Giles?*'

'Yes. Why?'

Sami looked puzzled. 'I couldn't say it before, but the pain seems…' he paused, testing some thoughts in his mind, '…to have dissipated now.' He took a breath. 'Giles was the name of the man I met at the Golf Club near Vavuniya in Sri Lanka. Giles Vitivelli – I thought his name was strange at the time, especially his surname.'

A jolt passed through Madeleine like an electric shock.

'*Giles Vitivelli?*' she said, incredulous, her voice emerging louder and with a higher tone than she intended. She swallowed and tried to speak normally. 'That's the name of the patron of the GHO, the man who….'

Her mind struggled to put this new piece of information in its place, but she was distracted by something Sami had just said.

'But why is his surname strange? Vitivelli sounds like a normal Italian name to me.'

'It's not Italian at all. 'Vitivelli' in the Tamil language of Sri Lanka means 'Morning Star'.'

And Morning Star was another name for Lucifer.

Madeleine felt ill. A sinking feeling inside felt like her stomach was contracting.

Giles Vitivelli was *Lucifer.*

Several emotions chased through her mind.

Despair… the hope that Giles might charge to her rescue had just evaporated. *Annoyance…* how could she have missed detecting his true intentions? Was he that good at masking his thoughts and feelings? She dismissed that thought. It wasn't possible. More likely, she'd been overawed and let her own emotions get in the way. She recalled she *had* been concerned at some of his *micro-movements,* but she'd overlooked those concerns because of the amazing opportunity he'd presented to her.

And *frustration…* how could she have been so stupid?

As if a veil had lifted, the pieces fitted together.

Giles Vitivelli's *name* was the information that Sami had been taken out of circulation to prevent him from revealing. The pain barriers wore off with time, so Sami couldn't be left on the street.

A horrifying question occurred to her. Why hadn't Lucifer killed Sami? And although her mind recoiled at the thought, she added: '…and Melda?' That would be a more complete and final solution. Was the fact that Lucifer was *now* resorting to murder to cover his actions just a reflection of his increasing desperation?

But wouldn't Lucifer know that the pain barriers wore off and that Sami could tell Madeleine about Giles Vitivelli? Either he'd forgotten that fact, or… or, it didn't matter to him that she knew.

With clarity, she knew the motive for her kidnapping.

Giles… or Lucifer… or whoever he was, intended to use her to force Logan to give up the cylinder and its contents.

CHAPTER TWENTY-SIX

The Magician vs The False Puppet…

Wednesday 11:15 am

Madeleine rested her hands on the table, which had been cleared and again set for three. In front of her was a plastic knife, a plastic fork, and an empty plastic plate. Sami and Melda were still in the bedroom. The man who had invited her, and only her, into the dining room, Giles Vitivelli, sat at the head of the table, next to her, his back to the exterior door.

Tanaka, who had accompanied Giles into the bunker and ensured Madeleine joined him in the dining room, had left and closed the door behind him.

There was a new item in the room. A video camera had been set on a tripod and pointed at an area of bare wall. As far as Madeleine could tell, it was not recording. Two cords connected the camera to sockets on the wall; one was a power cord, the other – Madeleine wasn't sure – it could be a connection to some network.

'I apologise for your experience,' Giles said. Madeleine's antenna was on full alert. Incongruously, his apology was sincere. 'Bringing you here was necessary to ensure that Mr Milan took me seriously, and would accept my invitation to visit me without delay. I know he has an item, a cylinder, that was buried at the *Arsenale* in Venice, and I would like to offer a trade for that item. I admit my treatment of you was heavy-handed, but I didn't have time for other options.'

Apart from the first sentence, the rest of his speech contained several lies, the first that Madeleine had heard from his lips. She had to remind herself that this was Lucifer sitting beside her – the man who had ordered Logan and Nico killed and the man who probably engineered the death of General Mastricht. She was appalled that he would describe her drugging and kidnapping as merely 'heavy-handed' treatment.

'When he arrives,' Giles continued, 'I intend to treat him with the respect due to a fellow practitioner of our art. We'll make an exchange, and you and he will go on your way. This will be over in a few hours.'

More lies. Madeleine noticed he didn't mention the release of Sami and Melda.

'I don't believe you,' she said firmly. 'I believe you're holding me hostage and will continue to do so until Logan does what you require of him. You will just take the cylinder in exchange for me.'

'Just *take* the cylinder? No, no – far too vulgar. One should strive for finesse in life, otherwise why bother. I do intend to propose a sharing of information. I have a manuscript dedicated to Sekhmet that any practitioner would give his little finger to obtain. My manuscript for his will be my simple offer.'

Madeleine watched him carefully while he talked and was surprised to find that he believed what he had just said. But why would he exchange manuscripts when he could simply demand Logan hand over the cylinder in exchange for her release? For the sake of finesse? It didn't make sense. Nothing made sense. Did he have something else in mind? She had no doubt that Lucifer was an unusually complex personality, and perhaps she would never understand him.

By using the words 'practitioner of *our* art' a few moments ago, he was admitting to using the power. Before she thought about it, she said: 'Did you force General Mastricht to take his own life?'

Giles' response was a narrowing of his eyes and a tightening of his lips. He lowered his head and sighed.

'I wanted this meeting to be as pleasant as possible, but I see my effort was wasted.' He lifted just his eyes and regarded her for a few seconds. 'So be it. Let's move straight to the endgame,' he said, his head rising, his voice hardening. 'I do so love the endgame.'

She caught a change behind his eyes. A veil lifted, and Madeleine felt in that instant she was seeing the man behind the façade. *Lucifer.* Whatever was coming next was the real reason for his visit. She was immediately on her guard.

His voice lowered and became monotone. She could hear him speaking, but the words were not intelligible. She recognised the sounds. They were similar to the ones Logan uttered when using the power. Her mind whirled on the verge of panic. How would she know what he intended? She had to hide the fact that she was immune to the power, but how? It seemed hopeless. If she only once didn't react as he expected, she would give herself away in an instant. She had to remember to keep her face as blank and unresponsive as both Tricola's and the Carabinieri Colonel's had been when Logan had used the power at the Crossroads Hotel.

Lucifer reached beneath his coat and withdrew a gun. Her heart leapt to her mouth. He held it with two fingers as if he found touching the object distasteful. Dangling from his hand, it looked huge and menacing. Was he going to shoot her and then Sami and Melda? She involuntarily tensed, but he didn't attempt to grip the gun. Instead, Lucifer bent forward, reached across the table and gently placed the gun on the empty plate in front of her like he was delivering a steak. Even with the gentle placement and the fact that the plate was plastic; to her ears, the gun clattered onto the plate with the noise of a crack of lightning.

Was this a test? Was the gun even loaded? Surely, nobody would give a loaded gun to a hostage – unless… they were supremely confident of their ability to control the hostage.

Still muttering, his hand reached again beneath his coat. Madeleine kept her gaze straight ahead, observing with only her peripheral vision. The hand emerged carrying a twisted stick with a loop at one end. He held the stick upright for a moment, then stretched out his arm and touched

Madeleine's left hand first and then her right with the looped end of the stick. It took all her willpower not to cry out and pull her hands away. He withdrew his arm and reverently laid the twisted stick, the talisman, on the table. With one finger, he traced its length, and when the finger had completed the circle of the loop, he said another unintelligible sentence but this time he said it forcefully. She was certain he had given her an order. He regarded her for a few seconds. Was her face blank enough? How could the turmoil of her mind not be reflected on her face? She was sure her hands were trembling. Was she expected to do something now? She felt a bead of sweat forming in the hairline above her eye. She forced herself to slowly blink. If he became suspicious, she resolved to grab for the gun and shoot. In her mind, she practised the movements she would need.

She jumped when his voice broke into her thoughts, speaking in clear English.

'When I leave, you will wait in this room.'

He rose and walked to the video camera. She watched him as closely as she could without looking directly at him. Had her reaction when he started to speak been noticed?

'When this recording light comes on...' he pointed at a small light on the side of the camera, '...you will stand on that spot against the wall in front of the camera. The camera is connected to a screen in the room where Mr Milan will be standing. Mr Milan will ask you if you are well and ask how you've been treated. You will answer in the affirmative. You are my guest. You will speak only to answer questions. You'll smile, and you'll be relaxed and happy. You have enjoyed your stay here.'

He resumed his seat at the table.

'When the recording light goes out...' he said, '...you will take this gun and shoot the two people next door. Both of them. Push the safety forward and shoot them both twice in the head. Then you will point the gun at your temple, right here...' He picked up the talisman and tapped it against her head. '...*and pull the trigger.*'

He paused, looking at her. Scrutinising her? Did he expect her to reply? She didn't move.

'Nod if you understand me,' he said.

She nodded, keeping it slow.

Lucifer stood up.

He put his hands on his hips and leaned back, stretching his spine. He drew in a long breath.

'Very soon now, my dear, this sad little interlude with its unwelcome distractions will be over, and I can concentrate once again on the realisation of my longer-term plans.' He regarded Madeleine, a pensive look on his face.

'It's sometimes good,' he said, 'to have a captive audience, especially one who will not live to see the end of the day.'

He wagged a finger in the air. 'I'm feeling generous. I'll tell you a secret of life.' Lifting his chin, he pronounced: 'To achieve greatness, you must think great thoughts.' He smiled at her and leaned his hands on the table. 'In less than three months, I will no longer be a Cardinal…' Placing a hand on his chest and, emphasising each word, he said: '*I - will - be - Pope.*'

His eyes widened a tiny fraction – for a man with his control that signified considerable excitement, then he smiled sadly at her. A twisted smile.

She focused on keeping a blank face, but she could read his thought sequence. First, he had expected her to be amazed at his revelation, then he'd realised that in her state, she wasn't going to react.

He looked up at the clock and straightened.

'Time to go. I expect Mr Milan to be arriving soon.'

He picked up the talisman and returned it to his coat; then, with a last glance at her, he turned for the door.

Shoot him as he opens the door!

Could she do it? Could she shoot a man? Even a man like Lucifer? She lifted her hand off the table. She laid it on the gun, fingers curling around the grip.

Lucifer turned back. Madeleine stopped breathing but managed to keep her face blank.

'This information will be of no use to you…' he said. His eyes fell to the gun on the plate – to her hand resting on the gun. He registered surprise, just a flicker, but he wasn't worried.

His eyes lifted to hers and he continued: '…so I can let you into another little secret. My manuscript will be inside a beautiful box covered in red velvet and edged in gold, with a solid gold clasp. Eighteen carat. But…' he paused dramatically, '…the lid of the box is impregnated with poison. An extremely virulent poison that was rumoured to be the favourite of Lucrezia Borgia. It's absorbed through the skin. One has only to touch the lid and… well…' he flicked his fingers. 'Bye, bye,' he whispered. 'A few minutes. No antidote.'

Her heart skipped a beat. He intended to kill Logan.

He was watching her for a reaction. She could see and hear his naked need to be appreciated – for his superiority to be recognised. She wondered if his alarming disclosure about the poisoned box was a final test – but by the time that thought arrived, she was concentrating so totally on ensuring a zero response to anything he said, that a bomb could have exploded outside the door and she would not have flinched.

His face softened and he regarded her with a gaze she would have described as tender in anyone else. His eyes moved between her and the gun and back again.

'Leave the gun on the table when you go to the camera.'

He folded his hands in front of him.

'A pity that this outcome is necessary,' he said. 'I admired you and your work. You're a beautiful woman and young. I think you would have had a stellar career. You had some excellent ideas. Ground-breaking…'

He shrugged and turned away. He lifted a hand and knocked twice on the door. Her hand gripped the gun, lifting it off the plate. It was heavy. She used her other hand to help hold the gun steady and pointed it at his back. Tanaka was probably waiting on the other side. She would need to shoot him, too.

The door opened. Lucifer walked through the door. She pulled the trigger. The gun didn't make a sound. Nothing happened. The door closed behind him.

The safety. *The safety!*

CHAPTER TWENTY-SEVEN

Nico in the field: the beginning…

Wednesday 11:30 am

Nico straightened slowly, using the tree trunk as cover.

He was dressed in a NATO army camouflage suit. A hood covered his head but he had rejected the addition of netting with attached branches and leaves that would have offered him full camouflage in favour of being able to move freely. He'd also refused the Beretta handgun that Serene had offered. She had insisted, however, on the combat knife in his belt.

'You may want to cut something,' she said.

He unclipped a breast pocket and withdrew a small pair of foldable binoculars. Slowly scanning the countryside, taking his time, he carefully inspected areas where a person could be concealed. He detected no unnatural movement.

Nico trained the binoculars on the buildings separated from the main house. The first group was a row of structures, open on one side — gardening or farming implement sheds and a workshop; a garage containing farm vehicles, tractors, and trucks with harvesting gear on the back; other smaller machinery, ride-on mowers. There must be an orchard somewhere, although Nico hadn't seen one. Perhaps it was on the other side of the house.

One of the other buildings had a row of windows, possibly an accommodation building. There were several smaller buildings whose purpose was unclear. He would need to search them all.

Satisfied that there was nobody between his current position and the buildings, he replaced the binoculars and, bending low, moved from behind the tree and headed towards a group of bushes.

He tapped the thread in his ear. 'Moving in on the outer buildings,' he said. 'No sighting of any other people.'

CHAPTER TWENTY-EIGHT

Mount Sinai…

Wednesday 11:45 am

Lucifer put the phone to his ear. His call was answered with: 'Yes, Your Eminence?'

Lucifer said: 'What have you found?'

'I'm sorry, Your Eminence, I've had difficulty with the decryption software. I've searched one of the servers. It does not seem to contain the information you're looking for. But I'm still searching the other two.'

'Does not *seem…?*'

'I've found nothing of interest on the first server.'

'From Tanaka's description of the room and its security, Milan kept something valuable in that room. It must be on those servers. Find it.'

'Yes, Your Eminence. If it's here, I'll find it. But Tanaka may have…'

Lucifer terminated the call.

CHAPTER TWENTY-NINE

Mount Sinai Showdown, Bast vs Sekhmet…

Wednesday 12:00 noon

Logan ascended the steps in front of the mansion on the estate Lucifer called Mount Sinai.

He heard Tricola's voice in his ear: 'All three servers are secure. He won't be able to find anything worthwhile.'

At the top of the steps, a broad flat area flanked by six large columns on each side led to a set of tall double doors standing wide open. The main building stood three storeys high and fifty metres wide. More columns ran in both directions from the main steps in a curving arc extending along the front of the building, becoming widest at the far edges, forming a vast covered courtyard in the shape of a pair of wings.

Several other imposing buildings flanked the main house. From the plans he had studied, Logan knew that one was a garage with room for at least a dozen cars, and the others were guest houses, but even these were substantial two-storey buildings.

Landscaped gardens featuring hedgerows, covered archways, sculptures, and playing fountains were visible to the left and right, and beyond these Logan could see rolling countryside.

In front of the main house, across the circular area where the driveway terminated, an immense tree-lined lawn extended a hundred metres away from the house and ended in a spectacular water display of several fountains playing in harmony. Behind this display and forming a backdrop, the land rose gradually, then more steeply to a flat-topped hill crowned with a grove of trees.

The gardens and lawns were immaculately kept. It was a beautiful and peaceful haven away from the city.

At the doors, a voice greeted him.

'Very punctual, Mr Milan. I see you have brought the cylinder. That's good. Please enter.'

There was a speaker and a camera somewhere, but Logan couldn't see it.

'The second door on the right leads to the Library. I am alone. I've sent everybody away. Please join me.'

Logan stepped through the doors. On the ground floor, several closed doors could be seen on both sides of the massive entrance hall, which rose the full three storeys and terminated in a glass dome, through which Logan could see thin clouds drifting overhead. Walkways on the second and third storeys were visible from where Logan stood, reminding him of an enclosed suburban shopping mall.

The second door on the right was open. Logan walked towards it, his shoes clacking on the marble floor.

He paused at the door and scanned the room. A man, presumably Lucifer, stood beside a table in the centre of the room. A block of four reading desks stood in one corner, and there were easy chairs scattered around the room. On one of the reading desks, behind Lucifer, was a television screen, turned off. All four walls were covered from floor to ceiling by shelves full of books. Halfway up the walls, a narrow landing allowing access to the top shelves could be reached via the spiral staircases located in each of the four corners of the room.

It was an impressive collection of literature that Logan would have liked to explore.

Lucifer stood easily beside the table, his arms folded.

'Mr Milan,' he said. 'We meet at last. You have been a thorn in my side lately.' His voice was deep and smooth, but there was a bite to his last words.

On the table beside Lucifer, sitting on an oval cloth of green baize, stood a box covered in plush red velvet. It was the size of a small briefcase but the lid was curved like the top of a ring box. The edges of the box were trimmed in gold metal, and the centrepiece at the front of the curved lid was an ornate clasp of gold shaped like a caricature face of the Devil, complete with small horns. Set into the gold face where the eyes would be were two large emeralds.

Logan walked forward until he stood a few feet from Lucifer.

'Where is my daughter?' Lucifer asked.

'She will be brought here once Madeleine Galli is safe.'

Lucifer's eyes narrowed.

'Safe?' he said, a smile curling at the edges of his mouth. 'What makes you think Madeleine is in danger?'

Logan didn't reply. Lucifer dismissed the thought and dropped his gaze to the case in Logan's hand. He stared at it.

'Is the Book of Thoth in there?' he asked in a whisper. 'Have you seen it?'

'I haven't opened the cylinder. I was arranging the proper conditions for the opening when I received your message.'

'The Book of Thoth and the was-sceptre of Sekhmet… *together.*' Lucifer seemed entranced with the thought, his face reflecting his desire.

Logan said: 'The length of the cylinder would indicate the was-sceptre is inside.'

Lucifer composed himself. He lifted his head and straightened his shoulders.

'Let us have a gentleman's agreement,' he said. 'From my information, you are sufficiently skilled. We will both recognise and react if the other attempts to use the power, so why not just agree to bypass that option.'

Nico's voice: 'I've searched the first group of buildings. She's not here. There's nobody here.'

Logan bowed his head. 'I've only come for Madeleine,' he said. 'Can I see her?'

'Of course.' Lucifer indicated the television screen. 'Madeleine is waiting in a guest room. You can be assured she is well by talking to her via this screen.'

He reached across and switched it on. Madeleine appeared on the screen, visible from the waist up. She looked calm and composed.

Lucifer inclined his head. 'Talk to her. Ask her anything you like.'

Madeleine was smiling, but the smile did not touch her eyes.

'Where are you?' Logan asked. 'Are you comfortable? The room looks bare, and I don't see any windows.' He was talking for Nico's benefit and hoping to get more information from Madeleine.

Before she could answer, Lucifer turned away from the screen to face Logan and said. 'I assure you she's comfortable, and the room is also comfortable. I expected you'd want to discuss *her* rather than her accommodation.'

'Are you OK?' Logan asked.

'I'm fine.' She had her hands held in front of her. She was twisting them nervously.

Logan gave her a signal for 'Go ahead' in his sign language. He understood she wanted to sign to him.

'Are you hurt in any way?' he asked.

'No, I'm not hurt.'

Her fingers quickly spelt: *D-O*

He gave her a sign to slow down. It was one of the shortcuts he had shown her at the café. If she became too urgent with her signing, Lucifer would notice.

'Are you being held against your will?'

Lucifer turned back to look at the screen, interested in this reply.

Madeleine's hands became still. 'Not at all. I'm a guest,' she said.

Logan looked at Lucifer, watching Madeleine's hands from the corner of his eye. He needed to take Lucifer's attention away from the screen.

'I'm satisfied she's well,' he said. 'You can bring her here now. You have the cylinder.'

Lucifer turned to him. 'All in good time.'

His voice became formal. 'Mr Milan,' he said, 'I'm proposing an exchange. Inside this box…' he waved his hand at the red velvet box, '…resides the *Dedication to Sekhmet* manuscript. It's the copy made in the time of the New Kingdom from the original of the first dynasty. I'm sure you've heard of it. It's genuine. It is the one item in my collection that I consider worthy of offering in exchange for the Book of Thoth.'

While Lucifer was talking, Madeleine spelt: *N-O-T*

Lucifer tilted his head and gave a condescending smile – a teacher reproaching a wayward pupil. 'Unlike you,' he said, 'I do not keep my collection of information in electronic form. Where's the beauty in that? My treasures and my writings lie here, in this room,' he swept his arm around the library, '…where I can see them and, in an appropriate manner, *touch* them.'

T-O-U

He gave an amused grunt as Logan's eyes scanned the room. 'You need to know where to look. They're secure enough.'

C-H

Lucifer turned his palms upward and raised his eyebrows. An invitation.

'So, Mr Milan, let us exchange gifts. As with all exchanges, however, both parties will naturally require verification. I'll need to verify the contents of the cylinder.'

'But surely you're not going to open it here? It needs a controlled environment. You could damage the manuscript.'

L-I-D

'I'm not going to contaminate the contents; just verify them. A short exposure will do no harm. I expect you to do the same with my offering.'

'Are you sure?' said Logan. 'If it's papyrus inside the cylinder, exposure to moist air could be disastrous.'

Madeleine signed: *O-F*

Lucifer looked at him quizzically. 'Papyrus? Why do you talk of papyrus? The Book of Thoth was written on calfskin parchment, probably vellum. If anything, it will be too dry and need moistening.'

'How do you know that?' Logan knew the answer; his source had indicated that parchment had been used, but Madeleine needed more time.

R-E-D

'The Sekhmet Temple paper, from the Clerveaux collection, showed clearly the parchment hieroglyph alongside the hieroglyph of Thoth. You were registered as receiving a copy of that paper. Did you miss such an obvious reference? Or did you not understand it? Perhaps you are not as advanced as I thought.'

Lucifer fixed Logan with a stare that was meant to be intimidating. His eye caught movement on the screen and he turned to it.

Madeleine had signed: *B-O*. She crossed her fingers to signify '*X*' then disguised her movements by continuing to wring her hands.

'Why are you so nervous, my dear?' said Lucifer, softening his tone. 'You've been well treated, haven't you? You can speak freely.'

'Yes, I've been treated well,' said Madeleine. 'I'm just anxious to return to Venice as soon as possible.'

'And so you shall. When we've completed our business here, I'll send a man to fetch you.'

Lucifer had previously said he was alone in the house. Logan wondered where this man was located.

To divert Lucifer's attention away from the screen, he said: 'Let's get to our business then, shall we? Open the cylinder if you must.'

A smile of satisfaction. 'Indeed,' Lucifer said. 'Time to proceed.'

Madeleine's fingers spelt *P-O-I…* She froze as Lucifer looked directly at her. He reached across and switched off the screen, then turned back to face Logan.

'I suggest we open our gifts at the same time,' he said.

Logan lifted his case onto the table. He flipped the catches and opened the box to reveal the gold cylinder inside. He turned the case around so it faced Lucifer.

Lucifer gazed for a moment at the gold cylinder, then used the baize cloth beneath the red box to pull the box towards Logan.

'Please,' he said. 'Open it. I assure you that inside, you will find the contents are exactly as I have described.'

Logan looked at the box. It was beautifully made, a worthy container for such a treasure.

'Was this box made specially to hold the Dedication to Sekhmet manuscript?' he asked.

'Yes, I had the box built,' replied Lucifer. 'It's very special.'

Logan reached his hands out to the box, taking hold of the green cloth to drag it closer.

In a smooth movement, he lifted the cloth and slipped his fingers underneath. Grasping the box with the cloth, he lifted the box and threw both the box and the cloth into the air towards Lucifer – a lazy throw with no force. The box separated from the cloth, rising in an arc, turning over in the air. Lucifer gasped. In a reflex action, he caught the box before it could fall to the floor. Instantly, he snatched his hands away from the red velvet covering as if the fabric was hot, turning his palms upright and staring at them as the beautiful box continued its descent and clattered onto the floor at his feet.

He stood perfectly still for a few heartbeats, his eyes betraying the realisation of what he had done.

His head tilted back, taking his gaze to the ceiling, his pupils unfocused as if he was looking outside the building to the sky or even the stars. He stayed in that position for a long time, then lowered his head and bent to pick up the box.

Logan tensed, ready to move should Lucifer try the same trick and throw the box at him. Lucifer checked the box for damage before carefully placing it on the table.

Logan remained alert. Would Lucifer attack him in desperation?

'If my information is correct,' Lucifer said calmly, 'the death is particularly painful.'

He regarded Logan.

'How you knew is immaterial. But if I must lose, then so will you. I want you to know that Madeleine Galli won't be joining us. At this moment, she is locked in an underground bunker. On my instruction, she has just shot the Sri Lankan banker and his wife dead, and then she has killed herself with a pistol shot to the head.'

Logan heard exclamations of disbelief from Serene and Tricola at the same time. He kept his face impassive. Madeleine would not have been under Lucifer's influence, although she must have led him to believe she was, so he didn't believe she had shot anyone. Nico would have taken note of Lucifer's revelation of Madeleine's whereabouts and know he didn't need to search the big house.

'So, Sami is also here,' Logan said, deliberately using the present tense.

Lucifer ignored him. He raised a hand and pointed a finger at Logan. 'Sekhmet won the original battle,' he said, 'and *I* will claim some victory in this one.'

He lowered his hand and thrust it into his pocket, pulling out a black object the size of a matchbox. His thumb hovered over a large red button. His eyes narrowed and his lips tightened to a snarl as he thrust down on the button with excessive force. A green light glowed on the top of the box.

'I planned for every contingency,' he said, his eyes glinting with determination. 'With this device, I've sealed the door leading to the bunker. It's a substantial door, built to survive a bomb blast. You won't get through it even with a blowtorch. No one can get in or out of the bunker now.'

Lucifer showed his satisfaction with a grim smile.

'A gas has also been released,' he said, watching Logan closely for his reaction. 'If anything has gone wrong and there are people still alive in the bunker, they will fall into a deep sleep from which they will never wake. The gas will continue to flow until it builds up to a toxic amount. In two hours, anyone alive now in that bunker will certainly be dead.'

He shook his head. 'You may find them eventually, but you'll only find their bodies.'

His dark eyes bored into Logan's. 'I'm also happy to inform you that Mr Bowers will not let you leave the house alive.'

'I heard that.' Nico's voice in his ear. 'Bowers and his crew are out here, probably covering the entrance. I'll find them.'

Lucifer shook his head again. The movement seemed to cause him pain, and his hand went to his head, his brow creasing.

A string of sounds came from his mouth. Immediately, Logan also began talking, recognising the spell Lucifer was using and issuing a counter to nullify its effect. Within the counter spell he was uttering, Logan interspersed a spell of his own, a technique he had practised the previous night. The spell was designed to affect speech and would have rendered Lucifer mute in just a few seconds. Lucifer's eyes showed his surprise, but he responded without hesitation, abandoning his first spell and countering Logan's spell instead. When Logan took a breath, Lucifer managed to place the seed of a coercion spell, but Logan burst the seed before Lucifer could augment it. Logan mixed two spells, one hidden behind the other, but Lucifer didn't allow either to take root. After a further half-minute of duelling with thrust and counter-thrust, Lucifer stopped, recognising the futility of continuing. Logan didn't press his advantage.

'I suspected that might occur with two sufficiently advanced practitioners,' Lucifer said. 'I withdraw my previous assessment. You...' he paused, his eyes registering momentary confusion. He took two quick breaths. '...are a worthy opponent.' He sighed heavily, looking suddenly tired.

His teeth showed between his lips in a forced smile, then his body jerked, and he frowned. A groan came from deep in his throat. He leaned against the table. Logan started forward to help him, then stopped himself. To touch the man might be fatal.

'I could have had the world,' Lucifer said, his words slurred.

'You followed Sekhmet. You took the wrong road,' Logan replied.

Frothy saliva gathered at the corners of Lucifer's mouth. His knees bent and his hands scrambled across the table in a vain attempt to hold him upright. He groaned again, the sound developing into a long moan forced between his clenched teeth, a white frothy stream running down his chin. His legs collapsed, and he crumpled to the floor, his body folding into a foetal position. His muscles contracted, pulling against themselves, stiffening his limbs and distorting his face, the cords in his neck starkly visible.

With a sigh as his last breath was expelled from his lungs, his head went limp, falling back onto the floor with a crack.

Lucifer lay still.

The room was silent.

'Logan?' Serene's voice. 'Are you OK?'

'Lucifer is dead,' Logan said. 'Nico, can you hear me? Have you seen any sign of the underground bunker where Madeleine is being held?'

Nico answered: 'No.' In that one word, Logan could hear frustration and hopelessness. Searching above ground for an underground bunker was an impossible task.

'Tricola…' he said. 'I saw nothing in the plans that might be a bunker. Did you know about the bunker?'

Tricola's voice answered in his ear. 'No. I've never heard of a bunker. I don't know where it is.'

'What about the door?' Serene said. 'It's probably a metal door. We should look for that.'

'The house is huge,' said Logan. 'And the door could be in one of the other buildings. It would take a long time to search for the door, and even if I can find the right door, I won't be able to open it.'

He imagined being at the door to the bunker, knowing Madeleine was close, knowing she was dying. He forced himself away from those thoughts.

Even if he broke the task before them into steps, each step seemed impossible. Find the entrance door: impossible. Get through the door: impossible. Find another way into the bunker: impossible. Get Madeleine and Sami and probably Sami's wife out before they died from the gas: impossible.

Tricola's voice said: 'Wait…'

Even if everything else was impossible, the first thing they had to do was find the bunker. Concentrate on that. Had Lucifer said anything that might reveal the bunker's whereabouts? He recalled their conversation. He couldn't find any clues in Lucifer's words. Except… Lucifer had said that Logan may find the people in the bunker eventually. Did that mean there was another entrance? Logan shook his head in frustration. More probably he meant that with the right equipment, they may eventually get through the door.

'They'd need air if the bunker was underground,' said Tricola.

In a flash, Logan knew what she was about to say.

'Tricola, ask Archie to drive you here as fast as he can. Minutes count. You'll need to show us where you hid in the brambles. Serene, mobilise your men. Bowers must be neutralised before Tricola arrives. Nico…'

'I have Dax and Siska in sight,' said Nico.

Logan opened his mouth to advise Nico what to do with Dax and Siska, then closed it again. He'd let Nico decide that.

Logan remembered Lucifer's comment that Mr Bowers would not let him leave the house alive. Did Bowers know what had happened? Was Lucifer in contact with him? If Bowers knew Lucifer was dead, what would he do? Cut his losses and run? Or come into the house to finish the job?

He should check Lucifer's ears… carefully… and look for an earpiece. In the meantime, he'd better stay away from the windows.

He cautiously approached Lucifer's body. The green baize cloth was on the floor beside the body. Lucifer had handled it so it would be clean. Using the cloth, he parted Lucifer's hair and peered into his ear. The ear was particularly small, only three or four centimetres across, just as Tricola had described. He saw no evidence of an earpiece. He turned Lucifer's head, careful not to touch his skin with anything other than the cloth, and got down on one knee to look into his other ear. Again, nothing inside.

Lucifer could have a microphone in the Library, but Logan thought it unlikely. That wouldn't allow two-way communication. Tricola had said Tanaka had tracked her with a recciver in his ear, so if Lucifer and Bowers were communicating, that was the more likely method. Bowers' instructions must have been simple enough to not require elaboration. He had to assume Bowers was watching the entrance and still waiting for him to leave the house.

Logan said aloud: 'Lucifer has no earpiece. I don't think he was in communication with Bowers. Bowers probably doesn't know what's happened. He'll be waiting for me to walk out of the house.'

His eye fell on the red box, sitting innocently on the table where Lucifer had placed it. Madeleine had told him the lid was poisoned. What about the sides, the interior, the *bottom*? He stared at the green cloth he still held in his hand. The bottom of the box had been in contact with the cloth. He breathed in. He felt a tingle at his fingertips. Real or imagined? The efficiency with which the poison did its job had been amply demonstrated.

Logic told him that when Madeleine had said the lid was poisoned, she meant *only* the lid. He had no choice. He had to believe the bottom of the box was not impregnated with the poison; that the cloth he was holding was safe; and that the poison was not, at that very moment, speeding along his veins to his heart. He waited a few seconds to see if the tingling re-appeared.

It didn't.

Was it worth the risk to open the box?

Logan took extra care not to touch the side of the green cloth that had made contact with Lucifer's face. He had no idea whether Lucifer's skin or sweat contained the poison, but it was possible.

He put the tip of his finger, covered by the cloth, underneath the Devil's chin and lifted it. The Devil's face turned upward. Logan continued to lift, raising the lid. Inside, cushioned by the velvet interior, lay a manuscript written on yellowed parchment.

Logan did not understand why Lucifer had chosen to put something so valuable inside the box. It seemed an unnecessary risk. Perhaps he was so confident of the outcome that he knew he would not be giving the manuscript up. Or, maybe he would not have wanted to risk Logan doing something rash when he realised the contents were not as Lucifer had described, before the poison had time to act.

Whatever the reason, the contents of the box were genuine, an ancient manuscript just as Lucifer had claimed. A manuscript protected by the equivalent of a poisoned chalice.

He bent close and knew with certainty what he was looking at.

Stillborn calves were prized in ancient Egypt because from them could be produced the finest quality parchment, called uterine vellum – the material on which this manuscript was written.

The text on the first sheet was Egyptian.

The first words read: *Dedication to Sekhmet.*

CHAPTER THIRTY

Nico in the field: the end...

Wednesday 12:45 pm

Dax and Siska lay on the ground ten metres in front of where Nico was concealed behind a fallen log. Dax had binoculars up to his eyes, observing the entrance steps to the mansion. They were positioned at right angles to the entrance and a hundred and fifty metres from it. On the ground alongside Dax lay a rifle with a telescopic sight. Siska squirmed from her stomach onto her side. She reached out with one hand for a drink bottle leaning against a backpack between their knees.

'Lucifer said Milan would be out again within thirty minutes,' she said in a bored tone. 'It's been forty-five already. I'm tired of lying in the grass.'

When Dax didn't comment, she said: 'We're only backup. Bowers wants to take the shot. You know we're not going to do anything. How long do we have to wait here?'

Dax put the binoculars down between them and took up the rifle. He put the scope to his eye.

'Do you see something?' Siska asked. She stoppered the drink bottle and flopped back onto her stomach. She picked up the binoculars with one hand. 'What did you see?'

'Why don't you shut up?' said Dax. 'You talk too much. It would be better if you weren't here.'

'*I* don't know what I'm doing here, either,' Siska said, 'I haven't even got a rifle. All I've got is this useless…'

Nico rose from his prone position, crossed the log, closed the distance and was on them in one smooth motion. Two fingers stabbed into the base of Dax's neck.

At the sound of Nico's approach, Siska had risen onto one elbow, dropping the binoculars, twisting toward him, her other hand coming into view. In the hand was an automatic pistol. She must have already been holding it. He hadn't anticipated that.

She hesitated, looking at him incredulously.

'You…' she said. 'How…?'

Nico started the move to knock the gun from her hand, then stopped. Even with the speed he knew he had, she could shoot him before he reached her. If he tried, she would pull the trigger reflexively before she thought about it. The gun was steady, pointing at Nico's chest.

She looked into his eyes.

Deliberately, she pointed the gun away from him. 'I don't want to do this anymore,' she said.

She opened her hand and let the gun fall to the ground. Nico picked it up and tossed it towards the log that he had hidden behind.

He checked Dax. He was trying to rise, but he was unable to move, his limbs paralysed. He grunted, struggling for breath. Nico reached over his shoulder and eased the rifle from his grasp. He also threw it in the direction of the log. It landed with a clatter. He checked inside Dax's jacket and found another pistol like Siska's, tossing that to join the rifle.

Siska watched him.

'Bowers, Tanaka, and Dopey are in front of that grove of trees on the hilltop over there,' she said, nodding toward a hill about two hundred metres distant, talking fast. 'Bowers will shoot Milan as soon as he leaves the house. Watch out for Dopey. You won't be able to take him alone. Tanaka's good; he's strong, but I've seen him hit Dopey with everything he's got and Dopey just laughed. I hope you have plenty of backup. If so, please do me a favour and take them out. If you don't kill all three, I'll be looking over my shoulder for the rest of my life.'

'I can't let you go,' said Nico.

'Tie me up,' she said. 'I won't cry out, but knock me out if you need to be sure. I'll take my chances. I want all this to be over. I hope it counts for something that I could have killed you, and didn't.'

'Take off your shoes.'

'What?'

'Take off your shoes and socks,' repeated Nico.

He waited while she did as he asked.

'Now, sit up,' he said.

She sat up, lifting her chin. Nico used the edge of his hand to hit her beside her eye. Siska's head snapped to one side, her eyes glazed, and she slumped to the ground.

Nico pulled Dax's arms together behind his back, pulling a plastic cable tie from his belt and zipping it around Dax's wrists. He pushed Dax into the recovery position on his side and zip-fastened his legs.

'You'll be able to breathe properly in a few minutes,' Nico said. 'Don't struggle or you'll make it worse.'

He took one of Siska's socks and pushed it into Dax's mouth, holding it in place with a plastic tie, then used Siska's other sock to gag her in the same manner. He checked that she was breathing easily, then he zip-fastened her hands behind her and did the same to her legs.

Nico picked up the rifle and the two guns. He'd discard them when he found a suitable spot.

'Dax and Siska are out of the picture,' he said. 'They can be picked up later. I assume you heard her.'

'We heard, but that was close. Please be careful,' said Serene. 'We're on our way. ETA ten minutes. The bus is a convenient cover, but it's slow. We'll meet you beside the grove of trees.'

NICO MOVED FORWARD a metre. He was balanced on his elbows and knees and with a slow crab-like movement, he crossed another metre of ground. Through the trees to his front, he could hear the accent of Tanaka and Dopey's high-pitched voice, but Bowers wasn't in the conversation. Nico expected that. Bowers would be ever the professional, concentrating on the target.

Another metre. Ahead was a tree Nico estimated would be between ten and twenty metres from the two men. He would be able to observe from behind that tree, a little closer than he would have liked, but the small grove was the only cover on the hilltop. His right arm moved at the same time as his left leg, and he crept forward.

He reached the base of the tree. The voices of Tanaka and Dopey were close, more like ten metres than twenty. They were talking about tomorrow's weather and the likelihood of rain. Nico wondered why Bowers was allowing them to talk aloud about such unimportant matters. They should be concentrating on the mission. Maybe Bowers wasn't there.

Nico deliberated whether he should try to rise up behind the tree. He was too close. If someone was looking in his direction, any small movement would be noticed. He decided to move back and wait for Serene. He moved his leg…

A weight hit him in the centre of his back, driving the wind from his lungs, a wave of pain surging from his bruised chest. He gasped, trying to draw in air, but the knock had interrupted the normal working of his diaphragm, rendering him temporarily unable to breathe. Nico tried to relax, knowing his diaphragm muscle would resume normal functioning in a few seconds. He turned his head and felt the prick of a knife at his throat.

'If you *can* move – don't!' said a voice that could only belong to Bowers.

Nico heard heavy feet approaching through the trees. Dopey and Tanaka.

'Having trouble with your breathing?' Bowers asked sarcastically. The knee in his back and the knife at his throat were removed.

'Dopey, pick him up.'

Bowers had been waiting for him. Nico had not seen him, nor heard him, nor smelt him. He felt Bowers remove Nico's knife from his belt. A heavy foot thumped down centimetres from his nose.

Nico gasped again, trying to force air into his lungs. His chest wouldn't move. The breathing movement started but then stopped as if his body had forgotten what to do next.

Dopey carried him through the trees, deliberately letting his head make contact with a tree. Nico winced but made sure he didn't cry out.

'Don't damage him,' said Bowers. 'I want to talk with him.'

'I want to talk to him too.' That was Tanaka. Nico could imagine the sort of talk that Tanaka wanted.

'You watch the main doors. Let me know the second you see anything.' Nico heard Bowers walking away. 'I'll check for any more trespassers.'

Serene's voice in his ear: 'We're close. Seven minutes from your position. Are you OK? Hold on, Nico.'

Logan's voice: 'If you need it, say the help word, and I'll show myself at the door to distract them.'

Nico found he could breathe tiny shallow breaths. His lungs were able to expand a little more than before. His bruised chest made breathing painful, and he couldn't talk yet. Dopey sat him down against a tree.

Bowers returned through the trees carrying a rifle with a telescopic sight.

'When you finish with question, I like to teach this man a lesson,' said Tanaka. 'He trick me before. He not trick me again.'

Bowers stood in front of Nico, rifle in his hand, looking down.

'Are you alone?' he asked.

Nico grunted. His breathing was improving with each passing second, but he had to stall Bowers as long as he could to allow time for Serene to arrive.

Bowers raised the rifle and struck Nico hard on the foot with the butt. Nico wore solid army boots, but the heavy blow on the top of his foot caused a flash of intense pain.

'I asked you…' Bowers began.

'I see Milan!' said Tanaka. 'Wait. Now he gone back inside.'

Bowers snatched up binoculars from beside Tanaka. He trained them on the doors of the big house.

'He come out, then he look like he forget something and go back in,' said Tanaka.

'Dopey, what did you see?' asked Bowers.

'Same, Boss,' said Dopey. 'I didn't see him come out, but I saw him go back in.'

'What's Lucifer doing?' said Bowers, frustration in his voice. 'If he's finished with Milan, why doesn't he send him out?'

Bowers was talking to himself, but his words were confirmation that Lucifer and Bowers had not been in communication.

Bowers looked at Nico.

'I don't have time for you,' he said. 'I saw no one else. I think you're alone. I'd shoot you, but Milan won't come out if he hears a shot.'

He looked at Tanaka and Dopey. 'Kill him. Both of you. No noise. I'll watch the doors.'

Tanaka said: 'Me first.'

Bowers said sharply: 'This is not a contest. *Both* of you, kill him quickly and quietly so we can concentrate on the job we're here to do.'

He stood with his back against a tree so he could observe the mansion entrance and also keep an eye on the action. Nico could see he was anticipating the spectacle as much as his men.

Nico got to his feet. He tested his foot. Sore but stable, nothing broken. He took a breath. His chest stuttered. Not yet fully functional, but he was getting oxygen.

Dopey giggled. He moved his shoulders and flexed his massive hands.

Nico stood with his back to the grove of trees. The small clearing in front of the trees formed a natural flat circle bordered by the trees on one side and the edge of the hill on the other. Over the edge, the land dropped steeply for twenty metres, then eased quickly to a gentle slope. At the bottom of the slope, Nico could see a row of fountains.

Tanaka moved forward, and Nico backed away from him.

'He scared,' said Tanaka.

Nico glanced at the trees and considered running through them. His bruised foot would slow him. He dismissed the thought. He needed to at least keep these men occupied as long as possible. Bowers caught his glance.

'If you run, I'll shoot you. Then I'll go inside the house and shoot Milan.'

Tanaka moved forward again. The hands he held in front of him were only partly closed into fists. Nico moved away but Dopey blocked his path. Tanaka gave a cry, leapt forward and threw a straight punch. Nico moved his head and the punch flew past his ear. Nico couldn't resist the opening Tanaka's extended arm presented. He bent his knees and punched Tanaka in his exposed side. A solid blow, it would hurt but not disable. Tanaka grunted and pulled back.

He switched his stance and advanced again. Nico recognised that Tanaka was using the Shotokan style of karate, a traditional style. He was unlikely to do anything unorthodox. Dopey also lumbered forward and Nico moved away from them both but he was running out of room and was being pushed into the trees. Tanaka moved to prevent Nico from entering the trees, closing the distance. He flicked a backhand blow at Nico's head. Nico easily ducked the blow and took another step back. Tanaka's punches were technically correct and fast but not *very* fast; a man who excelled in the dojo but not in the street.

Nico felt Dopey's presence. The big man was closer than he thought. Nico's shoulder was suddenly being painfully squeezed in a vice. One huge hand had caught him; not a blow, Dopey had simply lunged forward and grabbed Nico, his fingers digging into the flesh. The man was close enough to have punched Nico's head and if he'd done so, it may have been all over. But Dopey was used to winning with his strength, not by punches.

Dopey squeezed.

Nico felt as though his shoulder was about to pop. He twisted, bent his knees again and punched his fist into Dopey's hand from below, hitting the tender part underneath the wrist, his knuckles driving into and separating the tendons. Dopey howled in pain and let go. He shook his wrist.

Nico realised he could not afford to play a delaying game. If he tried to gain time by only defending and running, he risked getting caught again. He had to go onto the offensive. He shook his head. Even if he could disable both Tanaka and Dopey, he knew Bowers would be watching with a rifle in his hand — but he would worry about that later. He would try to circle and move closer to Bowers; he may get close enough for a surprise attack. He rotated his shoulder to test it. It was becoming a familiar story. Another part of his body was sore but functional.

'Five minutes,' said Serene's voice through his earpiece. 'Stay alive.'

Five minutes was too long.

Nico turned to face Tanaka and Dopey. Both of them were moving forward more confidently now.

Nico took the opportunity as soon as it appeared. Tanaka advanced in his straightforward style. Counting on him not to deviate from his current path, Nico leapt into the air toward Tanaka, feet forward, his body twisting and one knee bending. At the last moment, his foot flew out and the heel of his boot crashed against Tanaka's knee. Nico heard the bone break. He regained his feet as Tanaka started to fall, adjusting his stance for a twisting side punch. His fist twisted just as ShangWu's uncle had taught him, and even though Tanaka was falling fast, the projecting knuckles of Nico's hand caught Tanaka perfectly in the throat, crushing his larynx.

ShangWu's uncle had taught Nico to kill his opponent after delivering such a blow as the alternative death by suffocation was painful and unnecessarily prolonged, but Nico did not have time for such niceties.

He flicked his eyes to Bowers. Would he use the rifle now that Tanaka was down? He checked the distance between them. Still too far. Bowers would be able to bring the rifle up before Nico could reach him.

'One down,' he said, softly enough so only Logan and Serene would hear. Tricola was listening in too, he remembered. Tricola, who was speeding to the estate to help find Madeleine. Minutes were important. His resolve strengthened. He couldn't depend on Serene arriving in time. Nico had to stop these men himself.

Bowers looked at Tanaka, writhing on the ground.

'I did not like that man,' he said. 'Good riddance.' He looked up. 'But Dopey will catch you. There's nowhere to go.' He smiled. 'Your speed will not help you.'

Dopey had stopped when Tanaka had been hit, and he was staring at the man on the ground. Tanaka's hands were at his throat. A strangled, gurgling sound came from between his teeth.

Nico took a step then raised onto the toe of his foot, turning, jumping and sending a spinning back kick crashing against the side of Dopey's head. He had to reach high to make contact more than two metres off the ground, and it was a difficult stretch. Nico felt the jarring impact against his foot. It was the one Bowers had hit with the rifle butt and the renewed pain was sudden and intense. Maybe something *was* broken. He completed the spin and recovered his stance, limping as his foot struggled to hold him. He expected to see Dopey on the ground, but the big man had just staggered back and was still upright, shaking his head. Nico moved forward as quickly as his foot would allow. He wouldn't be able to kick with that foot again.

Dopey swung an arm at him, but he went underneath and hit Dopey with force in the solar plexus under the ribs. It was like hitting a plank of wood. The punch seemed to have no effect.

Nico heard Bowers laughing.

'Everyone makes the same mistake,' Bowers said. 'You can't hurt him. He's covered in an armour plate of muscle. And he only has to catch you once.'

Nico backed away from Dopey, shaking his arm as if he had hurt it, using that as cover to back towards Bowers' voice behind him. Could he get close enough?

Bowers was instantly alert. 'No closer. Take another step and I'll shoot.'

Nico stopped.

Dopey was smiling. He moved his head back and forth, already recovered from Nico's blow. The muscles in his neck must be immensely strong.

Nico remembered ShangWu's uncle telling him the story of Yim Wing Chun, the young girl who founded the Shaolin Wing Chun Kung Fu style. Wing Chun had developed the style to give smaller fighters like herself an advantage. In the legend, she had fought a much bigger man and used his size and strength against him.

Nico closed his eyes and calmed his breathing. He heard Dopey take a step toward him, then another. He felt the moment when Dopey thought he might catch Nico with his eyes closed, and the big man lumbered forward at a run to close with Nico. Still with his eyes closed, Nico ducked low. He heard and felt Dopey's arm swish over his head. He had the absurd feeling that he could continue this fight with closed eyes, so clearly did he feel the presence of his opponent.

He opened his eyes and bent lower. Pushing with his good leg, he struck the side of Dopey's knee with the heel of his palm. Again, the jar in his arm told him the blow had been true, but although he grunted, the big man seemed unaffected. Nico knew the blows he had delivered would have disabled a normal man. How could he defeat someone who absorbed everything he could throw? Dopey's legs were as solid as tree trunks and just as immovable.

Nico remembered the Wing Chun philosophy – multiple strikes against the same target would accumulate and eventually be successful. Dopey continued to swing and reach with his big arms in an effort to catch hold of Nico, but Nico borrowed again from the Wing Chun style and flowed around Dopey's slow and awkward movements. Nico hit Dopey's knee in precisely the same spot again and again, as well as striking pressure points on his spine, arms and neck. Striking these points would typically have resulted in significant pain or, as in Dax's recent experience, temporary paralysis, but in Dopey, the vital locations were enfolded in muscle and difficult to reach.

Nico noticed the change when it came.

Continually moving around the clearing and swinging those massive arms was taking its toll on Dopey. The big man was breathing heavily, his actions becoming slower and more laboured. Nico could see that being continually hit without being able to retaliate was also having an effect mentally. Dopey cried out in his frustration, the noise more a squeal than a roar.

He abandoned caution and rushed headlong at Nico.

Nico slid to the side and as Dopey's momentum carried him past, Nico was presented with a clear target of the knee with the luxury of extra time to deliver. He drew on another facet of the philosophy of his Chinese tutors at the Shaolin school and channelled his inner Qi, the life energy, striking with increased force. ShangWu's uncle had said that the energy of a Qi blow preceded it like a wall of air.

As the heel of Nico's hand crashed with extra power against the knee joint, Dopey stumbled. His damaged leg would no longer hold his considerable weight.

Dopey's gaze flicked to Bowers. 'Shoot him,' he pleaded in his high squeaky voice.

Nico seized the opportunity that Dopey's momentary inattention provided. He leapt to the side, twisted his body, and threw his entire bodyweight behind his shoulder, driving it into the giant's side under the armpit. There was a risk that Dopey could enfold Nico with his massive arms and trap him, and in the beginning, that's probably what would have happened.

But three things had changed. Dopey was tired, he was hurting, and he was standing too near the edge. Even a few minutes ago, he would have been able to save himself, but the solid leg that would have prevented him from falling, the one that Nico had hit a dozen times, gave way.

Dopey stumbled on the edge of the hilltop, his body still moving in the direction Nico's charge had forced him. The action seemed to happen in slow motion. With nothing but air to arrest his fall, the giant man toppled over the rim, and with his arms spread wide, uttering a high-pitched wailing sound, he dropped twenty metres before crashing to the earth. He rolled three times and didn't move.

The air was still and quiet.

Nico saw that Bowers was ready for him if he tried anything. Nico's attack had taken him away from Bowers to the very edge of the clearing – he was too far away. Any attempt to get to Bowers from this position would not succeed.

He spared a glance at Tanaka. The man was dead.

'If I hadn't seen that myself, I wouldn't have believed it.' Bowers straightened. 'Dopey was a particularly useful man. I'm sorry to lose him.' He shook his head in admiration. 'I've never seen anyone move that fast.'

'I almost hate to do this,' Bowers said, raising the rifle.

Bowers' hand moved to the trigger. From the corner of his eye, Nico saw Logan come through the doors of the big house at a run in a futile last-minute attempt to distract Bowers.

The shot echoed like a clap of thunder in the still afternoon air.

Blood and bone exploded from Bowers' head, flowing in a river down his face, reaching the end of his nose as his legs crumbled and he fell in a lifeless heap.

In Nico's ear, Serene said: 'Cavalry's here.'

CHAPTER THIRTY-ONE

A rescue attempt, a race against gas and time…

Wednesday 1:30 pm

Tricola pointed into the centre of what looked to be a natural thicket of tangled bramble bushes. If an air duct to the bunker *was* hidden under the brambles, it was efficiently disguised and protected. To the eye, there was no sign of any man-made structure apart from a raised hump in the centre.

'I crawled in there to hide. The pipe with the fan inside is in the middle.'

'I don't hear a fan,' said Logan. 'It must be quiet.'

Tricola nodded. 'I didn't hear it until I was close.'

'We'll need protection to get through that,' Nico said, pulling off his camouflage jacket. Logan took off his own jacket – an expensive *Brioni*.

Serene was standing with two of her men a short distance away. She took a phone from her ear and finished the call, walking toward Logan and Nico.

Two groups of four men had been dispatched to collect the bodies, two alive, three dead, from the countryside, and another two men had entered the house to retrieve Lucifer's body. Logan warned them not to touch the body or the red box on the table without protection.

Logan looked up as Serene approached. 'Serene, how long since Lucifer released the gas?'

Serene checked her watch. 'Sixty-five minutes since Lucifer's announcement.'

She handed him a small flashlight. 'Here's the flashlight you asked for. The soldiers all carry them as part of their kit. This belongs to the Sergeant.'

'Thanks. Were you able to talk to a doctor?'

'Yes. A doctor will be here in fifteen minutes. And Sir Brian has arranged for two ambulances also.'

'What about the Police?' he asked.

'They will not be involved.'

'The doctor, is he…?'

'He's known to us.'

'Thank you, and please thank Sir Brian.'

'Of course, but it's not necessary.'

Logan copied Nico, reversing his jacket and using the sleeves to protect his hands. Nico stepped forward to lead the way. Logan put a hand on his shoulder.

'You're limping. How is your leg?'

'Bruised. It won't slow me down.'

Logan nodded and Nico entered the thicket, pushing aside the thorny bramble stems. Logan followed, clearing the way for Serene and Tricola. Nico reached the centre and pulled apart some thicker stems to reveal that the hump was a mound of earth. Set into the mound was a metal pipe. When Logan peered into the pipe, he could see the fan Tricola had mentioned.

'I see the fan but it's not turning,' he said, frowning.

Serene said: 'That's a good sign. The fan would be stopped when the gas was released, so it's an indication this *is* an air duct into the bunker.'

'Anyone smell anything?' said Logan.

'The gas could be odourless,' said Serene, 'but, in any case, the air duct will probably have been closed by a shutter to keep the gas from escaping the bunker. You may have to break through the shutter to get inside.'

Nico bent to enter the pipe, but Logan stopped him.

'There'll be gas inside the bunker. We don't have masks. I'll go. If I slow my heartbeat, I can hold my breath for more than five minutes.'

Nico acknowledged and stepped back. 'Which means,' he said, 'after two and a half minutes, you must turn back.'

'If Serene's right, I won't meet the gas until I break through the shutter.'

Serene nodded. 'We should be able to hear you moving along the pipe,' she said. 'When you get to a point where you need to hold your breath and can't talk, tap twice on something every ten seconds or so to let us know you're OK. We don't know what the gas is, so we don't know how fast it operates. At the first sign of drowsiness or dizziness, get out as quickly as you can. We can regroup and try again.'

Logan knelt and entered the pipe. It was large enough to crawl on his hands and knees. At the fan, he eased himself between the blades. It was a tight fit.

'Nico,' he said, 'can you try and widen these blades to make it easier on the way out.'

He continued head-first down the pipe, hearing Nico enter the pipe behind him.

After ten metres, the pipe suddenly curved downwards. It was becoming difficult to see, so Logan switched on the flashlight. The light was bright. The beam showed a drop of two metres then the pipe curved out of sight. It would be difficult to get an unconscious person up this shaft single-handed.

'Ten metres in, there's a vertical shaft that drops two metres,' he said. He spoke normally, knowing he could be heard through the earpieces. 'Someone will need to be at the top when I return with Madeleine and the others. Nico, you'd better come to this point and bring the soldiers with you; there may be more sections like this.'

He dropped down the shaft, noting that the vertical shaft was wider than the horizontal pipe. He squatted, bending his neck, and shone the flashlight along the lower pipe. Only the faintest of light from the surface reached to this point. At first, it looked like the pipe terminated after another ten metres, but on closer inspection, he could see it was another downturn. He crawled forward. One metre down the second shaft, he saw a set of closed shutters.

'You're right, Serene,' he said. 'There's a second shaft, and the pipe has been closed off.'

He took a moment to assess his condition. He didn't feel sleepy. The air was a little stale but it was breathable.

The shutter did not look sturdy. It was designed to keep nothing heavier than gas on the other side.

'I'm going to hold my breath and kick through the shutter. You'll hear when that happens.'

Logan heard Serene's voice in his ear: 'Watch each other,' she said, her warning directed to Nico and the soldiers. 'If the gas is lighter than air, some may come up the shaft.'

Logan slowed his heartbeat. He breathed slowly and deeply a few times, noted the time on his watch, then raised his foot and kicked downward at the shaft. The closed shutter was metal, but a light metal like aluminium. His first kick tore the shutter free, and it fell another metre, clattering when it hit the metal floor of the shaft. Logan shone the flashlight into the hole. He couldn't see where the pipe went from the bottom of the shaft. He lowered himself down feet first and crouched at the bottom.

The pipe continued level for two more metres and terminated at another set of metal shutters.

Why would two shutters be needed?

He crawled forward. It wasn't another shutter – it was an open grill.

It was where the air duct met the bunker. He had to return to the second shaft to have enough room to twist around so his feet faced forward. He shuffled back to the grill and kicked out with both feet at the metal cover.

It came away in one corner. He kicked again, harder. Two more corners came loose. He kicked again at the last corner, and the grill fell into the room. The activity had caused a rise in his heartbeat. He calmed himself and slowed it again.

'Tap twice if you're OK.' Serene's voice.

He tapped twice on the side of the pipe.

Inside, the room was pitch black. Logan dropped onto the floor and shone the flashlight around the walls. In the centre of the room was a table and six chairs. Logan searched for an indication that Madeleine was here. It was an underground room, but was it the bunker they were seeking? There could be several underground rooms on the estate. Had he gone to all this time and effort only to work his way into a different bunker?

He moved to the table and swept the room again with the flashlight beam. This time, he noticed there was another item in the room. A video camera on a stand. Instantly, he knew this was where Madeleine had been when he talked to her. She had stood there against that wall and warned him about the red box.

But now the room was empty.

There were two doors and Logan crossed the room to one of the doors. He turned the handle. It was locked. It was a solid metal door, perhaps the one that had been sealed by Lucifer. He looked at the other door. It had no door handle. How did it open? There was a glass window in the wall beside the door. Logan checked his watch. One and a half minutes had passed. He was feeling good.

He shone the flashlight through the window.

He saw Madeleine first. She was on a bed, but rather than laying on top, she was kneeling, slumped upright against the wall. On an adjacent bed lay Sami Bandarakaianan and another woman, presumably his wife.

Logan picked up a chair and threw it against the window. The chair was light and bounced off the glass without damaging it. Logan strode to the video camera and yanked out the cords attaching it to the wall. He closed the three legs of the stand and picked it up, then returned to the window, where he swung the metal stand with the camera attached at the window as if chopping at a tree with an axe. The camera crashed into the glass, and the window shattered.

Logan slowed his heart again and shone the flashlight on his watch. Two minutes. He tapped twice on the window frame as a signal to the others.

Nico's voice said: 'I'm at the top of the second shaft with the sergeant. We've been here a while. No effects yet. Looks like the gas is heavier than air.'

If enough gas is released, thought Logan, it will expand and, after filling the bunker, without the shutter blocking it, the gas will eventually work its way up the air duct.

Logan used the legs of the camera stand to clear the glass from the bottom of the window frame and climbed through. He reached Madeleine and eased her out of her awkward position leaning against the wall. As he laid her down, he noticed words had been written on the wall. He illuminated the letters.

Someone had used lipstick to write a message.

L. Tried to block gas. Halothane. Save Sami's wife first, she most affected by gas. M.

Beside where Madeleine had been hunched, a square one-and-a-half-metre-high bulge protruded from the wall. Blankets had been piled on the sloping top of the protrusion. Logan could hear the hiss of gas.

Logan checked the pulse of Sami's wife. It was irregular and slow. Her breathing was shallow.

Several thoughts raced through his mind as he picked her up.

Madeleine expected him to come. They had tried to block the gas. That would have reduced its effect. She had continued to try to stop the gas until she had been overcome herself. Despite her desperate situation, she had not given up hope that he would somehow come for her.

He lowered Sami's wife through the window. He could feel the effect of his lack of air now. He dragged the table to the wall below the air vent and lifted Sami's wife onto the table. Pulling her along the pipe would probably be more efficient than lifting and pushing her, but he wouldn't be able to lift her limp body into the vent if he went first, nor would he be able to climb over her once he had lifted her into the vent.

He wanted to breathe. His heart rate was up again. He slowed it down. He could hold his breath easily for five minutes if he was standing still, but he was expending a lot of energy in physical activity.

Using a combination of lifting and pushing, he moved Sami's wife along the pipe to the bottom of the second shaft. A light shone down the shaft.

Nico's voice said: 'I can see someone.' Nico's feet appeared, straddling Sami's wife. He picked her up and lifted her up the shaft. Someone must have taken her from him because he crouched, and a bright light shone directly into Logan's eyes. He felt Nico take his arm and pull him into the shaft.

'I think the air is clean at the top of this shaft,' Nico said. 'Not sure about down here. I can smell something. Not unpleasant, but something in the air.'

Logan wanted to get higher before he breathed. With Nico's help, he pushed with his legs to squeeze past him into the shaft. He stood up and was about to climb when he felt hands lift him under his arms, pulling him up to the top of the shaft. He heard Nico ascending the shaft behind him. He saw that another person was ahead of Sami's wife, pulling her along the pipe with the assistance of the sergeant from behind.

Logan let the air stored in his lungs out slowly and took in a breath. He didn't smell anything in the air. In the light of the flashlights, he watched as Sami's wife was passed up the first shaft to someone at the top. The sergeant turned back, and Logan said: 'I just need a minute. There are two more people to bring out. I have to go back, and you'll be needed to help them up the shafts.'

As soon as he was breathing normally, he said: 'Serene, tell the doctor the gas is called Halothane.'

LOGAN KNEW THAT Madeleine would want him to take Sami next, before saving her. Logic told him the same thing. Sami was older and probably more vulnerable. Madeleine was young, and she was fit and strong. But, as he climbed again through the window, he saw her lying on the bed and his whole being cried out to him to get her to safety immediately.

He lifted Sami.

Serene's voice in his ear: 'The Doctor says Sami's wife is still unconscious, but she's breathing well and her heartbeat's good. She's improving. He thinks she'll be OK.'

Sami was taken out of the bunker in the same manner as his wife before him. Each person in the chain now knew what was expected of him, so Sami's exit was smoother and quicker than that of his wife.

At the top of the second shaft, Logan needed a little longer to recover before he was able to breathe normally. He shone his flashlight at Nico and received the thumbs-up sign. Logan repeated the procedure of slowing his heartbeat and holding his breath, then he squeezed past Nico and dropped down the shaft. A few seconds later, he stepped onto the table and into the bunker.

His heart skipped a beat when, at first, he couldn't detect Madeleine's breathing, but there it was, slow and deep. He checked her pulse, again slower than normal but regular. He picked her up in his arms.

Lucifer had said that two hours of exposure would be fatal. Madeleine had been exposed for around ninety minutes at this point, but hopefully, the blocking of the gas vent would have reduced the amount of gas entering the room. He shook his head. Calculating her exposure time was unimportant. What mattered was to get her out as soon as possible.

Logan lifted Madeleine into the pipe without difficulty. He paused there a few seconds and prepared himself, invoking a spell to reduce the pain. His arms and legs were taking a battering from crawling along the metal pipe. His knees were bruised, but even more damage was being dealt to his elbows and forearms. After carrying Sami's wife and Sami, his elbows were not only bruised, they'd also lost skin. He'd left his jacket at the pipe entrance to give himself more freedom, but now he regretted not having his arms better protected. Without the spell, every touch of knees or elbows on the pipe floor would have been extremely painful. He tried to minimise the damage by taking Madeleine's weight on his wrists and hands rather than his elbows, but his mobility was too severely affected. He shifted her back onto his forearms, reinforced the spell and carried her along the pipe to the second shaft.

He tapped on the pipe to let Nico know he was at the bottom of the shaft.

There was no response.

He expected to see the light from Nico's flashlight, but the only light in the darkness came from his own. He tapped again. Again, nothing.

Could he get Madeleine up the shaft on his own? Where was Nico? The sergeant should also have been close.

He couldn't waste time. He was feeling the accumulated effects of the need to hold his breath for several minutes three times in succession. For whatever reason, he was on his own; he had to get Madeleine up the shaft by himself. Logan invoked a spell to enhance his strength, knowing that asking more of his muscles would demand more oxygen, compromising his ability to refrain from breathing.

He lifted Madeleine's limp body, struggling in the cramped space to get her head and shoulders into the shaft. He twisted himself into the junction and tried to get his legs underneath him so he could push upwards. He could feel the struggle draining him; his lungs were burning, and his body had started to involuntarily shake as it tried to override his commands and initiate a gulp to force air into his oxygen-deprived lungs.

He managed to get a knee into a position where he could push with his legs. There was a dizziness in his head. Was that lack of oxygen, or had he breathed in gas without knowing it? He put all of his enhanced strength into a drive upwards, bringing his other foot to bear when the space allowed. His back, already strained by the bending and crawling, felt like it was about to break.

Madeleine inched up the shaft. Logan managed to get more of his shoulders under her, but he felt his strength fading. The effort had taken too great a toll from his body. He'd asked too much. A blackness swirled in his head. The shaking in his limbs was now constant. If he didn't breathe in the next few seconds, he would fall unconscious.

Madeleine had fought for him and Nico to a point well beyond normal capability. She hadn't given up on him, and he wouldn't give up on her.

He opened his mouth and screamed. A primaeval scream that came from deep within him as well as from the depths of humanity's distant past. When the scream ended, his lungs would be empty, and he would be forced to draw in new air – air that, at this level, was almost certainly mixed with gas. He summoned the last ounces of strength left in his entire body, thrusting upwards to get Madeleine to the top of the shaft and push her far enough into the pipe so she would not slip back. There was clean air at the top. She could possibly survive there.

When his shaking arms could push no more, he let her go and was elated when she didn't fall back. His energy spent, he collapsed to the floor of the shaft, gasping uncontrollably, unable to prevent his exhaustion from allowing the blackness to consume him.

Now he could smell the gas, a sweet odour.

MADELEINE OPENED HER EYES. She was staring up at the sky. She could see the tops of trees, leafy branches waving against white clouds. She felt the wind on her face.

She was lying once again on a bed. A stretcher. She drew in a deep breath, the clean air filling her lungs as memories of the last moments in the bunker came flooding back to her. The despair… She had hoped they would be able to block the gas vent, but first Melda, then Sami, had fallen unconscious. She had pressed down on the blankets covering the vent as firmly as she could, but she could still hear the insidious hiss, and she could smell a sweet, flowery aroma.

She lifted her head, expecting to see Logan. He wasn't there.

Then she saw him. He was talking in a low voice to a man she didn't know. Logan's shirt sleeves were rolled up, and his elbows and forearms were bandaged. He turned his head towards her, smiling when he saw her eyes were open.

'Sami and Melda are fine,' he said, anticipating her question.

He knelt beside her, placing his hand gently on her arm and rubbing it affectionately in a gesture she found pleasingly intimate.

'And, according to the Doctor, so are you,' he said.

'You saved me,' Madeleine said, her voice a croaky whisper. 'I knew you would. Thank you.'

'I had to be saved myself, as did Nico. It seems the gas got to us all eventually. We have Serene to thank for getting us out.'

The man Logan had been talking to, the Doctor, said in English: 'You should have no lasting side effects. Do you think you can stand?'

Madeleine raised herself on one elbow. A moment of nausea quickly passed.

'I think so.'

She reached for Logan's hand to help her from the stretcher.

She stood up and saw Sami and Melda in a group with Serene and Nico and some soldiers. Tricola was there too. Serene and Nico were looking towards her. Serene raised her hand in a wave. A huge smile lit up Tricola's face, and she ran towards Madeleine.

Madeleine returned the wave and felt a sudden light-headedness. She stumbled against Logan, her arms holding onto him. Logan caught her, and their eyes met.

His arms felt strong and secure.

He tilted his head and kissed her.

EPILOGUE

An Inheritance, a Deception, an Admission, and a Dream.

Thursday 10:15 am

Logan considered the desk in his computer room to be an imposing item of furniture. It met the criteria. It was big and solid. The edge of the desktop and the thick legs were intricately carved. The desktop itself was leather, as was his high-backed desk chair. It *was* an imposing desk.

The desk he now sat before was twice the size of his desk. Four people, himself, Madeleine, Nico, and Tricola, sat on one side of the desk, and one person sat on the other side. The chair in which that person sat was also twice the size of Logan's desk chair.

The lawyer's offices were on the third floor of a building at the foot of the Spanish Steps in the centre of Rome. The room was large but nondescript, the furnishings unremarkable except for the giant desk.

The man behind the desk resumed talking.

'The Grant of Probate has been correctly obtained, and the assets of the deceased have been apportioned according to Italian law,' the man in the huge chair said. 'The deceased having no other living relatives but you, young lady…' he raised his eyes to Tricola, peering over the top of a pair of ornate spectacles, '…as his legally adopted daughter – you are the sole beneficiary, and you will inherit all the assets…,' he paused, glanced down at his papers then up again, '…and *debts* of the late Giles Vitivelli.'

He adjusted the spectacles on his nose.

'It seems many of *Signore* Vitivelli's assets have been seized by the Carabinieri, and others are under investigation.'

The man gave a grunt of indignation that such outrage should be inflicted on one of his clients.

He continued: 'Nonetheless, the list of the major assets so far established to have been owned legally by *Signore* Vitivelli, and therefore included in the grant…' he looked up from the paper and scanned the people in the room, '…with other such assets as may qualify for inclusion in this list to be added once investigations are complete – is as follows…'

He proceeded to read from the paper.

'A Bank of America account containing seventeen point five million dollars. A fifteenth-century restored castle near Trento. An eighty-five-hectare villa in Tivoli. A State Bank of India account containing…'

LOGAN WAS THE LAST to leave. At the office door, the lawyer tapped him on the shoulder.

'I understand *Signore* Vitivelli accidentally poisoned himself. Is that correct?'

'Yes, that's true,' said Logan. 'The Cardinal's death was a tragic accident.'

'Cardinal?' said the lawyer. 'Oh no. It's been definitely established that Giles Vitivelli was *not* a Cardinal. I have no idea why he would want to make such a bizarre claim. Somehow, and for whatever reason, he *did* manage to convince a lot of people he was, in fact, as you say, a Cardinal. It is amazing he was able to maintain that deception for so long. He actually had residence at the Vatican. Can you imagine it? Unbelievable!'

'Yes,' agreed Logan. 'It is amazing.'

'WOULD YOU HAVE GIVEN UP this cylinder and its contents for me?' Madeleine let her fingers run along the smooth golden surface of the cylinder now reclining, once again, on the dining table.

Logan regarded her before replying. 'In an instant,' he said. 'That was my plan.'

She smiled.

Logan walked to a window and looked out over the canal.

'Several years ago,' he said, 'I located a manuscript purporting to be the Book of Thoth. Its credentials were solid, and the history had been authenticated. It cost me quite a sum, but a rigorous examination eventually proved it to be a fake – a good fake, but it was an important lesson for me.'

He turned back to face her.

'That fake is inside the cylinder. Lucifer wouldn't have been able to tell it from the genuine article without proper testing. I knew it would pass his visual examination. But, in essence, it's worthless.'

'So… you weren't risking anything.'

'On the contrary.' He joined her at the table and placed his hand on the cylinder beside hers. 'Inside this thin casing also lies the genuine *was-sceptre of Sekhmet*. I've *seen* it.'

He recalled the moment he had watched Dr. Sciazori slowly draw the ancient talisman from the cylinder, gradually bringing its full length into view. An object of pure power that had been hidden from the light of day for thousands of years.

'There was no way I was going to allow Lucifer to be in the same room as the full package. I could switch the manuscript, but I had no means of acquiring another was-sceptre in a few hours. Lucifer would have detected a substitute in a second. I had to gamble that he would release you if he got what he wanted and hope I had a chance to retrieve the was-sceptre somehow. With the benefit of hindsight, I know he didn't intend to release you under any circumstances. He planned to remove all of us from the field. Permanently.'

Madeleine stared at the cylinder as if she could see through the metal into the interior. After a few seconds, she gave the golden cylinder a gentle pat, stepped back, and slowly turned in a circle, letting her gaze roam around the room.

'I'll be sad to leave this apartment,' she said. 'In spite of the sometimes stressful circumstances, I've enjoyed it here.'

He nodded in agreement but didn't say anything. She walked over to him and slipped an arm around his waist, leaning against his shoulder.

'Have you considered the fact,' she said, when her eyes found his, 'that, using the criteria you have applied to some of the gods of ancient Egypt, *you* could now be considered to have god-like powers?'

He laughed. 'I would consider myself to be only a very minor god.'

She shrugged her shoulders. 'Perhaps…'

'One thing that still intrigues me,' she said, after a few moments, 'is the curious set of truly remarkable coincidences that brought us together and moved us forward at times.'

'I know what you mean,' said Logan. 'I, too, find coincidence intriguing.'

'I'm talking about the particular coincidences we experienced over the past week – the ones you said were pieces of a puzzle.'

'I know,' said Logan.

He wondered if he should mention the dream he had woken from that morning.

In the dream, he had been sitting alone late at night in one of the *Magari* lounges, a glass of Armagnac held loosely in his hand.

A pleasant voice behind him had said: 'Good evening, Logan.'

The voice was familiar.

'Good evening,' he had replied.

He had turned in the chair to see an elegant lady dressed in black.

Like her voice, she was familiar, but he couldn't place her.

'Forgive me,' he had said, 'but do I know you?'

'We have never met before, but, yes, you know me,' the lady had answered. 'You call me Bast.'

DISCLAIMERS

Insieme is a fictitious cosmetics company and trademark, and there is no *Insieme* store on the *Calle Salvadago* in Venice or anywhere else.

The *StadtPolizei* building on *Bahnhofquai* in Zürich does exist, but apart from the entranceway, which *is* a tourist attraction as described, all other rooms and personnel mentioned within are fictitious.

The National Archaeological Museum of Venice is located on St. Mark's Square, but the associated personnel mentioned are fictitious.

The towers at the entrance to the Venice *Arsenale* were constructed between 1377 and 1440. However, there are no apartment buildings adjacent to the towers as described in the novel. Claudia's apartment building is fictitious.

ABOUT THE AUTHOR

OWEN TREVOR SMITH

I now live on the Kapiti Coast of the North Island of beautiful New Zealand, but I have lived and worked in Australia, England, Germany and Switzerland.

I share my home with two dogs (Harry and Jacko) and three guitars (not named). I've travelled throughout the world for extensive periods of time, and I've sailed the Atlantic from England to Brazil in my 41-foot ketch 'Adastra'.

I have written poems (that rhyme), short fiction in diverse genres, and also children's stories and a two-act play.

The Pharaoh Of Venice is my second novel.

Visit www.owentrevorsmith.com

Email: owentrevorsmith@gmail.com

ALSO BY

OWEN TREVOR SMITH

<u>Seven Roads To Travel</u>

A collection of seven deliberately diverse short stories:

The Singer

An old man recounts the memory of a golden moment amongst the chaos of war

Chances

An adventurer experiences the extremes of dark despair and wild elation adrift in a raw South American city

Luck is a Lady Tonight

A desperate gambler finds luck has more than one form

The Man from Mexico

A western ranch-hand shares the challenges of high-country life with a mysterious companion and a hoard of old Mexican gold

A Smart Fish Story

A simple fisherman hooks a smart fish that's more than he can handle

The Tonic

A young couple obtain a bottle of quack tonic that seems to live up to its wildest claims

Boss

A Grandfather's enjoyment of a visit to the family fishing hole is colored by memories from the trenches of WW1

The Day Bonny Blue Raced For The Cup

A thrilling and moving lyrical descriptive poem of 66 verses in the style of legendary Australian bush poets *Andrew 'Banjo' Paterson* and *Henry Lawson*. Australian bush ballads are renowned for their easy-flowing style and comfortable rhythmic pace and this poem is a beautifully crafted example of that art.

A desperate Australian farming family caught in a drought and under threat of mortgage foreclosure in a few days forms a plan to enter their horse Bonny Blue in a horse race with 16-year-old son Jack to ride her. Jack and Bonny Blue use their bond and their fighting spirit to overcome inexperience, prejudice, and overwhelming odds in the race for the Carling Cup – a race destined to become legendary.

Lindisfarne: Fury of the Northmen

Feran Chronicles: Book 1

An authentic historical fiction set in England and Europe at the end of the turbulent 8th century CE. A tale of a clash of cultures.

On the 8th of June, 793CE, Fenn is a young apprentice scribe at St. Cuthbert's Monastery on the island of Lindisfarne in North-East England. On that fateful summer's day, he is violently torn from one life and thrust headlong into another. Dragon-headed ships appear on the beach, and savage raiders swarm ashore – the first Viking raid on English soil. Fenn is dragged across the sea to a life of cruel slavery in a harsh and foreign land; to a society that could not be more different from his own.

After months of brutal existence, Fenn seizes an opportunity to escape. Together with four other slaves, including a talented, beautiful and mysterious young woman, he sets out on a thrilling journey across a thousand miles of unforgiving landscape, pursued by a ruthless and relentless Viking leader as the events of the times unfold and whirl around them.

This is a story of courage and determination in the face of adversity, of despair and joy, and of loyalty and love.

Westerling: Prince of Wessex

Feran Chronicles: Book 2

Kaela knew the Queen had murdered Lord Orvyn the moment she learned how he had died.

A man who complains of stabbing pains in his stomach and a band of iron around his chest moments after drinking from his wine cup; who falls from his chair, face beaded with sweat and struggling to draw his next breath – the screams of a kitchen girl filling everyone's ears, and the wooden plate she had been about to place on the table splitting in two on the stone floor beside her Lord, peppering his contorted body with onions and peas – such a man has been poisoned.

And poison showed the Queen's hand as surely as if she had used it to thrust a knife into his heart.

This is the story of the birth of a dynasty that eventually would rule all of England. The Kingdom of Wessex at the close of the turbulent 8th century was a world of rivalry, betrayal, violence, and mystery.

The players: a cunning and ambitious Queen; a cruel High Reeve of Wessex; a bitter and ruthless usurper and his two menacing companions – a pair of barely-human twins; a strange lady of the forest who may have the gift of prophecy. And the ordinary folk, the backbone of every community – upon whose shoulders a new land can be forged.

Fenn and Kaela are two young outsiders with fresh dreams who find themselves thrust into the centre of the conflict. They must rely on their wits, their unique skills – and each other – to survive the danger threatening on every side as they strive to save the kingdom and ensure a new beginning for WESTERLING.

Visit www.owentrevorsmith.com for more information.